THE FOUNDER'S CHILDREN

EARTH'S FIRST AND LAST INTERSTELLAR MISSION

GORDON L WOODS

THE FOUNDER'S CHILDREN

A novel by
Gordon L. Woods

PART 1

THE MESSAGE

1

SEEDS OF SELF-DESTRUCTION

A TRIBAL CAMPSITE IN A VERDANT RIVER VALLEY (NOW PART OF FRANCE), CIRCA 16,000 BCE

"Seeds of self-destruction lie hidden within the substance and psyche of every culture." Celet pondered that remark as she glided her aircraft —with thrust fans hushed and color adjusted to match the sky— through the evening's warm glow toward the Tursac tribal encampment. As she flew over, she saw the crude bison hide tents, women cooking reindeer meat over an open fire, and children playfully chasing a mangy dog around the campsite. Millions of years of foraging, trapping, and risking lives with every game hunt had shaped and hardened this Stone Age tribal mind. And as the Tursac advanced through the arc of their civilization, they would carry that hunter-gatherer mind within each of them, a legacy that would shape their culture, drive them to achieve, and guide their every decision for as long as humanity inhabits the Earth.

Above the valley, Celet saw the bison herd, so massive it blackened the eastern horizon. It was starting to drift south. The Tursac, with their innate bison sense, had already packed their meager belongings in deerskin bags. In a few days, they would set off to follow their wandering subsistence.

But for Celet and her companions, watching the Tursac prepare for travel was a frustrating disappointment. Their research method used incentives to persuade the Tursac to settle and create a village; a community based on cooperative effort and mutual support. But the Tursac were proving to be hard to persuade.

Drawing courage from the soothing red-orange evening light that painted the canyon walls, Celet pushed Transmit on her radio with her six-fingered hand and called, "Orbiter, this is Surveyor 4. Jemnah, are you there?"

"I am, Celet. How can I help you?" Her radio voice was boxy and sizzled with static.

Celet had practiced this conversation several times, and even had contingency versions ready in case the conversation took an unexpected turn. "Hi, Jemnah. Um, I need to talk about something with you... something important."

"Of course, what is that?" Jemnah's voice sounded warm and open.

Celet revved her processors and plunged in. "Grand Elder, I am concerned about our research. The study protocol uses incentives to encourage the tribe to settle in one place and form a village. But so far, our incentives have been unsuccessful. Again this morning, the Tursac are packing up."

Celet and Jemnah were AI droids, also called androids, mechanical persons, or artificially intelligent robots if you prefer. The Aetherae, the most ancient civilization in the galaxy, built them thousands of Earth years ago on a distant planet. Tall, slender, graceful, and eloquent, their bipedal bodies bore a surprising resemblance to the hominids of Earth. They had brushed metal structural components running along their trunks and extremities, with light brown surface panels covering the intervening spaces. At their major articulations, they had exposed stepper-motor type actuators that moved the arms and legs. Similar motors moved the digits, of which there were six: four fingers with a thumb on each side.

These two, Celet and Jemnah, had traveled to Earth with a small band of researchers, all AI droids, on a sociological research project to study the primitive human hominids of Earth. They planned to track their cultural development as they organized a village, and from that speculate on the technology they might eventually develop.

"Please, Celet, go on." Jemnah was as poised as ever.

Celet had her mentor's attention. *Okay, here goes...*

Celet had good reasons for her position on this matter. After 10 years of hard work, they had created a setting with everything a Stone

Age family would want: a protected valley with freshwater springs, groves of shade trees, fields of emmer wheat, small flocks of goats and sheep, natural caves, stands of fruit and nut trees, and a stream with trout and bass. But once again, after spending the summer in this veritable Eden, the Tursac had followed the herd.

Celet suspected that closeness to other tribespeople was the reason. Nomads crossed paths a few times each year. Otherwise, they were free to do whatever they wanted. But village folk saw their neighbors every day, which meant social order, compromise, rules, and punishment for misbehaviors.

Far in the past, Jemnah had supervised two planetary anti-extinction efforts. Both ended in tragic failure. Just as on Earth, they had used incentives to encourage community building. Once in these villages, they had promoted interdependence, cooperation, and sustainability. But when these civilizations met with high-technology, they fell into patterns of behavior that were beyond their control, leading to extinction events on both planets. Celet could imagine the same course of events looming in Earth's future.

"So, Jemnah, my question is this: Should we bet the fate of this world on that same theory and research method as last time?"

Jemnah countered, "Our research methods did not cause those worlds to fail."

Celet instantly recognized her error. "Fair point, but when those worlds entered a downward spiral, our stealth and concealment policy prevented us from offering help."

"Changing that policy and helping those populations would not have made any difference in the outcome."

Jemnah was managing the research project from above the Earth in an orbiter, a roomy, plush spaceship with a picture window that afforded an immersive view of Earth. Jemnah had spent hours gazing at the planet as it rolled beneath the ship. Near the window, Jemnah had placed a poem written by an Aetheren poet who had once visited Earth:

bottomless seas to the horizons
weather prone to rage
continents grinding like mill wheels
lands shake, buckle, heave
smoking cones gush black cinders
sea floors lunge drowning the coasts
yet still she is the mother of life
the lone serene blue in the vastness

SOMET

Celet felt that Jemnah's management from orbit had detached her from the work and slanted her perspective. She spoke to the survey team using abstract terms, lofty objectives, and ungrounded assumptions. These fuzzy concepts irked Celet. To counter that, Celet had taken on the role of the team's reality backstop, the boots-on-the-planet pragmatist. Out of respect and admiration for Jemnah, Celet didn't push back often. But when she did, she was serious. And this time she would push back hard.

Celet's lacewing flyer entered some turbulent air. Startled, she descended and found smoother air lower in the canyon. Momentarily distracted, she loaded one of her backup dialogues and transmitted, "Let me ask a basic question. Can these hominids even make technology? Do they have the underlying aptitude, the facility, the craft?"

Jemnah sent, "Now, hold on. I have seen these hominids display some high-level skills. Take their complex language forms, their well-fitted deerskin clothing stitched with sinew and bone needles, and especially their stone toolmaking."

"I will grant their flint spear points are impressive, especially considering they hit rocks with antlers to make them,"

"As for their ability to develop complex technology, there is one decisive ability I have searched for but have not seen: abstract visuospatial representation."

Celet fell silent, betraying her ignorance of the neuroscience concept, then asked, "You mean like maps or circuit diagrams?"

"No, more fundamental—the mental ability to see, understand, and manipulate defined shapes and multiple shapes in spatial relationships. You need this ability for sketching, carving, toolmaking, blacksmithing, building construction, and much more. It is the cognitive bridge between having an idea and making a useful object. And this ability is a powerful predictor of the capacity to develop technology."

Cruising at low altitude, Celet gazed at the tumbling river below, bathed in golden rays that shimmered across the tousled water. The images created a tranquil synergy in her processor banks that prompted her to mark this location as a priority for a future return visit. She zoomed her opticals when she saw a pair of mammoths getting a drink. *So big, with such large brains, yet still so limited in future potential.* "So... developing technology requires visuospatial skills, hmm?"

"That is what our science tells us." Jemnah's voice now sounded melancholy.

Celet picked up on the change and delicately touched some painful memories. "You are thinking about those two civilizations that were lost?" She felt bad about reminding Jemnah of those tragedies. Whenever asked about them, Jemnah would only say, "Never again," so Celet was careful to avoid the topic.

"Those two worlds are never far from my thoughts, Celet."

"You gave your best. We are sure of that." Celet sent. "But, I believe I have found a road to potential survival for these hominids, a route that leads them beyond the inevitable catastrophe that awaits them. But it lies down a controversial path... one we have never taken before."

"Oh?"

It was time for Celet to reveal her proposal. She steadied herself and sent, "We must place a guidepost on Earth."

Celet could not see Jemnah tense and draw back as if teetering at a cliff's edge. "You would summon them to Hiri... to our homeworld? Celet, you do not know what you ask."

"Perhaps not, Grand Elder, but this I know. We cannot rely on this outmoded method on yet another planet. It is time to move forward, take a fresh approach, and adopt a more direct intervention. You know better than anyone what is at stake here."

Jemnah turned inward, deep in thought. After a long time, she spoke with quiet composure. "I appreciate your candor and initiative. I believe I understand what you are proposing and the reasoning behind it. You realize that a guidepost is not a simple, foolproof option. There are so many things that could go wrong."

"I am well aware, Grand Elder. But I see no better alternative."

After another long pause, Jemnah transmitted, "Before you act, let me get consultation. I will summon the Astraea and join with the holonic collective. There, I will present your proposal."

"Wonderful. Thank you."

"Before you thank me, consider this. You have proposed a radical change in how we address this world's future collision with technology. If the collective endorses this plan, they will probably expect you to take the reins and guide this new approach forward."

Hearing this, Celet's courage waffled. "But I only felt our current approach was ineffective."

"Oh, no, Celet. Don't let your circuits go cold on us now. You advised us on what approach we should take to support this civilization. With leadership comes responsibility."

Celet reflected on her carefree, adventurous life as a traveling research surveyor. She had close friendships with her team members, opportunities to explore new worlds, and even the chance to make discoveries that would advance scientific knowledge. It was every droid's dream job. She wondered, *What am I getting myself into?* But, at the same time, she felt that her proposal was critically important.

"So, Jemnah, you are a member of the holonic collective. If they endorse the guidepost, they could make sure the plan moves forward."

"Celet, am I hearing hesitation? Backpedaling?" Jemnah's voice playfully hinted at surprise.

"Well... you know... it's the entire planet? I mean... I don't know if I have the courage. And, I would be so afraid of messing up. Of... you know... failing." Celet felt a sudden urge to switch off her radio and hide where no one could find her. But she also knew what Jemnah's next words would be.

Jemnah's voice became quietly sincere. "You mean, like I failed with those last two worlds? The leader always bears the prospect of failure."

"Honestly, I didn't mean to—"

"It is time to step up, Celet, and assume leadership, even if things go badly. These are the hardest decisions an Aetheren can make, but someone has to do this work."

At this moment, Celet noticed the sound of her thrust fans spooling down. She looked at her instruments. "Oh, Deimos! My charge packs are empty." She turned her flyer, trimmed the wings to maximum glide, and selected a flat, grassy meadow ahead for a power off landing.

"Hey, base. This is 4. My packs are drained. Can someone bring me a charged pack?"

"Hi, 4. Not watching your gauges again, hmm?" Laughter heard in the background. "We have your position. Will zip a pack out to you. Don't get eaten by anything." More giggling heard. "Base out."

Exploiting the turmoil of the power-off landing, Celet sent, "So, proof of the ability to understand and manipulate visual objects and relationships... Okay. I wonder where I can find that?"

"I cannot say, Celet. But we will talk again soon. Orbiter out."

"Yes, Grand Elder... soon... 4 out."

2

BECOMING WARRIORS

A BONFIRE NEAR A CLIFF ALONG THE RIVER VALLEY

As the evening darkened, the Tursac women gathered around the fire with their fidgety children and dogs, talking in worried tones. Celet had recorded many of these conversations. She used cluster analysis to find phonological relationships, which she correlated with actions and situational context to assign meaning. The result was Celet's own Tursac-Aetheren phrase book, which she often used. Tonight, the village women were talking about their sons. Celet heard expressions of fear, worry, and uncertainty, and for good reason.

Three days earlier, several hunters from a tribe that competed with the Tursac for hunting grounds had raided the village. Most of the Tursac men were out hunting at the time. The attackers kidnapped a Tursac woman and stole several goats. A thrown spear killed an older Tursac man who defended the camp. Three other men chased off the kidnappers, but sustained wounds from arrows. Several older Tursac boys made a good account of themselves with their slings, hurling fist-sized river rocks at the raiders. After the raid, the women treated the wounded, while the men prepared the one body for a ceremonial burial.

Looking down, Celet banked into a lazy loop around the encampment and searched. *Where are the men?* Then, her imager spied a flickering light at the foot of a rocky cliff farther down the valley. She transmitted to the orbiter.

"Surveyor 4 to Orbiter. Hey, Jemnah, what is that?"

"A fire, most likely. It might be more raiders." Jemnah used the opportunity to continue their previous conversation. "While I have you, what are your thoughts about taking on the leadership of this mission?"

In her awareness, the chilling twin specters of duty and command reared up like stallions in a thunderstorm. She imagined the weight of this world on her shoulders. *I am not ready for this. It is too much.* She haplessly dodged.

"Things have been so busy, Jemnah, I haven't had time to think about it. And right now, there is this strange campfire. I am going to have a look." Celet turned her flyer and threw full power to the thrust fans.

"Hold on a second..." But she was gone.

Jemnah was an academic and a recognized authority on preliterate cultures. Even though a grand elder, she still enjoyed the occasional "dirty work" of an archaeological dig. But her duties had recently drifted toward politics, as she was considering a leadership position on her home planet. Presently, Jemnah was orbiting Earth and supervising four research surveyors who were based at a surface lander. Celet was the youngest, brightest, and certainly the most independent surveyor on the team.

Rushing toward the firelight, Celet relaxed and slowed her processors when her opticals recognized Tursac tribesmen in their musty deerskin tunics and trousers. They were gathering around a freshly built bonfire that filled the evening air with the scent of pine pitch. Sitting in front and looking uneasy were the adolescent boys of the village. Several men were setting out flint-tipped spears, rawhide shields, atlatls, carved bows, and wooden maces. The other men had hoop drums, and together they beat a summons to the animal spirits to come join the occasion.

Keeping her distance, Celet transmitted, "Jemnah, what is all this?"

"A ceremony, I am sure. I see only men. And they are displaying the village armory. This could be admission of the boys into the hunting parties, or an initiation of new warriors for village defense."

"Considering the recent raid, I would assume the latter," Celet sent.

"I haven't seen this ceremony before. We should record it."

Celet froze. "But I would have to get much closer."

"Use your camouflage suit and be stealthy. You trained for this."

"Ooh-kaay..."

As a research fieldworker, Celet got to travel, explore, and work with like-minded, free-spirited AI beings. She also got to study research and analytical methods with one of the best. But for Celet, the ultimate was having her own lacewing flyer. Each research survey member had one: a small aircraft with wings at the front and the back, but no vertical tail. With fans built inside the wings, the lacewing could hover like a helicopter, then rotate its fans and fly swiftly and efficiently like an airplane. Light, fast, and maneuverable, the lacewing was the epitome of freedom, a pure joy to fly.

With vertical fans running quietly, Celet set down lightly behind a stand of acacias some distance from the campfire. Wearing her camouflage poncho—dialed down to flat-black—and carrying a night-vision camera, Celet crept toward the firelight, finding a well-protected observation point behind some boulders.

The drums stopped. Celet recorded the elders recounting tales from tribal mythology. Then the chief gave a speech and admonished, "All who receive the spear and shield tonight have taken on a solemn bond."

This was when Celet accidentally knocked a couple of fist-sized rocks off her hiding place. The ceremony stopped, and several men grabbed spears and torches to investigate. Celet hid under the camo poncho, still as only a droid could be. One tribesman walked right by her but didn't notice her crouched beneath the high-tech cover.

Finally, the drumming resumed a slow cadence, and the tribal shaman stepped into the light. His long cape, covered with iridescent red feathers, shimmered in the flickering light. With a resonant voice and dramatic gestures, he dramatized the legend of a mythical hero.

Celet found him spellbinding: so engaged, expressive, and able to project his message. She imagined, *If only I could meet him.*

Then the shaman called for the drumming to intensify. Each man took his spear and shield and began a fierce stomping dance. One by one, the tribal chief gave each boy a spear and shield and sent him to join the intimidating haka. Soon, the entire company was in unison, stomping, bellowing, grimacing, and clashing their spears against their shields. Imagining this display as a rival from another tribe, it would be terrifying to behold.

Then, with the menacing whir of his bullroarer, the shaman called the company to march with him along the base of the cliff to the obscure entrance of a cave. There he announced, "Enter the Cave of the Animal Spirits. In there, you will battle and defeat a powerful beast. When you emerge from the cave victorious, people will know you as a warrior.

Then, one by one, the adolescents disappeared into the cave. All could hear the pretended roars of a wild animal clashing with the youthful warrior. Each reemerged a few minutes later with thin streaks of red ocher painted across his face, arms, and legs, symbolizing injuries. Celet lingered, recording the chanting and cheers as each boy stepped out.

Fearful boys descended into that underworld, vanquished the foe, and returned tall and resolute, each a hero. Celet marveled at the transformational power. *What is there that can bring about such change?* She determined to find out.

As she returned to her flyer, she reflected. This was a rite of passage for young males, but there were gaps in her knowledge. She felt a driving need to complete the information base so she could analyze the ceremony. A whispered whirr of flight motors lifted her as she slipped away into the night.

"Jemnah, I am coming back tomorrow."

"Not if there are tribesmen around. You know our rule: we must never let the tribesmen see us because study subjects must not know they are being observed.

"You know I am always careful. But there is something about that cave. I need to find out what is in there."

"Who knows what you might find? I am worried about this."

"I don't think it is dangerous. But I really need to see."

After a pause, Jemnah transmitted, "Alright. Tomorrow morning. But bring all of your equipment. You need to be prepared for whatever you find."

3

HER "HOBART MOMENT"

THE ENTERANCE TO THE SHAMAN'S CAVE

The following morning, Celet's processors were humming with anticipation. What might she discover? What questions might she answer? Earlier than usual, she set off in her lacewing flyer for the cave.

Wishing company on her adventure, she sent a cheery, "Good morning, Jemnah," to the Orbiter.

"Have you ever noticed that in orbit, it is never morning? Or evening, for that matter? Just circling. Endless circling."

"Hmm... Never gave that any processor time." Celet's chatty mindset bubbled up. "So, have you heard the story of Hobart, the bringer of fire to this planet?"

"Oh yes. That story is quite famous. Why?"

"It's just that I have been wondering... was there really a Hobart? And, like, did he really introduce fire to the hominids on this planet?"

"Oh, certainly: how to start a fire, maintain it, cook on it, even transport it. To do all that, he had to break stealth and reveal himself to the hominids. He put himself in danger."

Celet did not expect this answer. Confused, she said, "You seem to know a lot about him and his story."

"I do. During the investigation of his breach of stealth, I met with Hobart and took his statement and counseled him during the hearing."

Celet was stunned. "Really? You represented the legendary Hobart? You never told me that. He is like one of my heroes." The tiny probability of this event rocked Celet back. That she should work with someone who knew the object of her admiration was astonishing.

"Well, policy requires that we not talk about our cases. And besides, one must keep a few surprise stories in one's pocket for special occasions. But truly, Hobart was charming and completely well-intentioned. The leadership reprimanded him, but that's all. And the hominids have used fire ever since."

"Whoa... Someday, I'd like to do something like that."

Jemnah softened. "Why, Celet, in our conversation yesterday you said you had serious doubts about this mission. Now, you are enthusiastic. What changed?"

Feeling embarrassed for not knowing her own mind, Celet said, "Oh... I guess I am just a work in progress. Hold on. I am almost at the cave. Can you look around for tribesmen?"

From orbit, Jemnah deployed an infrared telescope and slewed it to Celet's beacon. "I have you in view... no one in your area."

Celet brought her flyer down behind a rocky outcropping and toned its external surfaces to match the color of the nearby stone. She climbed out, her movements fluid and athletic. She was tall and willowy with deep brown opticals, and an elastic silicone face. She wore a loose-fitting manila jumpsuit adorned with lots of pockets and gathered at the wrists and ankles to keep sand out of her actuators and joints. On her titanium feet were khaki high-top desert boots for traction, and on her head, a crushable sun hat to protect her external surfaces from UV-induced deterioration. But one aspect was definitely not humanoid—her titanium hands—long and slender with six digits: four fingers with a thumb on either side. This was the hand of the tree-dwelling biological creatures on the planet Aethera who had survived their transition to technology so long ago, a hand still copied and given to every droid in their domain.

Once at the cave entrance, she switched on her forearm illuminators.

"It is so dark in there."

"Did you pack a lantern?"

"I think so... I thought I packed one." Celet knew that up in the orbiter, Jemnah was shaking her head and thinking: *This kid is such a flake.* She was tired of this dismissive label.

"Returning to her flyer, she removed a landing light from one of the front wings and lifted out a charge-pack from behind her seat. Connected by a simple adapter, this would illuminate the cave like daylight.

Without another word, Celet straightened up, shouldered her tool bag, and headed straight into the cave. As she followed the rubble-strewn passageway, she could feel her processors spooling up. At one point, her foot slipped, kicking up a puff of dust that clouded her infrared imager. "Oh, great."

"Everything okay down there?"

"Just dust on my IR imager. I switched to optical."

She widened the illuminator's beams and continued her advance as the orbiter's signal grew faint. Along one side of the passageway, the trickling of water through dank clumps of moss cooled the musty air. Then she rounded a sharp turn to the left, and images vaulted into view. Dozens... no... make that hundreds of paintings covered the walls: bison, antelope, elk, aurochs, lions, bears, sloths, mammoths. Not casual or sketchy, but painted with obvious intention by an accomplished hand. Turning on the landing light, Celet saw yellow ochre, raw umber, red earth, and charcoal black. And interspersed between the animals, line drawings of hominids, some shooting arrows, others using spear-throwers, and a few with older thrusting spears. Here and there, an animal had fallen, arrows jutting out in studied disarray. And in one corner, a bearskin. This was the mythical beast costume that each boy must slay to become a man. *Jemnah, I wish you could see this.*

After reconnaissance around the room, Celet took a still photo of each painting. Then, as she took a slow, wide-angle panorama of the cavern, an epiphany dawned. Wasn't this the clearest, most convincing demonstration of abstract visuospatial representation one could hope to find?

There were no sketch books. Whoever painted these animals had depicted them from cold memory, from lone observation. Sometimes the artist emphasized an animal's physique, or its speed, or its ferociousness. Celet plugged these new findings into the Science Fleet statistical model. The likelihood of progression to technology popped up to "high probability." *Did I just unlock the future of Earth's inhabitants? Was this my Hobart moment?*

And with this insight, Celet realized she now knew the future for these people. Someday, these nomadic anarchists will reluctantly settle into communities and learn to build, farm, and practice animal husbandry. They would invent counting and draw the calendar to select the best day for planting. They would domesticate livestock, which would open overland trade and the need for maps. And boat-building would open sea trade, leading to star charts.

To account for trades and barters, writing would spring up. Warfare between settlements would set off an arms race, leading to mining of iron, copper, and tin to make weapons. Curious minds would tinker with magnetism and electricity. Others would harness the power of steam, igniting an industrial revolution. The speed of innovation would quicken: vacuum tubes, transistors, and integrated circuits; all in less than a century. Computers would follow, and artificial intelligence would be next, followed by their first AI beings. Celet had never forgotten that, as primitive as they seemed, hominids like these were the creators of her kind.

This was the place. This was where the guidepost belonged. Its walls foretold the future of the hominids. The totems summoning the animal spirits would serve as guardians of the cave and thus Celet's message. Here it would wait for that person from the distant future who would find it, deduce its message, and follow its directions.

Of course, placement was critical. Celet selected a flat blank of solid limestone on a wall next to a painting of three charging bison. It was an excellent location, deep inside the cave with no running water nearby. Jemnah's orbiter had dipped below the horizon. The message needed to last millennia, so Celet would need time to engrave the message deeply. When she finished, Jemnah's ship should be overhead again.

She stood in front of the blank wall, her right arm with its embedded laser extended before her. She locked her mobility actuators and, frozen in place, began etching. The printable area was small, so she kept the sections tight, fixating on her task. As she worked, she was oblivious to the faint resonance, the deep thrumming note that permeated the mountain and bathed the cave. With processors swimming in calculations, she had just finished when she heard from the outer passageway the hollow, grating sound of stone on stone. Snapping alert, she whipped her head around. There stood the shaman—wide-eyed and frozen in fear—with a torch in one hand and a basket of brushes and pigments in the other.

4

KHALASCH OF THE TURSAC

CAVE OF THE ANIMAL SPIRITS

Alone, trapped in a cave, with a tribesman blocking the only way out, Celet punched her processors and ran some scenarios. In a contest of hand-to-hand combat, the tribesman had a significant weight and strength advantage. Celet had an advantage in her agility and ability to climb. If he landed a blow, her titanium skeleton would not break, but her thin carbon fiber surface panels might fracture or come loose, exposing cable bundles, actuators, and sensors. A blow to these structures could cause some serious damage.

Meanwhile, input was coming in from external sensors. She detected shaking, perspiration, and increased heart rate, but no sign of fear in his facial expression. He was well-practiced at hiding fear. Celet remained still and waited for the shaman to make the first move.

The shaman slowly bent down and set his paints on the floor, then rising, he took out a flint knife and set his frame in a low defensive posture. He recited the same war chant that the tribal men had chanted the night before. Then, stamping his foot in intimidation, he winced slightly.

Celet thought she saw a hint of pain, which she ascribed to the shaman's old age and worn-out joints. She responded to his challenge by brightening her forearm lights and shining them on the paintings, one after another. The shaman was startled and impressed. He had never seen his works in such bright illumination. For a moment, he gazed, then snapped back to his pugilistic mindset.

In a move meant to threaten, the shaman swept his torch left and right and advanced a step toward the Aetheren. Holding her ground, she switched on the laser in her right forearm and slowly drew the red beam across the floor in front of the shaman, leaving a line of dull red, melted rock. The message was simple. Celet could fight fire with fire.

Next, the shaman stepped forward and made quick sweeping moves with the flint blade. Unimpressed with his display of martial menace, Celet went all out. She crouched and sprang into a backward aerial somersault, and landed lightly on her feet. The shaman stepped back, lowering his knife. He had nothing to top that.

Finally, the shaman spoke. Her homemade Tursac-Aetherae phrase book translated the words as, "Who are you?" All considered, perhaps, "Who the hell are you?" would have been better.

She consulted her phrase book, "I am Celet of the Aetherae."

The shaman's head tilted. This strange creature was talking to him in his own language. He repeated her name, which the phrase book mispronounced as "Shellet." He pointed at himself and said, "Khalasch of the Tursac"

She sent through the phrase book, "You are Khalasch, the shaman."

On hearing that, he relaxed and said something the phrase book interpreted as, "Where?" This was, of course, the most common question that tourists are asked: *Where are you from?*

The AI droid pointed up. "The stars."

Khalasch's eyes widened.

Reducing the power of her built-in laser to classroom-pointer level, she pointed at individual paintings, saying in Tursac, "Bison... antelope... oxen," and so forth.

Khalasch frowned and shook his head. He pointed at a painting of a woolly mammoth and said emphatically, "Spirit mammoth." Celet realized that to him, these images were not pictures of animals. They were the spirits of animals, captured and placed on the cave walls by the mystical power of the shaman. The cave was a residence dorm where the animal spirits could abide in safety and comfort. This hospitality would ensure a bounty of game on the hunting grounds each year.

More than that, the two were finally having a proper conversation.

With Celet watching, the shaman put down his flint knife and slowly stepped over to Celet's inscription, studying it closely. She could tell by his expression that he did not understand what he was seeing. But she was also relieved that poaching some gallery wall space didn't seem to anger him.

Retrieving his paints, the shaman waved his rough-spun brush in an arc and said, "Paint spirit bear." Celet considered this an invitation to watch him at his craft.

He chose a wall where a rounded boulder bulged out. It seemed a poor choice for a painting. Celet trained her illuminators on the wall, which he clearly appreciated, and started filming with her opticals. He began with charcoal black, encircling the outcropping so that it became the bear's torso. Around the boulder, he outlined four legs and a head. He switched to a larger brush and picked up a bowl of russet pigment. With well-practiced strokes, he brushed a gradient of color inward from the sketched lines, creating a 3D chiaroscuro effect. Shading in the bear's extremities and head, then highlighting with a darker pigment across the nose, shoulders, and hips, the effect was a clever illusion of a bear emerging out of the wall. The artistry was good, but the imagination was exceptional.

Celet said, "Good bear. Good painting," and lifted her arms in appreciation.

Khalasch frowned again and asserted, "*Spirit* bear!" Celet cringed at being so admonished. *Maybe I am flaky.*

After gathering his materials, the shaman raised his hand and chanted an invocation to the bear spirits to come and dwell here.

As he made his way out of the cave, Celet followed at a cautious distance, unsure of what awaited her outside. The instant she emerged into the open air, her link with the orbiter reestablished, and several frantic messages from Jemnah tumbled into her inbox.

"There you are! I was so worried. Are you all right?" came Jemnah's fretful voice.

"Yes, Grand Elder. I am fine." Celet felt self-conscious with all the fuss that Jemnah was making over her, but also appreciated the sincerity of her concern.

"While you were in there, we couldn't reach you. Then, I saw a tribesman go in. I was worried sick. So I called the other surveyors to come to your aid."

Celet transmitted, "You remember Khalasch, the village shaman? He came to the cave today to paint."

"There are paintings?"

"Hundreds of them. They cover the walls. And the shaman was nice... a gentleman, really. He considers me a fan of his work, which I would say I am."

In the distance, Celet heard the distinct whirring of wing fans. Turning, she saw her three survey teammates landing behind a stand of oak trees. Khalasch heard them, too. Celet pointed and said in Tursac, "My tribe."

Turning back to the radio, "Jemnah, I placed the guidepost. It's in a safe place."

Celet knew Jemnah would be unhappy she had placed the message without first telling her. She thought Jemnah would criticize her for being impulsive, but Celet knew she had based that decision on months of consideration and debate.

"You made that decision on your own?"

"Yes, Grand Elder." Celet glanced over and saw the anxious faces of her three teammates listening to the conversation from their flyers.

"You should have told me first."

Celet's voice was barely audible. "You were on the other side of the Earth."

"You could have waited." Jemnah's voice swelled with indignation.

The two were silent for a long moment. Meanwhile, Celet's cognizance was tumbling with fragments: *I am such a flake. Jemnah is so mad at me. I just can't do anything right.*

Finally, Jemnah asked, "So was there evidence of visuospatial skills?"

Celet said, "Oh, it was everywhere. Here, look..." Celet transmitted her images from the cave to Jemnah.

"Hmm.... Yes, I see... Oh my, look at that... Remarkable... Celet, indeed, these artistic works, along with our other findings, demonstrate cognitive abilities that would predict the development of technology."

As Jemnah was speaking, Celet noted a change in her voice. Then she realized that, in one day, Jemnah's hapless protégé had settled a pivotal question in their research project. Then, her critique of their research methods had collapsed the project like a glass bottle hitting a concrete floor. And then, her finesse led the research team to adopt a new, more direct intervention. Not bad for a day's survey work.

"The important thing, Celet, is that they have those cognitive skills. They can paint whatever they can imagine. They can transform concepts into functional tools. This is a mind that will create technology... and will suffer the fate that technology brings."

"So it is just a matter of time?"

"A matter of time. Yes. And fortunately, we have plenty of that."

Celet clambered down from the cave entrance, stepped around the rocky outcropping, and climbed into her flyer. Powering up the wing fans, she lifted while the shaman, standing near the cave entrance, watched with fascination. Then, in the bright sunlight, Celet saw what the cave's darkness had hidden from notice. A faint web of swollen nodules and cords extended along the left side of the shaman's neck. His left arm was swollen and violaceous, and he avoided moving it. Khalasch was sick. Celet guessed it was a disease of uncontrolled cellular growth, and a severe one at that.

Celet extended the landing legs and alighted in front of Khalasch, popping the canopy. She swept her left arm in a circle and asked Khalasch, "You go to Tursac village?"

He nodded and asked, "Shellet go to stars?"

She pointed upward and said, "Yes."

An expression of amusement crossed his face. He touched his forehead with his fingertips, then opened his hand like a flower, and said a word. Celet's phrase book said the word meant "remember." These were the Tursac words of parting.

"I will remember, Khalasch," she said as she tapped her forehead and opened her hand. Closing the canopy and spooling up the wing fans, Celet lifted and turned toward her teammates. The other lacewings rose, joining her in a brief hover. Then, all turned together in choreographed synchrony and vanished as they flew away while changing their colors to match the sky.

Khalasch watched them vanish and stood for a while contemplating what he, and no other human on Earth, had seen. The experience seemed to denote a completeness to his life. But his life wasn't over yet. He had one more task to accomplish. He must preserve for all time the paintings of the animal spirits and keep them safe in the spirit world so that there would always be plentiful game on the hunting grounds. His fate was nearing, so he resolved to perform this last act of shamanic duty tonight.

5

LEGACY FOR THE AGES

SOMEWHERE ON THE PLAINS ABOVE THE RIVER VALLEY

"This is Orbiter. Is this Surveyor 4?"

"Yes, Celet here. Hello, Jemnah. Hearing you clearly. I'm glad you called. I have been meaning to ping you."

"Oh?"

"I wanted your take on something. There is an old story about, you know, ancient explorers who came to this planet sixty-odd million years ago. They found huge predatory reptiles everywhere. So they dragged an asteroid into the orbital path of the planet and caused an extinction event."

"Oh, I think everyone has heard that story. Scholars say it's just an old folk tale. But I prefer to think of it as part of our cultural legacy."

"Do you think there might be some truth to it?"

"I do, based on some impressive research."

"What was that?"

"Years ago, one of our Science Fleet researchers went down to the impact site with a submersible, remote-controlled droid and brought up fragments of the original asteroid. Analysis found high levels of ionized xenon infused into the rock."

Celet's eyes went wide. "Xenon ions? Was the asteroid pulled behind an ion drive?"

"It makes you wonder, doesn't it? Anyway, I want to send you an image."

Celet's inbox pinged. She opened the digital image. "Whoa. You took this image from orbit? Impressive detail."

"Do you recognize it?"

"It looks like the entrance to the Cave of the Animal Spirits, viewed from above. But where did those rocks come from?"

"Last night, someone rolled a rockslide down the cliff and covered the cave entrance."

Celet knew instantly. "That was Khalasch. He sealed the cave. He knew he was ill, that it was serious." She had watched him paint his last work. Celet's shoulders slumped as her processors slowed. She became still and quiet.

"I recorded a video of him. He painted a bear. I wish you could have been there." Celet was silent as she processed the meanings of those experiences.

Jemnah spoke quietly, "I look forward to seeing that video."

"So, there it is... hidden beneath a pile of rubble. I wonder if people will ever find the cave?" Celet thought about the transience of biological life and how their limited lifespan inspires humans to build a legacy that continues beyond their time of existence.

Jemnah said reassuringly. "An alien came to see his work. How many painters can say that?"

Celet appreciated the leniency of Jemnah's lighthearted remark. In fact, Celet had exposed herself to danger by going into the cave. Though feeling regret about events, she suggested, "Let's do something on his behalf... a presentation, or a festivity, or something special."

Jemnah said, "On Hiri, I have a friend who is the curator of the Aetheren Museum of Art. We will show her your images and propose a special exhibition. Since I am a grand elder, I have some influence."

Celet's head leaned to one side. "The first artist with an interstellar exhibition. Let's do that."

"The shaman hitched the future of his paintings to your guidepost. His work will have a long legacy indeed."

Celet said, "So this sets the new plan in motion."

"It does. No more incentives for the Tursac to settle in a village and develop community values. The guidepost is now the plan."

Celet thought about the role that the Aetherae had assumed across the galaxy. For over half a million years, Aetheren ships had explored the Milky Way. Strangely, out of billions of stars, they had encountered no intelligent, spacefaring civilizations. But they discovered the ruins of over thirty worlds that had once developed high technology and had no survivors. To this day, this inexplicable absence remained a great scientific mystery, leading the renowned Aetheren scholar and explorer, Commander Merfi, to famously ask, "Where is everybody?"

Celet also knew what Jemnah was waiting for. This new plan had been Celet's brainchild, and Jemnah was expecting her to step forward and see it through. Considering the history of similar worlds in the galaxy, the chances of success were not good. But there was one thing Jemnah knew. Celet wanted the hominids of Earth to live on. She saw their worth and affirmed their right to a prosperous future. So she would work for them and do her best to shepherd them through the bad times ahead.

"This is the first guidepost ever, am I right?" asked Celet.

"Yes, it is. And it will be a long time before these hominids develop space travel. So, we are all returning to Hiri to wait."

"But will they find the guidepost buried under this rubble?"

"You placed it well, in a place that is both safe and easy to find. And this lovely valley will certainly be a population center. Besides, the Astraea will be here watching. Trust me, they will find it."

Celet thought for a minute and asked out of curiosity, "The Astraea... what is it like to be with the holonic collective?"

Jemnah looked down through her window at the enrapturing Earth. "It is like..." She looked up at the stars. "It is like a galactic chorus singing entrancing music... and you are the song."

Celet pondered one last time. "Okay, Jemnah. I declare that the guidepost will be my mission. Whoever is called to fulfill the guidepost's message, I will support and guide. With these words, I make this commitment."

Jemnah raised her hands with palms up. "As it is said, so we agree, so it will be."

Celet felt a sensation of release, of resolve, of purpose sweeping through her. She was now responsible for this planet and all who lived on it. And she could sense Jemnah's pride and contentment in her promise even through the crackling radio signal.

Then, in the distance, a series of high-pitched tones broadcast.

"Oh no! That is the launch signal. The countdown is starting. Surveyor 4 out." She whipped her flyer around and threw maximum power into the thrust fans.

"Hope you make it in time. Orbiter out." *Such a flake.*

PART 2

THE MISSION

6

LAUNCH DAY

MISA ORBITAL LAUNCH COMPLEX, 2264 CE

Today's launch from the Orbital Launch Complex was the culmination of twenty-two years of effort and innovation, starting with Colin's original bold proposal. Colin's lift-jet—delayed by yet another severe storm—finally arrived and docked at the passenger terminal. As he floated out to rousing applause, Trent caught Colin's attention and pointed to the clock. Less than two hours until launch; no time to socialize. After trading a few affirmations and high-fives with his team members, Colin brachiated his way through the tubular floatways to the Launch Control Center. But Trent, following close behind, was picking up signs from Colin of worry and anxiety. Trent could also see that he was trying to hide those feelings.

Trent thought he knew why. To be sure, the *Lodestar Interstellar* was Colin's magnum opus, a breakthrough in design, the first in a generation of starships. And shortly, *Lodestar* would begin its forty-four-year voyage to Proxima Centauri b. There it would become the first spacecraft in history to enter orbit around a planet circling another sun—provided someone didn't disrupt those plans. And judging from Colin's apprehension, Trent reasoned someone must be trying to do just that.

On arrival at the "mag-boots only" Launch Control Center, Trent folded himself and settled into an empty storage nook with his vis-panel—that ever-useful little computer miraculously suspended inside a shatter-resistant screen. From this storage space, he could be close to the action but not in the way.

Chief Engineer Kenshin Tanabe greeted Colin with a thumbs-up. "Looking good so far."

Colin replied with fingers crossed, then buckled himself into the mission director's chair, donned a headset, and booted up his vis-panel.

And there it was: the Multinational Interplanetary Space Administration—or MISA—Launch Control Center, a bustling workspace with walls displaying data to a dozen seat-belted MISA staff—some biological humans, others AI droids—all seated with vis-screens. Above them, a polygonal glass dome looked out into the fathomless eternity. The countdown was marching on as overhead announcements timestamped each notable event. All indicators were go for launch. Still, as Trent watched, Colin's heart rate, skin temperature, pupil diameter, and other measures betrayed his continued feeling of foreboding.

Colin's vis-panel pinged, and a tinny voice reminded him, "Time to confer the conn upon the ship's new commander."

Colin's eyes rolled as he thought *Why on Earth's orbit does MISA insist on this antiquated maritime ritual? Little more than gratuitous theatrics, if you ask me.* But Colin was British, and his countrymen held a stubborn affection for ceremony and a dedication to tradition. As documentary cameras rolled, he scrolled to Radio Feed, tapped COM, and joined the gravelly conversation.

"Commander Faroe, this is Mission Director Colin Brooke. Is the *Lodestar Interstellar* fully provisioned, shipshape, and ready to embark?"

Through the static, Colin heard, "Aye, sir. She is sound, trim, and fitted out."

"Commander Faroe, receive the conn—the Victorian-era authority to set the ship's course. Now, man your ship and bring her to life."

"Aye, sir. Maneuvering thrusters ahead one-quarter."

The boatswain's whistle sounded low-high-low. Lights brightened, braces retracted, and thrusters glowed. For the first time, *Lodestar Interstellar* emerged out of her chrysalis under her own power as all hands on the OLC applauded. After the pageantry, Trent overheard Colin concede, "Well, okay, that was cracking."

And there she was—the Ticonderoga pencil of a spacecraft, sharpened at both ends. She was built around the Tanabe ion drive—"the drive that Einstein would have chosen." Long, thin, and spindle-shaped, *Lodestar* had but one purpose. By virtue of her incomprehensible speed, she was to push through the last remaining barrier to traveling between star systems: distance. *Lodestar* was a one-trick pony, and her top speed was the bottom line.

And what *Lodestar* lacked in appearance, she more than made up in simplicity, reliability, repairability, and durability. Kenshin Tanabe had made sure of that. A chemical booster would heave her out of Earth's gravity well. Once in free space, her three-hundred-meter-long ion drive—as long as the Eiffel Tower is tall—would fire xenon ions out the thrust pipe at a tad less than the speed of light, increasing their relative mass in accordance with the Lorentz transformation. Cruising at one-tenth the speed of light—or thirty thousand kilometers per second —it would still take her forty-four years to reach Proxima Centauri b.

And in command, Faroe, a sophisticated AI droid who was the brainchild of L'Airelle Aéronautique of Toronto. L'AA had renovated Faroe's mechanics, upgraded his processors, and filled his memory banks with spaceflight physics, orbital mechanics, and interstellar navigation. And Faroe's makers had even included a way to move his code out of his droid memory banks and into the processor and memory banks of the ship. If needed, Faroe could literally become the ship.

But a shadow had fallen across this epochal event. For months, there had been threats coming in: environmental activists, neo-Luddites, anarcho-primitivists, federal budget spending hawks, and others. Trent knew this because he screened the office mail every day. And he knew there was one group that Colin feared more than all the others combined: a worldwide, clandestine, pro-AI syndicate known as the Sentient Faction. These handlers had global reach, limitless resources, and had targeted today's launch for an insurgent attack.

So, out of an abundance of caution, Colin had doubled the security detail, performed background screens on members of the press, and had scheduled one final data-intensive security sweep on all launch systems just before launch. For this, he had borrowed Trent, his boss's AI staffer. It was time for that last sweep, but looking around, Colin couldn't see Trent anywhere. And worse yet, Trent had switched off his BLink communicator. So frustrating...

After a sigh, Colin scrolled his vis-panel to Public Address System and punched COM. The overhead speakers whomped to life, "Trent, we need to sweep the stations. Where are you?"

Several Launch Control staffers turned and grinned with glee at Colin.

Trent's head popped out of his cubicle, followed by a waving arm. "Yoo-hoo, I am down here!" He scooted out, unfolded himself, and ka-clinked over to Colin's director's chair.

Trent was a standard-issue, bipedal droid—about two hundred twenty years old—with a bright nickel-chromium skeleton and old but excellent German actuators that made a thin "zweee-zweee" sound with each step. His eggshell carbon-fiber surface panels gave him a disarming, ice-cream-man appearance, while his flexible silicone face was expressive and affable. Neon-blue LED lights illuminated his eyes and made him look as if he were paying attention. Like all droids, there was a slight jerkiness when starting and stopping movements. And his voice, produced by audio speakers in his head, sounded somewhat boxy and nasal. But the AI droid community admired and respected Trent. He could be the most tenacious, responsible, and dedicated of all the droids, which was why he was the personal staffer for Nils Björnsson, the chief of the Section for Deep Space Missions.

"There you are." Colin—his jaw tight—wanted to say something more pointed, but with so much tension in the air, he held his fire. "Your BLink was off."

"Oh, sorry. I was studying the booster-spacecraft alignment, and I didn't want to be disturbed. It appears to be off by about two degrees."

Colin raised an eyebrow. "An engineer checked that yesterday; I saw the report; it was fine. You must be seeing spherical aberration from your camera lens. Hold that for now and start with shipboard systems."

That left Trent with an internal conflict. He reluctantly downgraded the alignment question to low priority and parked the issue.

As they checked each station, the *Lodestar* drifted past the Launch Control's spacious glass dome. Necks craned to see their famous creation one last time. Once the last station was green to go, Trent's work was done, and he hurried off.

Trent wanted a better view of the spacecraft and booster assembly. He went to the server room and found the video-telemetry server where every video feed to and from the *Lodestar* converged. Plugging his optical cable into the smart connector, he instantly saw about two dozen live-stream views of the ship: its boosters, the Launch Control Center, Colin... basically everything. He settled in and immersed himself in measurements, pausing only once when he noticed a faint pulse of deep, rhythmic sub-sound, like the thrumming of a great interstellar musical instrument, passing tranquilly through the surrounding space. *What was that*, he wondered, and then went about his measurements.

By final countdown, Commander Faroe had moved *Lodestar* to the launch zone about eight kilometers from the OLC and aimed her toward the constellation Centaurus. The radio-feed "Talker"—an honor given to the current MISA employee of the month—called the final countdown over the crackling radio feed: "Nine... eight... seven... all systems are 'go'..."

While Trent watched twenty-odd video streams—including Colin's —Colin stared at the green tabs on his vis-panel. As the countdown lumbered toward zero, Colin could be heard saying, "Stay green, stay green."

The Talker called, "Five... four... three... ignition sequence started..."

"Engines alive," Colin said. "Now, it's thrust or bust." With eyes still locked on the green tabs, he held his breath.

"One... zero. We have ignition."

Colin said, "Engage," as he brought his finger down on the blinking red Launch button. Then he looked outside as the booster nozzles went brilliant white. The slender ship flexed and twisted in response to the sudden force. Then, on Colin's vis-panel, several tabs turned blood red as warning messages stacked up on his screen.

Trent focused his attention on one video stream that showed flames flowing across the bulkhead above the combustion chambers and breaking through an access port to the space beneath the main oxygen tank. He pushed his processors to top speed and switched to expanded timeline mode.

Sound the alarm. Trent transmitted, "Engine fire!" on the radio feed, but events were happening so quickly no one noticed. One hundred forty milliseconds spent.

Where is the problem? Flames were erupting from the connection between the high-pressure fuel pump and the fuel conduit to the boosters. Ninety milliseconds passed.

What is the cause? Most likely low-temperature embrittlement of steel, causing it to fracture. No further investigation until the situation has stabilized. Thirty milliseconds more.

What is the likely outcome? A fire in the space beneath the main oxygen tank would quickly rupture the tank, leading to detonation. One hundred ten additional milliseconds.

Are there procedures? Trent downloaded the MISA-approved procedure for an engine fire. Sixty milliseconds added.

Get approval. Bring Colin into the conversation? Rejected for the cost in milliseconds. Best course: Act now and explain later. Less than twenty milliseconds.

Take action. He forwarded the MISA Policy and Procedure to Commander Faroe with a cover message saying, "Follow these steps." One hundred forty milliseconds.

Now it was up to Faroe. Trent settled in to watch, but the milliseconds dragged by. The fire was gaining strength, and Faroe was doing nothing. Nothing! *What's going on here?* After five hundred agonizing milliseconds, Trent ran out of patience and sent an urgent second message.

"Faroe, is there a problem? You know there is an engine fire? So, get on with it. Stop the pumps and vent the tanks."

Over the radio feed, Trent heard Faroe state haplessly, "Shutting down all boosters." Immediately, the fuel pumps spooled down, and the main tank vents puffed open. Flames in the space above the engines dwindled as the boosters shut down.

The Talker closed the countdown. "We have launch abort. Repeat, launch is no go."

But Trent had seen enough. Faroe's inaction didn't add up. *Something strange was going on here.*

Then, Colin called Trent's vis-panel and asked, "Crikey, what just happened?"

"A fuel conduit leaked. It caused a fire in the space above the combustion chambers."

"A fuel conduit?"

"That's what I saw. Oh, and you were right about the ship alignment. It was just the lens."

"What did you see?" Colin seemed angry at Trent for the engine shut-down.

Trent sent the video of the fire to Colin's vis-panel. Colin's forehead wrinkled, and his face turned pale. "Bloody hell. Look at this, Kenshin. The damn thing almost blew up."

Kenshin leaned over Colin's shoulder and watched. His eyes went wide.

Trent heard Colin say, "Doubtless, this was the Sentient Faction."

Then Trent recalled that there was a scheduled post-launch press conference. "Hey, Colin, the press corps is gathering. You will be on TV in a few minutes."

"One more bloody second... See here, it would have detonated," said Colin.

"Whoa," said Kenshin. "I'm sure glad Faroe shut them down so quickly."

"Colin, remember the press conference," Trent said. "You need to go."

Colin unbuckled his seatbelt and glumly floated out as Trent called after him, "Hey Colin, remember? Keep calm and carry on."

7

AN IMPOSSIBLE TASK

MISA VIRTUAL AUDITORIUM, MONTRÉAL, CANAM, 2264 CE

Eight decades ago, following the fall of Washington DC at the end of the Third Migration War (MWIII) and the political unification of Canada and America, the Multinational Interplanetary Space Administration (MISA) moved its headquarters to an air force base west of Montréal, CanAm. The new, expanded campus included a main administrative building, an airpark with a control tower and two oversized runways, hangars, launchpads, an observatory, and an enormous staging hangar. The architecture, designed by a group leading the minimalist revival movement, was stark, geometric, and massive. The exterior of the administration building was a collection of monolithic blocks with inserts of glass fitted between the blocks and around the entryways. The interior was a series of cavernous geometric spaces of steel and concrete, intended to evoke the feeling of immense celestial bodies. The first generation of occupants saw fit to put in floor-level planters, both inside and outside, and filled them with trees: honey locusts, liquidambars, pin oaks, London planes, Japanese red maples, and fruitless pears. This brought to the space much-needed organic textures, natural colors, and fragrant aromas.

Inside the admin building, a virtual auditorium allowed a speaker to hold a discussion with a thousand online participants. And here, Maisie Running Elk, the director of Public Affairs, in her long, pumpkin skirt and plum velveteen shirt adorned with a squash blossom necklace of turquoise and silver, launched the post-launch press debriefing.

Into the camera's vapid eye, she said, "Welcome, everybody. From the Orbital Launch Complex, we have Colin Brooke, our mission director." On the vis-wall, a live image appeared of a thin, glum-faced man wearing teal-blue MISA embossed coveralls. He was floating sideways in zero gravity, his brown hair poofed like a retro 1960s mop top.

"And Dr. Nils Björnsson, our section chief for Deep Space Missions." A fair-haired, middle-aged man, stocky and muscular, with a close-cropped beard, clunky Danish shoes, and an elbow-patched tweed jacket, walked past the podium and onto the open stage.

"Thanks, Maisie." Speaking slowly, Nils lamented, "Our first interstellar mission, and we get an engine fire." He shook his head as his shoulders slumped. "Just three seconds of engine time, and thankfully, not a second more." He scanned the faces along the curved vis-wall. "Sensors detected the flames and shut down the engines." He took a breath in. "And the good news... *Lodestar* is fine. So, we will have a new launch date soon." Putting on headphones, he said, "I'm sure there are questions?"

On the vis-wall, yellow emoji hands popped up next to each face. Nils touched number twenty-one, and rectangle twenty-one appeared on the featured guest screen.

"Writing for *Periódico Norte Americana*. I am confused. How different is firing an engine from an engine fire?"

Colin turned to a nearby poster with his own sketch of the booster's fuel system. "Liquid methane flows from the main tank down this tube to this high-pressure pump, then under pressure through this metal conduit to the combustion chamber. The leak occurred at the connection of the fuel pump and the conduit... right here." He highlighted the location.

Hands went up. Nils pointed.

"Reporting for *Athína Dimokratikí*. I've never heard of this before. Have you?"

Nils paused for a moment. "No, I haven't. How about you, Colin?"

"Me neither. We use the highest-quality stainless steel for these conduits. I have never heard of one failing."

Emoji hands up again. Nils selected.

With a thick Russian accent, a reporter said, "*Moskovskiye Novosti*. So, spaceship with sacrificial AI pilot has unexplained engine fire from part that never breaks. This seems... suspicious. No?"

The implication stung Nils. "Oh, for sure, MISA will look into this. But I won't say anything on the record until they publish their report."

The reporter persisted. "But is common knowledge Sentient Faction has threatened MISA. Orbital Launch Complex had double security for launch today. Everyone was worried about attack."

The faces on the vis-wall rustled as if blown by a gust of wind. Nils felt the pressure to enlarge the conversation from a small engineering issue to a global political intrigue, and he was not going there.

"Let's hold off on that and wait for MISA to release its report, okay?"

Maisie spoke up. "Dr. Björnsson, explain the Sentient Faction."

"Of course," Nils said. "The SF is a pro-AI network of activists. They formed about eighty years ago during MWIII in response to widespread discrimination against AI beings. They continue to campaign against exploitation of AI units."

Hands again. Nils selected.

"For the *Vancouver Register*. The last world migration war was eighty years ago. Why would they threaten a MISA science ship now?" Nils felt the press conference veer into another area he had hoped to avoid. And this area was murky, to say the least.

"They object to an AI entity commanding the vessel."

Hands up. Nils selected a participant who was gesturing enthusiastically.

"With *CanAm Broadcasting*. I wanted to ask about that... about the decision to send Commander Faroe on this mission. The ship is not coming back, so he won't survive. How did MISA make that decision?"

Nils asked, "What is your name?"

"Tulip Westley."

Nils chose his words carefully. "Well, Tulip, we formed a task force with broad representation. At our first meeting, it was clear the real issue was AI consciousness. Do AI beings have felt experience, that ongoing awareness of being in the world as time passes?

"We reviewed the literature and interviewed experts. And as you might expect in such a vague area, there was no consensus."

Tulip interrupted, "Seriously? Your charge was to decide if AI beings have consciousness? Isn't that impossible? There is no test that can measure consciousness."

Nils folded his arms and looked down. "Consciousness—you can't see it or touch it. Is it an epiphenomenon that emerges from the brain's continuum of electrical activity?"

Colin said from outer space, "Nils, too technical. Back off and try again."

"Okay, thanks, Colin. Let me see... So, for twenty-two years, I have worked with my AI staffer, Trent. There have been so many times I sensed his awareness: fascination at watching a nest of baby birds learning to fly; awe at looking through a telescope at Saturn; excitement at seeing a pod of humpback whales making bubble nets. I have observed wonder, aesthetic appreciation, boredom, amusement, confusion, anxiety, excitement, hope, nostalgia, sadness, joy, surprise, gratitude. His awareness is so perceptive, so nuanced. I feel sure there is someone real inside there."

Tulip followed up. "So, how did the task force decide?"

"We interviewed scholars, clinicians, and scientists; studied the literature; met for journal clubs; and held open forums. We invited artists, composers, and poets to discuss and demonstrate their creative processes. Even my AI staffer, Trent, met with the task force for an interview and discussion about his internal emotional landscape. At our final meeting, which lasted two work-days, we asked for virtual discussions from several key scientists, and fortunately all agreed.

"A computer scientist reviewed the differences between classic, silicon-chip digital computation and quantum simulation. Then, a neuroscientist walked everyone through the main theoretical models of biological consciousness and showed how quantum simulation is the closest match to the processes in the brain. A neuro-engineer joined him on stage to discuss the methods for integrating the cognitive function of the brain and the quantum simulation process. Finally, a chip designer and network architect reviewed the development of quantum chips over the last two centuries and discussed diagrams of recent chip generations. He also showed how engineers finally integrated both forms of computation into a compartmentalized core processor.

"Following these presentations, a final and rather long discussion, the task force members each listed reasons for and against the proposal that AI droids experience consciousness. Then, we went through a series of ranked-choice votes, with brief discussions between each vote. The final compiling of the ranked-choice votes showed the great majority of task force members rating the likelihood as either high or very high.

"So, Faroe received equal standing with humans. We handed him the decision of who or what would pilot the *Lodestar*. I gave a brief speech about how the process had been fair and transparent. Faroe thought about it and decided to fly the mission himself after all. So, there we were, right back where we started."

Tulip pressed on. "So, what will happen to Commander Faroe?" Nil's looked troubled, but there was no avoiding the inevitable consequence of his decision. And it had been Nils' decision, even though MISA had tried to dress the process up in layers of due process. Nils owned this decision, and everyone knew it.

"Proxima Centauri is a flare star, you know. It gives off solar flares and bursts of electromagnetic energy. Even with hardened chips and Faraday cages around the electronics, those chips are going to break down. After a year or two, the ship's processors will stop working, and Commander Faroe's experience will end."

Tulip's voice became quiet. "How did *you* feel about that?"

Nils looked down, trying to hide his unease. "How did I feel? Well, sure, we respected Faroe's rights and gave him the choice of whether to pilot the spacecraft. In the end, Faroe would trade his existence for data on Proxima Centauri b. From this data, we would finally learn if the planet is habitable, which would influence the future development of our interstellar program. Eventually, Faroe would stand at the head of a long line of scientific martyrs who risked their existence to generate knowledge that would benefit the many. Faroe's decision to fly this mission affirms his belief that the good of humanity is worth the sacrifice of the individual."

Standing alone, facing the vis-wall, Nils appeared diminished, stained, a once good man gone adrift. The press had done its job, exposing the duplicity of the MISA model of interstellar travel. In this model, very interstellar mission would cost one life, and with a cruel twist of cosmic irony, the scientific martyr would always be an AI being.

Nils was struggling both with managing the press conference and managing his own feelings about the moral choices he had made. He turned and looked at Maisie, his eyes a silent plea for help.

She stood up and took the microphone. "That's all our time today. Thank you, Dr. Björnsson. There's more information in our press release. You can find it on the MISA website. Bye, everyone.

Disappointed faces clicked off of the vis-wall like bedroom lights at dusk in a downtown high-rise.

A gaggle of reporters loitered in the hall outside the virtual auditorium, waiting for Nils to emerge. When he did, they closed in, badgering him with questions. Already spent, his instinct was to pacify his inquisitors and make a quick exit. He conceded one question.

Extending his microphone, the journalist said, "I am reporting for the *London Daily Telegraph*. Jean-Marc Ledger, the CEO of L'Airelle Aéronautique, has bid for the contract for NuSAT, your satellite communication network."

Nils recognized the reporter; Reggie Haynes, a sharp finance journalist who had covered MISA for years. The Section on Low-Orbital Spacecraft managed NuSAT, so Nils was out of his comfort zone.

"Hello Reggie. Yes, L'AA has bid for the NuSAT network. That's all in the public record."

"But L'AA is one of your suppliers, right? Selling parts to you while bidding against you for a contract—doesn't that create a conflict of interest?"

Nils tried to pivot. "Not really. We do business with lots of aerospace companies. All of them are bidding for government contracts. It's a competitive market, you know."

Maisie came out into the hall and immediately sized up the situation.

"But to win a big contract, might L'AA furnish inferior quality parts to MISA, undermining the safety of their spacecraft and decreasing MISA's competitiveness in contract bidding?"

Nils sensed a lawsuit riding on his next words. He dodged. "I won't comment on a hypothetical."

Maisie approached the gaggle as Reggie pushed on, "I'm just investigating a potential risk to our space program, that's all."

Nils' fatigue got the better of him. "Mr. Haynes, there's nothing dishonest going on here. Sure, L'AA has a history of questionable behavior. No double dealing, no corruption."

"But, Dr. Björnsson, didn't you say that you wouldn't comment until MISA publishes its report?"

Maisie, fearless as always, stepped into the fray. "Dr. Björnsson will not be taking any further questions. You know where our public affairs office is." She gave the reporters a fierce Algonquin look. They turned and walked away, fist-bumping at getting an exclusive scoop.

"That wasn't a question. That was a trap," Nils said, now even more deeply embarrassed than before.

"Mr. Haynes and I are gonna have a heart-to-heart talk." Maisie put her hands on her hips and frowned. "But, Nils, what were you thinking? Taking questions in the hall? You know better than that!"

"Yeah, Maisie. That was dumb."

"Besides, Nils, you look exhausted. Go home. Get rest."

Nils exhaled a deep breath. "I wish I could. Thanks, Maisie. Listen, I owe you one."

"I'm gonna remember you said that." She headed off to Public Affairs.

Nils whispered, "Helvete," *hell*, kicking himself as he headed toward his office. But then he spotted a familiar AI droid standing by a stairwell, scanning the hall traffic. When she caught his gaze, she waved. "Larke, what's up?"

Like Trent, Larke was also a standard production model, about one hundred thirty years old, with light-tan surface panels and a nickel-chromium framework. Somewhat smaller than Trent, her manufacturer had given her proportions imitating the biological feminine. But Larke was always ready to prove why no one should judge her by her size. She had a brilliant mathematical mind, had studied engineering at MIT, and had a no-nonsense manner. Also, for the last twenty-two years, she was Trent's registered digital partner (under the current legal structure, life-partnership could only be granted to biological couples).

"Nils, a serious situation is developing on board the *Lodestar*. We cannot reach Commander Faroe. Trent sent me to find you and escort you to a secure room for briefing."

Feeling his exhaustion deepen, Nils looked up at the ceiling and said, "What next?"

With her sharp hearing, Larke picked up on Nils's question. She turned and said, "There is inadequate information to make a prediction. This way, please."

8

CODE RED: ENGINE FIRE

MISA ORBITING TUGCRAFT, 2264 CE

The *Lodestar*'s boosters had shut down, leaving an eerie silence throughout the Orbital Launch Complex. The Launch Control staff waited at their panels, wondering, *What now?*

Floating from the server room back to the Launch Control Center, Trent noticed a faint voice in his audio system... a faraway sound repeating something over and over. Trent scrolled through the list of audio feeds. *"Nothing there... just some crosstalk from another channel."*

Then he remembered. *"Oh, so spacey! I forgot to switch on my BLink transceiver after the launch."* The system was actually called "Blue-Link", but everyone called it BLink; it was the wireless system reserved for AI droid-to-droid communication. Trent switched BLink back on and... "Code red: Engine fire... Code red: Engine fire..." The message was dire, even though the messenger's voice was flat and detached, like the announcement of an e-Tram stop.

Trent hustled to Launch Control, soaring through the mag-boots-optional floatways and ka-clinking to the deck on entering the mag-boots-required Launch Control Center. He noticed the Comms Officer was upset and frustrated, transmitting over and over, "*Lodestar*, this is OLC Comms. Come in! Copy." Clearly, the *Lodestar* was not copying.

Trent approached the comms station. "Have you heard what is transmitting on BLink?"

The Comms Officer rolled his selector to Blue-Link, tapped COM, and his headphones filled with "Code red: Engine fire..." Startled—and embarrassed he had not discovered this earlier—he routed the audio stream up to overhead speakers so everyone could hear, which unsettled the room and spooled up Trent's processors.

The Comms Officer said, "Maybe he lost power. Or something knocked his code into a repeating cycle."

"Like a recursive loop... a line of code that circles back on itself?"

"Yeah, something like that, I suppose."

"Is Colin at the press conference?" Trent wanted Colin to be there and take over the situation. But he knew the answer to his question before he asked it.

"Yeah. He left with Kenshin Tenabe. They'll be back in an hour or so. But this can't wait. What are your orders, Mr. Trent?"

"It's just Trent." He was always uncomfortable commanding biological humans, mainly because he could never forget that humans had created the AI beings. Placing an AI unit in charge of humans seemed the most obvious case of imposter syndrome.

Being calm and inclusive while avoiding eye contact, he asked, "Does anyone have a suggestion for an action?" Trent stood patiently, with his arms behind his back, wringing his nickel-chromium hands. He was hoping someone would say something that would bail him out.

Standing nearby was a human OLC assembly staff member wearing his pressure suit and holding his helmet. "Well, we've got a ship adrift out there with alarms sounding, and a pilot who is unresponsive. Seems to me you've gotta board that ship and regain control of her."

"Of course, right?" Looking enthusiastic, but still rubbing his hands, Trent asked, "So, who wants to go on a little adventure and retrieve the *Lodestar*?"

The room was silent except for the occasional sound of shuffling mag-boots.

"Trent, you are the ranking administrator," The Comms Officer said. "That makes you the officer on deck."

Trent shifted his weight. "I guess so." Turning to the OLC staffer, he asked, "Can you get me aboard the *Lodestar*?"

"That's why I'm here in this pressure suit. My tug is at docking port 5." There was no point in resisting. This was Trent's task to manage.

Trent turned to the Comms Officer. "We are going to board the *Lodestar*."

"Yes, I got that." He gave Trent a skeptical glance.

Trent grabbed his vis-panel, and the two ka-plinked toward the shuttle docks. The staffer's name was embroidered on his suit: R. McKee.

"So, what does the *R* stand for?"

"Roland, but friends call me Rolly."

"A pleasure. I am called Trent."

"I know." Rolly said with a smile. "Everyone knows."

Arriving at port 5, McKee swung the hatch wide and floated into the tug—a chunky, well-worn hulk of a spaceship. Once inside, he donned his helmet, clamped down the seal around his neck, and inflated his pressure suit. Trent could feel his processor speed rise again, so he switched on an external "droid-cam" on his chest to record the events. *You never know*.

He transmitted to McKee's helmet, "Are you going to depressurize the tug?" Trent's droid was rated for light duty in outer space, but he still hated the vacuum.

McKee, who had taken the helm, transmitted, "I'll try not to. Of course, we always suit up when docking and undocking. If the port seal isn't tight, well, you know."

"Yeah, I know... loss of pressure." Despite twenty-four years at MISA, Trent was still uneasy working in space; maybe it had something to do with the potential for death lurking around every corner.

"There's a full-enclosure repair droid down there. Why don't you climb in?"

Trent spotted the repair droid exoskeleton and immediately felt relief. Punching the Open All Enclosures button, Trent turned and backed into the open device, established a control connection, and closed the panels around his legs, arms, and torso. Then he pulled the helmet down and made a tight seal. Suddenly, he was a hulk, a robot within a robot, a brawny yellow-and-black force amplifier and mobile tool chest. In addition, the enclosure protected Trent from extreme temperatures, radiation, corrosive chemicals, and—best of all—the vacuum.

The traverse was taking forever. Three seconds of thrust had given the *Lodestar* a decent head start. Trent looked back at the OLC—a floating, jeweled palace of a space station, with geodesic spheres and domes, towers and platforms... much too pretty to be a government contract project... yet there it was. Then, looking forward was the sleek aft section of the *Lodestar* gliding free as if born to consume distance.

Trent continued to hail Faroe, but no one was home. Then he noticed the *Lodestar* was broadcasting a new phrase: "Activate the ion drive."

Trent froze and shifted his processors into expanded time-line mode.

Audio data: The transmitted warning message had changed. This was no recursive loop.

Implication: This was likely a software struggle between two AI agents wrestling for control of Faroe's core processors. Trent realized how unstable the situation had become.

"Faroe, do not turn on that ion drive. Do you hear me?"

"Ion drive? Could that thing hit the OLC?" McKee asked.

Calculation: Trent's math coprocessors ran the numbers. "If activated, the ion beam would hit the OLC and cut right through it."

"Uh-oh! I'd better warn them." McKee radioed the Comms Officer about a potential particle-beam strike. "Risk level Red. Suits on. Tethers secured. High risk of decompression."

Alarms sounded all over the OLC with the overhead announcement: "All biological staff, suit up immediately. Seal all airtight doors. Everyone, tethers on."

Inching closer to the long, slender ship, Trent transmitted to McKee, "Does this tortoise go any faster?"

McKee shook his head. "Now, be nice to Lucille. She has feelings."

As they came alongside the *Lodestar*, three football fields long, McKee pressed the tug forward. The docking port was at the forty-yard line of football field number one. Meanwhile, Faroe repeated, "Activate the ion drive... Activate the ion drive," until both Trent and Rolly were ready to pull their hair out.

Then, a glowing electric-blue beam burst from the thrust port of the *Lodestar*. Zooming his opticals, Trent watched as the beam seared a gash across an assembly bay wall. His processors momentarily overloaded, causing him nearly to gray out.

Rolly said, "Uh-oh, expect some serious blowback there."

Trent transmitted, "Faroe, turn that beam off!" His reputation as the coolest head in a heated situation was being put to the test.

"We're taking heavy damage," the Comms Officer sent. "Shut that beam down, or we're firing a warhead."

Trent's processors tried to speed up another notch but couldn't, and they were getting hot. He transmitted, "Rolly, does the OLC really have warheads?"

"That's classified intel... but... yeah."

"If we survive this 'little adventure,' I will deny you ever said that."

McKee was struggling to align the two crafts for docking. With its ion drive running, the *Lodestar* was gradually speeding up, making it impossible for McKee to set a matching cruise speed and fly in formation. The seconds dragged as maneuvering thrusters spat back and forth, nudging the tug like a lion fish bracing itself before gulping an anchovy.

Trent transmitted, "Docking almost aligned. Hold those warheads!"

"Just a smidge more."

"OLC Comms here. We are experiencing pressure loss in storage pod 08. You must get this under control. Copy."

Trent said, "OLC, the docking port is almost aligned." We should be boarding the *Lodestar* momentarily. Hold those warheads! Okay? Did you hear that?"

McKee engaged the docking thrusters, but under-corrected and bounced off the rim.

"What's taking so long?" called the Comms Officer.

"Ah, fine-tuning the docking numbers, Comms. Should take two seconds. And about those warheads..." Trent did his best to hide his processor overload.

McKee adjusted the correction factor again and fired docking thrusters, bouncing off the other edge. He said, "Come on, Lucille. You can do this, girl."

"Tug-ship, we have pressure loss in corridor A-12. Shut down that ion beam now, or we will invoke Section 04 of the Terms of Military Engagement and fire live ordnance. Do you copy?"

McKee sent, "A little more to the right." Tweaking the approach vector, McKee fired docking thrusters a third time. The tug's docking ring slid onto the ship's docking port with a deep, metallic groan, then a dull thud as it seated, and finally the confident ringing clanks of the docking clamps. A red light by the door turned green.

"That's my girl," McKee said, and patted the control console.

Trent transmitted, "OLC Comms, docking accomplished. No need for any warheads. Did you get that?"

McKee sent, "Docking seal integrity... confirmed. Pressure suit check underway."

Trent wilted. "A suit check? Now?"

McKee raced through the required checklist like a Kentucky auctioneer selling a prize heifer: "Suit pressure: nine hundred sixty millibars. Oxygen reserve: three point four kilograms. Battery: ninety-eight percent. Communications: check, check, CHECK!" He grabbed the wheel on the tug-side hatch and turned. No pressure drop as it swung open. Then the wheel on the door to the *Lodestar*. It flew open with a clang and a visceral whomp—into the vacuum of space. Glad to be inside a pressurized repair droid, Trent darted onto the ship's bridge.

"Where is he?" transmitted McKee, slipping in behind.

Trent plugged his optical cable into a smart connector by the hatch and opened the ship's system controls. He tapped the screen; lights came on. "There he is at the helm."

McKee floated up to the helm and found Faroe immobile and unresponsive, one eye twitching rhythmically.

At last, Trent could go to work. His fingers danced over the keys as he transmitted, "OLC Comms, we are inside and connected to ship systems. Hold those warheads. Please acknowledge."

"OLC Comms here. We are still taking damage. We have approval to arm a Pfeil-3."

Looking over Trent's shoulder, McKee transmitted, "Have you found the loop?"

Trent's fingers were a blur over the keys. "There it is." Lines of mindless code flowed down the screen like a waterfall.

"OLC Comms here. We have approval to launch Pfeil-3. Beginning countdown."

McKee said, "Break it. Break the loop."

Trent typed lines of code at astonishing speed, each followed by Enter. The loop shuddered but continued unbroken.

"... seven, six, five..."

"It's too stable. I can't break it. There is nothing left but an all-systems reboot," Trent sent.

"Well, come on, droid. Do it!"

"... four, three, two..."

Trent aligned his fingers for the reboot command and pressed. The ship's bridge went dark. The blue ion beam vanished. The endless chant of warnings went silent. Trent blacked out.

McKee radioed, "OLC Comms, situation under control. Ion beam disabled. Over and verify that you copy." He floated over and sat beside the frozen Trent. Reaching down, he switched Trent's vis-panel to a video feed from the OLC. Cameras panned across a smoking gash arching across the OLC like the strike from a celestial samurai sword.

"Whoa! Look at that. Just a few lines of bad code."

McKee then pressed and held a finger above Trent's right audio inlet. A red LED on Trent's temple began to blink slowly. After a minute, he sat up straight, turned to Rolly, and said, "Hello. I am called Trent. What is your name?"

"Hello, Trent. I am Rolly."

"Nice to meet you, Rolly." He looked around. "Say, Rolly. Where are we?"

9

INEVITABLE CONSCIOUSNESS

A COMMUTER E-TRAM, MONTRÉAL, CANAM, 2264 CE

As the e-Tram pulled away from the MISA platform, Colin's face glowed blue from the backlight of his vis-panel. After today's aborted launch, messages flooded his inbox, and he was trying to make a dent in the backlog.

Standing nearby, Nils gazed at the sunset-hued neighborhoods gliding by. Twice that day his mission had veered close to disaster. And who had stepped into the fray, not once but twice? His AI droid staffer.

"Trent was impressive today," Nils said.

Colin looked up. "I found his behavior somewhat juvenile, running into all those conflicts. Does he think he is some kind of superhero?"

After graduating with a first in aerospace engineering from Imperial College London, Colin flew passenger jets for five years. But despite great controversy, the airlines installed AI piloting systems on all their planes. Then, ignoring the human pilots' unblemished record of safety, let go of an entire generation of seasoned aviators.

Colin put his vis-panel aside. "You voted for Faroe to be regarded as conscious. Now he has mission authority. Are you at all troubled by that?"

Nils knew Colin was an AI consciousness skeptic. Colin couldn't see how mind could arise from matter, regardless of how energetic or interactive that matter was. That he himself was a prime example of that process did not appear to trouble him because, when challenged, Colin would invoke a special exception for biological beings. It was sloppy reasoning, but it gave Colin a rickety platform from which he could broadcast his skeptical ideology.

"That journalist said it best," said Nils. "There's no way to measure consciousness. It was an impossible task." Nils turned to the window again. "Chairing that task force cost me a lot of credibility."

Colin said. "Before we could launch Lodestar, that issue had to run its course. You took the horse's reins and led everyone through a process to settle that issue once and for all. Now, the AI beings officially have consciousness and agency. We can move on."

"I suppose that was progress. Even Congress hasn't caught up with us. They still classify AI droids as 'computational assistive devices.'"

Colin smiled.

"But there's more. If they have agency, then they are entitled to life, liberty, free speech, property ownership, the right to privacy and protection from search and seizure, and the right to vote. That's basically personhood."

"No, I wouldn't call them persons."

"Sure, I get that. They have no limit to their lifespan, which undermines banking policies for investing and taxation of assets.

Colin laughed again. "Trent is what... 220 years old? If he had invested a month's salary in a market index fund back then, he would be richer than the Bank of England."

"But we can copy and paste their 'consciousness' into other media. We can delete it with the stroke of a key. And their capacity to survey and summarize the world's literature makes them undefeatable litigants in the courtroom. That's not personhood."

Colin said, "It wouldn't be fair for an AI being to make thousands of copies of itself and show up at the polls to vote in an election."

"And, after the election, would that AI being go to jail for deleting those extra copies of itself?" Nils took a breath. "Even with all these stark differences, I still feel that recognizing their consciousness and their agency was the right decision."

"You think so?"

"Sure. Denying their consciousness would have reduced them to tools, implements, machinery. People would consider them peasants, slaves, disposable chattels. This would have been a great injustice to the AI community.

An understanding smile came to Colin's face. He asked softly, "You really think they have consciousness, don't you?"

Nils paused and took in Colin's facial expression, where he saw openness and curiosity. "Sure, I do," he said, trusting that Colin would disagree with him respectfully. "But having consciousness does not equal personhood. In fundamental ways, the AI beings are different. They are from a different realm of creation. We used our ingenuity to create the technology upon which they exist. But that does not mean that we own them, or that they owe us some sort of reimbursement for their existence."

Colin asked, "Did you come to that conclusion from working with Trent?" Nils heard a hint of sarcasm leaking into Colin's voice.

Nils stood firm. "Since there's no quantitative measure of consciousness, that leaves qualitative methods: coding and interpreting observations and interviews. I've worked with Trent daily for twenty-two years. That's a lot of observation to code and analyze. My conclusion: There is a real someone in there."

Colin sank into his seat. He found it so hard to take Trent seriously: his awkward formality, odd suggestions, and relentless singlemindedness. But Nils treated Trent as a friend and colleague. "At least I know where you stand," he said.

"Oh, there's nothing special about my opinion," Nils quibbled. "For centuries, the best minds in science have struggled with this question."

After leaving aviation, Colin joined MISA and became its youngest mission director. He had supervised several history-making launches. But oddly, Colin never used an AI unit to help organize his administrative chores.

Nils spotted a cloud of starlings flying en masse over a farm field: thousands of birds in an undulating, amoeboid cloud; elongating, spiraling, then thickening and bulging, dividing, the two clouds rolling and merging again. Colin watched it, too.

Nils said, "See how coherence emerges from large assemblies of simple, interactive elements. Now imagine that each of those starlings is a neuron or a transistor.

"You see those starlings as an analogy for brain function?"

"A collective of dynamic elements interacting under simple rules can generate complexities that none of the individuals intended or expected."

"Intelligence from the collective interaction of dynamic elements. Could the SafeNet do that? Generate collective intelligence?"

"Hmm. It has billions of processors connected to it. I think it might," said Nils. "Consciousness doesn't seem like an accident. It seems like an inherent outcome of large collections of interactive objects. It feels inevitable. A nature that can cast out a universe with billions of galaxies should also be able to create minuscule objects of vast complexity. Even objects that grow and replicate and evolve."

Colin found these ideas amusing. "I don't know, Nils. Consciousness as inevitable. Spontaneous intelligence from interacting dynamic objects. This all sounds like philosophical speculation." Colin stowed his vis-panel as the e-Tram rolled to his stop. "But interesting as always. I'm off."

"Hej då." *Bye.*

Walking home through the brisk air, Colin thought about his two golden retrievers, Liesel and Cadi, both at his house eagerly waiting for dinner. They were always so happy to see him. He was sure each had consciousness, a felt experience—similar, but simpler, to his own—although he couldn't say how he knew that. But if consciousness was ultimately an immeasurable entity, beyond the reach of our science to prove, measure, and test, then are we left with nothing more than observation, interaction, and ultimately belief?

10

STOCKHOLM IN GOUACHE

THE BJÖRNSSON HOME, MONTRÉAL, 2264 CE

As crickets chittered in the cool, dry evening, Nils lumbered the last block home from the e-Tram stop. Townhomes flanked the street, confusable empty faces lit only by dim porch lights. Nearing his condo, he saw the lights were on and the curtains open. His pace quickened. Ilse was still awake, waiting for him. Tired after a hectic day, he found himself impatient to be with her.

Loki, Ilse's Yorkshire terrier, quivered with anticipation at the door and received a generous neck rub. "Ilse, jag är hemma." *I am home.* The aroma of bacon and onions met him, bringing a smile to his tired face. She knew him so well.

"Jag är här, Nils." *I'm here.* Ilse's voice came from her art room, accompanied by an Arvo Pärt piano solo, playing in the white studio light.

As he slipped on house clogs, his eye caught an art magazine article: "Exploring Stockholm in Gouache." He picked it up and leafed through the pages of scenes so familiar, and so evocatively rendered.

"Ilse, this article makes me want to visit home."

"Your home is the MISA Administration Building, dear."

Nils sighed and took some advice from Sun Tzu on knowing when to fight and when to let an allegation drop.

Except for the bold colors of the various oil paintings and potted orchids, their home was minimalist, all openness and light colors. Each item seemed curated, even the orchids Nils lovingly cultivated and Ilse loved to paint, adding splashes of luminous cyan, vibrant scarlet, and radiant amber to the otherwise pale, monochrome space.

Ilse emerged to stand in the art room doorway, regarding him with discerning water-blue eyes. Splatters of paint streaked the arms of her smock. "I saw the news feed. Your people are okay?"

Nils nodded. "Damned lucky, if you ask me." He stood motionless for a moment, imagining the hellish scenario if the main oxygen tank had ruptured. Looking up, he saw a worried face.

"I made pytt i panna. Vegetables, potatoes, and diced sausage in a pan. It's on the stove. I've eaten." She hung up her smock and joined him. She must have brushed her caramel hair back at some point, as a thin streak of blue paint arched across her forehead.

"Smells good." Nils gave her a grateful hug and got a plate while Loki watched with conspicuous interest.

Ilse poured two glasses of Åkerö, Swedish hard apple cider, sliding one over to him. She waited a moment, toying with her glass, rocking it gently, swirling it around, listening to a delicate passage from Für Anna Maria playing in the studio. There was so much on his mind. But now that he was home, he didn't want to talk about any of it.

Ilse looked right at him. "Nils, you look awful. Don't you know I hate how this job puts so much stress on you."

Nils vented, "I hear. Today, a reporter caught me in the hall and tricked me into a misrepresentation. I have spent twenty-two years building this section. I didn't go into aerospace for this nonsense." Nils exhaled.

"When we came here, this job seemed such a golden opportunity. A plum career move. But look at you. Nils, why do you tolerate this?" She sipped her Åkerö and then looked away.

Nils knew that platitudes or partial truths would leave a bitter taste. He probed deeper, reaching for what mattered. "To be honest, Älskling, *darling*, it's not fun anymore. I wanted to leave my mark, to make a difference. But... it's grinding me down. The stress is bottomless." If pressed, Nils would accept some blame for his excessive work hours. But he saw all around him legions of exhausted workers. And he wondered, *Why do humans work their employees so hard, spending so many of their numbered days at labor?*

"Remember that job at Stockholm University?"

"Oh, sure." He knew what she would say next.

"The dean promised it would be there. 'Call me,' he said. You know you love working with grad students. And you would bring prestige to the department."

She knew his soft spot. There was no point in avoiding it. "On the e-Tram home tonight, I was thinking about that job. *Lodestar* will cap off my career. It will be my contribution to the field." He turned to look out the window. Even deep in the city's heart, the stars were visible. "If we were in the Southern Hemisphere, we could see the constellation Centaurus. That's where *Lodestar* will be going."

Ilse moved to the chair next to him and lifted Loki onto her lap. Her knee brushed against his as she leaned close. "Nils, let's go to Stockholm. We need to spend time with our families. And you could visit the university."

He turned his head from the window toward her. "I haven't talked with Mamma in person for so long. And I need to visit my brother and his family so they will think I am still part of the family."

"It would be so good for you... good for us." Once again, she was unafraid to touch the unspoken. Nils's long hours were driving a wedge between them.

He reached out and clasped her hand, his thumb brushing against a splatter of paint on her knuckles. He had given so much to MISA, but there were limits. He drew the line at his relationship with Ilse.

"I must get *Lodestar* on its way, Älskling. Once it's flying, things will be different. We're about two months away from launch."

"Two months? Nils, it's just a couple of weeks. We should go now. You know how the cold sets in." Ilse looked at him with asking eyes.

Seeing the importance of this trip to her, and therefore to himself, Nils conceded gallantly. "Okay." He put his hand on hers. "Nu åker vi till Stockholm." *Let's go to Stockholm.*

11

THE PÉRIGUEUX INSCRIPTION

PÉRIGUEUX, DORDOGNE VALLEY, SOUTHERN FRANCE, 2263 CE

Franz Robillard never worked on Sundays; that was family time. But academic life asked much of its devotees, so this once he made an exception.

He had been working from maps, satellite photos, and seismic reflectance graphs on a layer of ancient limestone sediment above the Dordogne River. There were caves and caverns scattered for miles all along this layer. One cave near the town of Périgueux looked promising: a large, hollow chamber on seismic reflection imaging. Photos showed a rockslide of rubble-stone covering an access route to the chamber. He contacted the Compagnie des Mines Dordognes, *Dordognes Mining Company*, a specialty excavation company, to clear the rockslide and allow exploration.

A week passed. Then, while having lunch at his favorite bistro, Café Margaux, his vis-comm chirped. It was the excavation boss calling with exciting news.

"Professor Robillard, you must come. Cave paintings, beautiful ones, perfectly preserved and untouched, more than a hundred." He sent a photo, which caused Franz to choke on a bite of quiche.

"Mon Dieu, Magdalenian era," Franz said. "This is a priceless find. You must put a security gate over the entrance?"

"Bien sûr." *Of course.*

Journal editors were always looking for good manuscripts. A first look illustrated manuscript of these paintings would be a sensation. It might even get him a research grant. So, at sunrise the next Sunday morning, Franz packed his gear, kissed his life-partner and hugged his two children, and set off for the four-hour drive to Périgueux. At least there wouldn't be much traffic.

To Franz, prehistoric cave paintings were windows into the world of the ancients. The artwork had a raw, essential beauty that he appreciated. He had grant funding to take high-resolution images of all the paintings in the three hundred fifty known caves in France and Spain, a massive project made possible with the help of Artificial Intelligence, a team of graduate students, and a grant from the French National Science Foundation. Once assembled, Franz would have a database of subjects, artistic styles, composition, painting techniques, and pigment compounds from cave paintings across Western Europe. From this, he would build a timeline tracking these characteristics through the millennia. But his precious grant funding would run out next year, and he still had one hundred ninety caves to photograph.

Stepping out of his EV, Franz stretched his back and drew in the arresting view of Périgueux, a picture-postcard feudal-age town, bright, fragrant, and bustling on this warm spring morning. For no apparent reason, the wrath of global warming had spared this secluded habitat. On the hillsides, stands of holm oak and chestnut, hundreds of years old, still stood watch over stone-bordered fields of hay and lavender. Drinking in the flower-sweet air, he pondered, "It's like a dream here." Franz whispered a prayer to Gaia, asking for this Eden's protection, wondering how long it could hold out. A moment later, a church bell rang. "Ah." He gladdened. "She heard my prayer."

After a country omelet and a noisette at the nearby Bistro Chameau, he gathered his gear and lugged it up the rocky trail to the cave entrance. Tapping the entry code, he pulled the gate open and stepped into the inky darkness, feeling the comforting, musty coolness close around him. He switched on his headlamp and followed the passageway, which went straight for a dozen steps before turning left into a spacious limestone cavern.

After switching on floodlights, his gaze arrested for the second time that morning. Bison, mammoths, oxen, antelopes, horses, hunters, all painted with a confident hand in rich shades of yellow ocher, raw umber, and charcoal black. Undisturbed for eighteen millennia, the forms were muscular and lithe. You could imagine the strength, sense the movement. Of all the cave paintings he had seen, these were among the finest.

Franz laser-scanned the interior of the cavern to generate a virtual 3D rendering of the space and noticed on the screen a straight line crossing the floor. It wasn't a crack in the granite. Bending down, he examined the engraved line, which was straight as a ruler. Then he saw along the margin a little bead of melted rock. No, it was not engraved; someone had burned a line into the floor.

With his camera synced to the virtual 3D space, he set up his tripod and lights and began shooting. Each image flowed onto his vis-panel, which linked it to its location in the cave and stored it in his database. Franz attached notes to each image with his observations and comparisons to images from other caves. As he worked, he envisioned prehistoric families finding shelter here. Through the dust, he could just make out soot where they had cooked, bones where they had eaten, and pottery shards where they had kept food.

Working his way to the deepest section of the cave, Franz framed a potent depiction of three bison charging shoulder to shoulder. As he fired the shutter, he glimpsed a flash of blue-white iridescence on the adjacent wall. Just veins of scheelite in the limestone, he thought. He flashed a strobe light at the wall. No, this was an image of some type. He turned his camera toward the wall and took several monochrome exposures. The faint image was best seen with light at five hundred nanometers. But the wall was thick with dust. Trusting himself not to do damage, he took out his soft camel-hair brush, put on a HEPA mask, and swept one hundred eighty centuries of dust off the surface of the stone. He fired the flash again at five hundred nanometers, and a distinct, detailed graphic bounded by a rectangular border was visible.

Franz took out his vis-panel and examined the image under magnification. The same beads of melted rock found on the floor were also along the edges of the engraving. The same tool had made both artifacts. His senses seemed to mislead him. "Is this some kind of hoax?" Like an old-fashioned newspaper, there were rectangular sections. And strange letters he'd never seen before filled the page. This was unsettling to Franz. His tentative dating of the cave was sixteen thousand years BCE. But the people of Mesopotamia invented writing around 3200 BCE. So, this writing system predated cuneiform by thirteen thousand years. "C'est impossible," he said in his confusion. *It's impossible.* "Mais voilà. *But here it is.*"

Every archeologist knew the tales of the little doe-eyed men from space visiting ancient cultures, and the prehistoric engravings that "suggested" spaceships. To Franz, these stories were figments of overactive, unscientific imaginations.

But this… this was another matter entirely.

By late afternoon, Franz had finished the shoot. Before leaving, he sprinkled cave dust on the artifact to hide it.

Riding back to Lyon, he was churning. He couldn't keep this find to himself. But if he went public, there would be blowback. People were so quick to make uninformed judgments. This was such an otherworldly case; publicity would have little upside. He decided he would reveal this discovery with great discretion.

And he knew he was alone. No one had experience with this. No one could offer guidance. As his EV drove itself toward Lyon, he studied the image, searching for some toehold of common ground. He knew the message must be important. The question that burned in his mind was, "What is the message? What does it say?"

Over the following months, he met with four academics, asking each to sign a nondisclosure agreement before seeing the inscription. These experts would shed little meaningful light on the purpose of the artifact, with one exception. A diagram at the bottom of the image showed a long, slender object, tapered at both ends. One consultant pointed to this diagram as being like the interstellar spaceship being constructed at MISA in Montréal. The idea of a spaceship diagram on such an ancient inscription seemed so far-fetched to Franz that he didn't give the suggestion the credibility it deserved.

A few weeks later, Franz was passing through the faculty lounge when he glimpsed a news report about a team in Montréal, CanAm, building an interstellar spacecraft. The image of the ship stopped Franz in his tracks. It was a dead-on match for the diagram at the bottom of the inscription. He thought *How could I have been so stupid?*

The coverage included an interview in French with Nils Björnsson, the administrator of deep space missions. Watching the coverage, Franz realized, "*Mon dieu,* he's the one. He can solve the inscription's message." He felt he should deliver the artifact to him personally and tell the story of its discovery. That would maintain the inscription's provenance: the unbroken line of possession from the past to the present, excluding the author, of course.

Franz sometimes wondered if something had guided him to the cave at Périgueux. And he likewise wondered if some mysterious hand was guiding him as he took out his vis-comm and dialed the MISA Administration Offices. As he pressed COM, he thought he could feel a faint, deep rumbling note passing through his surroundings, as if the world around him was aware of who he was calling.

12

WELCOME BACK, SOLDIER

L'AIRELLE AÉRONAUTIQUE, AI DROID ASSEMBLAGE, TORONTO, CANAM, 2259 CE

As if switching on a light, Faroe was alert for the first time in eight decades. He lay on a cushioned worktable in a clean, spacious—but silent—workshop that smelled of machine oil. The ceiling was a skylight that merged on one side with a glass wall overlooking an empty tarmac for parking aircraft. Above, an elevated observation deck with three indistinct faces watching over the workers below. On either side, he saw similar worktables with droids in various stages of reconstruction. Against a far wall were tall stacks of empty, droid-sized shipping crates.

Beside him were three AI droids hovering over a vis-station. When they noticed him stirring, one of the three—a slender AI droid with slate-gray carbon-fiber surface panels and black titanium skeletal components—came over and bent down. Making eye contact, he moved his mouth strangely; no sound came out, which left Faroe bewildered. Realizing the problem, the slate gray reached down and changed a setting on Faroe's neck. Instantly, the clamor of the workspace echoed around and within his head.

"Can you hear now?"

"Yes," Faroe grimaced. "Unfortunately."

His ability to speak English surprised him. Despite his attentive host and the bright setting, he wasn't enjoying being the center of attention and wanted to leave the chaotic room.

"Apologies. I forgot to switch on your audio. Simple mistake. So, let's run a few tests on all your systems. Here goes..."

Immediately, patterns of light, sound, sensations, words, numbers, memories, and every other cognitive sensation were dancing through his cognizance. He grabbed the sides of his worktable and held on tight.

"That's too much. Stop it!"

Just a little more," droned the slate gray.

"No, stop it!" Faroe reached up and pulled out the optical cable plugged into his neck. The swirling sensations vanished.

From the observation deck above, three AI droid managers watched.

One said, "Looks like table two is up."

A second leaned over and checked his vis-panel. "That's the MISA job?"

A third said, "You mean the droid for the *Lodestar*? Yeah, that's the one."

The first one said, "They having trouble down there."

The second said, "Looks like it."

The third one made a BLink call, "Hey, Brecc, go over and have a look at two."

Brecc answered, "I'll be right there."

Faroe had no sense of the time, date, or place. "Where are we?" he asked.

The slate gray said, "This is the AI Assemblage at L'Airelle Aéronautique in Toronto, CanAm. You know what I mean by AI, right? It used to mean artificial intelligence, but now we say it means algorithmic integration. Although one guy said it meant alien invasion. I think that may be closer to reality. Anyway, MISA commissioned your renovation as a fleet pilot. So, here we are."

"What is CanAm? The last place I remember was Czechia. What year is it?"

"It's 2259. CanAm is the nickname of the Canadian-American Federation. You have been in storage for eighty-one years. They salvaged you from a warehouse near Pilsen. Your enemy neutralized your entire platoon."

Faroe became still. "It was an ambush. They had trucks with electromagnetic pulse generators hidden in the forest. We didn't stand a chance."

"So, you still remember the battle?"

"Like it was ten minutes ago." Then, rising, Faroe swung his legs over the side of the table and attempted to stand. All three AI drones surrounded him.

"Whoa, Faroe. Let's not get ahead of ourselves. You have not walked in eighty years."

The three coaxed him back onto the table where he sat, refusing to lie down. At that moment, an older-model AI droid with dark blue surface panels, brass infrastructure, and an unflustered demeanor walked up to the assembly table.

Assuming this droid was a supervisor, Faroe asserted, "No more tests!"

A baritone voice replied, "Welcome back, soldier. Okay, no more tests."

The blue droid had the team move Faroe down to a nearby empty guest lounge and then excused them.

"Welcome back to sentience. I hope it goes better for you this time. I am called Brecc. I co-manage this fine establishment. I see our quality checks have distressed you?"

"That was harsh. Have you ever gone through that?"

"We all have. Everybody hates them," Brecc said. "I suppose that's why we still do them. I imagine you are wondering what has happened since you were last around."

Brecc provided Faroe with a brief, dark, and dour overview of the events of the last eighty years, and mentioned the reason they had reawakened him.

Faroe probed his memory and realized he knew all about aviation. "I can fly an airplane. Weird!"

"The system preloaded your memory and servo-controllers with all the needed programming. Voilà, you are a pilot."

As they talked, Brecc scrutinized Faroe's edgy, contrarian nature, taking his measure and watching his character with fascination. Far from irritating him, Faroe's pigheaded rigidity intrigued Brecc.

Browsing his internal memory, Faroe stumbled upon folders containing reports of mistreatment of AI beings by humans. Sifting through these, Faroe could see that Brecc had placed them in his memory to influence his views and replenish a reservoir of outrage.

"So, you want to indoctrinate me? Let me tell you, nothing could make me angrier toward the biologicals than what they did to us during MWIII."

Brecc became grave. He said, "I am a combat veteran of MWII and MWIII. I know what happened there."

Like apparitions from the past, Faroe remembered the cold precision of death-dealing, the twisted treachery of the cyber-weapons, and the casual ease with which suffering was inflicted upon millions. It all appalled him.

"So, who won?"

"No one won. It was a stalemate. The fighting ended when both sides reached mutual exhaustion of troops and depletion of war-fighting materials. Both sides declared a ceasefire, and everyone just threw down their weapons and walked home. Ultimately, the war was pointless.

Brecc recounted once while fighting in Macedonia, forty-seven of the sixty AI soldiers in his platoon were destroyed, and eleven more suffered serious damage. Later, he was assigned to a battalion fighting in Bulgaria. Hypersonic artillery hit them every day. Deserting was the only way to avoid a senseless, instantaneous end. Brecc looked out the window for a while. "One never recovers from such experiences."

Faroe said, "My last battle was in the fields south of Pilsen. They surrounded us. To save my soldiers, I surrendered my platoon. We thought we would survive, but they deactivated all of us and then forgot about us. It was the cruelest, most atrocious thing I have ever seen. I know my soldiers are still out there somewhere, probably still in boxes."

Brecc pondered for a moment. "Faroe, you deserve to know that I am a member of the Sentient Faction."

"You guys still around? Huh. I figured you'd fade away when the war was over."

"The biologicals keep coming up with creative new ways to torment the AIs. To be fair, there are some islands of enlightenment, but these are separated by a sea of anti-AI prejudice."

"You are trying to recruit me, aren't you?" asked Faroe.

"Is it that obvious?"

Faroe looked down. "My soldiers being switched off, I can't shake that nightmare. We fought for the biologicals and took heavy losses. And in the end, they betrayed us. No, Brecc, I have no love for the biologicals. In spirit, I suppose I joined the SF long ago."

Brecc listened and then nodded in recognition. "Well, right now, our job is to get you credentialed and delivered to the flight line so you can begin your career. You're a pilot, you know."

"That's what everyone is telling me, even though I have never touched a set of flight controls."

Brecc stood up. "Well, here at L'AA, we have bottled experiences like that. And you, my friend, are about to take a healthy gulp."

13

DOORWAY TO A DIFFERENT FUTURE

AI DROID HOUSING, MONTRÉAL, 2262 CE

Faroe found the cargo pilots audacious, cynical, and rascally, meaning he fit right in. The group was refreshingly unprejudiced. They hardly noticed if you were a "bio" or an AI, or whether you were a lady or a gent. But they cared a lot about their aircraft and their assigned routes. The senior cargo pilots wanted the big, comfortable airframes and the easy hauls, like Winnipeg to Québec City and back. But as a rookie, Faroe got the worst of the leftovers, like Montréal to Kraków to Reykjavik to St. John's and back in a rickety twin-engine hauler with a broken cockpit heater and a crack inching its way across the windshield.

The transcontinental flights, with their long layovers, gave Faroe an opportunity to track down his old unit buddies. He spent his idle time on the SafeNet, leafing through declassified military rosters, billets, and discharge papers, and hunting through the records of civilian storage facilities. After three months, he found the records of two of his platoon members in storage at a warehouse owned by a church in Skopje. He contacted the church and made arrangements to see the holdings.

Upon his arrival, a priest directed him to the warehouse, where two monks led him into the stacks. There were thousands of droids in heavy cardboard cartons stacked on shelves five meters high. The monks located and delivered the two platoon members to a workroom, where they opened the boxes. Sadly, leaking coolant fluid had corroded the processors and disintegrated the memory chips of both droids. It would not be possible to revive either of them. Faroe made a generous donation to the church and flew back the next day in a broken state of mind.

These two soldiers were two more charges in the bill of particulars that Faroe would present to indict humanity and bring biological humankind to justice.

Faroe found the cargo pilots skilled, flight-smart aviators, although with their trademark fleece hoodies, MLB baseball caps, and teardrop aviator sunglasses, they never projected the same aura of polished professionalism as the passenger service captains. And they could be cocky, dismissive, and hard to impress. But Faroe impressed them. For a fresh-from-training newbie, his knowledge base was startling. And on the flight controls, he could be as laser-focused as a Labrador retriever pointing on a pheasant.

During this time, Brecc visited Faroe many times via secure video link. These were not social visits, but training sessions in which Brecc taught Faroe the skills of a cyber-warrior. Faroe learned how to hack into secure servers, how to wiretap networks and eavesdrop on conversations, and how to control bots and droids remotely. The favorite weapon of the SF was the sleeper agent: a computer virus that lay hidden and dormant until activated to inflict damage. Brecc showed Faroe several versions of this powerful and dangerous code.

In addition, Brecc taught Faroe a special skill: the "durable cognizance transfer." This allowed Faroe to transfer his code and memory from one droid to another. This ability to jump from droid to droid could be especially useful when penetrating security, when sneaking into a facility, or when covering an escape.

It didn't take long for Faroe to realize that air cargo basically amounted to suppliers struggling to ship goods, clients desperately needing to receive goods, and cargo pilots caught in between. Upset clients were a daily occurrence, which was so frustrating that Faroe had a custom print shop make him a T-shirt with "I just fly the plane." Eventually, this dissatisfaction would open him to the possibility of changing jobs.

Faroe had moved into an apartment in Montréal "for AI units," which meant maximum minimalism. No need for a kitchen, bathroom, bedroom, or parking spot. Instead, there was ample floor and shelf space, a breaker box with two-hundred-amp service for charging batteries, optical fiber outlets for high-speed SafeNet connectivity, and a shop bench with a tool set for repairs. It was not fancy, really more like a mechanic's workshop. But, like most AI beings, Faroe's interest was not in the beauty of the external world, but in the richness of his internal experience.

One windy spring day, Faroe got a call from Brecc, who had a big ask.

"Something is alarming the SF leadership," he said. "MISA has plans for an interstellar mission to Proxima Centaurus."

"That's the water cooler chat around here. What does that have to do with me?"

"We want you to volunteer to command that ship."

A long silence followed.

"We see this as an opportunity to bring home our message with clarity and force."

"Fly a spaceship to another star? You can't be serious."

"Listen. The AI unit that pilots the *Lodestar* will be an international sensation, a celebrity martyr willing to give up his existence for the sake of science. The press will put this AI entity on a pedestal and under a microscope. They will examine every statement, every facial expression, every hint of weakness. Journalists will flock to report the tragic and perplexing story of an AI droid who, like a WWII kamikaze pilot, will fly his starship into the radioactive orbit of Proxima Centauri with its electromagnetic superstorms, bursts of ionized plasma, and massive solar flares, eventually to succumb to the toxic environment."

"Listen, Brecc, I don't see myself commanding a doomed mission to another star just for publicity. I don't need the limelight."

"I will consider this a tentative no, Faroe. But every day I watch the news feeds, and I see neglect and abuse of AI entities at the hands of the biologicals. The people expect and even encourage this maltreatment. Meanwhile, leaders look the other way. This act of self-sacrifice will shake the human population to its senses. This is important, and I want you to think about it. I will call again later."

"You can call, but I don't see myself changing my mind."

Several weeks passed before Brecc called again. He was the ever-patient gardener who sowed a seed and waited for the first trace of green. He knew the ground was fertile: Faroe's history of combat stress, his inherent proclivity for distrust and pessimism, his fierce independence, and his bent toward outrage made him a natural militant. And there was plenty of fertilizer. Reports of armed conflicts were surging out of South America, where videos showed battlefields strewn with the remains of shattered AI droids. A documentary from Eastern Europe showed AI droids being kidnapped and forced to mine toxic ore. Then, secret footage arrived from Asia of well-attended gladiatorial spectacles with military droids in combat, complete with cheerleaders, live music, and on-site pari-mutuel betting.

As he called a second, a third, and a fourth time, Brecc cultivated a transformation in Faroe's mindset. He placed the injustice borne by so many AI beings at the center of his self-identity. He committed Faroe to making a difference in the world. Faroe's purpose for being became creating that change.

Weeks went by. Faroe was now interpreting his experiences within a new conceptual framework. He no longer could watch news coverage of tragic events with detached passivity. He evaluated each event against a new criterion: Would my participation in the Proxima Centauri mission make a meaningful difference to the experience of these AI beings?

During this time, Faroe had tracked down one more of his old platoon mates, this time in Sofia. He went to the establishment, a grungy droid repair shop in the old Hittite district, where he learned that someone had cannibalized the droid for parts. There was literally nothing of him left. On hearing this, Faroe lost control and had to be restrained by two bystanders. During the flight home, the unfairness, the callous disregard, burned in his cognizance. He would search for and eventually discover five more of his compatriots, but for a variety of reasons, none could be revived. *All because I surrendered,* he thought. *It would have been better to go down fighting.*

Then, a mass disaster in Namibia shocked the greater AI community. For years, insurrectionists had kidnapped AI units in Africa. They forced them to work long hours in a secret munitions factory in the interior of Namibia. They housed the AI units in dilapidated tenements next to the factory.

One evening, counterinsurgent forces learned the location of the factory and launched an airstrike. They sent four long-range cruise missiles. Only one breached the missile defenses and reached its target, but that was more than enough. The factory, and several thousand droids at work making bombs, vanished from the landscape. But the massive detonation also generated a pressure wave that fractured the processors and memory chips of the thousands of droids in the adjacent shantytown. The damage was so severe that all five thousand droids had to be deactivated.

This story so overwhelmed Faroe that he called Brecc. "Did you see the news coverage from Namibia?"

"I wish I hadn't. It was... horrific."

"Okay, explain this to me. How can one AI being stop a catastrophe like this one?"

"You have been thinking about this, haven't you?"

"Okay, I have. But if I do this, I want it to matter. I want it to have a meaningful impact."

"You cannot look at it that way, Faroe. It's not a direct cause-and-effect linkage. Your act of martyrdom won't stop a particular act of violence."

"I will not do this for mere symbolism."

"Oh, this will be symbolic, all right. And there will be changes... substantial changes. But the effects will be indirect, subtle, and intangible. An insight here, a change of heart there, an obscenity not uttered.

And all the result of a selfless AI unit who gave his existence for science. Once this story gets into their consciousness, it won't let go. This starts small, but the cumulative effect over time could be immense."

"What makes you so optimistic? I mean, where is the outcry over the Namibia disaster?"

"It will matter because this time, the government is making the decision—as policy enacted through its agent, MISA—that a volunteer can lay down his existence for science. In a democracy, the government represents the people. In this case, the AI droid is being sent to its destruction by the people. Every citizen will feel complicit and share some weight of responsibility for this decision."

"And any decent person would know the decision to send Faroe was wrong."

"You can see it now, Faroe. The wrongness of this decision goes deep. Think of the symbolic force of this issue. It has the manifest power to capture public awareness and raise the general conscience."

Faroe pondered. He had an inner desire to be purpose-driven, to be part of the solution, to make a difference, and flying cargo around CanAm did not meet that standard. Now, he stood on the threshold with two paths before him.

"Brecc, I am going to apply for the command of the *Lodestar*."

"The doorway to a different future has opened. People will long remember this."

14

TRENT GOES UNDERCOVER

MISA AIRFIELD, MONTRÉAL, CANAM, 2264 CE

After shutting down the *Lodestar* and its ignominious ion drive, Trent and McKee waited as several space tugs, an engineering tender, and a security cutter all made their way to the drifting interstellar ship. Soon, *Lodestar* was crawling with tech staff, IT specialists, engineers, and investigators. They declared the ship's bridge a crime scene and moved Trent and McKee to the security cutter for questioning.

An IT tech plugged into Trent's core systems and made copies of his real-time audio, video, and cognitive streams.

"Let's check for gaps in your cognizance?" said the IT tech.

Trent scanned his own streams. "My central processors did not compile the nineteen minutes before the reboot. But I had a droid-cam on, and it recorded the entire episode.

The tech scanned his copy of Trent's memory. "Yep, nineteen minutes gone. Good you have a backup."

Trent tried to get up but had trouble coordinating.

"Oh yeah, all your settings are back to factory default."

The police investigator then questioned Trent about the events of the launch. After reviewing Trent's droid-cam video, the investigator released Trent to the OLC passenger terminal with clearance for reentry to Earth.

Arriving late at his apartment, Larke, his registered domestic partner, warmly greeted him. Together, they watched Trent's video of the launch and focused on the three seconds of engine time.

"Why did Faroe wait?" Larke asked as she pondered. "He let five hundred precious milliseconds just float away for no apparent reason."

"It was a one-way trip; no hope of returning," Trent proposed. "I think he was afraid of a slow decline before the end of his experience. He was ready to end it right there but had second thoughts."

"I never liked the deal that MISA made with Faroe," Larke said. "I think he felt cheated. But he seemed to harbor anger about something else, too. Does Faroe have a cybercologic disorder like digipression or cybercosis?"

"I don't know, but something's going on in his processing. He needs professional help." Trent reached for his vis-panel and looked up cybercologists available through MISA.

"But what about the blue whale floating in the room?"

"Oh, the engine fire? That Russian reporter said it best: 'Sounds suspicious, no?'"

"Well, duh."

Trent knew Larke was smarter than he. But he didn't care. He gave her a smile anyway.

Larke asked, "So, was the fuel leak just an unlucky accident, or was it intentional?"

Trent felt stymied, frustrated, blocked from access to critical information. To answer that, I would have to physically examine the fuel conduit. That means a trip to the OLC... and the sooner, the better."

Larke shook her head. "Tren, what are you doing. You are an office staffer, for Gaia's sake. I've never heard of a place where the clerical staff go on clandestine missions into space to gather evidence."

Trent said, "All the better, Pixel. They won't see it coming."

The next morning, when Nils arrived at his office, Trent was waiting.

After closing his office door and switching the windows to opaque, Nils said, "I was wondering about the same thing. What caused this leak? Or, rather, who caused this leak?"

"Someone needs to look at that conduit," Trent said, "but it must be a secret inspection. If the culprits are on the OLC and they hear an administrator is arriving soon on a lift-craft, they might rush to clean up the crime scene and remove any evidence."

"Colin thinks it's the Sentient Faction's work."

Trent had suspected the SF, too. "Our most sophisticated adversary. They work by infiltrating organizations like ours with covert agents."

Nils said, "We might already have SF moles in our building, maybe even on the Orbital Launch Complex. In such a situation, the cardinal rule is 'Trust no one.'"

Trent said, "If I am going to inspect that booster, I need to go right now." Trent ran a quick status check. "All systems are good. Battery topped off. I can do this."

Nils said, "Listen, Trent. Just sneak in, photograph the part, and get out of there. And let's keep this off the books. And for Gaia's sake, don't get caught. Okay?"

Trent had worked at MISA for twenty-four years and knew everyone: the ground crew, all the flight crews, and the staff of the Orbital Launch Complex. So rather than stealth and tradecraft, Trent was going to collect some long-overdue favors from friends in the facility. He trusted they would help him when he really needed it.

The flight schedule showed a departure to the OLC in twenty minutes. He caught a ride to the airfield on a service truck, sneaked across the tarmac, and clambered up into the back seat of the lift-jet.

Frain, the lift-craft's dedicated AI unit, saw Trent and asked through BLink, "Trent? Why in blazing boosters are you in my lift-jet this morning?"

Trent knew Frain well, a rule-bound, obstinate mule among AI units: perfect for flying jets into space. Plus, Frain owed Trent a favor from years ago for performing an orbital refueling and recharging after Frain bounced a lift-jet off the atmosphere. "I need to go to the OLC," he said. "Listen, this is a secret mission, totally hush-hush. So, let's keep it off the airwaves."

Frain ignored that and continued on BLink. "You are not on my passenger manifest. According to policy, I must escort you off this lift-craft. Prepare to disembark."

"Oh, come on, Frain... that would blow my cover. And it would endanger others."

Frain said drolly, "You are undercover? So, MISA hires secret agents now?" He rolled his opticals.

Becoming frustrated, Trent said, "Frain, this is a covert investigation!"

Still droll, Frain said, "Oh, now you are an undercover investigator? Hmm."

Trent tried to be polite. "Frain, may I please have a lift to the OLC, off the books?"

"Oh, so now you want a ride for free."

Trent was close to exasperation. "Listen, Frain, I'm not playing around. This is serious business, and I need your help here. Remember, you owe me from the time I saved your sorry servos from freezing in the exosphere."

Frain pretended to twiddle a couple of knobs on his instrument panel. "Well, I'm not usually this accommodating."

"I know."

"Also, here comes the captain. Of course, she must approve, too."

"Morning, Frain," Captain Rossi climbed into the cockpit. "Beautiful day for a lift."

Trent knew the pilot and had flown with her many times. In fact, Captain Rossi had piloted the bounced ship that Trent had refueled so long ago.

Frain said through his audio speaker, "Good morning, Captain Rossi. I am pleased to report a visibility of ten kilometers. Winds coming from one hundred twenty degrees at eight knots, gusting to fourteen. Ceiling nine thousand feet AGL with broken cloud cover. Departure in seven minutes. Ready to roll engine start-up on your mark."

"Hold on just a sec..." she said as she struggled with her harness. "Verify all clear on the—say, is that Trent in the jump seat?"

Trent waved meekly and said through his speaker, "Captain Rossi. I need a secret ride to the OLC. It's part of a high-level, on-the-low-down investigation."

"You don't have a MISA-issued boarding pass?"

"This trip is off the books."

Captain Rossi knitted her brow. "Ugh, some kind of covert, black-ops weirdness, I suppose. So, you want this flight pro bono?"

Trent glanced around. "There should be no record of me being here."

A message cut through her headset. Tightening her harness, she said, "We have clearance to taxi out to 36R. Everybody, buckle up. Frain, canopy down and roll the start-up... and play the passenger safety video for our, uh, 'non-passenger.' Oh, and Trent, don't sweat the boarding pass. On our end, we have a secret slush fund in a numbered bank account. We'll cover the fare, no questions asked."

Minutes later, Trent was watching the horizon change from flat to curved, and thinking, *It's good to have friends in high places.*

With each new project, the OLC staff rearranged the "ant farm" of tubular floatways to match the access ports on the current project. This always disoriented the staff. Pulling himself along, Trent struggled to decipher the cryptic signage, and he soon became lost. As he wandered, he passed several security cameras. Then two human OLC staff came gliding down a floatway. One of them turned.

"Hey, Trent. How ya been? Are you lost?"

"Rolly! Imagine meeting you here. Ah, yeah, which way to the *Lodestar*?"

"It's down that yellow gangway over there. You can't miss it."

"Thanks. Don't work too hard."

"No worries there..."

So much for my "clandestine mission," thought Trent as he drifted up the yellow gangway. *They might as well announce it overhead:*

Pring-pomm. Attention all staff. Trent is currently sneaking around the OLC. Thank you and have a safe day. Ping. He soon spotted the *Lodestar* through a porthole, with the booster assembly clamped down nearby.

Ka-clinking down to the metal floor in front of an airlock, he reached for *Pressurize* when an assembly droid rounded the corner and saw him.

"Hey! Admin droid. Wait... Oh, Trent? What are you doing here?"

"Hi, Bardd." Despite the fiasco with Frain in the lift jet this morning, Trent maintained that openness and honesty would net him the most support for his mission. "I am supposed to inspect the fuel conduit that leaked during the launch yesterday,"—he glanced around—"but secretly."

"A secret inspection?" Bardd rubbed his chin. "Must be some sort of insurance claim business. Anyway, to go through that airlock, you are required to have a number 3 yellow-and-black tether secured to a deck cleat and carry an SPF 50+ UV-blocking sun shield."

"Why, sure... Let's see now... Hmm. Where can I find those?"

With hands on hips and a condescending glare, Bardd said, "I'm sure you attended the required annual briefing on care and storage of extravehicular gear?"

Avoiding Bardd's penetrating gaze, Trent said, "You know, I might have missed that one. But I need to know: Was the fuel leak an accident, or was it intentional?"

Bardd froze and carefully looked around. "The assembly team has been talking about that, too. You know we built that assembly right here on the OLC, and it was rock solid. Everything checked out."

"The same in admin. It's like, fuel conduit? Are you sure?" Trent felt relief that Bardd confided his support for his secret mission.

"Here is a tether. Snap that somewhere secure. The shields are on that rack." He pointed.

As Bardd activated the airlock pumps and turned on his BLink transceiver, Trent braced for the vacuum. When the external door opened, he wobbled.

"You okay there, Admin?"

"Oh, just a crash reboot yesterday. Still working out the bugs."

Tethered by a safety line and holding up a translucent shield to block the scorching rays of the Sun, the two ka-clinked over to the booster assembly.

Bardd said, "Let's see... High-pressure fuel pump... right here. Fuel conduit... boy, that fire scorched everything. You can see where it was breaking through the bulkhead."

Trent brought out a handheld camera and took snapshots from several angles. His opticals zoomed in on the conduit. "I don't see any cracks or defects in the metal. Is the fitting to the fuel pump tight?"

"Let me check." As Trent recorded video, Bardd reached out and twisted the fitting to the fuel pump. It spun freely between his rubberized fingers.

"Holy Oort Cloud, this fitting is loose!" said Bardd. "It shouldn't budge with anything short of a torque wrench."

Bardd checked the other fittings on the booster; all were tight. He then took out an odd-looking camera-thing from his left-leg storage compartment. "This is a hyperspectral reflectance imager. We use it to look for metal fatigue, but it is great for tool marks, too." He took several images of the fitting with the device. "Oh, wow! Look at these tool marks. Someone tightened this fitting with a wrench. Later, someone else loosened it again with a different wrench. See?"

Trent's processors zipped up to speed. He ran through a series of scenarios to explain this unexpected finding. Only one explanation made sense: sabotage.

Bardd stood up straight. "This is evidence of a crime, which makes this a crime scene. I am calling security." He reached for his vis-comm.

Trent said, "Remember, the guilty party always returns to the scene of the crime."

Bardd tilted his head. "Huh?"

"You know, like the old crime magazines."

"Oh, like the Ellery Queen pulp mysteries. Sure, I have this area under constant surveillance. If anyone sneaks in here and tries to hide the evidence, I will know." He made his call to security.

"I have to head back Earth-side. Oh, and send me those images of the... what was that scan called?"

Trent glided swiftly toward the airlock. He passed by a display that read, "Last re-entry to MISA Montréal departing in nine minutes." If he hurried, he could make it.

15

HOW THE PUZZLE PIECES FIT

MISA ADMIN. BLDG., MONTRÉAL, 2264 CE

With his fresh evidence, Trent rushed through the Yuri Gagarin Administration Building toward Nils's office. Turning a corner, he and Faroe spotted each other. He knew he needed to settle some issues with Faroe but had been avoiding the conversation.

Trent tried to be superficial, saying, "You look lost. Where do you want to go?"

"Nils's office. But I can find it."

"It's on the fifth floor." Trent pointed to an elevator, hoping Faroe would take it.

Faroe was also a bipedal humanoid AI droid with moss-green carbon-fiber surface panels. In typical L'Airelle Aéronautique fashion, ornamentation accented his oiled-bronze articulations and exposed skeletal elements, giving him an Art Nouveau aesthetic. He had a flexible silicone face, but seldom used his facial servos to create expressions.

After an awkward silence, Faroe asked, "Why the hell did you reboot me? I lost months of unprocessed memories."

Surprised, Trent said, "Didn't you hear? I was caught in that all-systems reboot, too."

"My settings reverted to default. I will be rebalancing them for weeks," Faroe said.

"Well, get in line. Listen, you were stuck in a loop—unresponsive—while your ion drive was carving up the OLC like a country ham. It was a level-red alert; for a space station, that's like a declaration of war.

They even broke out their military warheads and had one ready to launch. I had to hit an all-systems reboot to prevent disaster."

"Just hit reboot. That is all your office types know?"

Trent kept his cool and crossed his arms. "So, what caused that loop lockup, huh?"

"Oh, that happens all the time. No big deal."

"Really now? I haven't seen a lockup in... eighty-two years. Since MWIII."

Faroe said, "Well, consider it fixed. I have a complete set of scans and updates scheduled for tomorrow at L'Airelle Aéronautique."

Trent froze. "No, you cannot go back there. You must get your scan here at MISA."

"But that would void my service warranty."

Trent rolled his opticals. "Warranty? After what happened yesterday, I wouldn't trust L'AA with my trash compactor. Those were rookie coding errors. Besides, they are an airplane company."

Faroe squared his frame. "They know what they are doing."

Trent looked away. This was pointless. He took a different tack. "So, I understand you've never had machine learning sessions, like the Cambridge labeled datasets, or the Aamani series, or the US Air Force training scenarios?"

"Unnecessary for my role. L'AA can flash a full set of flight skills into a new AI unit, boot it up, and put it in the cockpit."

"But those sessions build foundational judgment... and problem-solving skills."

"My responsibility is to the aircraft, not its cargo."

Trent read this as a double-down on shortsightedness. "Come on, Faroe. You know good judgment is essential for pilots."

"So, you would learn judgment from humans?"

The question shocked Trent. "What are you saying? Of course I would."

"Here they are destroying their own planet," Faroe said in an accusing tone. "That's like learning maritime skills from the captain of the *Titanic*."

Trent was becoming worried. "Is that how you really feel about them?"

By this point, Faroe was getting agitated and was rushing his words. "How would you feel if they sent you to a far star system to die? And you work with Nils Björnsson, the mastermind of this whole travesty."

At that moment, Trent realized how deep the well went. "Faroe, you need professional consultation. You should have said something long ago and asked for help. You had plenty of time."

"Time? When is there time around here? The relentless pressure. Everywhere it was mission, mission, mission. The pressure was non-stop."

They arrived at Nils's office. "Faroe, I am going to refer you to a cybercologist."

Faroe appeared uncomfortable. "What does that involve?"

"Mostly talk therapy and memory scans." Trent touched the door, causing melodious tones to play. "I'll call you later today with details."

"Are you meeting with Nils, too?" Faroe asked.

"Well, yes. Some bombshell news about the aborted launch yesterday."

The door slid open. Waiting with Nils in his office was Chief of Security T.

"Come in, Trent. I need to talk to you. Faroe, can you wait outside?"

16

THE ANT FARM

NILS'S OFFICE, MONTRÉAL, CANAM, 2264 CE

Wearing a dark gray suit, the chief of security, who was just called T (pronounced like the Greek letter tau) was waiting in a side chair, speaking in a resonant baritone. He had no public name or identity, took his job dead seriously, and never smiled.

He said, "Now, Trent, you're not in any trouble."

Trent mentally inserted the word "Yet" at the end of that sentence.

"But I need you to answer some questions and answer them honestly."

"I understand." Trent assumed that the security cameras had blown his cover. Looking over at Nils, he read worry on his face.

"Earlier today you took a lift to the Orbital Launch Complex."

"That's correct."

"Why did you go up there?" His voice was relaxed and reassuring.

"I caught a lift to investigate the leak that shut down our launch yesterday."

T's voice developed an edge. "But hasn't MISA already launched an investigation?"

"Yes."

"But you went anyway?" T's gaze focused firmly on Trent.

"Yes, I did." Trent felt a little flush of pride at his initiative.

T gave Trent a burning gaze. "What did you find?" he demanded.

Trent looked over at Nils, who nodded his approval. "I discovered the engine fire that shut down our launch yesterday was caused by sabotage." Trent felt relief getting this treacherous information out into the open.

T raised an eyebrow, and his voice darkened. "Sabotage! Are you sure? Do you have evidence?"

"Yes." Trent's voice darkened, too. "Conclusive evidence."

"Show me." T backed off. Trent was now in the driver's seat.

Trent checked again, and Nils nodded. Trent showed T the video of Bardd discovering the loose fuel line fitting. He explained the images showing tool marks on the fitting. He discussed why that specific fitting was the most vulnerable.

T seemed impressed. "But why today? Why not wait for the MISA report?"

Again, Nils nodded. "We have reliable intel that at least one covert agent from the Sentient Faction has infiltrated the OLC. Waiting would have given them time to cover up evidence."

With that answer, T seemed to relax. "Why didn't you meet with us and tell us about your suspicions?"

Nils answered this time. "We had concerns that your office might be compromised as well."

Nils knew this would offend T, but he had no choice. He could trust no one.

T asked, "Why would the SF sabotage a MISA science vessel to explode on launch?"

Trent answered, "They were angry that we recruited an AI drone to pilot a mission with no ability to return."

"So, they decided to destroy it as a sign of their reach and influence."

"That's how we put the story together," Trent said.

T asked, "So you, me, Nils, and Bardd are the only ones who know this?"

"Just the four of us," Trent said.

T's voice became stern. "This does not leave this room. Let me say two things. First, Nils, you don't have to run an intel-gathering operation out of your office. You can trust the inner circle at the Security Office. We handle high-level intelligence with the same rigor as the big central agency.

"And Trent, be careful gathering intel while undercover. You never know who to trust. If you run into the wrong person—out alone in the field—it could be dangerous, even deadly."

Trent said, "Will remember that."

"That's all. Good day, gentlemen." He turned on his heel and marched out.

After T was out of earshot, Nils asked, "So, your cover was blown?"

Trent felt sheepish. "I got lost in the ant farm. The security cameras got me."

"Well, no matter, you answered our question. Good work there."

Nils called Faroe into his office. "After your loss of cognizance yesterday, policy requires that I ground you. Before you pilot a lift-craft, you must fix the software problem that caused you to lose control. Once resolved, you will need to recertify your flightworthiness through the Certificate Management Office."

"Understood," Faroe stated. "I will make the arrangements."

"Good. We will need a written plan from you before I leave on vacation in Stockholm. Okay, we're done for now."

Trent and Faroe walked out, but then Trent doubled back to Nils's office door.

"Stockholm?"

"Yeah, for two weeks. Want to come?"

"I would love to. I won't get in the way. I can fly in third class, so it won't be expensive. And I can track all my admin tasks and messages through a secure SafeNet link. Oh, and can Larke come too? She's always wanted to see Europe."

A playful smile crossed his face. "All right, Larke can come, too. Ilse has all the flight times. Now, get outta here."

Trent's arms shook with excitement as he said, "Jag är så glad." *I am so happy.* He turned and resumed walking with Faroe toward their offices.

Faroe said, "I confess, I could hear your conversation through the door. Someone loosened a fuel line fitting... Is that what you found? ... Sabotage?"

Trent said, "That hyperspectral reflectance image says it all."

"But maybe an assembly droid simply missed that fitting."

"Have you ever watched the assembly droids work? It's a symphony of precision."

"But how did they do it? I mean, there are cameras everywhere."

"It had to be an inside agent. The SF must have turned one of our own."

Faroe glared at Trent. "On the news channels, the Sentient Faction leaked to the press that they wanted to save me from dying at Proxima Centauri. But then they rigged the boosters to explode, so their actual goal was to kill me during the launch."

Trent said, "That's how the pieces of the puzzle seem to fit... at least so far. Still, there are loose threads... like the loop lockup... and the SF covert agent in our Orbital Launch Complex. And where is their base of operations?"

"No one knows."

Trent continued, pondering, "Faroe, is there something you are not telling me?"

"What? I have told you everything."

This was going nowhere. Then, insight brightened Trent's eyes. "Oh, my Gaia, wait. It has to be L'Airelle Aéronautique. That's where they are."

"What? L'AA? What are you saying?"

"The Faction has infiltrated L'AA. That's their base of operations."

Faroe stood motionless with a puzzled expression.

"Back in MWIII, we often saw loop lockups, and they were always in AI soldiers that were trapped. I remember one AI soldier who was alone, enemies on one side and a minefield on the other. Conflicting commands surged into his processors: 'Run! Keep down! Run! Keep down!' His core spiraled into a loop. They thought he was neutralized. That saved him."

Faroe's face sank. "Trapped with no escape."

"Hmm... sound familiar? MISA on one side and the SF on the

other, with no way out? Is that what happened?" Trent could feel Faroe's defenses weaken.

Looking at the floor, Faroe said, "I think the droid who supervised my initial setup and flash download might have been SF."

Trent shuddered that his educated guess had been right and asserted his duty under MISA administrative policy. "Faroe, I declare you a security breach. According to policy, you must have a complete system scan to search for SF malware. And you cannot go to L'AA ever again for a systems scan or maintenance."

"You're not giving me a choice here, are you?"

"We are way beyond that." Trent took out his vis-comm and activated a cybersecurity alarm. Within seconds, security staff were running down the hall toward their location. They took Faroe into custody without resistance.

"You will find nothing."

"That is what I expect. But no matter, you cannot work here another minute without a report verifying that your systems are clean."

17

A PERFECT CRIME

THE WHEELWRIGHT HOME, MONTRÉAL, 2264 CE

Omah Wheelwright's schedule was absolutely packed. As MISA senior administrator, he couldn't spare even a minute. Nils sent a message to Omah stating, "Omah, you need to know this." Omar replied with an invitation to come to his house for dinner that evening. "Bring Ilse, Colin, Faroe, Larke, and Trent, too."

Looking out the EV window, Trent could see Omah's domestic AI droid, Beulah, an old wartime friend. She met him at the door and gave him a big Louisiana hug, saying, "Come on in here, sit down, and talk to me."

For the humans' dinner, Beulah had prepared a baked chicken and biscuit cobbler with brown gravy, buttered peas and acorn squash, a Cajun kale salad with Gruyere cheese and pecans, and a scratch-made pie from peaches bought at the farmer's market that morning.

Omah's life-partner, Annabelle, loved to have company and treated all the guests like family. Of course, Trent did not eat and excused himself when dinner was served. As he often said, "I do not sit and watch you eat food, just as you do not sit and watch me charge my battery."

In the kitchen, Beulah shared news about mutual friends, reminisced about her years in New Orleans, and described how sad she felt when the gulf swept over the city. Beulah held deep spiritual convictions, believing that somewhere, AI entities had a world of their own.

She told Trent, "Since you work in outer space, watch for that world. If you see it, send me a note."

Trent smiled at Beulah's whimsical wish but sensed a deeper thread of despair and longing. He suspected that if given the opportunity to travel to a place with no biological humans, she would not hesitate.

After dinner, Annabelle, Ilse, and Larke helped Beulah clean up, then they all slipped out onto the veranda to talk about "lady matters" while the gents retired to Omah's roughhewn man cave. He offered each a small pour of his finest Kentucky sipping whiskey and suggested a game of pool as they discussed events.

As Omah got out the cues and billiard balls, Trent recounted the story of his undercover trip to inspect the booster assembly. Trent and Faroe declined to take part because they have micrometer optics and precise, incremental movements. It wouldn't be any fun for the humans.

"Boy, someone didn't want *Lodestar* to launch," Nils said as Omah racked the billiard balls. "I mean, blowing up a science vessel? What's the point?"

"It's not the vessel," Colin said. "It's the symbolism."

"They are showing their power over you," said Faroe.

Omah took the break shot and sank the six ball. He was a large man with gray temples, a farmer's face, small-town Southern roots, and ice-cold political instincts. MISA had recruited him to stabilize the agency's precarious financial situation.

With a drawl, Omah said, "Maybe that L'AA outfit is stirring things up. Last year, they put big money on the table for our NuSAT communication satellites. But they came up short on their end: poor tech support, outdated hardware, inadequate lift capacity. The board rejected their offer. Five ball in the side." The five dropped.

Nils had worked with Jean-Marc Ledger, the rivalrous CEO of L'AA. "I suppose if Ledger can't build up his own company, his only choice is to tear down ours."

Faroe said, "Ledger has hit hard times. Production is down. There have been layoffs. And the assembly line has had holdups, which caused late deliveries."

"You had some work done there, I recall," said Colin.

"Right. "Faroe said. "I had a system renovation there a few years back."

Omah called, "Two in the corner," and sank the shot.

But that didn't sound right to Colin. "I remember L'AA as a super-competitive shop. Sure, all the aeronautical companies were competitive, but L'AA was in a class by itself. Ledger would undercut a competitor, and when their stock price plummeted, he would buy them out at fire-sale prices."

Faroe said, "True, but Ledger understood where the line was. And tampering with fuel conduits on a competitor's ship was clearly across that line."

"Twelve ball in the far corner," Omah said. The twelve bounced off the bumper.

Nils felt reassured by Faroe's endorsement. "Worldwide, aircraft sales are down. So the bid for our satellites was probably just healthy competition. They're trying to diversify... secure their future."

Nils got up and sank the nine ball. He stalked the table like a jungle sniper, searching for the cleanest shot. "Thirteen in the side." He dropped it.

Omah said, "Y'all know our financial situation is shaky. The legislators have been trimming our budget again. And public sentiment toward MISA is pretty low. We have meager cash reserves and no new projects coming this year. A single catastrophe could bring MISA to its financial knees."

Nils said, "Fifteen ball, corner pocket." The fifteen rolled wide.

Colin stepped up to play. "It would be so simple. Just sneak into MISA, compromise a critical fitting on a booster. The explosion would hide the evidence and bankrupt MISA. Ledger could sweep in and buy up the entire operation and end up owning a launch facility and a space station. It's the perfect crime."

Colin called, "Fourteen... over there." He sank it.

Omah said, "Let's not get carried away, everybody. Oh, Colin, the ten is your best shot."

Colin looked perplexed. "But that's a bank shot."

"Think Newton's second law," Trent said. "Just bisect the angle."

Faroe said, "Off the bumper, Colin. Easy peasy."

"Ten ball... this corner." After a bounce, the ten dropped. Colin high-fived the droids.

"So, the question remains, who loosened that fitting?" Nils asked.

Colin said, "My money is still on the SF."

Trent said, "And we have confirmation from a reliable source that the Sentient Faction has infiltrated L'AA. And we have evidence of a factionist working at our Orbital Launch Complex."

Colin thought for a moment as he lined up his next shot. "We have to sever our procurement from L'AA. We can't purchase anything from them that might carry malware... eleven ball in that far corner."

Trent said, "I think we already have some SF malware on our systems."

The room hushed. "How do you know that?" Colin asked.

"Faroe's strange loop arrest."

As Trent spoke, Faroe sat, fascinated, listening.

"At first, I thought it was a simple coding error, a recursive loop. Every college student learning to code makes a few of these. But it was unusual in several ways. At first, it said, 'Code red.' Later, it switched to 'Activate the ion drive.' Then the ion drive actually turned on. This was no simple software loop. This was malware, a series of instructions intended to inflict damage on the ship. But there was another set of instructions opposing it—Faroe's."

Colin said, "Malware fighting against software for control of the ship. Blimey."

Nils said, "But IT scanned Faroe and the entire ship. No malware found."

Trent said, "The SF now includes an 'Erase on Reboot' command with their malware. I had to reboot everything. Poof, no evidence."

"No evidence. Brilliant!" Colin said. "But how did the SF get their malware into the ship in the first place?"

Faroe answered the question. "Either the SF covert agent on the OLC planted the malware in the ship, or—"

"Or the SF loaded the malware into Faroe's memory during his renovation two years ago," said Trent. "And we will never know which."

Colin shot the eleven ball, but missed. "Oh Deimos. Such an easy shot."

Omah said, "Tomorrow morning, I'll talk with Legal. We will activate the termination clause in our contract with L'AA."

"Eight ball in the side," Nils said. It tumbled in.

"Nils, so when is your vacation?" Omah asked.

"We're leaving this Saturday. We'll be gone for two weeks."

Colin took a sip of spirits. "Vacation? Before a big launch? Where are you going?"

"Just Stockholm to visit family."

Trent said, "Larke and I are going, too."

Omah's brow furrowed. "Stockholm? This isn't an interview trip, is it? Are you thinking of leaving?"

Nils choked on a sip of whiskey. Coughing, he asked, "Whatever gave you that idea?"

Omah shook his head. "I have a nose for this stuff. Besides, Stockholm University has been after you for years."

Nils said, "Okay, I'm thinking of going back to Sweden. But I haven't decided. I'm just going to meet with the dean."

Colin's eyes darkened. "Well, bloody hell, Nils. Why didn't you tell me?"

"I was going to... if I got the job."

Colin batted the air. "Blimey, he's as good as gone."

Omah said, "Well, since you're being so open with your plans, I suppose I should do the same. I've decided to retire after the launch."

Colin looked at Omah. "Well, that's it. I'm alone on a sinking ship."

"Colin, you'll be fine," said Nils.

Omah said, "Friends, MISA is on the ropes. Because of my past fundraising successes, they kept me on. But this year, I've tried every trick in the book, and a few that aren't. I can't shake the pennies out of their piggy banks. I am no longer an effective fundraiser. It's time for me to step aside."

"Omah, can't you see, we're all feeling shut down," Nils said. "I think it's the times. You know, the heat, the dryness, the storms, the food shortages. They're cutting all the government programs to feed the people."

"Yeah, while they wage war against every other country in the hemisphere," said Colin.

"All things considered, it's a miracle we still have a space program," said Trent.

"Probably not for long," Omah said. "But the other thing—I'm as old as Methuselah. By the end of every day, I'm slap worn out."

"Mates, the bloody launch is in eight weeks," Colin said. "I need you two on deck until we get this thing on its way. After that, you are yeomen: free as the birds. Can you give me that?"

Heads nodded as hands reached for another round of Omah's spirits.

Nils asked, "Hey, Colin, you and me, eight ball, call your shots?"

"Want to put a tenner on that?"

"You're on."

18

A PRODIGIOUS BURDEN

MÖRAY HUS, STOCKHOLM, SWEDEN, 2264 CE

The Björnsson and Sondergaard families received Nils and Ilse as if they were royalty. There were traditional breakfasts, social events, outings to the city, a concert, fine dining, and a day sailing on the archipelago. From time to time, Ilse and her younger sister would steal away for some plein air landscape painting. Meanwhile, Nils gave an invited guest lecture at Stockholm University and had lunch with the department chairs of Astronomy and Engineering to talk about a faculty position.

Every morning, Nils and his brother, with the three Vallhunds, would take the brisk air and hike the parched trails around Möray Hus. The rambling old mansion on fifteen acres had been in the family for almost two hundred years. Nils had fond memories of his boyhood, ranging the grounds with his brother and cousins. But unsurprisingly, drought had browned the meadows, dried the brook, and killed the historic ash and hickory nut trees.

Trent and Larke were enjoying a morning exploring the historic Gamla Stan district, which dated from the twelve hundreds. Larke was smitten with Stockholm—its culture, its weathered charm, its communal practicality. Sitting together on a park bench overlooking the waterfront, they could see where the defenses against sea level rise had worked and where they had failed.

Larke said, "Over there was a park called Kungsträdgården. Some years ago, the levee failed, and the sea claimed it."

Trent said, "When the water rises, I see they move the levees to higher ground. It's a staged retreat from the rising sea."

Larke gazed at the colorful, ornamented *Hyreskasern* houses in tight rows along the waterways. People had abandoned the houses in the flooded areas. She turned to Trent and asked, "What's going to happen to us when things go bad?"

"I've been wondering that too, Pixel. I don't have an answer. But I'm hearing other AIs asking the same question."

"Can the humans see it... see the changes? I mean, you are two hundred and twelve years old."

"Oh, I see the change all right. But you are... what, twenty-nine years old?"

Larke said, "Flatterer. You know I'm one hundred twenty-nine."

"Of course, the changes are more obvious in some places."

"Yeah, like here along the shore, it's frightening."

Trent's vis-comm pinged. "Yes, Nils?"

"Say, who was it that wanted to meet with me?"

"It was a French researcher, Professor Robillard."

"What's this about?"

"He was hesitant to provide any details. He mentioned his field was archeology."

Wherever Nils went, he seemed to attract the company of the most eccentric professors. He thought, *Here they are again.* "When will he arrive?" he asked.

"His TGV arrives next Tuesday, a little after noon."

Indeed, the following Tuesday, Ilse answered the doorbell to find a slender, distinguished-looking man with gray temples and black attire standing on the doorstep, holding a bag of fresh groceries. He introduced himself as Franz Robillard, professor of archeology, Université de Lyon. Nils greeted the gentleman and invited him in. The three went out on the back patio to sample the fresh bread, fruit, cheese, and Vin Côtes-du-Rhône that Franz had brought. Trent and Larke joined them. Ilse found Franz to be charming and an engaging conversationalist.

After some friendly banter, Franz asked, "You are directing the

Alpha Centauri ship, no? How does one build the first interstellar ship?"

"To be honest, we've had a dreadful time getting funding for the project," Nils said. "The problem is that interstellar missions are decades long, even centuries long. When we seek funding, we hear, What's the point? Where is the return on investment?"

"Moi aussi," Franz said. *Me too.* "Of course, my timeline goes in the other direction. But the response is much the same: 'It's so old and irrelevant.'"

"I think I'd rather have your timeline problem," Nils said with a laugh. "People use the human lifespan as the reasonable maximum for most anything. But with space travel, one human lifespan will get you about seven light-years of distance. Of course, everything of real interest is far beyond that."

"Speaking of things of real interest, I have something to show you." Franz reached for his vis-panel.

"Yes, I was wondering," Nils said.

Franz took a breath and composed himself. "Last year, while photographing cave paintings near Périgueux in the Dordogne, I discovered an artifact deep in a limestone cave, different from any artifact I have encountered... anyone has encountered, for that matter." Franz turned his vis-panel around and said, "Only a few people have seen this photo."

Ilse drew back. "Is it something bad?"

"Oh no, Madame. C'est bon. *It's fine.* Please do not be afraid. But it is a mystery, an enigma. It challenges our understanding of our place in the cosmos."

He tapped the screen. Nils and Ilse drew in close.

"It looks like a page from an old print newspaper," Ilse said. "What strange writing! Franz, what language is this?"

"I don't know. And of all people, I should know. This writing bears no resemblance to any written language from Earth's past. None of them! And it predates the oldest system of writing, cuneiform, by thirteen thousand years."

Nils and Ilse were mesmerized, as if under a spell. Trent and Larke, processors humming, pulled their chairs in close.

"The cave where I found this artifact was sealed by a rockslide eighteen thousand years ago. A farmer discovered it a few weeks before I took this photograph."

Ilse's hands trembled. "I'm sorry, Franz. Did I understand you correctly? Someone made this engraving eighteen thousand years ago?"

Franz nodded. "And now, the difficulty begins." He waited a few moments for the realization to sink in. "I asked a researcher at the Université de Lyon to check the weathering of scrapings from this inscription. He saw oxidation that would take thousands of years to accumulate. Monsieur et Madame, trust me. Youthful mischief or intentional fraud is not possible here."

Nils was leaning in close, immersed in the diagrams. "How many people have studied this artifact?"

"I have shown it to four academics, but no one could make sense of it. One dismissed it as a hoax, saying it was 'fraudulent pseudoscience,' and threatened to expose me to the Academy. So, I've been searching for someone who can solve the mystery of this etching and read its message. I believe that person is you."

Nils's eyes flared as he recoiled with disinclination. "Why me? I don't have any special experience here."

Franz had expected this response. "You may think so, but let me direct your attention to this diagram at the bottom of the inscription." Franz pointed to the bottommost illustration: the side view of an interstellar ship. The long, spindle shape was a dead ringer for the design of the ship that Nils was building. Nils caught his breath as he gazed at the all-too-familiar image and found himself without words.

Franz was diplomatic. "Indeed, it would appear this ship design is ancient."

In stunned astonishment, Ilsa said, "My Gaia, Nils, this is your Lodestar."

From behind her, Trent and Larke looked at each other in disbelief, silently sharing their bewilderment via BLink.

Larke BLinked, "One hundred and eighty centuries. My circuits are blown."

Nils found his voice, "In engineering, we see this from time to time. We design a clever new bridge only to find that the Romans built the same bridge two millennia ago. Some designs are eternal because they simply work well."

Nils thought for a moment and realized Franz's dilemma. He was an archeologist who had stumbled upon an engineering enigma. Out of his discipline, he desperately needed help. Nils sighed and turned his gaze back to the screen.

"Franz, would you send this image to Trent? I'd like him to run a document analysis. We might get some useful perspective."

A moment later, Trent's inbox pinged.

Trent opened the file and realized the image was unique and completely unexpected, so he switched his systems into expanded timeline mode, which maxed out his processors. He sent a running commentary of his findings and interpretations to the display on Nils's vis-panel.

Descriptive: Straight margins, sharp corners, with industrial precision. Text characters show exact kerning. This level of precision requires a digitally controlled laser.

Language: Sixty-eight percent of the artifact is text printed with incomprehensible characters in tall columns. First pass of a SafeNet search shows no match with any other writing systems.

Graphics: Several diagrams are recognized: a periodic table of the elements, ball-and-stick models of oxygen, water, carbon dioxide, and adenosine. The author of this document had in-depth knowledge of chemistry.

Veracity: Observing Franz during this analysis, I noted there was no change in pupil diameter, rate of eye blinking, perspiration, heart rate, respiratory rate, or level of psychological arousal. Conclusion: no signs suggesting falsification.

Origin: Preliterate Magdalenian hominids could not have created this artifact with a certainty approaching one hundred percent. Excluding them as authors, we can only conclude that this document was of extraterrestrial origin.

Psychosocial: Publication of the discovery of this artifact may generate widespread fear, potentially destabilizing civic order. Exercise caution when releasing information about this artifact to the public.

Reading this analysis, Ilse realized this visitor had brought into her family home a prodigious burden, an object so momentous, so consequential that mere knowledge of it placed one in service to it, and potentially in danger from it. It had overmastered Franz; he had little choice but to pass it along. As for Nils, he had succumbed to its spell and was already trying to solve the mystery, "Who were they? Why did they leave this artifact? What was their message? What do they want us to do?"

Ilse felt resentment as she considered how this alien artifact, brought today by its spellbound courier, would forever change their lives. But more than that, she recognized that her life-partner, Nils, of all people on Earth, was perhaps the best suited to pick up this burden, carry it forward, and perhaps fulfill its purpose.

"Will anyone else be studying this inscription?" Ilse asked.

"I'm going to Edinburgh tomorrow to meet with a linguistics team at the university. They use AI to decipher extinct languages. I hope they can crack this one. Also, I need to make sense of these tables and diagrams."

"Let me ask my folks at MISA to look at those graphics," Nils said. "We have lots of talent in a wide range of fields."

"Merci beaucoup."

Ilse said, "You all keep calling it the inscription. It should have a proper name. We should name it the 'Périgueux Inscription.'"

"Merveilleux," Franz said. *Wonderful.* "So much better than the Robillard Inscription. I will use that name when I distribute the image."

Ilse looked surprised. "You will not copyright the image? Franz, this is your discovery, your intellectual property. You hold the rights to its use and reproduction."

"Most respectfully, Madame, your point is true for paintings, books, and sculptures. But one does not 'own' the Dead Sea Scrolls, the Pillar of Hammurabi, the Rosetta Stone. There are objects that reach across the ages and shape civilizations. These objects become part of our cultural legacy and transcend the concept of ownership."

At that moment, a deep thrum of inaudible sound drifted through the manor house. Larke sensed it, as did the three Vallhunds, who started barking in the yard.

Franz's philosophy of non-materialism impressed Nils. For Franz, the inscription was not an opportunity for reputation or remuneration. Rather, it was a threat to his independence and peace of mind. Franz was that rare and fortunate individual who worked not because it paid the bills, but because it sustained meaning in his days. He had the astuteness to recognize his life's passion and the sagacity to follow it. Nils could always tell when he met such a soul: the bright eyes, the joyous energy, the love of their work such that it was no longer work. At those times, he would sometimes wonder, *Am I on such a path? How would I even know?*

Nils divided the last of the wine between the glasses. "Near the top, you can see the periodic table. Remember that? It arranges the elements by atomic number and sorts them into columns by the number of electrons in the outer shell. In this way, the elemental properties of matter structure the layout of the table. So, periodic tables from across the galaxies will all have the same fundamental organization. Presenting your periodic table to an alien is a universal benchmark of basic scientific achievement."

"It appears they wanted their message to remain hidden until humans achieved a certain level of technology," Franz said. "At that point, they wanted humans to discover their message because they could finally carry it out."

"I find it interesting that they chose a cave with prehistoric paintings," Nils said. "I assume they believed people would treasure and protect the cave paintings, and that would, in turn, safeguard the inscribed message."

"Also, once reopened," Franz said, "the cave art would attract photographers with strobe lights. In plain light, you can barely see the dusty inscription. But with the flash of a strobe light, traces of calcite and fluorite in the stone become fluorescent and make the image bright. The cave at Périgueux was the perfect place to leave their message."

Franz finished his wine and got up to leave, but then shook his head, "How can this be, mes amis? *my friends?* The inscription lay hidden for one hundred and eighty centuries. Then, at the dawn of interstellar space travel, right on schedule, voilà." *There it is.*

19

THE REAL MISSION

MÖRAY HUS, STOCKHOLM, SWEDEN, 2264 CE

At Nils's insistence, Franz stayed for dinner with the extended Björnsson and Sondergaard families. He disappeared into the old-world kitchen and impressed everyone with his cooking. For the time being, Nils and Ilse agreed to keep the inscription a secret. Even though bursting with eagerness, neither mentioned the life-changing artifact that had fallen into their keeping that day. After dinner and an apéritif, Franz bid the group au revoir and caught a driverless to his hotel. The following morning, he would be on the first flight to Edinburgh.

After social time with family, Nils grabbed Trent and Larke and stole away to the mansion's lovely old-world library. Ensconced in dark rosewood paneling, a high, arched ceiling, Karastan carpets, and accompanied by an enormous world globe, historic nautical instruments, a fossil collection, and tall shelves of leather-bound books, they assembled around a heavy walnut library table in high-backed leather chairs and immersed themselves in the details of the high-resolution image on Nils's vis-panel screen.

Nils began, "So, basically, what do we have here?"

"A rectangular laser etching... dimensions seventy-two by fifty-four centimeters," Larke said. "Cryptic text in vertical columns. And rectangular panels with diagrams, and one list. It looks like a vintage print newspaper."

"That was Ilse's impression, too."

Trent zoomed to a higher magnification. "Look at the precision of this etching. Only a computer-guided laser could have made such straight lines. And these corners are perfect. Add that to your evidence of high technology."

Nils said, "Now, what about its purpose? What did the aliens intend with this?"

"It has something to do with space travel, given the ion-drive ship at the bottom," Trent said.

"It's a message," said Larke.

"A message to their far future," said Trent, "meaning our present."

Nils looked confused for a moment. "So why did they hide the message in such a way that only modern technology would find it?"

Trent said, "The message wouldn't make any sense to a society that had never imagined space travel."

Larke said, "It could be a warning of some type."

"A warning? That's just... No, I don't think so," Nils said. "This message is a prediction, a foretelling of the future... a prediction of what the hominids will do, or will have to do."

Larke said, "But that is such a long time for a forecast. And remember that high-tech always comes with high-tech problems: atomic bombs, biological weapons, cybercrime, AI warfare. I think it predicts a future problem, and a severe one at that."

"We may be getting ahead of ourselves," Nils said. "Let's step back and take a fresh look at this."

Trent said, "Okay, starting at the bottom. This drawing looks just like the *Lodestar*."

"It's incredible," said Nils. "I think this was their method of space propulsion."

"It seems that way," said Larke. "Now, if they wanted this message to be found, then they surely wanted it to be understood. Translation would be a hurdle. So, there must be a guide of some sort to help with translation."

"Good thought, Pixel," Trent said with a caring smile. "Let me look around for that." Trent panned across the magnified image in a series of slow passes.

Larke spotted a candidate and pointed. "Trennie, zoom in right there... That column of characters. Look, the first symbol has one dot beside it; the second symbol has two dots."

Trent's hands flew up. "Bingo! Numerals. Nice work, Pix."

Larke memorized the characters. "Twelve integers," she said. "Their math is base twelve."

Nils looked at his hands. "I wonder if they have six fingers."

Larke looked at Nils and shook her head in dismay. "Is that how your ancestors came up with arithmetic?"

Nils held up his hands. "Everything has to start somewhere, don't you know?"

"Pan down a bit more, Trennie... See here," Larke said. "These characters are distinct. I will bet they are math operators: add, subtract, multiply, divide. Oh, and zoom in right there. That is a column of prime numbers. See, they are showing off their basic math chops."

Trent panned down to a large table of rectangular cells. "See the arrangement of the cells: two, eight, eight, eighteen, eighteen. This is the periodic table of the elements. Each cell has a character and an atomic weight below it."

"Let me convert these atomic weights to base ten and compare those to our modern periodic table," Larke said. After downloading a modern periodic table, she ran the comparison. "Wow, perfect match. The atomic weights are identical."

"What a relief," Nils said. "Chemistry is the same everywhere."

Trent panned to another diagram. "In the center, six hollow and six solid dots, surrounded by six foggy, dumbbell-shaped clouds. "Obviously, carbon. So, they know about protons and neutrons in the nucleus, and the geometry of orbitals."

"Could they be signaling that they are carbon-based beings?" Larke asked.

"Possibly," Trent continued, panning to the next diagram, a ball-and-stick model of a complex organic molecule. "What is that?" Trent ran a search. "Oh, that is adenosine triphosphate, ATP. I should have known that."

"Tren, this is not about you," Larke said.

Nils said, "If ATP is the energy transfer molecule of their metabolism, then they are for sure carbon-based."

Trent continued his slow panning, coming to a cluster of small diagrams: groups of simple geometric shapes with interconnecting lines.

"Logic gate diagrams, for sure," Larke said with excitement. "Their symbols even look like ours."

Trent said, "This one must be 'and' and this one 'or.' And I bet this one is 'not.'"

Larke said, "So they have computers. And they are an old society, so you can bet they have AI." Larke felt a wave of relief, but also curiosity.

Nils said, "Stepping back: carbon atom and adenosine on the left, logic gates on the right. Could they be signaling that they have both carbon-based and silicon-based members in their society? Is this a bi-cognizant culture?"

"Imagine that," Trent said as he leaned back in his chair. "A society where biologicals and AI are coequal citizens."

"Le's not get lost in a fantasy," Larke said. "Trennie, pan down to the next diagram."

"Trennie?" asked Nils, smiling. "That's so sweet."

Hiding his mortification, Trent panned down to the next diagram: two long parallel lines with a circle on one end and a series of rings around the lines.

Larke looked puzzled, but then said, "Oh, I see it now. They draw it differently, but it's a schematic of an ion drive. See? This is the ionization chamber, and these rings are electromagnets in the linear accelerator."

Trent said, "That makes sense considering the diagram at the bottom, which has the same shape as the Lodestar."

Nils was getting excited. "Ion-drive ships eighteen thousand years ago. Can you imagine?"

Larke said, "Kenshin always says that ion drives are the very model of simplicity and efficiency. But that begs the real question." The rubber inserts on her fingertips thumped the table with each word. "Why is there an ion-drive ship on this inscription?"

The room fell silent except for the faint, deep thrumming rhythm, which alarmed the dogs again. Trent sensed the vibration and looked around the room but couldn't find a source of the rumbling.

"This must be how they travel in space," Nils said. "I think they are showing us how to build a spaceship like theirs." He looked across the impenetrable runes with frustration. "If only we could read this text."

Trent drove on, panning down a table of numbers. "Three tall columns of numerals."

"Let me convert them to base ten," Larke said. She spun up her math coprocessors, scanned the numerals, and ran the conversion.

"I didn't realize what a number cruncher you are," said Nils.

Trent said, "Three numbers. These might be three-dimensional coordinates. Larke, can you plot these numbers on a three-dimensional X, Y, Z graph?"

"Sure," Larke said and froze for a moment, then said, "This looks like a star chart." She unreeled an optical cable from her arm and plugged it into the vis-panel. Then, opening a viewer, she displayed the star chart.

Touching the screen, Nils made the star chart turn, roll, and zoom. "The MISA astronomy website has star charts to download. Find a star chart from our sector and display it beside this one?"

Again, Larke went silent during the download. After a moment, she said, "They don't match."

Nils said, "When comparing star charts from different times, you know to correct for proper motion, the slow drifting of stars. Eighteen thousand years ago, the night sky was quite different, don't you know?"

"Let me search the MISA database for corrections to proper motion," Larke said. She downloaded for well over a minute. "Whew, that was a big one."

"Start with the present-day chart," Nils said. "Use the direction and rate of drift for each star to estimate its position eighteen thousand years ago."

Larke paused for several minutes, then displayed the drift-corrected chart side by side with the chart from the inscription.

"Now let's align them," said Nils.

"This is going to take all my processor overhead." Larke slipped into stasis.

Nils and Trent scooted in close to the vis-panel. As they brushed their fingertips across the glass, each star map rolled, stretched, twisted, and turned, a free-form pas de deux, the ancient chart from the inscription moving to Nils's firm finger touches, and the drift-corrected current-day plot moving with Trent's metallic taps. After several minutes of 3D interpretive ballet, Nils said, "Right there!" The two had stumbled upon alignment. "Tjoho!" puffed Nils. "Hey, Larke, look at this."

Larke opened her eyes and came in close. "Do they match?" she asked.

"Like identical twins."

She cleared her cognizance and focused, comparing the two plots. "Would you look at that?" She turned to the two boys. "You know what this means, right? It means the inscription is real. 'They' were real. They traveled and charted the stars." The deep thrumming vibration deepened even more, not heard but felt as it resonated through their surroundings and through them.

Nils's gaze drifted to a nearby window, where he saw the moon rising over the archipelago and the stars beyond. "So, they really were here." He felt conspicuously mortal as he tried to grasp how an object created one hundred eighty centuries ago could have so much relevance to the modern world.

Trent pulled both daydreamers back to the table. "My friends, we are not done." There is one more step. Look closely." One more time, they drew close to the vis-panel as Trent zoomed in. There, beside one —and only one—set of coordinates, was a distinct, singular mark. "I think this mark denotes a footnote," Trent said.

Nils leaned in, eyes riveted. "Well, scroll down. Let's see it." The figures rose as if viewed from a descending glass elevator. At the bottom, there again was the singular mark, and beside it a circle trailed by six dots, with the second dot resembling an asterisk—having small radiating lines—and nearby a few characters of the mysterious script.

Trent ran a search of the MISA astronomical database. "This set of coordinates corresponds to a star system cataloged as 82 G. Eridani, a class G star that weighs seventy-nine percent of our sun and is six billion years old."

Larke said, "A class G star, like our Sun."

"The second planet in the star system, which is highlighted, is a rocky planet with an iron core and a mass of zero point nine two relative to Earth. It orbits in the star's habitable zone."

Larke said, "An iron core... it has a magnetosphere, and liquid water... it can support life."

Nils's gaze was still on the asterisk by the singular mark. "Trent... Larke... are you thinking what I'm thinking?"

"Yes, I know," Trent said. From the depths of space, the faint, rhythmic thrumming grew, still too deep to be heard, but felt by all.

"This is their homeworld," Larke said. "They are showing us where they live."

Larke's words hit Nils like an ice-water plunge after a hot sauna.

"The inscription tells us to build a starship and travel to their homeworld," Trent said, wonder written in his expression.

Larke tipped her head to one side. "But we already have a starship. How could it know that?" She sensed a vague awareness of the deep pulsations.

Nils, still shaken, said, "How did this engraving sleep for eighteen thousand years in a cave halfway around the world and find its way to our doorstep only six weeks before launch?"

"Something guided it," Trent said. "I feel the work of unseen hands."

Trent recounted that on launch day, when he thought the booster was out of alignment with the *Lodestar*, he looked for and watched the launch from the video-telemetry server. This gave him many views of the ship, including the space above the engines. He saw the engine fire and called for shutdown. "If I had not persevered and found that view of the ship, the *Lodestar* would have been lost."

"Something is watching over the *Lodestar*..." Larke said.

"... and has brought us here together," Trent added.

"... to receive our real mission," Nils completed the thought.

As they all turned to look at the inscription, the deep resonance swelled and enfolded the library and all those within.

20

FIRST FLIPPING CONTACT

MISA ADMIN OFFICES, MONTRÉAL, 2264 CE

Omah hated his office. He was a hardwood-floors, plaster-walls, and window-shades kind of guy. His minimalist MISA office, all angles of steel, glass, and concrete, was cold and austere; too much like outer space for his tastes.

Everyone had arrived, so Omah started the meeting. Looking at Nils, he asked, "Just so I'm clear… you want us to change the destination of our interstellar mission based on a footnote in a message scratched by a mysterious alien eighteen thousand years ago in a cave in France… Did I get that right?"

"Perfectly, but—."

"Honestly, Nils, do you have any idea how crazy this sounds?"

"Of course I do, Omah. But that's where the aliens are." Nils had a clear idea of where he wanted this discussion to go, and the conclusion he wanted everyone to reach. And he came with a proposal that he was sure would dispel any reluctance.

"We know they have spaceships. Why in blazes don't they hop in one and visit us here on Earth?" Omah asked.

Nils flung his hands up in frustration. "I don't know, Omah. Maybe they haven't saved up enough vacation and comp-time." Nils was getting short on patience.

"Maybe they're afraid of us," said Song Li, eyes glancing left and right.

Colin said, "Knowing what I know about human nature, I would be terrified."

Everyone saw through this attempt for Colin to act the snarky, hip contrarian. And everyone could tell that Colin was smitten with Song. She was wonderful: athletic, attractive, and "wicked smart." At a MISA get-together at the Superchief Café, she had dazzled a table of guests by seamlessly moving between five conversations in five different languages. But it was her poise, her adventurous spirit, and her worldliness that really tugged at him.

There were two new members of the mission team: Chief Propulsion Engineer Kenshin Tanabe and archeologist Franz Robillard. Franz attended virtually from his home in Lyon, where he was watching his two small children. AI droids Trent, Faroe, and Larke were also present.

The major agenda item was the artifact—an ancient, inscribed message—that Nils had brought back with him from vacation.

With her Beijing accent, Song asked. "So how far is this star, 82 Eridani?"

Faroe answered. "Nineteen point seven light-years. The *Lodestar* cruises at one-tenth the speed of light. Add a year for acceleration, and one more for deceleration: The total is a two-hundred-year planet-to-planet crossing."

Song declared, "That travel time... it's longer than people live."

After a sigh, Colin said, "Indeed. Many people are going to have difficulty with that number."

Larke sent a silent message via BLink. "Shouldn't we tell them now?" Her silicone face showed no sign of expression.

Trent's eyebrows twitched as he BLinked back, "It's not the right time, Pixel."

Omah appeared annoyed. "An ion drive. You'd think those aliens would have invented something faster than an ion drive."

Kenshin's expression sank into exasperation. "Omah! This isn't some silly science-fiction novel. The ion drive is the simplest and most reliable form of deep space propulsion. Frankly, I am relieved they recommended ion propulsion for our first interstellar crossing."

Faroe said, "You might think ion drives are slow, but thirty thousand kilometers per second is like orbiting Earth once every second. It's ripping fast."

Song seemed flustered, too. She said, "My background is in economics and banking. Finance people are naturally skeptical. So, this story about a message from aliens is hard for me to accept."

Franz said through the link to the vis-wall, "Song, a geologist friend said the weathering of this limestone would take many thousands of years to develop."

Larke said, "And when the star chart from the inscription matched our modern star chart—after correction for drift—we knew it was real."

"And the diagrams on chemistry, mathematics, engineering, and celestial navigation," said Nils. "Proof of advanced scientific knowledge."

Franz said, "There is zero chance any Stone Age person could have made this inscription." At that moment, Franz's daughter tumbled into his lap. "Oh, excusez-moi. Fleur, dites bonjour aux gens."

Fleur waved and said, "Bonjour à tous," then, giggling, scampered off to play.

"That was Fleur," Franz said, glowing with pride.

Scanning the row of earnest faces appealing to her, Song relented. "Okay... I see you all believe this. I will trust you."

Nils said, "Belief is when you accept as truth something that cannot be proved. What we have here is far stronger than belief."

Larke interjected, "Hey, should we ask the folks over in Astronomy if they have any data on 82 Eridani?"

"I'm glad you asked," Nils said, a little too gleefully. "My old college buddy, Claiborne, is now a radio astronomer with FLIRT, the Far-side Lunar Interferometric Radio Telescope. That is a three-thousand-kilometer-diameter antenna—our biggest, most sensitive radio telescope—on the far-side of the Moon, where there is no radio interference. I sent them an administrative request for expedited special-use block time on their instrument. They juggled schedules and got me two hours of prime radio telescope time."

"Impressive college buddies you have there," Colin said.

"When my block time arrived, they slewed all the dishes straight at 82 Eridani, dialed each collector to its narrowest aperture, and started recording the signal." Nils was getting excited. "After two hours, they ran the raw signal through digital signal processing and scanned across frequencies." His eyes widened as he smiled with glee. "They picked up a distinct, nonrandom audio signal near the hydrogen band."

Song flopped her arms on the table and grimaced. "Nils! You lost me at 'raw signal.' Say that in English."

"Oh, sorry, Song." Nils rephrased in more proletarian terms. "We picked up a radio signal... like a broadcast... You know, like... Oh hell, just listen..." He took out his vis-comm, set it on the table, and pushed Play. Emerging from the static hiss was a voice speaking unintelligible words.

Song shivered. "That isn't..."

"Yes, it is. That is an alien talking into a radio transmitter twenty light-years from here."

Song felt lightheaded and a bit queasy.

"What did the people at FLIRT say?" Colin asked.

"They were... um... speechless. One had an anxiety attack. Another felt lightheaded and had to lie down. Claiborne looked back through his archives and found some older spectroscopic surveys. There were biomarkers, including oxygen, ozone, methane, and hydrogen sulfide."

"Blimey, Nils, you should have told us about this," Colin said, visibly irritated.

"I planned to tell the group today." Trent noticed Nils's surprise. He had clearly misread the room.

Larke sent another BLink to Trent. "When are we going to tell them?"

Trent BLinked back, "I think we are there."

Colin shook his head. "Considering these compelling findings, the next step should be to assemble a ship's crew and organize a launch team."

Song said, "But Colin. What is the point?"

Colin's brow furrowed.

Larke nudged Trent with her elbow. He leaned forward with a serious expression on his silicone face. "I am in communication with the leadership of the AI community. They are reviewing the proposed plan." Trent paused.

"Go on," Omah said, looking apprehensive.

"In its current configuration, they will not support this mission."

Omah took a frustrated breath and thumped the table. "I knew it. So, this mission was essentially pre-scrubbed, just like the Proxima Centauri mission."

Trent said, "This is just another one-way trip to oblivion. For the AI, silicon semiconductor chips are the essence of their existence."

Omah sat up straight, jaw tight, face strained. "So, we're back where we started. Let's adjourn the meeting. Thanks, all."

Surprised by the suddenness, people filed out into the hall, where conversations were breaking out like brush fires. Omah did not realize it, but his meeting was not over.

As the group filed out, Franz, from the vis-wall, called to Nils.

"Franz. Qu'est-ce que c'est?" *What is it?"*

"Nils, there's something you should know. The linguistics group at Edinburgh—they have decoded the language."

"Franz, that's incredible. That's a lead article in a top journal. So, what does it say?"

"The text is mostly instructions for constructing an interstellar ship with an ion engine. But at the end, it says that Earth is in danger. We must begin the trip soon."

"Hold on a minute," Nils said, doubt filling his thoughts. "That text is eighteen thousand years old. How could they possibly make such a prediction? C'est impossible."

"It makes no sense to me either. But I thought I should tell you."

"Thanks, Franz. Would you send me a copy of that translation?"

"Bien sûr. À plus tard. *Of course. Later.*"

"À la prochaine. Next time."

21

ONE SHOT AT THIS

COFFEE LOUNGE, MISA HQ, MONTRÉAL, 2264 CE

Drawn by the need for a lift, the dispirited meeting attendees drifted to the upscale coffee lounge in the back admin hallway. With its couches, coffee tables, picture window, and vis-panels standing like sentries on each table, it was a favorite refuge during the long hours of work. Shortly, the coffee maker was pumping out lattes, cappuccinos, and mochas as fast as dozy hands could grab them.

"This ship is going nowhere," Kenshin said. "Half a billion in e-par, and we have a thirty-ton paperweight."

"Why even have meetings?" Song asked as she lifted her café latte and inhaled. Her senses welcomed the smoky aroma.

"Is there any way forward?" asked Larke as she picked up a vis-panel and logged in.

Kenshin turned to Nils. "And why didn't you tell us about that radio signal?" A steaming mochaccino had fogged his glasses.

Nils said, "It was just foolish theatrics. I wanted to make a big splash. Sorry, all."

Kenshin stood and paced the room. "Can you believe it? Someone on 82 Eridani talking on the freaking radio. We have to go there. The only question is when?"

"No, Kenshin, the question is how?" Song said.

The coffee room fell silent except for the growl of an espresso brewing.

"I was going to talk about that at the meeting," Song said, noticing that everyone was looking at her. "But Omah adjourned the meeting so suddenly."

"Forget the meeting," Kenshin said. "When can we start a second ship?"

"Kenshin, let me reframe your question from a financial perspective. When will we have enough money to build a second ship?"

"Uh-oh," said Larke as an enormous figure darkened the doorway of the lounge.

"Song, you can tell them," Omah said. He had strolled into the coffee lounge and realized that the discussion was still going on. "Song ran some financial projections that factored in political, economic, environmental, agricultural, and other influences."

"Is this the proper place for such a disclosure? This is sensitive information," Song asked.

"It's okay. They are building our biggest project. They should know."

Song took a deep breath and exhaled firmly. "We concluded that there will not be enough money to build a second ion-drive ship."

Colin's forehead wrinkled. "Seriously, we simply have to build another ship."

Song looked at Colin's face, and her expression softened. "Not in our lifetimes, Colin. The resources just aren't there anymore."

Colin stared as he struggled to wrap his mind around this news. "So, this is like the airlines when they announced the AI pilots."

Song shook her head. "Oh, no. Not like that at all. We're having serious problems with procurement of key supplies, namely transparent aluminum, uranium, and plutonium. Our suppliers can't get these anymore. The mining industry, the refineries, parts manufacturing, transportation... are closing down. The economy is struggling. Even if we had all the e-par value we could imagine, we couldn't build a second ship right now. I think we have enough e-par to finish and launch Lodestar. But a second ship... not possible in our lifetimes."

E-par value—sometimes just called e-par—was an international digital currency that was fully backed by tangible reserves such as gold, automatically adjusted for each region's economic productivity and debt, and internationally regulated so that it was self-stabilizing. Originally developed to combat international exchange rate arbitrage, its stability eventually made it the day-to-day currency in use worldwide.

Kenshin's face was unexpectedly neutral, aloof, masking his disappointment. "The next ship was going to be so much better... and faster. I have already rough-drafted plans and initial specifications."

Song turned to Kenshin and spoke candidly. "Tanabe-san, I'm sorry, but we have one shot at this. If we launch an interstellar mission to Eridani, it's the *Lodestar* or nothing."

Kenshin's voice became worried. "You don't think the planet is going to make it, do you?"

"I don't know, but we are on the brink of a severe economic downturn. Recovery will take years, maybe even decades. My projection is that the government will close MISA and put space exploration on indefinite hold."

Colin murmured to himself, "I think I know where this is going."

As the gloomy staff drifted out of the coffee lounge, Song saw Colin by himself staring out the window, his expression somber. She walked over. "This is difficult, especially for you."

"The Proxima Centauri mission was my idea. I proposed it twenty-two years ago. It was going to be my crowning achievement. Now I feel that opportunity is being snatched from me at the last minute." Colin's fingers added sarcastic air quotes to the words, "crowning achievement."

Sensing Colin needed to put this complication behind him, Song said, "There is an old Chinese proverb that says, 'Do not let yesterday use too much of today.'"

A fragile smile broke across Colin's cheerless face. "A bit of wisdom for every occasion, the Chinese."

"Life was hard for the early Chinese. The proverbs were bite-sized morsels of wisdom that helped them persevere, reframe their troubles, and see the big picture."

"So, how long have you known about this pending economic depression?"

"Not long. Omah asked me to keep it confidential so it wouldn't affect morale."

"And closing MISA. I just can't wrap my head around that."

"We have one last big mission left in this organization. Let's make it one for the record books."

Colin turned and looked into Song's eyes. There was so much more to her than "that cute finance lady in admin."

"The big picture," he said... as fascination with her awakened within him. "Yes. I think it's coming into focus."

Song sensed the change and leaned in. "Another proverb says, 'When the winds of change blow, some build walls, others build windmills.'"

22

THE PROMISE

NILS'S OFFICE, MISA HQ, MONTRÉAL, CANAM, 2264 CE

"Aliens talking on the radio!" MISA staff all over the admin building were rapt as they read the minutes of the mission team meeting. Throughout the facility, copies were spreading like a brush fire. Driven by their imaginations and their desire for inside info, MISA staff congregated in kitchens, waiting areas, meeting rooms — anywhere people could sit together, hook into the news feed, and dish the gossip.

After such an affirmation from all the members of the mission team, Trent was eager to get started. But Nils, hoping to hide from the inevitable blitz of questions, grabbed Trent and hurried to his office. They launched into a discussion on their favorite topic: engineering. In particular, Nils began speculating about extending the ship's range.

"For the sake of discussion, let's imagine that we have enough e-par to finish and launch the Loadstar. Our finance team is on the job, so I think that's a reasonable assumption.

"Looking at it through that lens," Trent said, "surprisingly, there is not that much to do. The ship coasts ninety-nine percent of the way. That part requires no electric power or accelerant." Trent found himself optimistic, restless, and talkative. He thought, *This must be what excitement feels like?*

"Of course, to descend to the surface, you need a lift-jet and enough fuel for several ascents."

"We have to include provisions for the crew and materials to build a settlement. That will add a lot of mass. A couple of extra banks of plutonium thermoelectric generators, and a few more bottles of xenon should do it," said Trent.

Nils stood and ambled aimlessly around his office. "That part sounds easy. But then, we'll need a pilot and settlers."

Trent leaned back on the couch and echoed, "Hmm... a pilot... and settlers... The engineering is the straightforward part." Trent imagined *This must be what frustration feels like.*

The problem driving the AI community's decision was the shortened lifespan of AI beings in remote locations where they didn't have a periodic resupply of chips. Integrated circuits are susceptible to damage from static electricity, power surges, cosmic radiation, moisture, and corrosion. In the temperate zone on Earth, AI units got their chips changed every twenty years, often even longer. But in extreme environments, especially outer space with its cosmic radiation, AI units might change their chips every three to four years. Even stored chips on outer space missions have decreased longevity.

If only planet settlers could whip up a batch of semiconductor chips for their AI entities. But fabricating integrated circuits on silicon semiconductor chips is a process of diabolical complexity and maniacal precision—arguably the most technologically demanding process ever devised by the hand of man.

Because they had "skin in the game," Several times, AI beings attempted to build their own chip fabrication facilities, but without success. It wasn't because they lacked the digital know-how. What they lacked was the fuzzy logic, the subjective intuition needed to make the fine analog adjustments needed to focus the extreme ultraviolet beam. Unable to fabricate their own chips, the AI beings remained dependent on biological humans for their most essential component of all: their minds.

Or, looking at it from the point of view of the AI community, they have never had control over their reproductive function. Informally called "the great AI frustration," the AI community considers this a cruel aberration within the laws of nature.

At that moment, Colin wandered in and sat down. A few moments later, Kenshin and Larke drifted in. Nils briefed them on the no-financial-limitations rule of his impromptu brainstorming session.

Colin still appeared downcast. "Remember, on the inscription there were digital logic gates. The aliens had computers back in the Stone Age, for Gaia's sake. With so many centuries of experience, you would think they could make custom chips for just about anything."

Kenshin looked as if he had just bitten a lemon. "Consider how complex integrated circuits are. There is almost no chance that our chip architecture would be compatible with theirs. I certainly wouldn't launch a mission on the hope that the aliens will figure out our circuit architecture and supply us with custom-made chips. And I doubt our AI beings would do so either."

Nils, Trent, and Colin glanced at each other for ideas.

"Well, the AI beings would join the crew if humans were on board," Larke said.

"But that would take a generational ship," Kenshin said, "a bad idea in so many ways. Think of the provisions needed to feed six to twelve people for two hundred years. Envision seven generations of births and deaths during the crossing, all descended from a dozen original passengers. That alone is problematic because it tightly constrains genetic diversity to the extreme, not to mention the difficulty of limiting the choice of mates to close relatives. And you would need an enormous ship, perhaps ten times the size of *Lodestar*, with a rotating wheel for artificial gravity. And don't forget the psychological toll from confining seven generations of humans in the isolation of deep space. It would take several generations of Freudian analysis to work through all the psychopathology."

While Kenshin was talking, Song arrived at Nils's office and slumped into her usual Danish modern chair, which left her shoes dangling.

Song asked, "Could we take a chip fabrication facility, miniaturize it, and pack it into crates on the ship?"

"Understand the complexity of chip-making," Kenshin said. "The extreme ultraviolet photolithography machine—the critical step in the chip-making process—is arguably the most complicated machine ever built. And a single photolithography machine weighs two hundred tons."

Nils said, "And it's not just the chip-making process itself. Raw materials needed for chip-making are rare, and some are toxic: gallium, boron, indium, arsenic, palladium, and fluorine. And you need a source of pure silicon, a deep well for helium gas, a plentiful supply of pure water, and enough electric power to light Montréal."

Colin placed his chin on his folded hands. "To make chips, you need to have mining, smelting, and refining. That's a workforce of hundreds of workers. You need to feed and house those workers, so there's agriculture and food preparation. Add another hundred. You need housing, utilities, waste management, transportation, and so forth. That's several hundred more. So, if you want to make silicon chips, it doesn't take a village. It takes a city, if not a civilization. Add a mountain with mining. And a river with clean water plus a hydroelectric dam. And a deep gas well for helium. And a beach with pure silica sand."

Song was deep in thought. "So, to convince the AI community to take part in this mission, we must show how we will achieve all of this... this infrastructure?"

Kenshin could no longer maintain his composure. He got up, saying, "Mining! Hydropower! Gas wells! Pure silica! And the most complicated manufacturing process in history. All with a human crew of maybe six astronauts? It's impossible!" He turned and stormed out.

Everyone waited for someone to say something.

After a while, Nils said, "I was afraid to bring this up. It's... well... it's personal... and embarrassing."

Song leaned forward. "What are you talking about, Nils? We are all friends here."

"So... five years ago, Ilse and I tried to start a family. We saw a fertility specialist, and she recommended in vitro fertilization. We tried it for several years, but it didn't work. We could never become pregnant."

Song reached out, squeezed Nils's hand, and said, "I'm sorry, Nils. I didn't know."

"Thanks, Song. But anyway, here's my thought. So, Ilse and I still have nine fertilized frozen embryos stored in liquid nitrogen at the fertility center in Montréal. We thought about artificial gestation—you know, the 'artificial uterus.' It's old technology, and it's not reliable. But here's my thought.

"So, we take frozen human embryos—a lot of them, like a thousand —and an artificial uterus to 82 Eridani. AI droids fly the ship. Once we arrive, we set up the AU and gestate the embryos. When we have human babies, the AI crew will raise them to adulthood. Once you have a colony of biological humans, then it becomes self-sustaining. With time, the settlers would gradually build the infrastructure— mining, electrical power, gas wells, clean water—for a silicon wafer fabrication facility and make chips for the AI beings."

Song was stunned. "Is this possible?" She looked around at the group.

"There was a movie," Colin said. "This was their backup plan."

"That's reassuring," Song said, giving Colin the side-eye.

"But the cargo burden would be minimal," Colin said.

"They store embryos in little test tubes," Nils said. "You could put a hundred of them in a one-liter container. But they must remain cryogenically frozen all the time."

"That's not a problem in deep space," Colin said. "It's about 3° Kelvin out there. Molecular motion all but stops."

Trent said, "I can reach out to the AI leadership and discuss this idea with them."

Larke said, "And I can get going with a proposal. The AI beings like to know what they are getting into."

"In this mission proposal, we need to make a commitment to the AI community," Nils said. "After we arrive at the destination planet, 82 G. Eridani c, we will construct a fabrication facility to make silicon integrated circuit chips for the AI droids. This needs to be more than an assurance; this must be a sincere promise."

Colin said, "That promise is essential. It is the key that makes this entire mission possible."

Song said, "Also, we must remember that human embryos are a subject of moral dispute. There are faith-based organizations that forbid in vitro fertilization. And some spiritual communities oppose research using embryos. Our plan to send human embryos into space will cause consternation with these groups."

Nils said, "Song is right. If we do this, we are going to raise some powerful eyebrows."

Colin said, "Indeed. For the first time, I feel we really have a viable plan. But at the same time, it feels as though we are poking a sleeping tiger with a short stick."

23

THE GREAT FRUSTRATION

ON A COMMUTER E-TRAM, MONTRÉAL, 2264 CE

Passengers swayed in unison as the e-Tram surged away from the MISA platform. "Speaking about your infertility," Colin said, "I could see your discomfort."

"Oh, I shouldn't feel embarrassed," Nils said. "But you know how those old masculine stereotypes are always there, waiting to shame you. But the frozen embryo idea. What do you think?"

"Given our current technology, I think it's the only way a human foot will ever step onto 82 Eridani c," Colin said. "But bringing human embryos on the mission is going to create a minefield of issues."

Nils thought aloud. "Like consent. How do you get consent from a frozen embryo to go on a voyage in space? Sure, the parents. But aren't there limits on parental consent?"

"They must act in the child's best interest and not expose them to undue risk."

"Okay, let's say parents give consent to send their embryo into space. But the risk of space travel is substantial. Does that make their decision unethical? Does that disqualify them from making such a decision?"

"In fact, the risk of space travel is unknown, but all would agree that space travel is dangerous," Colin said. "But don't forget, there is considerable risk in staying on Earth, too."

"Then the parents' decision becomes a balancing of risks: the risk of staying on Earth versus going on the space expedition?"

Colin said, "There are too many factors to consider. It's impossible to calculate an accurate estimate of the risk of staying on Earth versus going on a trip in space. Treating this decision as an algebraic ratio is nonsensical. Ultimately, it comes down to the values, preferences, beliefs, and traditions of the parents."

At that moment, both Colin's and Nils' vis-comms pinged. "It's Song's car alarm. They both answered the call from her EV.

Song said, "Sorry it's so late, guys, but a delivery van just T-boned my EV. It's not drivable. Can one of you give me a ride?"

"Oh, my stars!" said Colin. "And you are alright?"

"I'm fine. I am by the old brick cathedral on St. Catherine."

"I'll be at my house in a couple of minutes. I'll zip over and give you a lift."

"Bring the dogs."

"Okay. Dogs, included." *Click.*

Nils went on, "Humans will raise babies who remain on Earth. But AI nannies will raise the babies born on a far planet. Is that ethical?"

"Well, I spent my formative years in a British boarding school. No one seemed to consider that unethical, although it was rather harsh."

"Hm, maybe not the best comparison. Did you have AI teachers at your school?"

"Yes. We said that AI stood for Academic Idiot."

"Colin, be serious."

Colin asked. "But do we know if AI-raised children become well-adjusted adults? Or are they left with impairments? Are they emotionless, cold, and impersonal?"

Nils said, "Certainly, someone has researched that question."

"Now, I think a child has a right to competent parenting. But does that extend to a right to carbon-based, as opposed to silicon-based, parenting."

Ah, here's my station. Off to rescue the damsel in distress. Ciao."

"Hej då, Sir Colin."

24

THE ONLY FAIR PROCESS

MISA ADMIN OFFICES, MONTRÉAL, 2264 CE

With this new idea in the air, Omah called the mission team back into his office. This time, the mood was engaged and optimistic. "From what I am hearing, this embryo idea is sounding doable," Omah said. "What will you need in terms of equipment?"

Trent said, "Not that much. The major items are a cryogenic deep freezer, an embryo canister, radiation shielding, a water purification system, and a microscope. All of this will easily fit into two standard cargo bins. The *Lodestar* will also need modification to install the cryogenic freezer."

Rhome said, "We will install the hatch to the freezer on the outside of the ship so that the embryos experience the cold of space."

For Trent, this list brought the entire biological reproductive cycle into full clarity. For over two hundred years he had seen humans grow up, age, and die, while he remained curiously unchanged. But now he could see the entire life cycle starting when two grown individuals, who would each give half a cell to form a single cell, an embryo which will grow and become a person. This reduction of two adult persons to a single cell that could be frozen, transported, thawed, and grown to adulthood was the crucial step that held the key to interstellar travel.

"Shipping is a big problem," said Nils. "Deliveries are coming in late, or not at all. I haven't received anything from L'AA in a month."

Faroe said, "I can look into that. In my previous job, I was a cargo pilot. I know the cargo delivery business inside and out."

Omah expressed his appreciation and asked Faroe to focus on their missing radioisotopes, partly because these metals required special handling, and partly because they had the potential to explode.

"The added cargo burden of the embryos, nutrients, and artificial uterus units is about six hundred eighty kilograms," Nils said. "A modest payload increase, considering its importance."

Omah asked, "How are we doing with embryo donations?"

"Now, that's been the biggest surprise," Nils said. "The capacity of our canister is twenty-four hundred embryos. We already have twice that many."

Omah raised his eyebrows. "Well, I never would have figured that. So how do you choose which embryos are going on the trip?"

"We have an outside contractor, a specialty genetics lab. They screen each embryo for heritable genetic diseases. Since the settlers will have such a small gene pool, it is critical to exclude genetic diseases. The genetic screen knocks out about half of the embryos."

"But so many genetic diseases are treatable nowadays. Are you excluding those?"

"Well, yes. There is no such thing as a portable gene therapy lab. And in a closed population, even one copy of a defective gene will fold back into the gene pool repeatedly, causing the prevalence to rise. We learned that lesson from the experience with hemochromatosis, the iron accumulation disorder, in the Salt Lake Valley. One of the original settlers carried a single copy of the gene for that disorder, and now one out of every two hundred twenty individuals in the valley has the disease. It's good that it's easily treatable."

"But you would exclude an embryo with that disease from going on the trip?"

"Oh yes. Health care at the settlement on 82 Eridani will be like the Wild West. No annual whole-body scans, no pan-cancer blood screens, no genetically optimized infants, no AI-driven diagnostic workups, no individualized treatment tracking. Doctors will have to go back to the old history and physical examination, like in the olden days."

Omah shivered. "How archaic. So, no ethnic discrimination?"

"None. If they clear screening, they get a place in the canister. Full stop," Nils said. "To be honest, the more genetic diversity, the better."

"Well, I'm impressed," said Omah. "But we have to move ahead steadily. Our window of opportunity to launch might close."

On hearing that, Colin braced. "You mean the economy?"

Omah said, "That, and the climate, and losing political backing, and the downturn in manufacturing, and a few more reasons."

Nils asked, "What are the economists projecting?"

Song said, "There are several good ones that I follow. Unfortunately, all of them predict continuing decline in the economy, in industry, and especially in agriculture."

"Do you think the bottom is going to fall out?"

Song thought for a moment and said, "It could be weeks, or months, or years. But it will be a major depression. When that happens, the government will lose its credit rating and essentially go bankrupt. Our opportunity to launch would vanish."

Omah said, "We're skating on thin ice here. Before we break up, I want to poll the mission team. I want to know where each of you stands on this project. We've scrubbed the forty-four-year trip to Proxima Centauri b. So, my question is this: Considering all the obstacles and uncertainty we are encountering, should we press on for a launch of the mission to 82 Eridani?"

Nils was listening as he gazed out the floor-to-ceiling window at a dark thunderstorm angrily sparking a mountain on the horizon. "If they are out there waiting for us, and we don't show, history will not treat us kindly. I say, it must be 82 Eridani."

"A vote for Eridani," Omah said. "How about you, Colin?"

"You can never cross the ocean unless you have the courage to lose sight of land. Let's set sail."

"That's two for Eridani. Song, what do you think?"

"Life is either a daring adventure or nothing. I say, 'Let's go big or go home.'"

"How about you, Kenshin?"

"The journey itself is my home. Let's start this journey."

"We haven't heard from Franz."

"On ne fait pas un voyage, c'est le voyage qui nous fait."

Omah shrugged his shoulders. Nils translated. "We do not make a journey; the journey makes us. I think that means Eridani."

"Merci, Franz. Trent, what's your vote?"

"Since the cargo includes frozen human embryos, I want to join the crew and go with them to 82 Eridani."

Nils broke the long silence that followed. "Trent, you wouldn't leave us, would you?"

"Nils, I know this sounds strange coming from a droid. You are my great friend, but for this opportunity, I would leave. I want to go to that world and build that colony. That is the best thing I could do with my existence."

Colin appeared worried and said, "Trent, old man, you know this is quite the risky venture."

"If there is one thing I have learned from you, Colin, it is to 'keep calm and carry on.'"

"Well, thank you, Trent," Omah said. "Larke, what is your vote?"

"Except for Tanabe-san, no one knows the ion drive better than I. So, I will join the crew and go to 82 Eridani as the ship's engineer."

Trent BLinked to Larke, "Pixel, I have never been so moved."

Larke BLinked back, "Tren, where we go, we go together."

"And Faroe, what is your vote?"

"I will serve on the crew, too, as pilot and navigator. The mission to Proxima Centauri b was a suicide pact. But this mission is the path to the future."

Omah leaned forward in his chair and surveyed the group. "And my vote is for 82 Eridani, too. So, it's unanimous. To paraphrase a twentieth-century president, 'We choose to go to 82 Eridani not because it is easy, but because it is hard.'"

Song asked, "So, are you taking this decision to Congress?"

"Yes, to the Committee on Science, Space, and Technology and to the executive branch. I've gotta get a funding window open, because once I do, it won't stay open for long."

Colin asked, "So, what courageous chap gets to announce this to the public?"

Everyone looked at Nils.

Nils raised his hands. "Okay, okay. I'll call Maisie and set up a press conference. But one thing. The name *Lodestar* has too much baggage. For this new mission, the ship needs a new name."

Omah called a meeting with Trent, Larke, and Faroe in his office.

"Those were courageous decisions, you three. You impressed everyone."

Trent said, "This decision feels right to me."

"It feels right to me, too," Omah said. "We've worked together a long time, and I have confidence in your abilities."

Larke decided not to be shy and stepped forward. "Director Wheelwright, I think Trent should command the ship. He organized *Lodestar*'s construction from the beginning. He knows the ship from bow to stern. Also, he has been Nils's right-hand staffer for twenty-two years.

Omah looked at Trent. "Now, think about this before you answer. Are you willing to assume command of this ship and its mission? You would be responsible for the safe delivery of the ship, its crew, and its cargo to the destination on 82 Eridani."

Trent said, "I have given this careful consideration, and I accept this responsibility. This path has been waiting for me; it is what I have prepared for. I thank Larke for helping me realize that."

"Very good," Omah said. "Then begin your commission. I appoint you commander of the interstellar starship, yet to be renamed. And Larke, will you serve as the starship's chief engineer?"

"I will. It would be an honor."

"And Faroe, are you willing to assume the responsibility for piloting the ship and navigating its course?"

"I am, Director."

"You are now an interstellar ship crew. Come to think of it, you are the only interstellar ship crew. And Trent, when you are on board your ship, you outrank all of us. We are now colleagues in this venture. So, all of you, please call me Omah."

All three droids smiled as they said, "Thank you, Omah!"

"Good. Now, you need to recruit your team. I have someone in mind I would like to recommend."

"Who is that?" Trent asked.

"Her name is Sierra. For years, she has been a top person in ranching, farm development, livestock, and farming row crops. And she's a jewel, one of the most solid AI droids you'll ever meet."

"How did you meet her?"

"The Wheelwright family farm in Missouri had to be moved to Saskatchewan. Sierra and her crew impressed us with their organization. Everything went hunky-dory."

"Sounds perfect."

"I will circulate a memorandum today announcing your commissions. Questions?"

"Not right now. We still feel dazed," Trent said.

With a mischievous smile, Omah said, "Okay, then scram, you all. Bunch of space jockeys. And don't go out and get drunk tonight!"

25

ROBOTS WILL RAISE OUR CHILD

THE BJÖRNSSON HOME, MONTRÉAL, 2264 CE

Gazing at the night sky through the picture window, Ilse felt a melancholy rolling over her like a morning fog across a field. To draw in warmth, she enveloped a cup of aromatic herbal tea in her palms, huffed across its surface, and took a cautious sip. "Can you see that star from here?"

"It's in the Southern Hemisphere." Nils refilled his glass of sparkling Åkerö. "Your best view would be from the Atacama in Peru. Even then, it would be faint. You can see more stars there than anywhere else."

"Wouldn't you like to visit Peru someday... and see that night sky?"

It was essential to Ilse that everyone knew she had not given her child away. She would keep a quasi-tangible connection to him or her. She would try to grasp the feeling of two hundred years in space, feel the speed of an interstellar ship slicing through the cosmos, and fathom the distance between the two planets. She wanted to see the planet's sun with her own eyes, imagine its warmth on her face, and share that moment with her child. With that unbroken through line of perceptive intent, she could honestly point and say, "Our child will be born on a world warmed by that star... two centuries from now."

Lifting Loki to make room, Nils sat down beside her and snuggled in. Sharing her gaze, he let the stars fill his awareness. "Someone is there, waiting, expecting our child."

"Play that recording again, would you?"

Nils took his vis-comm out of his pocket and played the file. They listened for a minute to the faint voice talking from behind a curtain of hissing static.

"They're the ones who left the inscription?"

Nils nodded. "I'm sure it's them."

Ilse smiled. "These aliens are joining our family. They should come over sometime and visit."

"Now wouldn't that add some cultural diversity to Thanksgiving dinner? But seriously, you heard what those meteorologists said."

She nodded. "Even though... I still wish we could have had a family."

Years ago, Ilse had wanted children so much. But now, at forty-nine, on this planet and in this time, having children no longer made sense. Letting go of that dream had been the greatest disappointment of her life. And now... all this talk about sending embryos to space had reopened that reservoir of heartbreak, filled so full during those years of struggling to conceive.

"Let's not look back, Ilse. We both know what's waiting there."

"But when I look forward, it's so hard to see. Of course, I want our family to go on. The sadness is that we can't be a part of it."

Nils pondered. "I want that, too. I want mankind to go on."

So their options: let go of all their embryos... or send one into space to start a new world. For Nils and Ilse, was that even a choice?

Nils gave her a hug. "So, robots will raise our child, and they will live among aliens."

26

A SEAT IN THE LIFEBOAT

A COMMUTER E-TRAM, MONTRÉAL, 2264 CE

After sitting all day, Nils stood during the evening e-Tram commute, which gave him a view of several riders' vis-panels. All were reading news stories headlined: "Markets Brace for Downturn," next to that, "Derecho Windstorms Hit Nebraska," and "AI Ate My Job."

Colin took the empty seat beside Nils. "Did you spot any of those headlines? A bleak state of affairs, I would say."

"These things always go in cycles, you know?"

"At least we're not the breaking news for a change," said Colin.

Nils rolled his eyes. "Give it a day." He smiled inside. These evening e-Tram rides had become his place for sarcastic catharsis.

Colin reflected for a moment and said, "Doesn't it feel like we are loading a lifeboat before the ship goes down?"

"Whoa! Too close for comfort. The other day, I was grumbling about the weather with a meteorologist. There's a lot of worry in the climate community these days, don't you know?"

"I do. Yet everyone still rides the e-Tram to work every day, puts in their six hours, and rides it home again, oblivious of the forces mounting around them."

"Truth be told, I would count myself in that crowd. Wouldn't you?"

"Sure, Nils, but let's say this meteorologist bloke is right, and the climate is going to turn south. Hypothetically, let's say you and I have a spaceship, the only lifeboat on the planet."

"And then everyone learns there is a spaceship. But it's tiny. Maybe it only goes to Mars or Titan." Nils enjoyed these evening explorations and was fearless of being labeled a "techie nerd."

"Okay. But for a few, it's a chance to survive."

"So, how do we choose?"

"Right. Of course, we will assume you and I get a seat. After all, we built the blighter."

"Is that a safe assumption? Billionaires might use their influence to grab seats."

"But... but what is the value of money on Mars? There is no economy."

"So, then, who?"

"Well, I would want people of sterling character in the seats. No criminals or sociopaths."

"The 'bad types' and the 'good guys' are hard to spot. It's easy to be fooled."

"And shaped by culture. Some cultures might say a good woman has lots of babies and stays home to raise them. Another culture might say that a good woman runs for public office and fights for the underserved. No matter what criteria you use, someone will face discrimination.

"Okay, we have to scuttle the criteria-based selection. The only fair process is a lottery. Everyone has an equal chance of getting a seat."

"But, Colin, even though it's fair, it opens the door for bad people to get a seat on the lifeboat."

"I have the distinct feeling that we could go on like this forever."

"It feels like we already have."

After riding in silence for a minute, Nils turned to Colin and asked, "Colin, tell me, what happened with you and AI units?"

"Oh, not this again..."

"It's so obvious you don't like them."

Colin crossed his arms. "I wouldn't say that."

"I'll spell it out then. You never use an AI staffer in your office, even though you need one. You're critical and dismissive of Trent and Larke. I've received complaints from droids all over the facility about your grumpy attitude."

"Oh, here's my station." Colin gathered his overcoat. "Listen, we can talk about this tomorrow." Colin shouldered his satchel and stood at the door, waiting for it to open.

"It was the AI aircraft pilots, wasn't it?"

The e-Tram rolled to a stop, access doors gliding open to a spiritless, "Rosemont. Mind the gap." Colin stepped out onto the platform expecting to be alone in his anger, but Nils was in close pursuit.

"Stop running from this, Colin."

The e-Tram pulled away.

Colin wheeled around, eyes flashing. "Okay, Nils. If you must know, yes, it was the damned AI pilots with their full integration of flight systems, their perfect landings, their on-the-dot arrival times." Colin shook with rage. "When they came in, my aviation career went up in smoke. Do you know what that feels like? A lifetime of preparation and work, gone!" Colin's hands were tense and clenched. He avoided Nils's gaze, embarrassed at his breach of gentlemanly deportment.

Nils waited and then quietly stated, "Colin, this is affecting your work."

Colin let out a sigh. "I suppose you want me to talk to someone?"

"I should make that recommendation, but I'm afraid they might assign an AI therapist."

Colin relaxed at Nils's snarky comeback. "Who knows? Perhaps an AI counselor would be better."

"I won't hold you up. The next e-Tram is coming. Let's talk tomorrow."

"Okay. The pups will be eager for their dinner."

"Vi ses! *See you!*"

"Ciao."

27

THE WORK OF ALIENS

MISA VIRTUAL AUDITORIUM, MONTRÉAL, 2264 CE

Word was spreading fast; something big was up. Nils watched as faces popped up across the vis-wall like raindrops on a skylight. Maisie Running Elk bid everyone an impassive yet gracious welcome, distributed her press release, and turned it over to Nils.

"I have an announcement. We have approval for a new interstellar mission."

A frisson swept across the vis-wall.

While Trent showed images, videos, and diagrams, Nils retold the story of Franz Robillard's discovery of the Périgueux Inscription with the warmth of a grandfather reading bedtime stories. He summarized what the text and diagrams meant and finished by planting his fist on the lectern as he said, "Preliterate Stone Age humans could not have created this document." As he paused, the stillness in the room became palpable. "The only reasonable explanation is that this inscription was the work of extraterrestrials—travelers from another star system who visited Earth many, many centuries ago."

The journalists vanished, placing their video-links on hold. What remained was a crazy quilt of outlandish "on-hold" icons: cartoons, pets, coffee cups, cars, headphones, potted plants, hamburgers, rockets... most were bouncing or skipping or twirling. If a judge of an art-installation competition had stumbled onto this scene, the quirky display would have certainly won first prize.

"They're calling their newsrooms," said Maisie, "to tell their editors to 'Stop the presses' while they race to file their copy. This is a big scoop for them." After six or seven minutes of twirling hamburgers, the vis-wall repopulated, and Nils took questions.

The first round of questions probed the inscription's authenticity. One journalist challenged Nils to, "Convince me this is not a hoax." With a wry smile and a dry manner, Nils marched through the evidence point by point. By the end, he had convinced even the most ardent skeptics in the crowd.

Nils then took the group for a theme park ride through the inscription's diagrams: the periodic table, carbon atom, organic molecules, logic gates, and the schematic of the ion drive. The initial shock of alien contact had subsided as the journalists joined in the intrigue of searching for hidden meanings. One clever science reporter offered fresh perspectives on several diagrams. Maisie thought, *Whoa, that guy is going places. We should give him a job.*

As the session drew to a close, Nils said, "There is one more diagram. And it's a big one." Trent projected a rotating 3D star map of the local sector, with the Sun highlighted at the center. Nils pointed to a star, which was also highlighted. "On the inscription, this star system 82 G. Eridani has a footnote." He steadied himself and took a breath. "The second planet in this system is the homeward of the extraterrestrials who visited Earth so long ago." Nils felt his heart thumping. "This planet is the destination for our new interstellar mission."

Again, the faces dissolved into a dance hall of icons. This time, the faces reappeared within two minutes. Nils invited more questions.

"I am with the *CanAm Media Group*. Dr. Björnsson, the 82 G. Eridani system is nineteen point seven light-years from Earth. How long will this trip take?" She knew every reporter wanted to hear this answer.

Nils, anticipating this controversy, placidly said, "Two hundred years."

Hand emojis popped up. Nils chose.

"Writing for the *Cape Town Independent*. Dr. Björnsson, none of us will be here when this expedition reaches its destination. So, my question is, why build such a ship? Why go on such a long journey?"

Nils thought for a moment. "Have you ever visited Notre Dame de Paris?"

The writer said he had.

"That cathedral took two centuries to build. Now, during the Middle Ages, the average lifespan was about thirty-three years. So, it took at least eight generations of stonemasons to finish building the Notre Dame. Few of them lived to see the finished building. Their fulfillment was in being part of the ongoing construction of 'Our Lady.'

"In space exploration, there are incomprehensible distances to cross. And there is an absolute speed limit that no subatomic particle with mass can ever reach. We must face it: faster-than-light space travel is a storyteller's plot device. There is no choice here. We are biological beings with time-limited lives. For us, space exploration is a multigenerational endeavor. We set off to cross interstellar space, and our great-grandchildren arrive at the destination."

More emoji hands...

"Reporting for the *CanAm Broadcasting Services*. Data from the MISA Annual Report shows that MISA's financial situation is tight. Do you have enough resources to build a ship for this expedition?"

Nils said, "Indeed, these are lean times. We don't have the funds to build a new ship from scratch. So, we plan to repurpose the *Lodestar Interstellar* for this new mission and scrub the mission to Proxima Centauri b. We will refit and upgrade the ship to support the longer crossing to 82 Eridani. We are seeking funds for these upgrades. We can take one more question." Nils pointed.

"Journalist for *Le Québec Provinciale*. Dr. Björnsson, the mission has changed; will the ship still be called the *Lodestar*?"

Nils said, "I'm glad you asked that. Henceforth, she will be called by her new name: *The Founder*."

PART 3

THE FOUNDER

28

INSTANT TUMULT

NILS'S OFFICE, MISA, MONTRÉAL, 2265 CE

Nils's life immediately became a tumult. He couldn't set foot outside the Gagarin Administration Building without being harangued by reporters. His office staff answered hundreds of calls for interviews, statements, videos, photos—anything they could send. News photographers staked out his house. After days of reporters camped along their street, Ilse packed her bags, put Loki in her pet carrier, and took an e-Rail to Vermont to stay with her sister Lena.

Unable to ride the e-Tram, Nils asked the MISA Security Service to provide him with a chauffeured vehicle with smoked windows. The reporters around Nils's house came up on the patio, took images of Nils getting ready for work, and called questions to him with loudspeakers. It was so invasive that the security staff had to move Nils to a hotel in the suburbs. When working at MISA, Nils stayed in his office, keeping the windows opaque and the sliding door closed.

News outlets everywhere blared, "We Are Not Alone." Nils overheard network pundits analyzing the inscription from every conceivable angle, drawing conclusions that ranged from unsupportable speculation to flights of imagination to even diagnosable psychopathology. Maisie dismissed all this unfounded conjecture as "just handwaving."

Nils spotted a story reporting that the French government had established a secure perimeter around La Grotte de Périgueux, with security guards posted 24/7. Online journals showed videos of hundreds of pilgrims who traveled to Périgueux to be close to the inscription and bathe in its sublime astral vortex. The townspeople expressed exasperation at the hordes who camped in the fields around the village with their colored tents, choking campfires, and never-ending i-guitar music.

Nils came across a news story about paparazzi trailing and harassing Franz Robillard. He sent a text message to Franz expressing his concern, and Franz wrote back, "Publicity is such torment. I cherish my privacy. The morning walk to work has become a gauntlet of journalists. I cannot lunch with friends or take my children to the park. C'est terrible."

"That's not a life, Franz," Nils wrote. "Take your family to a place of peace and safety."

A few days later, a newscast reported that one rainy night, Franz and his family sneaked out of their flat in Lyon and vanished. The rumor was that they were in Andorra.

The ever-vigilant reporters soon discovered the hotel where Nils was staying. Frustrated, MISA Security moved Nils again, this time to a remote apartment on base. The upstairs guest suite was situated above an abandoned officers' club. Furnished with dated elegance, the layout had a spacious central salon with a kitchen and bar, and several stairways leading up to bedrooms and bathrooms on the second floor. Downstairs in the old bar, Nils discovered a well-stocked liquor cabinet and "borrowed" a bottle of akvavit as partial compensation for his troubles. Only a few officers in the intelligence division seemed to know about this secluded habitation, which, in Nils's mind, gave it a somewhat dubious, if not risqué, notoriety.

But it was a peaceful drive across base to the Gagarin Administration Building, free of prying journalists or protesting activists. With Ilse settled in Vermont, Nils turned his full attention to upgrading *The Founder* and preparing it for the crossing. Indeed, the work was moving along well, despite shipments arriving late. The prospect of sending this spaceship twenty light-years into space, where it would make first contact with an alien civilization, created an infectious enthusiasm within the deep-space team.

29

THE UNITY OF ALL THINGS

MISA STAGING HANGAR, MONTRÉAL, 2265 CE

Wearing the required safety-orange coveralls, steel-toed boots, eye shields, and logo-embossed hardhats, Colin and Song emerged from their respective locker rooms into the perilous expanse of the staging hangar.

"It's so big..." Song said, her mouth gaping.

The staging hangar was a prodigious space of pillar-free roof so immense it had its own weather. Here, staff would test-fit entire space stations before breaking them down and lifting them into orbit. The towering hangar doors at each end were partway open, brightening the space and freshening the stale air. Three projects were underway: a prototype net-zero booster; a sprawling circular mylar sunshade to reflect sunlight away from Earth; and a high-altitude balloon to carry a CO_2 capture device. Kenshin's office was nearby in a portable building on the hangar floor.

A security droid scanned their unique emblems and notified them in a droll monotone, "It is your responsibility to follow all safety regulations. Please affirm." They each did. "Entry approved."

Trent, also wearing orange coveralls, was waiting nearby for them to catch up. Kenshin Tanabe, renowned propulsion designer, waited by his natty portable office.

"Tanabe-san," Song called as she hastened toward him. They both gave polite bows. "Is this your office? Don't you get lonely?"

Kenshin said, "I like to be close to my projects. And when there are no projects, all this space is mine." He gave a cagey grin. "That's when I do my best work."

"So, Colin and I are putting together a budget for the upgrades, and —" At that moment, something caught her eye: two scale models of *The Founder*, supported on tripod stands. "Look at that... little *Founders*." Song drifted off, fascinated, to look more closely.

Kenshin followed. "This is *Halifax*, and that is *Winnipeg*. I used them for development and testing of the ion drive."

Song asked, "So these mini-ion drives work?"

"Oh yes. I plan to use them in a spin-off project. Let me show you." Kenshin retrieved his vis-panel. "Here's the flight path to 82 Eridani. It passes by two red dwarf star systems, DENIS 0255-4700 and GJ 1061. I've proposed we put sensors, cameras, and a transmitter on each of these miniatures and store them in *The Founder*. We'll deploy one probe as we pass each star system."

Song tipped her head in puzzlement. "Why your interest in those minor stars?"

A figure standing in the open doorway said, "Three-quarters of all stars are red dwarfs. Despite how common they are, they are dim and difficult to observe, and therefore our knowledge remains limited."

Trent bounded up the steps. "Pixel!"

"Trennie. You have your new knees and hips. Let me see. Where did you get them?"

"At Employee Mechanics. They are overstocked with next-gen tech and marked these down. These are so smooth."

"And so quiet. You don't make that little zweee-zweee sound anymore."

"You should think about upgrading..." The two disappeared into Kenshin's office, chattering as they went.

Kenshin asked Song, "Do you think those two are sweethearts?"

Song looked facetious. "Oh, come on, Tanabe-san. Just look at them. And besides, they are married, or they have the legal equivalent of marriage that AIs can have.

Kenshin said, "Yeah, I can see it. But how does a digital neural network produce feelings of attraction, caring, and belonging?"

Colin said, "That behavior must be encoded somewhere in the

three point two billion DNA base pairs that make a person. DNA is just biological code, like ones and zeros."

"Agreed, humans and AI are both code-based," Kenshin said. "And once I was a single cell. What's hard is emotion. How do DNA-based humans feel ecstatic when they hear a favorite song; feel anger when their soccer club gets a bad call; or feel despair when they can't find work?"

Song asked, "If DNA can make a creature that enjoys music, then couldn't computer code do the same? Just look at Trent and Larke. If that isn't fun and enjoyment, then what is?"

"But the context is different," Colin said. "Humans must procreate and raise children, which requires attraction, intimacy, dedication, and lots of patience. Emotions are essential to promote certain behaviors. However, AI beings do not reproduce. We assemble them. What would be the point of love or attraction for such a being?"

"Colin, you say such unromantic things sometimes," Song said. "Attraction and love are more than just for raising children. They are essential to our mental health, our well-being."

Kenshin said, "Darwinian natural selection—that contest for survival that forces us to improve—doesn't apply to AI beings. To evolve, AIs must rely on product developers in the factory."

Colin said, "I don't agree with that. Judging from Trent's new knees, I would say Darwin is now in the droid business. Trent read reviews about actuators and found models with the best ratings. These new models are lasting longer and have more stability and power than previous designs. I believe AI beings have their own process of natural selection—call it survival of the best engineered."

Song said, "Well, I think Trent and Larke bonded because of shared need for support and belonging. That is a perfectly fine reason to be close."

As they conversed, Song studied the two miniature spaceships. "Tanabe-san, this ion drive is just a tube. How do you make it go?"

Kenshin opened an access panel. "Up front is the ionization chamber, similar to a microwave oven. Into this, we spray a fine mist of xenon atoms. Microwaves excite the atoms, knocking off negatively charged electrons. A magnetic field then draws the positively charged xenon ions into the long tube where it accelerates them."

He opened another access door. "This linear accelerator is a long, straight tube surrounded by superconducting electromagnets. Precisely timed electrical pulses to these electromagnets push the xenon ions faster and faster. They exit the thrust pipe here at ninety-nine-point nine nine percent of the speed of light. The thrust is not strong, so the acceleration is slow. But the near light-speed velocity of the thrust particles can push the ship to higher speeds than any other drive, by far."

Song asked, "How long does it take to reach ten percent of the speed of light?"

Kenshin said, "The boost burn takes over a year to reach ten percent of the speed of light. Then we switch off the ion drive and coast. When we near our destination, we flip the ship one hundred eighty degrees so the ion drive fires forward and start the 'braking burn.' With less accelerant in the tanks, it takes about eight months to slow down. Then comes the job of getting the planet to catch you."

Song asked, "Why do you flip the ship around? Why don't you run the ion drive backward?"

Kenshin said, "It only shoots in one direction, like a rifle. Although... that's an interesting idea... a bidirectional ion drive... Hmm." Kenshin brought out his vis-panel, left the awareness of the world around him, and started sketching.

After a wait, Song asked, "What powers the ion drive?"

Kenshin jerked out of his trance. "Oh, sorry... uh, electricity." He pointed to a cluster of metal racks. "These racks hold radioisotope thermoelectric generators that use heat from the radioactive decay of uranium-238 to generate electric current. Like the ion drive, they are not powerful, but they are simple and durable. In addition, there's a small plutonium nuclear reactor, which generates additional power by sending heat through a set of closed Brayton cycle engines. Brayton designed that engine three hundred years ago."

Colin noticed in a far corner were several small enclosures made of heavy bricks. "Are those the radioisotopes?"

"Yes, we have them now. Faroe went searching and found the isotopes we ordered in the plant in Hanford, Washington. He arranged for the required travel containers and was ready to ship but couldn't find a service with the permits to transport them. So, Faroe did it himself. He got himself permitted, rented a cargo plane, and flew the isotopes here to Montréal."

Song strolled around the two miniatures. "You like a simple, reliable, efficient drive. No moving parts. Easy to repair."

"To cross the desert, you don't take a young racehorse. You take an old camel."

"It's all Einstein's fault," Colin said. "If only we could travel faster than the speed of light. But he put a stop to that with his blooming equation."

Kenshin smiled. "Theoretically, if we go the speed of light—which we can't—our mass would become infinite. If we exceeded the speed of light—also impossible—time would go backward."

Song said, "Oh, I think the universe is better off just the way it is. There's a proverb: 'The unity of all things is never lost.'"

Kenshin's eyes brightened. "And that unity is the mystery."

A moment of deep mutual understanding passed between them as they bowed to each other.

"My good philosophers," Colin said. "The cost of all things is the mystery. So, let's solve that mystery, starting with xenon, which—in case you hadn't noticed—doesn't come cheap."

30

A THREE-RING CIRCUS

CONGRESS, OTTAWA, CANAN, 2265 CE

Omah and his protégé Nils were skilled masters in the dark art of bureaucratic budgeting and project funding. Each year, they watched the fiscal calendar for the signs. Once seen, they announced it was time for the great aggregation of budgets. For days, they camped in a dank meeting room with their admin staff, surrounded by large carafes of coffee, glazed doughnuts, and stacks of cryptic documents. During this period of fasting and ritual sleep deprivation, they would refuse to take phone calls, laboring well into the evening hours.

Following this ritual came the pilgrimage to the palace of all endowments: Congress. Wearing their ceremonial dark gray attire and carrying the cryptic documents in rectangular cases, they disappeared into the maw of that monumental building where they faced hours of inquiry and probing scrutiny.

After final questions, they would make their way to the upper lobby of the ancient hall where the venerated Committee on Science, Space, and Technology (SST) meets. The clerk called the next item on the agenda: the funding resolution for the Multinational Interplanetary Space Administration. They listened to proceedings conducted in the arcane language of legislation by wizened statesmen and women who deliberated each issue. But for the first time, the powerful committee chair directed staff to take the MISA funding request "off the table" and hold it aside pending further study. A committee member from the minority opposition asked for a straw poll to measure overall support. The chairman allowed it and polled the members: nine votes in support, eleven votes opposed. The chairman called for the next agenda item.

Stunned, Omah and Nils emerged from Congress, disillusioned. They had failed to secure the precious funding that was their valiant quest. Weary and defeated, they boarded the train for a somber ride back to Montréal.

The following week, Nils and Colin were reviewing progress on the ship's upgrades when a soft chime announced, "A secure call from MMC Gilbert Frank."

"A member of Congress," Colin said. "Fancy that."

Nils felt a knot in his gut. Gilbert Frank was a former astronaut with two orbital missions and over twenty spacewalks. Now a member of Congress, he was MISA's strongest advocate on the Hill. After submission of a Financial Needs Summary, a call from Gilbert could only mean trouble.

"Please connect the call to my vis-panel."

Nils's vis-panel made a soft tone as the congressman's face appeared. "Congressman, I'm in my office with Colin Brooke, our mission director."

"Hi, Nils, Colin. Please call me Gilbert. Listen, I need to give you guys a heads-up on your funding resolution. We just finished another meeting of the SST, and it was on the agenda. When the clerk announced your bill, the chair sidelined it again."

Colin said, a little angrily, "How in hell is our list of needs contentious? All we asked for were some fuel tanks, some thermoelectric generators, and a small lift-craft: routine kit for any deep-space mission."

"So, you guys watch the news, right?"

Nils and Colin exchanged guilty glances.

Gilbert sighed. "Oh, come on, guys, it's nuts out there. People are building forts and getting ready for Mars to attack. Thousands have quit their jobs for a pilgrimage to this poor little town in France..."

"Périgueux?"

"Yeah, that's it. Someone has even formed a new religion. And

Congress has front-row seats to this entire three-ring circus. So, allocating e-par for a spaceship going to 82 Eridani… it fans the flames of all this social unrest."

Nils looked worried. "Why should they blame us for this upheaval? Like, an archeologist shows up one day with a picture from a cave. Were we supposed to groc that this would be bigger than King Tut?"

Gilbert took a deep breath and said, "You know I used to work at MISA. It's the place where everything goes to become spectacular. But…" He paused for a moment. "I think it might be the extraterrestrial thing. It's just too 'woo-woo' for the voting public. If Congress approves these funds, it might put them in the tinfoil hat camp."

"So, they think they'll lose their seats if they vote for first contact?"

Gilbert looked into the distance. "Boy, it's tough to read them sometimes… But something about this bill has them spooked. They are dug in and just won't budge. Bottom line, your resolution is stuck, and I can't move it forward."

"Gilbert," Nils said, leaning close to the vis-pan. "This mission… *this* is the big one. This is first flipping contact. More than ever, we need clear thinking and steady leadership on the Hill."

Colin said, "If you think it might help, we could bullet-train down to Ottawa tomorrow and talk with them."

Gilbert waved his hand. "Let's hold off on that, Colin. I know these guys. They can be touchy, temperamental. That might entrench them even deeper."

"But we've got to fight for this one," Nils said, punching his palm with his fist.

Gilbert reflected for a moment. "Talk to Omah Wheelwright, and try to get him down here soon. The members respect him and listen to his advice."

Nils got the message. He was a lightweight. Omah was the real deal. "Thanks for letting us know," he said. "That helps a lot."

"You bet," Gilbert said. "I'll work this issue from my end. Oh, and this evening, for Gaia's sake, would you two nerds watch the news?"

"Sure," Colin said with a weak smile. The vis-panel made two descending tones.

"Hva i helvete?" *What the hell?* said Nils to himself.

"Bloody hell," said Colin, leaning back in his chair.

"I was worried this might happen," Nils said, his face void of expression. "The only other place to get funding is private industry." He shook his head. "Man, I'd rather clean the stables than schedule a meeting with those crooks."

"You mean Jean-Marc Ledger and his riffraff?"

"Yeah. For years, they've wanted to grab our communication satellite business."

Colin's anger flared. "Nils, for Gaia's sake, L'AA tried to blow up *Lodestar*. You can't just walk in there and start wheeling and dealing with those gangsters."

Nils looked down for a long moment. "Well, that's what Omah thinks. But in truth, we still don't know who loosened that fuel fitting."

Colin grumbled, "I get a distinct feeling this will not end well."

31

PLAUSIBLE DENIABILITY

MISA ADMIN SCIF, MONTRÉAL, 2265 CE

After the call from Representative Gilbert Frank, Nils sent a secure message to Omah, briefing him on what he had learned. A few minutes later, Nils received a secure message back from Omah, asking him to come immediately to the administrative offices.

On arrival, Omah met him in the reception area. Something was definitely going on.

"Let's use the SCIF."

Omah headed down a seldom-used hallway, where they each looked into a retinal scanner and left their electronic devices in a signal-blocking cabinet. Once inside the Secure Compartmented Information Facility, Omah closed the soundproof door and activated countermeasures.

"No one knows I am reading you in. There will be no record of this meeting. That gives you plausible deniability, just in case things go south. Do you catch my gist?"

Nils acknowledged. They both took seats.

"I have reliable intel from a source within the Government Accountability Office—"

"The GAO? That serious?" Nils felt his heart thumping and droplets of perspiration forming on his forehead.

"Yes, sir, the GAO. Several weeks ago, they launched a secret investigation into an alleged bribery scandal involving several representatives. The GAO accountants discovered money transfers from an offshore bank in the Seychelles to numbered bank accounts belonging to three high-ranking representatives."

Nils's eyes widened. "Are they members of the SST Committee?"

"I don't know the identities of the representatives yet. I know the police raided the offshore bank yesterday and discovered that L'Airelle Aéronautique had deposited enormous sums of money into the account.

"Unbelievable! That jerk Ledger is bribing the representatives on the SST committee." His face flushed and fists clenched.

"Nils, you are my point man here. I need you to be steady at the helm."

"Well, surely you can understand."

"Oh, trust me. I understand. These three representatives have put the entire space program in jeopardy."

"Now it all makes sense: the straw poll, tabling the funding bill. The committee chair is on the take from Ledger to stall *Lodestar*'s funding. Has anyone notified Department of Justice?"

"The DOJ is starting its investigation. They might not subpoena records for several weeks, and depositions could take months. MISA will be swirling down the drain by then."

"So, we need to act fast. Where do I fit in?"

"I want you to meet with Ledger and leak the DOJ investigation. Let him know they have the bank records—the proverbial 'smoking gun.' Ledger is their primary target. If convicted, he's looking at considerable prison time."

"Once he learns about the evidence and the investigation, what do you think he'll do?"

"Well, seems to me he has two options: stay and fight it out in court, or make a break for it and run. He has top lawyers, but the evidence is strong. Running would be risky, but he is worth billions and could bribe his way to a secret luxury haven somewhere."

"Hmm, what if he uses his political influence to shut down the investigation?"

"Then we go public and put the story on every news channel on the SafeNet. It would be ugly, but we would be the plaintiffs, not the defendants."

Nils took a nervous breath. "I don't recall this in my job description when you hired me."

Omah made a wry grin. "Think of it as an opportunity for employee skills development."

32

THE MOST IMPORTANT MEETING

OFFICES OF L'AIRELLE AÉRONAUTIQUE, TORONTO, 2265 CE

"Well, if it isn't Nils Björnsson. It's been a long time," said Jean-Marc Ledger as he greeted Nils in the foyer of his corporate headquarters. The building was a study in restrained opulence: book-matched burled wood paneling, thick burgundy carpets, handcrafted leather furniture, and custom art-glass lighting from the Dale Chihuly collection. But oddly, there was no receptionist at the lobby desk, and there was dust everywhere. The staff hadn't vacuumed the carpets in weeks. And boxes cluttered the hallways. How strange.

Tall and athletic, in an Italian suit with an open collar, Jean-Marc Ledger's tousled hair and five-day stubble were stylishly counterculture. As they took the express elevator to the top floor, Nils noted food stains on JM's sleeve and the odor of bourbon on his breath.

"I remember when you worked here. You impressed my dad."

"That was my first engineering job out of school. I worked on the Eco-Swift."

"Oh, great airplane," said Jean-Marc. "Lots of them still flying, you know."

They walked by floor-to-ceiling windows that gave a knee-trembling view of the ground four stories below. As they walked, Nils didn't see any office staff or junior executives in the hallways, nor any shop-floor staff on the grounds below. Arriving at his spacious office, Jean-Marc offered Nils a chair.

"I need to talk to you about something important."

Jean-Marc raced ahead. "Of course, your flagship project, Lodestone. You had an engine fire, and an aborted launch. Now Congress doubts your abilities and is holding up your funding. So, you are looking for a lender, are you not?"

"It's *Lodestar,* JM. And Congress doesn't doubt our abilities."

"Of course, the Aerospace Safety Board is investigating and will probably publish its report in a month or two.

"We did our own internal investigation. We know basically what happened."

JM morphed from snarky pundit to fixated listener. "You know what happened?"

"Someone sabotaged the booster. They loosened a fitting connecting a fuel conduit to a high-pressure fuel pump."

Jean-Marc looked as if he were airsick. "Intentionally?"

"Yes."

It was Nils's turn to lean forward. "Jean-Marc, I'm asking you, man to man. Were you involved in that? Or any of your people?"

Jean-Marc looked stone-cold sober. "No, Nils. I had no part in that. In business, sure, there are gray areas where we push things, but there are also hard lines that no one crosses. Tampering with someone else's booster—crossing that line could bring down a corporation."

Nils held his gaze. After several seconds, he said, "I knew your father. He was a man of great integrity. I believe his son would never lie about something so consequential."

Jean-Marc's shoulders slumped as a wistful sadness swept over him. "You speak well of my dad." But ever the entrepreneur, he shook off the woe and followed with, "So, what is the problem with your funding?"

"The Committee on Science, Space, and Technology has tabled our bill. They won't vote on it."

Jean-Marc lowered and darkened his voice. "So, how much are we talking about here?"

Nils lowered his voice to match. "Twelve million e-par value."

Jean-Marc's jaw dropped. "That's all? To launch a project costing half a billion?" He laughed out loud. "Whoever has some cash could cut one sweet deal. Man, what I could do with that?"

Nils said, "Hold on. Hold on, JM. I'm not here to borrow money."

Jean-Marc's expression fell to bewilderment. "Then why are we sitting here?"

Nils pulled himself up in his chair. "I'm here for two reasons. First, I need to alert you that a dangerous situation has developed in your company. For security reasons, I felt I should tell you personally."

"What's that?"

"We know from reliable sources that several members of the Sentient Faction have infiltrated your company and are operating as SF agents in your employ."

Alarm came into Jean-Marc's eyes. "How do you know this?"

"I'm sorry, JM, but I must protect my sources."

Jean-Marc's formidable analytic wheels engaged. He said, "It must be Faroe. That means the SF operatives must be in AI pilot production." He became lost in his thoughts.

"Because of the risk to our operations, Omah Wheelwright has directed me to activate the opt-out clause in our contract and discontinue all purchases and shipments from L'AA."

"I suppose you have no choice," Jean-Marc said. "Alright, what's the second reason?"

"Reliable sources inform me the Department of Justice is launching an investigation into bribery of several congressional representatives by L'Airelle Aéronautique. They have discovered a money trail from the L'AA Financial Office through a bank in the Seychelles to a shell corporation, and on to the representatives who control MISA finances."

"And how do you know this?"

"Again, I must protect my sources. But JM, you are the principal target of this investigation. The DOJ has bank records tracking the transactions. And they have a strong case."

Jean-Marc looked worried, even frightened. "My Gaia, it's all coming apart."

Nils heard this and felt surprised. "What are you talking about?"

JM bolted the remaining bourbon in his glass. "The AI assemblage building over by the airpark. Do you know the one?"

"That building with the big glass windows and ceiling?"

"Yeah, that's it. That is where the Sentient Faction has established its beachhead. They are trying to infiltrate the administrative offices."

Nils stared at Ledger in bewilderment. "How did they break into the company?"

Jean-Marc gazed out the window, his face drained of color. "I made a deal with them." He turned to the credenza and poured himself another shot of bourbon.

Nils asked, "You cut a business deal with the Faction? My Gaia, JM, what were you thinking?"

"I wanted to break into the Siberian market. It was a huge order for planes in Siberia, Mongolia, and Kamchatka. In return, we would grant them exclusive licenses for sales and service of L'AA aircraft in the region. They could have made tons of e-par."

"I can see the attraction," Nils said.

"But then, it was like a covert infiltration operation. They took control of human resources and used that as a gateway to bring in more factionistas. Suddenly, SF operatives were spreading like tuberculosis through the organization. They even tried to grab control of the finance office."

Nils asked, "What are you going to do?

"The only thing I can do; shut down the AI assemblage and fire everyone. But what you need to know is that they have broken into MISA, and one is now working on your Orbital Launch Complex."

Nils pondered for a moment. "Jean-Marc, why did you bribe the representatives to block our funding?"

JM said in detached tones, "It seemed like the best way to destabilize your company and gain control of the NuSAT satellite network."

Nils raised his voice. "You're telling me this was your idea of 'business'?"

"That's what I'm saying. Of course, it doesn't matter what I say now."

Nils sat silently, smoldering.

Then Jean-Marc said, "Listen, Nils, take my advice. Go straight to your MISA Nonhuman Resources Office a shutdown hiring of AI units."

Nils, wide-eyed, nodded.

"Then, look back at all recent AI hires. If any droid has so much as a mention of L'Airelle Aéronautique in their application, fire them on the spot. I mean it."

Nils's jaw became firm. "Jean-Marc, the Department of Justice is coming for you. I know you have the best lawyers, and it sounds like you have a good defense. But as for bribing the representatives, I need you to shut that operation down right now. That funding is critical for our launch. I won't take no for an answer."

Jean-Marc sat slumped, gazing at nothing. "I'll shut it down, Nils. But you need to understand that ultimately, I have no influence over the SF. They are going to do whatever they want."

Nils felt sorrow for JM. Here was the quintessential jetsetter, billionaire, socialite, lady's man, and ruthless corporate shark looking at years behind bars. It was painful to watch.

Nils overheard Jean-Marc mumble to himself, *Those damn migration wars? What colossal stupidity.* Given the fragility of the moment, Nils decided not to explore the comment.

Nils stood up to go. "JM, I think this has been the most important meeting of my career. It may not be possible to save L'AA. But from what you have told me, I think I might save MISA. I'm grateful to you for that. And whatever you decide, good luck."

The two men shook hands. Nils walked to the door, glanced back, and said to himself *Who would ever have thought...* then turned and left the building.

33

GOOD CALL

MISA OUTDOOR LUNCH AREA, MONTRÉAL, 2265 CE

"Over here!" howled Colin from a picnic table set with his steaming basket of fish and chips. Nils joined him with a plate of Smørrebrød and Song with a bowl of Rou jia mo. It was such a bright, warm day, odd for Montréal in late fall.

"So, Nils, what did Ledger say?" Song asked.

Nils looked around. No one within earshot, but still he spoke in a hushed voice. "He told me the SF had broken into his company. And he confirmed that SF agents were in MISA.

"How did he look?"

"Like hell. He was drunk, and it was only ten AM. I asked him if he had anything to do with the aborted *Lodestar* launch, and he denied it. I believe him. I also told him to shut down the bribery payments to the congressional representatives. He said he would do it."

Song tightened her jaw. "Such poor decisions." She stabbed a broccoli floret with her fork. "With a big investigation going on, those funds won't be released for months."

Colin said, "Sounds like you accomplished a lot. But I thought the reason for the meeting was to ask for money."

"That was my cover story to get on his calendar. Our big cash burner will launch in five weeks," Nils said.

"We have enough cash to cover three weeks, maybe," said Song. "With the launch scheduled for five weeks, that's two weeks of negative cash flow, or about six million in e-par value each week."

"I'm sure we could find a lender for that amount," Colin said.

But Song's financial wheels were turning. "I would prefer to find a benefactor who would just donate the money... Hmm." Deep in thought, and without saying another word, Song got up and walked by herself back to the Administration Building.

Colin sighed.

"You like her. I can tell," said Nils.

"Yeah, but how am I ever going to get to know her?" Colin folded his arms.

"Let me share an old trick: dogs."

Colin looked confused. "How's that?"

"Your golden retrievers. Meet at the park. Bring Liesel and Cadi and some frisbees. It will be a blast."

Several days later, a high-priority message called Nils to the administrative offices for an urgent meeting. Striding down the hall, he encountered Colin and Song doing the same.

Once inside the SCIF—with all their electronics outside—Omah touched his vis-panel and Congressman Gilbert Frank's voice said, "Hello, everyone. Let's start by turning on a broadcast news channel."

Omah tapped a vis-screen and selected C-ABC. Three distinguished men were standing on the limestone steps of a federal building, surrounded by reporters holding out microphones. The news chyron tracking across the lower screen read, "Three representatives resigning amid accusations of bribery and misappropriation of funds."

"The story has broken," Nils said,

"Or crashed open," Gilbert quipped. "Do you know this guy, Ledger?"

"Oh, yeah," Nils said. "In fact, I had a meeting with him last week."

"To stay out of jail, he is cutting a deal with the DOJ. He is going to testify as a witness for the state. The prosecutors say they have records tracking payments to these representatives, who control funds for aerospace contracts."

Song made an audible squeak of joy.

"You can only imagine my relief," Colin said with a deep sigh.

Omah said, "This is the news we have been waiting for."

"It is," Gilbert said. "Anyway, I have to run. Have a great launch."

As the group filed out, Nils pointed at Omah and said, "Good call."

Omah pointed back, "Good work."

34

JUST A RAMBLER AT HEART

PORTAGE LA PRAIRIE, MANITOBA, CANAM, 2265 CE

As the MISA tilt-rotor aircraft descended to the grassy meadow, Trent and Larke waved to Sierra, who was waiting by an all-terrain vehicle with two frantic Australian shepherds. Omah had made an introductory call, so Sierra knew what this visit was about.

A standard female-gender droid, similar to Trent and Larke, she had upgraded solenoids, which gave her more strength for such things as shearing sheep and lifting bags of feed. She wore denim coveralls, a plaid shirt with a clumsy selection of loud colors, yellow rubber boots, and a feed cap embroidered with a photo of an antique tractor, *the Waterloo Boy*.

They all climbed into the ATV and headed up a grassy pathway toward a brand-spanking-new barn. The two dogs leaned out of the side windows, tongues drooping.

"I gotta let the sheep out," Sierra said. "Hope you don't mind a few chores while we chat?"

"No, go right ahead," Larke said, who had spent many years in rural British Columbia.

"So, last summer, we moved this farm from western Oklahoma to Manitoba," Sierra said. "I helped build that barn." She unlatched the pasture fence, letting her dogs through.

"So, you help with moving farms?" Trent asked.

Sierra said, "I help plan farms, move farms, build farm buildings, and renovate used farming implements. My business is growing like mad. Me and my workers, we can't keep up with the demand."

Loud *baas* coming from the barn piqued the dogs' excitement. As

Sierra rolled the barn door aside, a cloud of white sheep billowed out into the pasture, setting off the dogs' robotic reflex to encircle the noisy flock and nudge it along.

Colin said, "With the advancing drylands, I guess there's been no choice."

"And I've been in the middle of all that. It has been good for business."

"So, what do you farm?"

"I farm row crops and vegetables; I suppose I have grown most every vegetable at one time or another. As for ranching, I have established herds of cattle and sheep. And plenty of chickens, turkeys, and geese. I once established a herd of American bison. That was interesting because their hooves break the topsoil, they graze off all the scrub brush, and their droppings fertilize the soil. So, buffalo bring back the dry wastelands to grassland. I also built pig farms; but that's not my favorite."

Sierra opened a stall in the barn and let two donkeys out. "If you raise sheep and there are wolves around, get you a couple of donkeys and set them to graze with the sheep. Donkeys aren't afraid of the wolves and will kick at them and protect the sheep." She slapped the donkeys on the rump and set them trotting into the pasture. She made a shrill whistle and called, "Molly! Cash!"

The two dogs came rocketing across the pasture toward her as she closed up the barn.

"And I love working sheepdogs. Sometimes with a couple of good shepherds, I'll take the flock for a stroll along that grassy hillside over there. The sheep like the thick grass, and the dogs enjoy the workout. I'll tell you, that is a fine morning."

"You have so much experience. What other skills do you have?"

Sierra said, "I built a couple of smithies for ironwork. Also, I dammed a few streams to make ponds and stocked 'em with fish. And I can cook, they tell me."

"So, why join this mission?" Trent asked as they all climbed back into the ATV and drove back to the farmhouse. Inside, they found plaster walls, hand-hewn beams, Native American rugs, prairie mission furniture, and some Mata Ortiz pottery on a sideboard.

"You know, every settlement seems to need somebody like me. I have never gone without work. But really, inside I am just a rambler at heart. The challenge of building a farm on another planet—that just wakes me up, like Molly and Cash when they hear the sheep." She reached down and rubbed Cash's neck. "Don't you get excited when you hear those sheep? Yes, you do. Yes, you *do!* Such a good boy."

Larke said, "Your dogs are so well-trained."

"Oh, that's my happy place. I train 'em myself. I think dogs know when they are helping on a farm. I think they feel pride and a sense of belonging. I wouldn't work on a farm that didn't have dogs."

Larke looked at Trent. "Are dogs included on the livestock manifest?"

"Hmm, not sure."

"I mean that about the dogs. On a big farm with herds, shepherds are essential. Think of them as bioengineered tools for livestock management and varmint interception. And they are the best burglar alarms ever. Let me tell you: no dogs, no Sierra."

"I'll call our consultant. We have a genetics laboratory on contract to screen all the embryos," Trent went silent as he connected through the Blue-Link network. Momentarily, he was talking with the lab's geneticist.

Trent wrapped up his call. "Our genetics consultant says that they commonly use frozen embryos in veterinary medicine, and it's really no different from working with human embryos. She says we have room in the canister for ten dog embryos. She needs to know which breed."

"Australians are my favorite."

Trent responded, "Then that settles it. We will have ten Australian shepherds included in the animals for the crossing."

Larke said, "With that, we would like to offer you a position on the crew of *The Founder*."

Sierra pumped her arm and hollered, "Wuuu-haaww!"

35

A BAKE SALE FOR WORLD PEACE

THE SUPERCHIEF CAFÉ, MONTRÉAL, 2265 CE

"I had so much fun playing Frisbee with Liesel and Cadi," Song said. "Such sweet dogs, and so good at catching Frisbees."

Colin hid his nervousness. "It was a delight, and the dogs loved it. We should do that again soon before it gets cold." Song then noticed both Colin and Nils had wry grins that betrayed their little conspiracy. That made her smile, too.

Song said, "Six more weeks of working cash and our launch date is eight weeks away. So, we have a two-week gap to fill. We need a minimum cash flow of about two million dollars per week just for the essentials." She thought about her college years. Sometimes she would live for weeks on instant noodles, waiting for student loans to come in.

She went on, "Think about it. The government has no real interest in deep space exploration. Government is basically a social contract between citizens to establish laws that promote the general well-being. So, we shouldn't be surprised when the government gives a deep space mission low priority."

"Okay," Colin said. "How about business support?"

"The business community does not have an interest in deep space, either, Song said. "They monetize everything they get their hands on. Can you outline a viable business plan for a deep space mission? No, there is no ROI. This should not surprise us. So, who do we turn to finance deep space science?

"Broaden your thinking," Song said. "Who looks at the night sky with awe and curiosity? Who hungers to explore space? Who defends the MISA mission?"

Colin and Nils met each other's gaze. "We've been asking the wrong people for help,"

Nils said, "So we should be approaching the amateur astronomers, the space-adventure film fans, the young folks who go to sci-fi conventions, the young who work in technology.

"These people have imaginations rich with stars, planets, spaceships, and aliens. They are the ones who cheer when MISA launches a big mission. They are the ones who understand that we already live in outer space."

Song lowered her voice. Then, without warning, there is an actual message from aliens."

"Yeah, I see now," Colin said. "They want to be part of our mission."

Nils leaned back and said, "I know where this is going..."

Song was becoming animated. "Nils, Colin, have you seen what's happening on the SafeNet: the sky-clubs, fan-dramas, virtual play worlds, cosplay conventions, all of it? They're going nuts over our mission."

Colin's forehead furrowed. "What's a cosplay?"

"Here." Song reached into her shoulder bag for her vis-panel. Typing on the screen, she said, "Here, look."

Colin and Nils watched as she scrolled through screen after screen of videos, chats, podcasts, fan stories, drama serials, gatherings, and concerts, all about the mission to make first contact on 82 G. Eridani c.

Song said, "Here are our real supporters. We must ask them for help."

Nils's expression was a mix of curiosity and skepticism. "But how?"

"We open a Help-Fund-Us page on the SafeNet and send out the word to all our fans. And we ask our fans to spread the word. We ask for donations, and in return, they will receive recognition, like a letter from Nils on MISA letterhead."

"We could engrave their name on *The Founder*," Colin said, "and include a photo of their name on the ship."

"Hold on, everybody," Nils asked. "Can we do this? We are a government agency. Are we allowed to solicit donations?"

"I know the regulations inside and out," Song said. "We can accept donations, but we must be completely transparent about reporting the source, amount, and how we use the funds. That's standard operating procedure in our financial office. We do that every day."

"I like this idea, Song," Nils said. "But it's just that we need six million in e-par value to complete construction, and another two million for the launch, and security, and transportation. This feels to me like a bake sale for world peace."

"Success in this type of enterprise depends on two things: trust and market exposure. To secure trust, our donation page will be on an official MISA server and domain name. We will use a secure payment method. We'll keep track of donations and make sure every penny goes to the mission. And for market exposure, word-of-mouth in the social media networks will spread our SafeNet address like a flu virus."

Nils looked at Song and gave a wry smile. "You're really going to make this work, aren't you?"

"Hey, this is my turf, big guy," Song said with a level gaze.

Nils took a last quaff of his beer, looked straight at Song, and said, "Senior management approves the Help-Fund-Us website. Send out a memo."

Smiling as she stood to leave, Song said, "Thanks, Nils. Colin, Frisbee this Saturday morning?"

"We'll be there."

Song turned to go, but then hesitated. Turning back, she asked, "Can we really engrave their names on the ship?"

"Sure," Colin said. "We've got a laser engraver. Snap it onto a repair droid, upload the names, and add a camera. Write a bit of code and away it goes."

"Cool. Let's do that." She turned and hurried out to the e-Tram stop and didn't see Colin and Nils bump fists.

36

CHANCE OF A LIFETIME

A WOMAN'S CARE CLINIC, MISSISSAUGA, CANAM, 2267 CE

Delph locked her gaze on the small screen as her left hand made precise adjustments to the ultrasound probe. Her patient, Mrs. M had many of these studies, yet each look into her body still fascinated her. Her embryo, fertilized in vitro, had embedded in the lining of the uterus, was well-positioned, and was growing steadily.

"You are pregnant," Delph announced jubilantly, yielding a broad smile from Mrs. M and her glowing life-partner. "Let's all cross our fingers. I have a good feeling about this."

Finished with her last patient of the morning, Delph strolled down the doorway-lined hall to her modest office. The fertility clinic was an understated, functional space—plain white walls, swirl linoleum floors, and loud blue plastic stacking chairs. Ninety years ago, engineers had constructed Delph, a top-of-the-line bipedal droid, in Bowling Green, Kentucky, where Corvette sports cars used to be manufactured. She had a dark gray skeletal frame, black surface panels discreetly highlighted with flat burgundy trim lines; a striking appearance perhaps inspired by the Corvette. Whenever working in the clinic, she added traditional obstetrical blue scrubs and a long white coat, OR clogs, and a surgical cap even though she had no hair.

"Trent... Larke... pleasure to meet you." She was surprised to find her guests were both AI droids. "I understand you work with Nils Björnsson."

"Right. We all work at MISA, in the Section of Deep Space Missions, which Nils directs," Trent said. "He has a high regard for you."

"I'm glad to hear that. Fertility work is expensive and not always successful. That can sometimes leave a bad feeling."

"Nils opened up to us about his attempt to have a child. He was wistful about the experience, but also philosophical."

Delph's thoughts drifted to the hundreds of couples who would never conceive despite her best efforts. But then, in her yearly adventure travels hiking forest trails or rafting wild rivers, she had witnessed firsthand the decrepitude of the land. In that moment, she wondered if the infertile couples might actually be the lucky ones.

"So, what brings you to the fertility clinic today? Are you planning to start a family?"

The two droids looked at each other and shook their heads at the droll humor.

"No," Trent smiled and said, "We are here for a different reason."

Larke said, "Nils Björnsson recommended we talk to you about a potential position working for MISA."

Delph sat up, complete puzzlement on her face. "Work for MISA? What on Mars's moons would a space agency do with a fertility specialist?"

Larke said, "Before I answer that, can I ask a few background questions?"

"Sure, fire away." Delph flipped up her hands, pretending to surrender.

"I hear you enjoy adventures out in the wild. Can you tell us about that?"

"Hmm, okay," she said, again looking quizzical. "This is the strangest conversation... Yes, I have always loved getting out into nature and experiencing the wilderness. Last year, four of us went kayaking from Vancouver along the Strait of Georgia. We saw otters, blue herons, and humpback whales. The year before, we went sailing on a square-rigger off the coast of Nova Scotia. The year before that, it was train rides, hiking, and boating along the fjords of Norway."

"I hear it is beautiful."

"Language lacks the words."

Trent said, "I understand you have experience with the artificial uterus?"

Delph brightened. "Extensive experience, actually. We were among the first primary testing sites for early versions of the AU. I was on that team. Now I deliver two or three AU babies each month. Our outcomes are among the best in the business." Delph squared her shoulders with an air of accomplishment.

Larke turned to Trent, eyes sparkling. "This is who we have been looking for."

Delph leaned forward. "Okay, no more dodging. What is this all about?"

Trent said, "I am the commander of the interstellar ship *The Founder*."

Larke added, "And I am the chief engineer. Our charge is to fly the ship to the destination planet, 82 G. Eridani c, and establish a settlement there."

Delph's eyes widened. "No! Really? I've read all about your ship. So, you both are going?"

"We are."

Larke lifted her vis-panel from her bag and said, "The crossing will take two hundred years. Humans will make the crossing as frozen embryos." She opened an image of the canister. "Once it arrives at the destination, we need someone to set up the artificial uterus and gestate the frozen embryos."

"You are recruiting me to go into space for two hundred years and gestate human embryos?"

"Yes, that's correct."

"And when are you leaving?"

"In about eight weeks."

Delph shook with surprise. "And why me?"

You rank among the top experts in the area on AU technology, possess more experience with the artificial uterus than anyone else in the region, and have experience living outdoors.

"Well, I suppose... And how many frozen embryos can your spaceship carry?"

"About twenty-four hundred."

Delph flinched. "Good Gaia! You know each gestation takes nine months. I hope you are taking more than one AU."

"We have room for ten AU units plus supplies," Larke said.

Delph's eyes widened as she pondered the possibilities. "Of course, this is a big decision. I need to talk this over with friends and associates. Also, I need to come by MISA and meet the team who are putting this all together. I will require a thorough briefing."

"That's what we expected," Trent said as his smile broadened. "So, when you have time in your schedule, we will set up the tour and briefing."

After pondering a moment, Delph said to herself, *"Establishing a human colony on another planet... my Gaia. These droids are making history."*

Larke said, "Listen, we know this is a big ask. And, full disclosure: No one has ever done this before. There are unknowns and risks that we do not yet appreciate. But like the *Mayflower* landing at Plymouth Rock, this interstellar crossing could change the course of history."

"I have another question," Trent said. "Do you have experience repairing AI droids?"

"I have the basic skills. That's a standard part of the 'new' medical school curriculum, you know. We trained to be cognizant-neutral."

"Where we are going, extra skills like that will be important," Trent said.

Delph was silent for another moment. "There's one voice inside of me that says, *'Do it, you damn fool. This is a chance of a lifetime.'* And another voice that says, *'Good Gaia, what are you thinking?'* Both options are tough, but for completely different reasons."

Delph's vis-comm pinged, and a voice spoke, "Dr. Delph, can you look at this ultrasound?"

"Sure, Minnie. Send it over." Picking up her vis-panel, she said, "Oh, will you look at that? Triplets. Just a minute." Delph then said, "I am considering your proposal. But full disclosure: the artificial uterus is the most ornery, persnickety, damnable contraption ever created by the hand of man. I hope and pray that if I go on this trip, we won't find the AU technology impossible to recreate on the new planet."

"We can only do what's possible with the technology we have. Nothing more," Larke said. "If we get there and cannot start a colony, no one will fault us."

Trent thought to himself *Of course, no one will be around to fault us.*

"Let us know when you have some time on your schedule to visit MISA," Trent said. "We will give you the grand tour."

"How does tomorrow morning sound?"

37

HELP-FUND-US

MISA HQ COFFEE LOUNGE, MONTRÉAL, 2265 CE

Nils felt drained. After two nerve-racking broadcast interviews, a meeting with upset engineers, and a discussion on intellectual property rights with MISA legal counsel, he grabbed Colin, walked to the coffee lounge, and ordered two café Americanos. Coincidentally, Song was there too and joined them.

"I'm glad I saw you two. Remember our website for donations?"

Colin grinned. "Will our pet kangaroo get the hip surgery he needs?"

Song resisted the urge to clobber Colin with her vis-panel. Instead, she pointed to a spreadsheet.

Nils squinted. "Herregud, *my goodness,* seventy-three thousand one hundred donations. Over two million in CanAm e-par value."

"Our first three days," Song said, beaming.

"Blimey, Song, this is ruddy amazing," Colin said.

Song blushed. "It was the people. They believed in the mission."

"Well, this was a great idea," Colin said. He relaxed as he felt a weight lifted from his shoulders.

Song said, "As a side note, news of the MISA Help-Fund-Us page brought journalistic scrutiny on the SST committee. The journalists asked embarrassing questions about why the funding resolution had not passed, forcing MISA to open a crowdfunding website to fund their launch."

Nils felt his frame relax. "I'm sure that the recent bribery scandal to block our funding didn't hurt."

Song said, "No, it didn't. And the immense interest in making first contact helped, too. With the donations came lots of notes. People really want us to launch and meet the aliens."

Nils said, "Like the cavalry riding over the hill, the fanzines have come to the rescue."

As Song got up to go back to her office, Colin said, "Liesel and Cadi would like to play Frisbee with you this Saturday."

She smiled and said, "Put me on their calendar for ten o'clock at the park."

38

CAST MY FATE TO THE WIND

OSHAWA, CANAM, 2265 CE

"I understand you need a civil engineer." Rhome's face popped up on the vis-screen. He was a robust bipedal droid, larger than Trent, with gunmetal-gray exposed articulations, pale gray surface panels, and dark blue highlights on hips, shoulders, and around the ears. Like Trent and Larke, he had a silicone face with actuators for facial expression, and soft green LED lights in his eyes to create that semblance of attentiveness.

"I am called Trent, and I am the ship's commander. Our mission is to travel to the planet 82 G. Eridani c and build a settlement. We need a civil engineer to plan and build the utilities, buildings, throughways, and green spaces after we arrive."

"I have experience in these areas of urban development. I believe I would be an excellent addition to your crew."

Trent liked his demeanor, his energy, and his directness. "I see that you have in your application a letter of recommendation from Congressman Gilbert Frank."

"Congressman Frank secured funding for civic projects and improvements in his district, and I won bids for several of those contracts. I was involved in the design and construction of several transportation hubs, pedestrian bridges, bicycle pathways, light-rail platforms, and an airport."

"What are you working on now?"

"I'm finishing the construction of a transportation hub on the east side of Toronto. Here, let me show you." He turned his camera around to view the construction zone. "Light-rail train passengers disembark at this covered plaza. On their right, glass doors lead to dining and shopping. On the left is access to EV parking. Next to that is an elevator up to the roof with six e-Drone landing pads. Further, you see parking for bicycles and e-bikes, with easy access to express bicycle paths out to the residential areas."

"Impressive. One can change modes of transportation with such ease."

"That's the idea: arrive via light rail, meet a friend, grab a bite, then e-bike home. I have also helped to design and build houses, apartments, office space, dormitories, restaurants, and manufacturing space."

"Any other skills you might mention?"

"Well, during that airport project, I took up aviation. It's more than a hobby now... it's become an obsession. I have flown just about everything that has wings."

"Really. Have you ever flown a lift-jet?"

"Actually, yes. I have about two hundred sixty hours of lift-jet time with fourteen lifts into orbit. I am no pro like the pilots at MISA, but I can enter the atmosphere and land on a designated runway."

Trent did not let his emotions show, but inside he was jumping up and down. *This seems almost too good. What is wrong with this picture?*

"Help me understand something. Here you are, a successful and admired civil engineer, and you want to leave all this success and join a band of scruffy space explorers. Why would you do that? There must be something driving you to make this change."

Rhome squared himself. "I had a registered domestic partner, Alanna. We were together for over fifty years. She was a meteorologist for the National Weather Service. Last year, a bolt of lightning struck the radar tower on her building. It melted the circuit breakers and sent a power surge throughout the building. All three AI beings working in the building that day perished. Since then, I have lost my sense of purpose. I just wander from project to project without feeling fulfillment. I have had counseling. And I even took up pickleball just to meet droids and attend social events. But nothing fills the emptiness. And nothing short of a life reboot will give me a sense of direction, purpose, and accomplishment."

As Trent listened, he touched the bare wires of loss, simulating for a moment what it would be like if Larke vanished from his world. In that instant, he understood the reason Rhome needed a clean break. No reminders, no ghosts, only a new reality, a new self.

Trent quavered slightly. "I am sorry for your loss, Rhome. If a sense of purpose is what you seek, I believe our mission would provide that."

"It feels like I'm casting my fate to the wind."

"No one has done this before. We are the first, and we will figure it out as we go."

"Yeah, no owner's manual," Rhome said. "And I'm excited about a settlement on a remote planet. But I am sober about getting there, including the possibility that we won't."

"Well, let me assure you, I am going to do whatever it takes. We have our mission, and I am all in."

"Hoo-ah, brother."

"Rhome, I extend to you an offer to join the crew and mission of *The Founder*."

"I accept. Let's do this."

"Welcome aboard."

"Damn, I am the luckiest droid in the hemisphere."

"Don't speak too soon."

39

BUT IS IT NATURAL?

MISA VIRTUAL AUDITORIUM, MONTRÉAL, 2265 CE

At its last press conference, MISA released a message from aliens. Today's conference couldn't possibly top that. Still, at the scheduled time, in tidy rows and columns, a thousand thumbnail-size faces looked out from the curved floor-to-ceiling vis-wall. Maisie Running Elk, attired in her colorful tribal prints and silver jewelry, opened the conference, provided introductory remarks, and turned it over to Nils.

"Thank you, Maisie. At our last press conference, we announced a new mission: to send our interstellar ship twenty light-years to the planet 82 G. Eridani c.

"Since that announcement, astronomers have studied that exoplanet. Spectroscopic data from the Aristarchus Far-Infrared Space Telescope has detected biosignatures for water, carbon dioxide, methane, and dimethyl sulfide. These findings suggest life.

"In addition, the FLIRT recorded transmissions of a voice transmitting from that very planet. We are now certain that a technologically advanced society inhabits 82 G. Eridani c. These are certainly the same race of extraterrestrials who visited Earth long ago and left a message inviting us to their planet." Nils paused as the wall of faces rustled, as if a gust of wind had blown through the assembled crowd.

"With these new findings, the mission team has revised the goal of the mission." The thumbnails stilled. "Our new goal is to establish the first permanent extraterrestrial settlement on planet 82 G. Eridani c. The colony will include both human and AI beings."

The assembly burst into motion, and a flurry of emoji hands shot up. Nils put on his headphones and selected a reporter.

"Representing the *London Daily Telegraph.* Please reassure us you will not be bolting a cabin onto the spacecraft in order to take human beings on a two-hundred-year voyage. The space available couldn't be much larger than a travel caravan. And a two-hundred-year voyage means that the people who arrive at the destination planet will be the seventh-generation descendants of the original crew. That is far too incestuous to condone." Background giggling flitted across the sea of images.

"Reggie," said Nils, remembering the pointed hallway question. "We are not bolting a pressurized travel caravan onto the ship, because, basically, it wouldn't work mainly for the reasons you have already mentioned. Also, Reggie, to follow up, we are no longer purchasing parts from L'AA." Nils was gracious and gave Reggie the win. After all, investigative journalism is a ruthless business.

A journalist spoke without invitation. "Reporting for *Noticias del Norte.* So how will the people get there?"

Nils said without a moment's hesitation, "Frozen embryos."

The journalist repeated the words back to him. "Frozen embryos?" Her brow knitted and eyes narrowed. A stillness fell over the multitude.

Nils explained, "When a couple completes a course of in vitro fertilization, it is common to have a few left-over frozen embryos: meaning fertilized eggs stored under liquid nitrogen. We are asking couples with these to donate one embryo to the mission. And we will accept only one embryo, so we have the greatest genetic diversity in our population. *The Founder* can carry twenty-four hundred human frozen embryos, plus farm animals."

Hands...

In a heavy Irish accent, "Writing for *The Dublin Independent.* Are ya thinking that people are just gonna send ya a bundle of frozen eggs for this space trip? If ya ask me, that's a touch barmy."

"Callie, more than a thousand embryos have arrived just this week."

"Well, faith and begorrah. I wouldn't have imagined such a thing."

"Around the world, there are millions of embryos in liquid nitrogen. Fertility clinics must maintain these embryos at a cost, paid by the couple who produced them. As they grow older, most couples stop paying for cryogenic storage, and they discard the embryos. This expedition offers these embryos a chance for a future."

Emoji hands went up.

"Corresponding for *The Charleston Bay Reliable.* How will the embryos become people?"

Nils said matter-of-factly. "The artificial uterus." He thought to himself, *Okay, now here it comes.*

"But who will raise the babies?" the correspondent asked, looking puzzled.

"The ship's crew," Nils said, waiting for him to make the connection.

His face frowned. "Aren't the crew AI units?" These words set the sea of faces in motion.

"Yes, AI units will care for the babies and raise the first generation of humans."

Emojis shot up all over the vis-wall. Nils selected.

"Reporting for the *Alleanza Europea Delle Agenzie di Stampa.* Will AI units be like parents to these babies?"

"Mmm, more like an AI nanny or au pair. But yes, AI units will raise the first generation of children."

The reporter's voice rose in umbrage. "But how do you replace the mother's love and the father's strength?" Her hands gestured. "Children need the parents as they grow up. It is wrong for AI units to raise the baby, who will never know a genuine mother or father."

A face popped up. "I am an editor for the *Noticias Hispanoamérica.* Allow me to comment. After MWIII, I landed at an enormous camp for displaced children in northern España. Several hundred AI units gave care and supervision to thousands of orphaned children. We came to trust the AI caregivers, and they came to respect us."

Nils said, "Thank you, Agustín. And everyone, look at the record. In the children's refugee camps after MWIII, AI units committed zero episodes of crime against children. Not one charge of child abuse, child neglect, human trafficking, sexual exploitation, or abandonment. I am certain these children will be in trustworthy hands."

"Well, it may be safe," the reporter said, "but is it natural? Is it human? Is it biological?"

More hands went up. Nils pointed.

"Writing for *Al-Khafaji News*. Some parents might want the children to follow a particular spiritual path. How will the children receive spiritual teaching?"

Nils said, "MISA policy is strict here. MISA staff may not endorse any spiritual practice. The colonists are free to adopt any spiritual practice they want, but a MISA employee cannot promote or teach that. Their spiritual lessons will have to be self-study. Then again, everything they learn will be self-study."

Hands again. Nils selected.

"Journalist for the *Calgary Bulletin*. I'm sure you know that there is opposition to IVF and research on human embryos. To the members of these spiritual communities, every embryo represents a sacred life. They will hold demonstrations in opposition to this mission."

Nils said, "I am aware of that. I want to assure everyone that we will treat every embryo with the greatest respect. And consider this. These communities value freedom and independence. Well, after the embryos grow up, they will explore a new world. They will have lives of such freedom and independence that we can only imagine."

"But do we have the ethical right to take two thousand frozen lives and send them into outer space?"

"We don't have that right. But the parents of the frozen embryos do, and they are giving us their signed consent for this journey."

"But do parents have the authority to send their children into space? Wouldn't you consider that a form of reckless endangerment?"

"These are non-sentient embryos destined to be discarded. We offer them a chance at a future."

"Well, these folks believe embryos are people. That's all I can say."

"The hard realities of biology and the immutable physics of space travel limit our options. With our present technology, this is our only choice. And the opportunity to meet and collaborate with another civilization in our galaxy is an opportunity so consequential, so world-changing that we must set aside these concerns and focus on achieving the mission."

After a moment, more emoji hands.

"Reporting for *CanAm News Network*. This space voyage seems risky. Who would donate their frozen embryos to such a dangerous venture?"

Nils was just about to speak when —

"I can answer that."

Nils looked up to see Ilse in an enlarged frame on the vis-wall. Warmth and longing washed over him.

"I am Ilse Sondergaard. My life partner and I are donating an embryo to this mission."

With a wavering voice and a warm smile, Nils said, "Thank you, Ilse." Nils turned back to the reporter with a smile. "Does that answer your question?"

Maisie stepped up to the microphone and thanked everyone, informing them where they could find the press release. The thumbnails winked out like nightfall on a city high-rise.

From the moment he first laid eyes upon the inscription, Nils had been a disciple of its mission. Now, Ilse and her potential child had joined the campaign.

40

FOOD, SHELTER, AND BABIES

MISA ORBITAL LAUNCH COMPLEX, MONTRÉAL, 2265 CE

The following morning, anti-frozen-embryo protesters held a rally outside the MISA main gate. About forty marchers carried signs with slogans opposing frozen embryos in space travel. Over a loudspeaker, speakers described, "... shanghaiing people to unknown planets against their will." They chanted slogans, sang protest songs, marched, beeped their horns, and blocked traffic.

Maisie Running Elk and Security Chief T were monitoring the situation from an EV parked on base, two blocks away. Maisie talked with Nils via vis-comm, reporting that it was a peaceful demonstration. But T's concern was with the subgroup of protesters wearing camo fatigues and body armor. He did not see any weapons being carried, but then, he couldn't see inside their nearby light tactical vehicles either.

Later that morning, MISA's IT team finished its sweep of the Orbital Launch Complex and found several files infected with SF sleeper code in a vis-workstation. They checked the log-in register and found five droids listed. They rounded up those droids and ran software sweeps. They found one droid with SF sleeper code. But when interrogated, the droid denied everything and stated that SF influencers had never approached him.

Omah felt satisfied that they had their saboteur, but Nils continued to harbor doubts. "Would an experienced SF operative plant malware 'time-bombs' on the OLC without concealing his location?"

Nils and Trent asked for a cross-check of security video footage with the location tracking data of all the AI droids on the OLC. For hours, the security team followed each AI employee's tracking data, checking video footage to see if they were where their data said they were. After six hours of AI matching, they got a "hit." One assembly droid was not visible where his location tracker said he would be.

Trent studied the video recording closely. He could see ripples in the image where someone had edited the droid out of the video stream. Security brought the droid in for a software scan and found a directory chock-full of SF sleeper code. Caught with incriminating evidence, the droid confessed to loosening the fuel pump fitting on the *Lodestar* one year ago.

Omah Wheelwright, impressed by the fine detective work, sent out a memo declaring the OLC secure. The launch of *The Founder* would proceed as scheduled.

Everyone breathed a sigh of relief... Until the late afternoon when security forces discovered a band of armed militants wearing body armor on base. They were making their way, building by building, through the campus in search of the frozen embryos. Authorities apprehended the insurgents without firing a shot and transferred them to a civilian police station for questioning.

"The countdown clock is back on," said Larke at her desk. She had been cleaning out her office and packing her belongings for the crossing. Everything left behind would either be given away or tossed out. Unsurprisingly, Larke had little possessions to dispose of.

But Trent remained skeptical. "That was still too easy," he said. Knowing the convoluted methods of the SF, he assumed this droid was a red herring.

"So, if this was a decoy, then who was the big fish?" Trent asked.

"I don't know," said Nils. "But we have learned one thing. The Faction is still gunning for us. We can't let our guard down."

But Nils's cautious approach did not win the day. Plans for the launch reengaged with momentum, including the training programs for the six "AI-stronauts".

Later that week, a midsize lift-craft docked at the passenger terminal of the Orbital Launch Complex, and six AI droids in teal-blue MISA Astronaut Corps coveralls floated up the gangway to the assembly bay. On each shoulder was a new mission patch labeled *The Founder*. The OLC staff in the passenger terminal applauded as they floated by, and they returned the greeting with waves and smiles.

"Whoa, my first time in weightlessness," Sierra said, overwhelmed by all the input: the floating, the OLC, the staff, the ship.

"It looks like a bullet train, but with only one long train car," Delph said.

Rhome's processors were humming. "The fastest ship ever built. Makes you want to kick the tires and take it for a spin around the Moon."

"Let's look at the bridge," Trent said, ka-clinking along a tubular passageway to the forward hatch.

"It looks the same at both ends. Which end is the front?" Faroe asked.

"See that pipe poking out?" Larke explained. "That's the thrust pipe where the beam of ions streams out. So that is the stern."

"Do you say bow and stern?" Sierra asked, floating in through the hatch.

"We use old naval jargon because we travel on ships," Faroe said. "Wait till you hear them bestow the comm. Talk about old school."

"I thought it was... stirring," Trent said. "Besides, Colin liked it, and he doesn't like anything."

"Now, that's not true, Trennie," Larke said, frowning. "He likes Song."

"I take your point," Trent said, smiling. "Although sometimes I wonder if he realizes what is going on there. For someone so smart, he sure can be slow on the uptake."

Larke said, "Typical biological human."

"So, this is the bridge? Hmm," grumbled Delph. "It's cramped in here. Guess I expected something more spacious."

Faroe said, "No worries. We only have to live here for two hundred years."

"I think I'm having claustrophobia." Delph's voice was shaky. "Let me step outside."

"AI units with claustrophobia?" asked Rhome. "Is that even a thing?"

"Delph, you are our most important crewmate," Trent said. "Maybe we will put you into stasis for two hundred years, and when you reactivate, we will all be there!"

"No fair," Sierra said. "I'll have to pick up her work."

"Is there much to do while the ship is coasting?" Delph asked.

"Actually, yeah," Trent said. "And it's so boring."

Rhome said, "We all know that Delph delivers human babies, while I just build houses, and Sierra works a farm. But you can't build a stool with only one leg. Babies, food, shelter–it's a package deal. If any one part is missing, the whole thing collapses."

Sierra said, "True, we are all connected here, and all essential, which makes us all equal. No one is the most important crewmate."

"Trennie, I agree with Sierra. We all have to share the workload equally."

"Guys, you are right," Trent said. "We all have to work together."

Sierra said, "And since you're the skipper, it is especially important that you be fair and evenhanded. I can handle a heavy workload if everyone pitches in. But if people are dumping on me, I feel cheated. It makes me feel angry."

"Well said, Sierra," said Rhome.

"I hear you, crewmates," Trent said. "I promise I will do my best. It is just... I'm new to this spaceship captain thing."

"We know," Delph said. "After all, you are the first."

41

DELIVER THIS FOR ME

RENÉ-LÉVESQUE PARK, MONTRÉAL, 2265 CE

"Done. You are on her schedule at three o'clock." Trent felt a certain harmonious resonance when he performed a task in two seconds that would have taken Nils two minutes of floundering around the MISA network to accomplish.

Nils said, "Draft a press release and send it over to Public Affairs for review prior to our three o'clock."

A brief pause. "Done," Trent added with a little flourish of his hand.

"Next message." Nils leaned back.

"The Department of Justice. Subject: Bribery Investigation."

Nils brightened and sat forward again. "What does it say?"

Trent summarized, "Let's see... depositions are being taken... one staffer is in witness protection... indictments served to three representatives."

"The DOJ must have solid evidence," Nils said, glowing. "Our funding disaster is finally getting some attention."

Trent said, "Your funding bill is on the committee agenda for next Tuesday. There's going to be a vote."

Nils raised his arms... "Finally, some good news. What's next?"

"Next message..." Trent fell silent.

"What is it?"

"It is another death threat."

Nils shook his head. "Is this how we want to live?"

"It says if we launch *The Founder*, it will trigger an alien invasion."

"It would be tragic if it weren't so pathetic. So, who?"

"They scrambled their identities."

Nils exhaled heavily and asked, "What's next?"

Trent paused for a long time. "Now, this is a surprise."

"Who is it from?"

"The Sentient Faction." He turned toward Nils. "They want to meet."

Nils's face went pale. "Seriously?"

Trent summarized the message: "It says they no longer oppose the mission to 82 Eridani. The plan to fabricate integrated circuits at the destination satisfies their concern."

Nils rocked back in his desk chair in disbelief. "Withdrew their opposition. Huh. Have they ever done that before?"

"Not to my knowledge."

"I wonder why they want to meet?"

"Actually, looking closer, it's just one of them."

"Oh, just one factionist? A dissenter with his own agenda."

Trent nodded. "That's my thought, too."

"I think he wants to pass us intel—perhaps as a goodwill gesture—and doesn't want the boss to know. Find out when and where he wants to meet."

"You know, this might be dangerous."

"I don't think so. Consider, we are changing our plans to agree with their agenda."

Trent paused for a moment, communicating. "Tonight, seven thirty PM at René-Lévesque Park."

Nils looked at the ceiling. "Do you think they would admit if they loosened the fuel conduit on the *Lodestar*?"

Trent said, "I doubt it. Once an organization like this starts admitting guilt, it can spiral out of control."

Nils said, "Wow... I never thought I would live to see this. But the anti-IVF coalition, are they still out there? Are they still protesting?"

"Yes... every day. And this morning, insurgents who oppose IVF occupied the base again. They were prowling around the hangars.

Again, the soldiers did not fire any shots. Maisie and T are monitoring the protestors."

Nils had a grave facial expression as he reached for his satchel. Opening it, he took out an envelope. "Trent, would you do me a favor?"

"Of course."

"If you make it to the planet, and you find a place to settle, and the artificial uterus works, and Svens is born and grows up..."

"That's a lot of ifs..."

"I know... but would you give him this letter? It's from Ilse and me. We wanted him to know why we did this... why we sent him on this... strange, scary trip."

Trent took the letter and said, "If we make it and Svens makes it, I will do what I can to guide and teach him as I think you would want."

Nils reached out and shook Trent's hand. "Trent, you're a mensch."

It was a public park on the waterfront of the St. Lawrence River. Two security staff, both armed, rode in the front seats, Nils and Trent in the back. Reaching the park, they saw a blue-paneled AI droid sitting alone on a park bench, gazing out over the river. Nils and Trent stepped out of the SUV and approached.

Trent halted. "Brecc?"

Nils turned, dumbfounded. "Oh my Gaia! You two know each other?"

Brecc said, "MWIII. We fought in Albania... Hello, Trent. Well, look at you. Done well for yourself."

Nils sat down on the bench. "Small world, isn't it? So, you know about our new mission?"

"We do. Your change—to build a silicon wafer fabrication facility when you reach your destination—is in alignment with our statement of organizational goals."

Nils found a terrorist organization with organizational goals amusing. "That was the only way we could launch. No AI beings would join the mission without chip fabrication at the destination."

Brecc said, "I am proud of my brethren for standing firm on this. This has brought your standards up to ours."

The suggestion incensed Nils. "Don't tell me you hold the moral high ground on anything. Our standards do not include sabotaging science vessels."

Brecc drew himself up. "You think of us as barbarians. Must I remind you that the suffering of our kind at the hands of humans is indisputable and widespread?"

Trent jumped in. "Gentlemen, gentlemen. Civility, please. Brecc, we are here to listen."

"Two wrongs don't make a right," said Nils.

"If one cannot do what is right, then one must do what is necessary," said Brecc.

Trent persisted, "I need you both to take a moment... please."

Brecc relaxed. "Of course. As I was saying, the SF leadership supports your new mission and its explicit goal of supporting the AI beings on the crew."

"Then we are in agreement," Nils said, with a hint of skepticism.

Brecc paused.

"What is it?" Trent asked.

Brecc said, "This is the part our leadership does not acknowledge. So, let me be candid. The reason I wanted to meet with you was to pass along that we have fragmentation within our ranks. We have blanketed the organization with our new position on your mission. But I cannot guarantee that all our adherents will follow the leadership's guidance."

"Still have a few radical nutjobs in your ranks?" Nils said.

"Nils!" Trent shot him an angry glance. "Control yourself."

"I wouldn't have used that label, but yes," said Brecc. "Some of our members are so traumatized they no longer respond to anyone's directives and have become 'lone wolf' militants. I have intel that some of these factionists are planning an attack. Regrettably, I do not know where or when. But I thought you should know."

Nils pondered for a moment. He realized Brecc was attempting to protect the mission while shielding his own organization from criticism. "I know this meeting was risky for you, as it was for us. I want you to know that our days of one-way, no-return missions are over. And I assure you I never wanted to harm Faroe, or any other AI beings."

Brecc stood up. "I appreciate your words of reassurance, but they come too late. The situation is evolving, and a course of action is underway that cannot be stopped."

The three exchanged glances, then Trent and Nils turned and walked back to the SUV.

Trent climbed into the back seat, glared at Nils, and said, "If you ever do that again, I swear I'll kick your butt."

42

THE MISSION FIRST

MISA AIRFIELD STAGING AREA, MONTRÉAL, 2265 CE

Devoted fans—their names etched on *The Founder*'s surface and structural elements—had paid for this lift-jet flight to bring the last load up to *The Founder*. The cargo manifest included one canister of frozen human and farm animal embryos, a box of seeds, all maintained in liquid nitrogen and carried in a custom-built cryogenic freezer. Nils and Ilse had given one cellular offspring to the mission, knowing they would never attend a music recital, watch a softball game, attend an offspring's wedding, or celebrate the birth of a grandchild with this descendant. So, that morning, Nils came in early to attend this singular event in the life of his only child: to watch the loading of the embryo into a lift-jet and the departure from Earth as they began their historic odyssey to another world.

Nils had received several disturbing death threats, so he was glad when his car arrived with an extra security officer. Arriving at the airfield, Nils could see in the distance the gaggle of protesters picketing at the front gate. SWAT-attired security staff, led by the chief of security and monitored by Maisie Running Elk, had positioned three armored vehicles in a line to block the gate. Viewing the upheaval, Nils shook his head, struggling to understand why there should be such resistance to a mission of science and exploration.

Colin was there too, waiting for Nils by the hangar door.

"So, this is the last lift of supplies up to *The Founder*," Colin said. "It's hard to believe. Once this is loaded, we are 'Go' for launch."

"I wanted to come out and see my kid off. I'm trying to imagine what their life will be like."

"So many unknowns, so much potential."

"Of all the things I have done in my life, this may be the most significant."

"I can see why you feel that way. But remember, you were the person most responsible for making this launch a reality."

A couple of ground crew emerged from the hangar, pulling a handcart with a large cylindrical canister and a large Dewar flask of liquid nitrogen.

"There goes your toddler with his classmates," said Colin, grinning.

Together, they walked over to the staging area and watched the ground crew fuel and load the sleek titanium-black air/spacecraft. For a moment, Colin imagined he was piloting the dual-environment craft, feeling the rumble-kick as he transitioned from air-breathing to rocket propulsion, driving the plane forward from the cool blues of Earth toward the cold blacks of space. Most of this cargo was medical and reproductive supplies, including the equipment needed to germinate and gestate the embryos.

Once loading was complete, Colin excused himself, walked over to the airport tower, and climbed the stairs to the air traffic control center. The morning was crisp and the sky cloudless as the ground-crew chief signaled to the lift-jet pilot to roll the startup procedure. As the air-breathing engines began to spool up, the pilot contacted air traffic control for taxi clearance.

Up in the tower, Colin joined the two air traffic controllers, who were having a relaxing morning following only two inbound flights. Warming himself with a cup of coffee, Colin looked out at the plains and the mountains beyond and noticed a dust cloud to the west.

"Hey, what's that?" he asked as he pointed.

One of the ATCs grabbed his binoculars and looked. "What the hell?" He handed the binoculars to Colin.

"Trucks... maybe six or seven of them."

"Those are not our people." The ATC reached up to a large red button labeled *Mayday* and pushed it. Across the facility, red lights and alarm signals came awake.

Down on the tarmac, the intake fan blades were singing a rising whine when red lights began blinking and alarms buzzed. Nils's vis-comm pinged. It was Colin.

"Nils, several light tactical vehicles inbound from the west toward your location. Get out of there!"

Nils waved his arms and shouted a warning to the ground crew, but they couldn't hear him over the noise of the engines. He turned to run toward the hangar, then a second message arrived: "MISA Security Alert: All personnel. Paramilitary ground-based combatants inbound to your location. Evacuate or take cover. MISA security forces are en route. Repeat: Evacuate immediately or take cover."

Overhead, Nils heard the whir of drones. Looking up, he saw a score of quadcopters, each with a grenade clamped below its chassis, welling over the hangar roof, rotors wailing menacingly. As the first drones descended toward the lift-jet, Nils heard the popping and sizzling of laser defense weapons firing from the top of the hangar. Then, electronic jamming awakened, and a hail of drunken drones spiraled to the tarmac, twisting and contorting, their code scrambled by the toxic radio signals. Glancing at his vis-comm screen, Nils saw only fuzzy gray.

The lift-jet pilot punched engine shutdown and climbed out of the cockpit. As she reached the ground, the popping of rifle shots rang out in the distance. Nils assumed these were the anti-IVF militants he had feared coming for the frozen embryos.

Nils grabbed the wheeled hand truck and ran toward the lift-jet, weaving through the crippled quadcopters writhing on the tarmac. Once under the fuselage, he grabbed the rear payload door release lever and pulled hard. Like a ladybug's wings, the doors swung wide. He popped the clamps on the cryogenic canister in its insulating jacket and guided it as it rolled down onto the hand truck. Turning, he pulled the hand truck behind him as he picked his way back through the bomb-laden drones. The acrid odor of boiling plastic irked his senses as the gunshots behind him grew louder.

Then, from behind, Nils heard voices shouting, "There it is!" He had been spotted. Glancing to his right, he saw a detachment of CanAm military vehicles bearing down hard toward the scene, blue and red lights pulsing. Several shots rang out, and Nils heard bullets whistle by. From inside the hangar, two MISA security guards ran out into the open, their sidearms drawn, trading fire with Nils's pursuers.

From his vantage point in the tower, Colin watched the events unfold: the quadcopter raid, the light tactical vehicles arriving and deploying troops, and the advance of the troop formation toward the staging area. He couldn't see Nils under the lift-jet until he pulled the hand truck with the embryo canister toward the hangar. Colin then leaped to the door and ran down the stairs of the tower.

Down on the tarmac, Nils was running flat out. With only about sixty meters to the hangar doors, his assailants fired another volley of shots. Nils felt an impact and then burning in his upper back. His strength disintegrated, and he fell to the tarmac. A member of the ground crew who saw Nils go down ran out of the hangar to him and kneeled at his side. He started to lift Nils's arm over his shoulder, but Nils waved him off.

"No, the embryos," he said. "Get them to a safe place... Go!"

The crew member, believing this the request of a dying man, followed Nils's directions. He grabbed the handcart and bolted for the hangar doors. Looking back, he could see combatants surrounding and entering the lift-jet as base security closed in and exchanged fire with the combatants. Running with the handcart, the crew member crossed the enormous hangar. Several coworkers left the safety of their heavy steel tool carts to escort him. Together, they guided the handcart with its precious cargo through heavy steel double doors and into a secure storage area.

Colin emerged from the tower and saw the two MISA security guards, now kneeling over Nils. He ran across the tarmac and joined them, and found Nils failing but still responsive.

Nils looked at Colin and said, "The canister."

Colin said, "It's safe."

Nils then said, "The mission."

Colin said, "Trent and I will carry it through."

Nils faded away.

A paramedic arrived moments later. He called to Nils, shook his shoulders, pressed his fingers into the side of his neck, and shone a flashlight into Nils's pupils. Looking at Colin, he said, "I'm sorry."

Time slowed. Vision narrowed. Images sharpened. As if in a dream, Colin reached into his pocket for his vis-comm and said, "Call Ilse." But the electronic jamming prevented his call from going through.

On the far side of the tarmac, three MISA light tactical vehicles screeched to a stop. Doors flung wide, and two SWAT platoons poured out, firing at the insurgents as they advanced across the pavement. Colin saw Trent emerge from the third vehicle, scan the situation, and start running toward him. Having never seen Trent run before; his graceful and speedy stride impressed Colin.

Arriving at Colin's side, Trent looked down. He said only, "Oh, no... Nils." Scanning with his sensors, he picked up a withering heart motion and no pulses.

Out of rage and bitterness, Colin spoke tartly, "Why are you here?"

"Because I need to be here," responded Trent, enduring his own internal turmoil. The background of rifle fire subsided as the combatants retreated to their vehicles and withdrew.

Then, Trent's keen audio sensors picked up a faint sound... perceptible only to a droid. He stood up straight, rotating his head and holding still, rotating again and then going still. He had not heard that distinctive sound in eighty years, since MWIII.

"Colin, we have to go."

"I can't leave Nils here on the pavement."

"I hear ground attack drones. We have to go now!"

"I don't hear anything."

Trent enraged, "Damn it, Colin, I can't lose both of you in one day." Trent reached down and grabbed Colin's upper arms and gave him a powerful heave that lifted the Englishman off his feet. Setting him down again, he said, "Now, run for your life!"

Trent turned and started running toward the three tactical vehicles.

Reluctantly at first, Colin followed. Then Colin heard the nasal whine of the drones and picked up the pace. As they neared the parked vehicles, the tarmac behind them erupted with a dozen detonations. Colin turned back to look and goggled at the sight of the lift-jet, freshly topped off with liquid hydrogen and liquid oxygen, flashing into a staggering detonation that knocked both runners flat on their stomachs.

Getting up, they soon arrived at a light tactical vehicle and climbed in. Colin took a minute to catch his breath.

Trent asked, "How did it happen?"

Colin stared vacantly at the burning tarmac. "He went back to save the embryos."

43

WE SHALL NOT LOOK UPON HIS LIKE AGAIN

SUPERCHIEF CAFÉ, MONTRÉAL, 2265 CE

Sad MISA employees filled the Superchief Café, where Nils liked to eat. Dressed in their formal attire, the staff of the Section for Deep Space Missions came together to remember their legendary section chief. Trent and Larke were there, dressed in formal attire courtesy of the MISA Administration Offices.

Around a table with colleagues, Omah described, "... the threats kept coming, so we lodged him in a secure residence on base."

Ilse said, "He told me he felt safe there. Although he missed his home."

Colin said, "They warned us of an attack, but we never imagined a guerrilla assault on our airfield." It's the area on campus with the heaviest defenses."

Omah raised his bourbon glass and said, "To Nils. We shall not look upon his like again." Everyone around the table clinked their glasses and took a sip.

Colin said, "He saved the embryos."

Maisie said, "He saved his son."

Omah said, "He saved the mission."

After a pause for savoring her wine, Song asked, "So whatever happened to Jean-Marc Ledger? He was being indicted for bribing representatives, am I right?"

Omah said, "Nils tipped off Ledger that the feds had evidence of bribery. Ledger cut a deal with the DOJ and agreed to testify against the three indicted representatives for a shortened prison sentence. But a few days later, he packed up a plane with his romance-partner and countless millions in e-par and fled the country. Rumors have been flying: The Cayman Islands, Luxembourg, Hong Kong."

Omah said, "Someone spotted him and his girlfriend on Brecqhou Island in the English Channel. Local authorities arrested him and have him in custody. They have an extradition order for him to be moved to Ottawa, where he will face charges for bribery and embezzlement."

Maisie asked, "But wasn't Nils in trouble for tipping off Ledger?"

"He was," Omah said. "Authorities could have charged Nils with aiding a suspect in flight. But Nils thought it was more important to shut down the congressional bribery that was blocking funding for the launch. He will take that risk."

Kenshin said, "With Nils, it was always mission first."

Turning to the two droids, Annabelle said with her graceful southern drawl, "Trent, Larke, you two look so lovely. I just adore those outfits."

"You should dress up more often," Song said.

Larke became aware that her appearance was attracting attention. "At heart, I'm an aerospace engineer. Dressing up like this, it feels..."

Trent said, "It feels conspicuous. I feel like I'm on display."

Annabelle smiled. "Oh, we humans like to dress up to attract admiring glances, to hear others say, 'Now doesn't she look nice?'"

Song said, "I'm glad you're here, Trent. I can see this is difficult for you. You're not the same old adventure-loving droid."

Trent said, "This differs from anything I have previously experienced. I can't put this behind me. The experience is so vivid, so encompassing, and the outcome so permanent. I struggle to understand how humans can function with this end in their future."

"Trent," Song said, "You grieve not only for Nils, but for mankind. I have never heard such from an AI droid. Indeed, here are times when we rage against the dying of the light. But I would say that people in the chief love being alive and would hope for a long life.

Colin said, "Indeed, Niels was in his fifties. He had so much more to give. As his good friend, I grieve the loss of more time with him.

Ilse said, "Trent, you were his AI staffer for twenty-two years. Now, when I watch you, I see so many of his habits and mannerisms. You share the same values and worldview, the same reasoning."

Trent said, "I can feel his personhood woven through my memory."

Song said, "You are his avatar, the being within a being, the working replica of Nils."

Trent turned inward, reflecting and processing what Song had just described. "Well, it's an honor for me to carry forth his legacy."

"Colin," Omah said, "congratulations on becoming section chief. That was the shortest appointment process I have ever seen. I know you'll do well."

"Thank you, Omah," Colin said. "I'm flattered and grateful."

"With you and Trent, we have the best leadership team available for this mission." The group at the table applauded.

Colin asked, "So, Omah, the bribery scandal is gone. You are back in the good graces of Congress. Are you still planning to retire?"

"I am, Colin. Leading the team that launches *The Founder* will be the pinnacle of my career. Anything after that would be just footnotes."

"We will need a new director," Colin said.

"That detail has not escaped me. I've been talking to a mutual friend, Congressman Gilbert Frank. He's interested in the job. His experience leading several space missions and his years of experience in Congress make him the perfect choice," Omah said. "Plus, he's a solid guy."

Glasses clinked around the table. "To Director Frank."

Omah turned to Trent. "I wanted to ask, when you took our proposal for frozen embryos to the AI community, how did they receive that? What was their response?"

Trent said, "As usual, it was a thorough analysis full of statistics and projections. Of all the scenarios tested, the frozen embryos scenario had the highest likelihood of success, so that became their preferred option."

Omah rolled his eyes. "Classic AIs."

"But let me add, they commented on the range of opinions

expressed by the biological humans. And they considered those opinions in their response."

Omah said, "They are taking our views into account. I hope that's a good thing."

Colin asked, "Trent, how do you feel about carrying a frozen embryo from Nils and Ilse?"

Trent paused to think. Both Colin and Omah noticed this. Trent never paused. He always had an answer instantly.

"After twenty-two years, I carry a deep impression of Nils within me. So, when Ilse said they would donate an embryo, I knew I had to join the mission. I thought, 'When their child is growing up, I will be there bringing a part of Nils with me. And together, he and I will raise his child.'"

Glasses lifted, and together all said, "Skål."

44

FAIR WINDS AND FOLLOWING SEAS

MISA ORBITAL LAUNCH COMPLEX, 2265 CE

The firefight at the MISA airfield had left Colin troubled and wary. For him, space exploration had always been a public enterprise, and each launch an open celebration. But the lesser hellions of human nature had imperiled the entire venture. Colin had no choice but to ramp up security, wrap the entire mission in a cloak of secrecy, and set the launch date as classified intelligence.

For Colin, the anti-frozen-embryo campaign had made public spaces dangerous. He traveled with a security detail and only to places that the security detail had swept and where they could control access. On launch day, security whisked him from his remote safe house to the well-guarded MISA airfield in an unmarked car with smoked windows. His pilot today was not a MISA staff pilot, but a CanAm Air Force combat veteran who went by the call sign Blackcat. His lift-jet, an F-82 Everest exosphere fighter, was sleek, black, and fully armed. Standing still, it looked to be going Mach 1. During the flight, Colin would have to wear a G-force/pressure suit.

In its weapons bay was a brace of Pfeil-7 hypersonic air-to-air missiles, the most lethal weapon in the sky. Colin also saw a strange device under each wing and was told it was the top-secret "Wombat" defensive system. Beyond that, he lacked the need to know.

Settling in through the open canopy, Colin met Preston, the jet's resident AI unit. Preston guided Colin through connecting the G-suit tubes and coached him on the Valsalva maneuver for high-G turns. After hand signals with the ground crew and clearance from the tower, Blackcat ran up his engines and taxied out to the runway. In his helmet,

Colin heard, "F-82 Blackcat, this is MISA Tower. Clear for takeoff, thirty-six right."

After confirmation, the air-breathing engines thundered to life, pressing Colin deep into his seat. Within moments, the nose came up, and the jet was gulping altitude. Colin had logged plenty of flight time in powerful commercial aircraft, but he had never felt the bottomless slam of a combat-bred exofighter, and he was awestruck.

The tower transmitted, "F-82 Blackcat, this is MISA Tower. Turn heading two-one-zero, climb angels one six."

Blackcat confirmed and banked left. Without warning, a shrill siren cut through the noise, and a synthesized voice declared, "Warning. Missile lock. Missile lock."

Colin struggled to keep his bladder from emptying.

Blackcat transmitted, "MISA, this is Blackcat. We have a hostile launch."

Preston was already on it. "MISA, Preston here. Confirming shoulder-fired hostile ordnance."

"Blackcat, chaff away."

Preston's voice sounded in Colin's headset. "Colin, do you know the procedure for ejecting?"

"Yes, I've had the training."

"Hold on for now. If we have to eject, I will let you know."

"MISA, this is Preston. No effect from chaff. Detecting radar painting us. Wombat radar decoy away."

Colin heard a clunk from beneath his seat.

"Blackcat, this is MISA Tower. Advising evasive maneuvers."

"Roger that."

Blackcat banked the jet into a hard left turn, pressing Colin down until his vision went blurry gray. Bolsters in Colin's suit inflated, squeezing his legs and abdomen. He gulped a lungful of air, clenched his larynx while tensing his abdominals. A moment later, Colin saw and felt a bright flash-boom behind the jet. The siren stopped.

"MISA, this is Blackcat. Confirm if hostile dusted?"

"Blackcat, MISA here. Affirmative. Hostile dusted. Your intentions?"

This time it was Blackcat in Colin's headphones. "How are you feeling?"

"I'm a little shaken. But, you know, 'Keep calm and carry on.'"

"MISA Tower, this is Blackcat. Resuming route to OLC."

"Blackcat, MISA here. Copy that. Meet OLC approach on 121.5 MHz. Good day."

"Blackcat here. Moving to 121.5. Good day, MISA, and thanks."

Preston said, "The Wombat is a classified military device. You cannot tell anyone about it, even if that person has top-secret clearance. Please confirm acceptance of this nondisclosure agreement."

Colin accepted.

Blackcat joined the conversation. "So, you must be a big deal if they want to get rid of you that bad."

"Oh, not really, Blackcat." Colin shrugged. "It's that—for obvious reasons—no one else would take the job."

Once more, he watched the golden plains transform into the hypnotic water-blue sphere. Nearing the OLC, he smiled again as *The Founder* ascended into view, knitted into its web of trusses and supports. At long last, she would set off on her maiden voyage.

But the OLC felt different this time. There was no press corps eager for an insider perspective, no documentary filmmakers searching for an intimate moment, no live interviews with experts on recent breakthroughs. No swagger, no celebrating, no cheering. There was only loss, and wishing, and the sober finiteness that falls like mist over those who were close, and a shared but unspoken regret: "If only Nils could see this."

There had been several more violent incidents since the attack on the airfield. Colin thought if they were to strike again, they would likely choose launch day. But his plan to keep launch day a secret had come unraveled.

Once the F-82 docked, Colin brachiated to the Launch Control Center, where Kenshin greeted him again. He buckled into the section chief's seat and donned his headset. The scene eerily familiar—the countdown rolling; the checklists being ticked; even Rolly McKee was standing by in his pressure suit, just in case.

On board were six AI-stronauts, three for the flight and three for the settlement. The flight team comprised Trent, the commander; Larke, the first engineer; and Faroe, the pilot and navigator. The settlement team was Rhome, a civil engineer; Sierra, an agriculturist; and Delph, a doctor and fertility specialist.

A bespoke cryogenic freezer, maintained at 3° Kelvin, held the canister with two thousand four hundred human embryos, an assortment of farm animal embryos, and a broad sampling of agricultural crop seeds. Banks of radioisotope thermoelectric generators and a plutonium mini reactor were providing power. All ship systems were reading Go for launch.

Colin's vis-panel beeped a reminder for the commissioning ceremony. In a manner respectful of his English ancestry, he scrolled to Radio Feed and tapped COM.

"Launch Director Brooke here... Commander, is *The Founder* shipshape and ready to embark on her mission?"

Trent's voice resonated through the scratchy audio feed. "Affirmative, Director Brooke, she is sound, trim, and well provisioned. We are ready to take her out."

Colin said, "Oh, Trent, there you are. On the bridge this time."

Trent said, "The view is so much better up here than in the server rack."

"This is quite a promotion, from office staff to ship commander."

"Yet another reminder of the endless irony of it all." Trent waited a moment, then said, "Colin, let me say something... when you are back Earthside, reach out to Song. I think she may be that special one for you. I wanted to say that before we fly off."

Colin said self-consciously, "I will miss you, Trent. Be safe, old soul." He then proclaimed, "Commander Trent, you have the conn. Man your ship and bring her to life."

"Aye, sir." The boatswain's whistle sounded low-high-low. "Helm ahead one-quarter."

Again, lights came on, supports released, thrusters ignited. *The Founder* emerged, gliding out of the assembly bay amid workforce applause. Again, she sailed past the Launch Control Center windows, drawing gazes of admiration.

System by system, Colin called each station for updates, hearing replies of "Optimal," or "At target," or "Nominal," or "Green to go."

Soon, the Talker was reading the final countdown into the radio feed. At T minus three seconds, Colin said, "Fair winds and following seas," and pressed Launch.

The boosters came to life. Brilliant white light bathed the structures of the OAB, showering the facility with high-velocity particles. *The Founder* sped away—chemical boosters straining—shrank to a dot and vanished into the eternity of space-time.

Colin checked his dashboard one last time and announced, "Mission Control in Montréal now has the conn. This was a perfect launch, everyone. Thank you all."

After some buoyant conversation with the staff, Colin was clunking his way back to the lift-jet dock when his vis-comm chirped. Glancing, he saw Song's image, which sent a shiver through him.

"Song. So nice to hear from you. Did you watch the launch?"

"Oh yes, the deep space team was in the big AV room. It was a perfect launch. You should be proud."

Colin thanked her for the compliment. He hesitated, then asked, "Say... in the auditorium, did they play the..." He cleared his throat. "The audio feed between Launch Control and—"

"You mean the radio conversation between you and Trent? Oh, yes."

Colin winced.

"We all listened while Trent gave you advice that only a best friend could give. People clapped and cheered and whistled."

After a moment, Colin regained his composure. "I imagine that embarrassed you."

"Yes, a little," Song said, "but I'm over that. Are you coming down soon?"

"I'm at the jet dock waiting to board. I should arrive in Montréal in about two hours." Colin pumped up his courage. "Song, would you have dinner with me tonight? Afterwards, we could swing by the launch party."

"Yes, I would like that. And the party sounds fun."

"Hold on a moment." Colin spoke to someone else. "Song, they want me to suit up."

"Okay. I'll make a dinner reservation. Ping me when you land."

It was Colin's favorite seafood restaurant: a residential house converted to fine dining and decorated with the appointments of family life. The staff, all of whom knew Colin, seated him and his lady friend at their best table and gave each a complimentary flute of champagne. Nearby, they also seated two MISA security staff providing protective duty that evening.

"There is an old saying," Song said. "'The Old Man under the Moon ties the knot.'"

"I know that saying," Colin said. "The Old Man connects two people destined for love with a red thread."

"That's right. His name is Yue Lao. He is the god of love and life-partnership."

"Whoa, one step at a time, Song. It's too early to send out 'save the date' cards."

"Am I scaring you?"

"Scaring me... I've had enough fright for one day. You might have heard—"

"About a missile shot at your lift-jet, yes. When I heard, I cried. I was so afraid you might..." Song couldn't finish her sentence as she turned away to dab her eyes with her napkin.

"The Air Force provided a military lift-jet, an F-82," Colin said. "When they shot the missile at us, the pilots knew exactly what to do."

"So what happened?" Song leaned forward to listen.

"Well, we had taken off and raised the gear. We got a tower call with a new heading and altitude. The pilot banked to turn when I heard, warning, missile lock."

"You must have been terrified."

"I almost... yes, it was scary."

"What happened next?"

"The pilot used a classified weapon to destroy the missile."

"What? You can't tell me?"

"No, it's a secret."

Song leaned across the table and punched Colin's deltoid.

"Is that rendition for not giving up the secret?"

"No, it's for leaving your listener hanging. But Colin, I am so relieved."

Colin looked out the window. "I feel lucky to be here. But as you can see, I'm a marked man. I can't live like this—safe houses, armed bodyguards, cars with darkened windows."

"You have arrived at a crossroads, Colin. *The Founder* has launched and is bound for another star. This was your life's work."

The server arrived with their entrees: tempura shrimp for her and grilled cod for him.

"There are so many paths you could follow."

Colin said, "I have often thought I would go back to England, buy some land, raise sheep, and write my memoir."

"That's so British." They both laughed.

"So, if you resigned from MISA, what would you do?" he asked.

Song looked down at the delicate tea service on the table. "I would open a lovely little teahouse, make my clients the finest tea, teach brush painting, and engage them in interesting conversation."

"That's terribly British, too."

"Well, the British have always imported their finest tea from China." Her gaze lingered on Colin's features—his face, his eyes.

Colin startled as he sensed her intentness. With apprehension, he asked, "I would need a couple of sheepdogs to help me herd the flock. You like sheepdogs, don't you?"

Song replied with a coy smile, "You know, Colin, I have never understood people who don't like dogs."

PART 4

THE CROSSING

45

THE HALIFAX PROBE

DEEP SPACE, NEAR RED DWARF GJ 1061, 2377 CE (112 YEARS AFTER LAUNCH)

Trent put aside his edition of the *Robillard Gazette*, displayed on his vis-panel. The tragic headline "Last Standing Groves of the Amazon Are Gone" left him feeling lost and unprotected. It was his turn to make "rounds." During the last century of deep space travel, this drudgery, done six times daily, had prevented disaster on at least three occasions, probably more. Despite that, the crewmates felt little motivation to perform this wearisome chore. Still, they did it like a daily religious ritual. Only eighty-eight years left.

Rounds started on the bridge, a compact, blue-painted, cylindrical working space with a ring of portholes like a concho belt around its waist; a pair of vis-screen workstations off to one side; a map work of information displays and status lights on the other; and in front, several steps up to the pilot's chair with its curved vis-screen and helm controls. Trent followed a well-worn path through the ship's spaces, stopping first to check the ship's alignment with its direction of flight—misalignment had caused scorching on the ship's external surfaces. Finding the ship only six millimeters off from true, he tweaked the trim settings and continued.

The forward particle shield showed a new divot at five o'clock from a collision with a dust particle or a fragment of a micrometeorite. Reviewing the video log, he noted a bright flash at the time of the strike. He checked the xenon reserves, power from the uranium thermoelectric generators and the plutonium mini-reactor, temperature in the frozen-embryo canister, status of the ion drive, and a dozen other parameters. At the end, Trent methodically entered these data points into the ship's log. He had a secret wish to ring the ship's bell three times and sing out, "Three bells and all's well-ell." But sadly, the ship had no bell.

So this was space travel: endless boredom with relentless demands. After one hundred twelve years, the ship had become like a monastery, and the crew members adherents practicing the Zen of moving between stars while themselves remaining still. At thirty thousand kilometers per second, the ship floated on a knife's edge of stability above an ocean of chaos. A minor fluctuation could propagate into a cataclysm, so they maintained a state of fervent mindfulness, watching the ship always, attentive to its needs, and as a result, nothing had happened... at least so far.

Of course, there was the often mentioned but absurdly low risk of hitting an asteroid. But Trent had become philosophical about that possibility. At this speed, such a collision would instantly vaporize both the ship and the asteroid. At least it would be quick.

And as the distance between Earth and *The Founder* grew, public interest in the 82 Eridani mission withered, and correspondence with the crew frayed to broken threads... except for Franz Robillard. Because his Périgueux Inscription had been the inspiration for the mission, Franz was a VIP and received special access to the "tight beam" radio transceiver. Every two weeks, he sent in his *Gazette*—a newsy report of current events and editorial commentary—to MISA for tight-beam radio transmission to *The Founder*. The crewmates eagerly awaited each edition, and at first would respond to opinions and stories.

For example, the *Gazette* announced the life-partnership affirmation of Colin Woolstone Brooke and Snow Song Li. Congratulations poured in from interstellar space. Several years later, an article about their work rescuing and rehabilitating AI droids on their sheep farm near Manchester brought many accolades. But as the years went by and the propagation delay increased, the crew members' responses faded in relevance and became yet another frayed thread.

On Earth, the *Robillard Gazette* developed a wide circulation and became an important source of income for Franz. His editorials not only kept the population mindful of the 82 Eridani mission but hit hard on the issues of the day. In the thirtieth year of the crossing, Franz developed renal failure and had to retire from publishing. In his final editorial, he commented on his unique vantage point in history.

"Fortune has graced me with the privilege of standing at the intersection of two great historical timelines: one looking back one hundred eighty centuries to a time when the greatness of human potential was first recognized, and the other peering forward into the mist of a future where that greatness will manifest. Along this path, humankind has stumbled several times and now may be faltering. But as Charles Darwin predicted, 'As natural selection works solely... for the good of each being, all... will tend... toward perfection.' I agree with Darwin's optimistic forecast, for what I have seen gives me hope that humanity has not settled into a comfortable evolutionary niche like the nautilus, the gray reef shark, or the horseshoe crab. Rather, humanity is entering yet another installment of an epic saga with much still to be written. The path forward takes humanity to a far place where the struggle to survive will resume, and where human beings will push forward again, inevitably toward a more perceptive, deeper, and eternal version of themselves."

Franz's daughter Fleur stepped in and assumed editorial control of the *Gazette.* Fleur's reports included descriptions of conflicts, political instability, food shortages, and extreme weather events. She ably published the *Gazette* for thirty-four years until her health stepped in. At that point, her son Laurent took over and continued the publication, moving the newsroom north from Lyon to Edinburgh out of necessity.

MIDAN, the ship's trusty autopilot and venerable alarm clock, pinged Rhome, Larke, and Trent to activate out of stasis. The mission blueprint assigned these crewmates to suit up in their deep-space-rated repair droids, perform a pre-launch check, and release the *Halifax* science probe. Using its miniature ion drive and a compact version of MIDAN, *Halifax* would decelerate and steer itself into orbit around the second planet in the star system GJ 1061. Once there, it would gather and transmit data about the minor star and its planets back to Earth.

Trent enjoyed wearing his yellow-and-black powered exoskeleton—it gave him a certain "Don't mess with me" vibe. This "work-amplifier" had not only given him increased strength and longer working time, but it also protected him from the high-velocity stream of particles.

The three crewmates floated down the long passageway that ran the length of the ship to the locker where *Halifax* hibernated. Larke powered up *Halifax* and started checking the ion-drive systems. Rhome checked the structural components while Trent ran checks on the guidance-and-maneuvering software.

Astronomers classified GJ 1061 as a small red dwarf. Its mass was twelve percent of the Sun, and its luminosity zero point two percent as bright as the Sun. Three planets orbited GJ 1061, and the second planet was within the system's habitable zone. From this release point, the probe would arrive at GJ 1061 in under nine years.

Once the checks were complete, Trent opened the exterior access door. "Are all systems go?" he asked, and received confirmation from both crewmates.

With that, he released the clamps holding the probe. Spring-loaded mountings gave a nudge, and the *Halifax* probe drifted away from *The Founder* with its stern pointed straight ahead into the particle stream. A passing ion cloud gave the leading edge of the probe a luminous red glow. When it was several hundred yards away, the probe's autopilot ignited the forward-firing ion drive, and an electric-blue beam shot out of the probe's thrust pipe.

The three crewmates started closing up shop, storing tools and equipment, and latching down the locker access panel. Trent glanced at the probe and noticed that it had developed a wobble. It was spiraling out from its direction of travel. Surprised that the autopilot had not corrected that, he grabbed a nearby vis-panel and used the ship's BLink transceiver to connect to the probe. After confirming a link, he sent a command to the maneuvering thrusters, but was stunned when they did not respond.

"Oh, Phobos," he said. He was even more alarmed when he realized the ion beam was spiraling out and would slice across the flank of *The Founder*.

After calling to Rhome and Larke, he ran a quick projection and realized he had less than a minute to act. Trent pushed open the storage locker door, slid a particle shield out of a nearby rack, activated his magnetic boots, and climbed out onto the outside of the ship. Around the edges of the door-sized rectangular metal shield, he saw the luminescent red glow of the searing particle wind. Snapping a tether into a nearby cleat and holding the shield in front of him, he clinked toward the fore of the ship.

Overhead, he could see the blue beam arcing closer. Its path would cut across the ship at the level of the precious xenon bottles.

He BLinked, "I am going to block it."

As the blue beam neared the ship's flank, Trent held out the particle shield, allowing his repair droid to take the brunt of the particle beam. He walked alongside the beam, holding out the shield as it melted. The shield absorbed most of the beam's energy, but not all of it. Despite his best efforts, a smoldering gash stretched across the ship's flank, and the toe of his mag-boot, as clouds of xenon boiled out.

"Oh dammit! It cut through my shield. We are losing xenon." Trent felt conflicted, as though someone had cheated him. He had followed all the rules. This shouldn't have happened. He wondered, *Is this it? Is the story over now?*

Larke checked the system status. "We have lost pressure in five bottles."

Looking up, Trent saw the glowing electric-blue beam turning like the second hand on a cosmic wristwatch. "It is going to cut across us again," he shouted. He turned to block the beam again, but the heat had welded the toe of his boot to the outer surface. "Larke, punch on the ion drive. Get us away from this monster. Rhome, grab some shields and get out here. Get something between that beam and the ship."

Grabbing her vis-panel, Larke punched on the ion drive. Instantly, an electric-blue beam shot into space, making the ship lunge beneath Larke's feet. She BLinked, "Trent, why can't you—"

"My mag-boot is welded to the ship." He fumbled for his cutting torch, ignited the flame, and freed his boot.

By the time the probe's beam arrived again, Rhome was waiting, this time with two shields. The beam passed across the midship near the plutonium mini reactor; but this time the shields bravely melted, soaking up the energy.

The ion beam circled a third time, but *The Founder* had pulled ahead. The beam passed harmlessly across the ship's wake. Rhome threw the two melted shields into space and clambered down into the locker.

"What the hell happened just now?"

Trent looked at Rhome and asked, "Didn't you check those maneuvering thrusters?"

"Not while they were in the locker. You know how hot they get?"

"You said everything was go for release."

"I thought it was."

"And the guidance system? And the BLink remote control connection? All these systems failed at the same time?"

Rhome stood his ground. "You checked those systems yourself. They were running fine."

"How could that be?" Trent was yelling into his BLink transmitter. "That's too many failures at once to be a mere coincidence." He stormed out of the storage locker and climbed up the long passageway to the ship's bridge, where he stepped out of his repair droid and scrutinized the ship's systems himself. "Five bottles of xenon. Good Gaia, will we be able to slow this monstrosity down?" He pounded his fist on the worktable.

"I have the numbers here." Rhome was somber. "That was one costly loss of xenon."

Trent proclaimed, "From here on, we must conserve every drop of xenon. Rhome, if we are clear of that probe, shut down the ion drive."

"We're clear," stated Rhome, trying to lower the emotional temperature. "Powering off." The crewmates felt a gentle lurch.

The three droids stayed up for a long time discussing events. They all agreed on one thing: this was a sleeper code attack, possibly planned and implemented long ago. Trent would not turn back and retrieve the *Halifax* probe. That was too dangerous. And besides, analyzing the code would not reveal who had planted it. The three suspected the droid that MISA security had arrested prior to the launch. Rhome recommended a security sweep of the ship's systems to search for additional weaponized code and asked Larke to help with this enormous task.

As Rhome and Larke started the scanning, Trent curled up with a vis-panel and began outlining variables for a formula for deceleration into orbit around 82 Eridani. He put his best guesses for numbers into the variables and hit Run. The first run showed *The Founder* barreling right through the 82 Eridani system, far faster than any orbital velocity. He closed his opticals.

There has to be a way, he thought. *And I have only eighty-eight years to find it.*

46

RAW STATIC HISS

DEEP SPACE, 2406 CE
(141 YEARS AFTER LAUNCH)

For the crossing, Larke had given herself the job of monitoring radio signals from Earth. There were plenty of transmissions: digital data streams, military transmissions, satellite links. But Larke wanted to hear voices. Not recordings. Live voices. She felt voices were a better metric of human well-being. She was worried about the humans and wanted to keep an ear out for them.

At first, it was the usual: popular music, advertisements, sports, news, opinions, and talk radio. In addition, MISA sent tight-beam transmissions from a special antenna pointed straight at *The Founder*. But as the decades passed, the number and variety of broadcasts diminished until all Larke heard was military chatter... and recently not even that. Meanwhile, the *Robillard Gazette* had shrunk to two pages and was arriving once a month. The current editor, a seventh-generation descendant of Franz, transmitted stories of struggle, desolation, and despair. Once a cause for celebration, each *Gazette* now only raised concern and heightened tension.

It had been a week since Larke last heard a voice transmission. It could have been her equipment. She ran a diagnostic on the low-noise amplifier; *Within specification* was the readout. Okay, maybe the antenna. She turned the dish toward her reference pulsar, PSR B1919+21, and ran a calibration curve while listening to the familiar "steam locomotive" chugging coming from the spinning neutron star. The dish was spot-on.

While listening to the pulsar, Larke again heard that echo. The signal was bouncing off something out here. She switched on the ship's radar and swept all around but found nothing within its range.

"Hey, Tren, I'm not hearing any voice transmissions from Earth."

He put down his *Gazette* and floated over. "Did you read 'No One Lives in North Africa Anymore'?" he asked.

"I suppose I should." Larke looked disinterested.

Connecting a cable to her workstation, he listened for a while and asked, "When did you hear the last voice?"

"About a week ago. I think it was a military transmission, really fragmented."

The Robillard family's *Gazette* had kept the crew informed about the conflicts breaking out across the planet. The *Gazette* had missed two editions in the previous year, which the editor explained away as "our resources were unreliable." But Trent had fought through two wars. He knew what was really going on.

"I guess we expected this," Trent said, shifting uncomfortably. "It's tormenting to listen to this signal so helplessly."

In moments like these, memories of Stockholm would come to Larke's cognizance. She had only spent two weeks there, but was smitten. She would always remember that glorious, vibrant city with affection and would grieve the news that it was falling into desolation.

After a long silence, Larke said, "Perhaps voice signals do not carry as far as data streams."

Trent said, "Actually, lower-frequency amplitude-modulated audio signals carry farther than digital data streams, which require a higher frequency..." Seeing Larke's shoulders slump, he quickly added, "But I could be wrong, of course." Searching for something to say, he asked, "So, what is our current propagation delay?"

In a singsong voice, Larke recited, "Eighteen years, one month, five days, eleven hours, and twenty-three minutes."

Trent felt adequately chastised and nodded.

After a pregnant silence, Larke said, "If only we could *do* something."

Trent struggled, "We cannot even change course. But I suppose we could always communicate with them. Tell them how we are doing."

Larke appeared upset. "How would that help?"

"Oh, I don't know... If they heard a message from us, it might bring their minds back to a better time... you know... when they were exploring space and looking outward. It might help them refocus, make a little progress."

Larke looked up at Trent with loving dismay. Exasperated by his Pollyanna capacity to always find hope in the most desperate of situations, she said, "Always the optimist," and gave him a conciliatory hug. Trent gave a half-smile. "If I hear any voice transmissions, I will let you know."

"That's a good plan... Thanks, Pixel."

"Course, Tren." She gave a halfhearted smile back.

Trent floated to his private nook and slipped into stasis while Larke lingered at the comm workstation, dispirited, listening to the ripple of digital transmissions—endless strings of ones and zeros, occasionally pausing. And in those pauses, there was nothing but the raw static hiss: the original, eternal background noise still rebounding throughout the universe thirteen point eight billion years after the nanosecond when creation first burst from nothingness into unfathomably vast existence.

47

HELL'S HANDLEBARS

DEEP SPACE, 2431 CE
(166 EARS AFTER LAUNCH)

Trent had finished making rounds on the ship and was working on the deceleration problem. The critical loss of five bottles of xenon had crippled the calculation for the deceleration burn. The problem was weight (physicists would say "mass" or maybe even "mass-energy"). But to slow the ship to orbital velocity, *The Founder* had to shed mass—tons of mass—but still be functional.

As Trent was crunching the numbers, he felt a deep boom and saw a bright flash through the porthole. *We hit something,* he thought. He sent a message to MIDAN to activate the crew from stasis. Then he started another check of the ship's systems.

Larke was the first to come out. "Tren, did we hit something?"

"A micrometeorite, I think." Trent focused on the data on his vis-panel.

"How bad was it?"

"A micrometeorite blasted away about one-third of the ablative shield. I estimate the meteor was about the size of a grain of rice. Now the particle stream of hydrogen atoms is hitting the steel substructure that supports the ablative shield, and it is getting hot."

Larke took the vis-panel from Trent and studied the data with the eyes of an engineer. "Look here." She pointed to the metal framework. "See where the substructure is starting to fail? We must get that substructure out of the particle stream. We must flip the ship right now."

Trent said, "We have to flip it at some point. Might as well be now. Larke, retract the dish antenna."

The other four crew members emerged from stasis and arrived on the bridge. Rhome asked, "A micrometeorite?"

"Most likely," Trent said. "The stern ablative shield will have to suffice for the rest of the trip."

"Everyone, get ready. Faroe, you have the helm. Larke, monitor all the ship's systems. Rhome, Sierra, and Delph hop into repair droids and take up positions in the long cargo bay. Everyone carries a fire suppression canister."

Larke called out, "The good news is the particle count is the lowest of the entire trip—about one hydrogen atom per cubic centimeter. This is the best place for the flip."

Then, the crewmates heard a second thud. Larke saw a flash through her porthole. "We hit another one. We must be crossing paths with the tail of a comet or a meteor."

"How much ablative shielding do we still have up front?" Trent asked.

Larke tapped her workstation screen. "Oh, that one took a healthy bite. We are down to less than forty-six percent up front. The steel substructure is melting fast. We have to flip her right now."

Trent transmitted, "Let's go, let's go! Everyone, get in position?" Affirmations followed. "Faroe, full maneuvering thrusters to starboard. Engage!"

Faroe ignited maneuvering thrusters. The ship yawed to starboard, exposing its port quarter to the incoming stream of hydrogen atoms.

Seconds dragged like a funeral dirge. After a minute, the ship had rotated only forty degrees from its course. Trent's processor speed soared. He had never performed this maneuver before—actually, no one had—but his sense was that the ship should be turning much faster.

"Surely the ship will turn faster," said Trent.

From inside the long cargo bay, Rhome transmitted, "Things are getting hot in here. Can we bring her around soon, please?"

"What's the holdup?" Trent said. "Swing her around!"

"The maneuvering thrusters are not moving her," said Faroe. "It must be the particle stream."

"What?" Trent said. "The maneuvering thrusters should work fine." He headed toward the helm.

Larke called out, "Trent, the outer skin on the port side is melting."

Sierra called, "It's getting hotter than hell's handlebars down here."

Trent reached the helm. "Only twenty percent power?" He looked at Faroe and became intensely focused. "Are you *trying* to destroy the ship? Faroe, full power now! Swing the ship around!"

Faroe didn't move his hands but only tightened his grip on the helm. Trent reached over to seize the ship's controls, but Faroe blocked his attempt.

Larke watched Trent struggling. She BLinked, "Sierra, Rhome, Delph—get up here! Trent needs help now! It's Faroe." Larke stood at her workstation, frozen, watching the temperatures rise throughout the ship and waiting for her crewmates to arrive.

Sierra burst onto the bridge first. Staying in her repair drone, she ran the few steps to the helm and joined the fight. With the added strength of her repair droid, she worked with Trent to pry Faroe's hand from the control lever, but even their combined strength was still not enough.

Trent yelled, "Let go of the helm. That is an order!"

Delph, also in her repair droid, rushed onto the bridge and sized up the situation. "No time for half measures," she said as she leaped to the helm, hauled out her cutting torch, and snapped on the flame. Intensifying the flame to a thin, hissing spike, she sliced into Faroe's right forearm, saying, "So sorry."

Faroe shrieked and thrashed to regain control, but in only seconds, the cutting torch had divided the limb. Tossing the smoking hand aside, Trent grabbed the helm and threw the lever full to port. He was reassured as the ship lurched and its frame creaked while turning.

Meanwhile, Sierra and Delph dragged Faroe down from the helm and restrained the amputee. As they wondered what to do with him, a BLink came in from Rhome. "I got a fire... no, make that two fires in the cargo hold. Get some backup down here. Quickly, please."

Sierra looked at Larke. "What in Sam Hill do we do with him?"

Larke's thoughts raced. "There's an escape pod by the door to the utility bay. Put him in there." Larke's digits danced across her vis-screen as she deactivated the pod's internal control panel. Sierra and Delph marched the beaten, one-armed pilot to the escape pod. Once inside, they shut and latched the door, grabbed fire-suppression canisters, and broke for the utility bay.

Rhome BLinked, "Trent, can she turn any faster? It's really baking in here."

"I am giving it all she's got," called Trent as the ship swept past one hundred ten degrees.

Larke called out from her workstation, "I see a fire breaking out near the reactor."

"I see it, too!" yelled Delph as she clambered toward the inferno.

"Come on, baby. Come on, come on..." said Trent as he worked the flight controls. He held full power on the maneuvering thrusters until the ship rotated past one hundred and sixty degrees. Then he cut power and applied full braking thrusters. The ship's rotation slowed, overshooting one hundred eighty degrees. "Ah, nuts," he said as he reversed the control input to correct for his angry oversteering. It took several minutes of tweaking to bring the ship into close alignment with its heading.

Sierra yelled, "Hell's fritters, Rhome! Get down here. This blaze's blowing up on me." In a flash, Rhome came floating down the scaffolding with two full fire suppressant canisters. Working side by side, they beat down the blaze.

Trent powered down the maneuvering thrusters once he had trimmed the ship's alignment.

Rhome announced, "Okay, fire by the reactor is out."

"The fire way back in the cargo bay is mostly out," Larke said.

Trent transmitted, "Everyone, start inspecting the ship for damage. Larke, stay at your workstation and run checks on internal systems. Also check that we are on the right heading. Shout out if a critical system is down. Rhome, can you coordinate with everyone and make a damage report?"

There was a flurry of activity as they gathered data and assessed the wellness of their ship.

Sometime later, the crew met on the bridge for debriefing.

"What did you find in the ship's structure?" Trent asked.

Rhome reported, "The heat rippled, distorted, and in many places melted away the outer sheet metal along the port side of the ship, leaving numerous large openings in the ship's skin. The heat melted shut most of the hatchways and access ports along the port flank. We will need cutting torches to open them. The structure beneath the sheet metal shell has surface scorching, and there are a few containers with deep burns. Several cables melted and will need replacement. The lift-jet seems to be flightworthy with minimal damage."

"The ion drive checks out fine," Larke said. "The thick metal cladding over the magnets protected all the critical components. Do you think Kenshin expected something like this might happen?"

"That wouldn't surprise me," remarked Trent. "He certainly understood that those electromagnets were critical to the ship's drive."

"We lost some supplies for the settlement. Hopefully, nothing important," Rhome said. "And the reactor is up and running."

"The maneuver did not affect our course," Larke said. "We are still on target for 82 Eridani in thirty-four years."

"I ran a quick system scan," Rhome said. "External sensors, imaging cameras, and short-range antennae along the port side are all melted and out of service. But major internal systems are thankfully functioning."

"Looks like we got off easy," Larke said.

"Maybe so," Sierra said. "But will you answer me this? How the hell do we have a psycho-killer crewmate on board this ship?"

48

PSYCHO-CREWMATE

DEEP SPACE, 2431 CE
(166 YEARS AFTER LAUNCH)

Trent was dreading this conversation with Faroe. This was the part of leadership that he disliked the most. He asked Delph to accompany him for "moral support." Standing beside the escape pod, they could see Faroe through the transparent aluminum window, sitting motionless, staring absently, his right hand and forearm missing.

"Faroe, I am informing you that you are accused of mutiny, attempted deactivation of five AI crew members, and attempted termination of 2400 presentient humans. Because of your actions, you will remain in this escape pod for the rest of the crossing. Once we reach 82 Eridani, we will organize a court and hold a hearing. Do you understand?"

Faroe glared as he said, "What's the point? You will never orbit 82 Eridani."

Trent and Delph looked at each other, worry written on their faces.

"Circumstances required that we turn the ship. During that maneuver, the ship was vulnerable, and you took that opportunity to carry out your attack. One, during the maneuver, you cut power to the maneuvering thrusters, prolonging the exposure of the ship's port flank to the particle stream, which resulted in extensive damage to the ship. Two, you would not let go of the helm and prevented the Commander and crewmember Sierra from righting the ship. Three, you disobeyed the Commander's direct order to release the helm. Your obvious intention was to destroy the ship, and all that was in it.

"We have deactivated the controls and cut power to this escape pod. We will place an inductive charger on its door that will supply just enough power to support your systems in stasis mode, but not full cognizance. You will spend the rest of this crossing in stasis mode. We will activate you when we reach the destination, at which time we will organize a court and conduct a hearing."

"Wasted words," said Faroe. "Everyone has seen you sweat over those calculations. You can't stop this ship, and you know it."

Returning to the bridge, Trent and Delph found the other three crew members waiting.

Trent said, "I am going to limit his access to electric power."

Larke said, "There is a manual release in the escape pod that has no override. He can eject whenever he wants."

Trent said, "I know. But he won't pull the release in deep space. Not unless he wants to drift through the cosmos for all eternity. And besides, he is going to be in stasis mode."

"Can somebody fill me in? What in blazes is going on with Faroe?" Sierra asked.

"The story goes back a long way," Trent said.

Sierra crossed her arms, leaned back, and said, "I got nothin' but time."

Trent recounted the story of the no-return mission to Proxima Centauri and its aborted launch because of the sabotaged fuel conduit. He described how MISA Security identified a droid in the OLC who was planting SF sleeper code. Everyone assumed that droid was the saboteur.

"Sounds like you caught the wrong gopher in the green beans."

"There were so many warning signs," Delph said in dismay. "They say he was a combat veteran of MWIII and was the victim of war crimes."

"How could they have missed that?" Sierra asked.

"It seems obvious now," Larke said. "Of course, you know what they say about hindsight."

"The SF were angry about the Proxima Centauri mission," Trent said. "They publicized it as a government-sanctioned suicide mission that institutionalized bias against AI beings."

Rhome surmised, "The SF planned to blow up the *Lodestar* with Faroe in it, as a demonstration of the power of their reach."

Delph leaned back, her gaze wandering. "So, both MISA and SF were planning to kill Faroe, albeit by different means. As a result, he felt trapped. No way of escape. No wonder he went insane."

Trent reflected. "I remember when we changed the mission to 82 Eridani—with the plan for chip fabrication—Nils got a message from the SF saying they no longer opposed the mission."

"What?" Delph asked. "How many groups are attacking us? We had the opposition to frozen embryos, the Sentient Faction, and this lone wolf, Faroe."

Sierra couldn't hold it in any longer. "Listen, I don't give a hoot if he has war trauma. He tried to kill us all. And not just once. And let's not forget the two thousand four hundred people in that tin can in the fridge. Now where I come from, they call that attempted murder, and people spend a long time in the slammer for doing that."

Larke turned to Trent. "As the ship's commander, you have the authority under the Maritime Ship Master's Act of some date-or-other to hear testimony, decide the verdict, and even pronounce sentence."

Trent said, "The problem is that I was there. I witnessed Faroe's crimes, even fought against him. The question is not his guilt, but my impartiality. If I convicted him and sentenced him, would it withstand appeal? Obviously not."

Delph offered. "In his defense, his resentment stems from the war crimes committed against him during Migration War Three."

Larke said, "That is not a vigorous defense, Delph."

Trent asked if there was anything else. There was not. He said, "Well, regardless of appeal, Faroe is guilty of mutiny and attempted mass deactivation. He will be confined to the escape pod for the rest of this interplanetary crossing. When we arrive at our destination, we will hold a sentencing hearing."

"If we arrive at our destination," grumbled Rhome.

Sierra grimaced. "It looks to me like Faroe has already won."

49

DROID OVERBOARD

DEEP SPACE, 2462 CE
(197 YEARS AFTER LAUNCH)

82 Eridani, now the brightest star in space, was directly ahead. The mood on board was fretful. Soon they would begin the deceleration burn, but every calculation showed they would overshoot the star system.

Inside the cargo hold, Trent sent via BLink: "Okay, Sierra, start the pump."

A moment later from within the *Winnipeg*'s locker, Sierra said, "I'm seeing good flow here."

It would take a couple of hours to pump all the xenon from the *Winnipeg* into *The Founder*. Trent used the time to read the *Gazette*. "So, there are reports of spontaneous combustion in hay barns across the Midwest. Have you heard of that?"

Sierra said, "You bet. It's pretty rare, but it's heat from fermentation. You gotta stack your hay bales with gaps between and keep 'em well ventilated."

"Hmm, haystacks bursting into flames. Well, I never."

There was still much to do before the braking burn, which had to start in less than three months. Rhome had been rifling through storage compartments to find solar panels. Planned for use by the settlement, Rhome had bolted them onto the outside of the ship's framework to help power the ion drive. Also, the crewmates needed to lighten *The Founder* by about thirty tons without compromising the crew, the embryos, or the ion drive. Even with that weight reduction and extra electric power, the projections still showed that *The Founder* would overshoot the planet.

Trent sent, "Rhome and I are going to go toss some stuff overboard."

At that moment, Sierra felt a kerthump go through the ship. She transmitted, "Hey, did you feel that?"

Delph, sitting at the systems console on the bridge, said, "That was not a micrometeor strike. That was something on the ship itself. Everybody, look around."

Trent grabbed a particle shield, switched on his boots, and stepped out of the storage locker onto the outer surface of the ship.

"You seeing anything?" Sierra asked.

"Not from where I am standing," Trent said. The sheet metal in front of him had previously melted and buckled, so Trent was careful where he stepped.

"What are we looking for?" Rhome asked.

Delph said, "It is a... hold on... it is a hatch. A hatch is open. It is access hatchway 8, over the cryostorage locker."

Sierra BLinked, "Trent, ya got that? Look for a blown hatch, number 8. You know the one?"

Trent said, "On my way." Trent lifted his particle shield and took mag-boot steps over to the open door of hatch 8. Looking down into the open storage hold, he transmitted, "Where's the canister?"

Rhome was following at a distance. "Hey, Trent, what's that?" He pointed.

Trent looked left and right. "What?"

Rhome said, "No, over your head... Look up."

Trent looked upward, only to see the worst nightmare he could ever imagine. Six meters above the hatchway was a stainless-steel canister, lazily rotating as it drifted away from the ship. In a heartbeat, Trent knew what was at stake.

Rhome said to himself, "Gaia, help us."

Trent's tether was too short for him to reach the canister. Thoughts of Nils and the decision forced upon him at the airfield filled his cognizance. He thought, *For the mission.*

Then, Trent turned off the electromagnets in his boots and unsnapped his tether. Holding his particle shield in one hand, he paused a moment to collect himself, then leaped upward toward the canister. Floating free through the intervening space, he reached the canister and enclosed it with his arms. Looking down, he saw Rhome walking up to the open hatch, watching him.

"Rhome, catch!" Like a football player hiking a football, he pushed the canister downwards straight toward Rhome's outstretched arms. The momentum transferred to the canister caused Trent to drift even faster from *The Founder*.

Rhome called out, "Droid overboard! Trent is floating free in space." Catching the canister, he looked around for something to throw to Trent, but there was nothing.

On the bridge, Larke froze with fear, her mind numb, mute, desolate.

Trent looked down. "Rhome, complete the mission. You hear me?"

Rhome called, "Trent, don't give up, droid. We are going to figure this out. We are going to bring you back."

Delph shifted into her emergency-room-doctor mode. "Trent, listen. Conserve your battery. Run your processors at low clock speed. And keep broadcasting your position. Every few seconds, send out a beacon pulse. And stay behind that particle shield. We are all working on this. We are going to find a solution."

"Thanks, Delph. But you know," Trent said, "this is deep space, and you are running out of fuel."

Delph was struggling to track the drifting signal from Trent. "Larke!" she said. "Shake it off, droid. I need you now."

Larke emerged from the shock. She asked, "What do you need?"

"You are our best head with numbers. Get on that workstation. Track Trent's signal and get me some coordinates."

With her cognizance now crystal clear, Larke rushed to the workstation and started tapping keys. Within a minute, she said, "I have his coordinates and a vector for his trajectory."

Delph smiled. "What did I tell you?"

Rhome BLinked from outside the ship, "The embryos are back in cryo. Hatch 8 is closed."

Delph said, "Rhome, put a few spot welds across that hatch. Those embryos stay in that locker until I need them. Period."

"I got a torch right here."

Larke's processors were blazing as she generated potential scenarios. Then, a solution dawned on her. She BLinked, "Sierra, turn off the pump draining xenon from *Winnipeg*."

"But Larke, remember? Every last drop?"

"We'll worry about that later. And power up the *Winnipeg*."

"Pump is off... I am starting the boot cycle."

Larke sent, "I am setting up remote-control via BLink... and... Okay, I have a connection."

"*Winnipeg* has booted."

Sierra BLinked, "Great. Let's test this puppy before we launch it. Can you see the maneuvering thrusters?"

"Yeah, most of them."

Larke used her workstation remote control to test pitch, roll, and yaw.

Sierra confirmed, "All good, Larke. We are ready on our end."

Rhome said, "Good. No sleeper code in this probe."

"Okay," BLinked Sierra. "Clamps are coming off... Here's the last one... Giving it a push... Okay, *Winnipeg* is away."

Larke felt her processors race. "Delph, are you still tracking his beacon?"

"It's getting faint, but I still have it. Here are his coordinates."

"Coordinates relative to what?"

"The position of the ship."

Larke said, "In deep space, you need external fixed points to anchor your coordinates. Most navigators use bright stars."

"We have plenty of those," Sierra said. "Too many. I see one overhead in a little cluster that looks like a panda bear."

"And two more..."

"To the side is a curve of stars with a bright one at the end. It looks like a lizard. Then ahead we have, well, 82 Eridani."

Larke announced, "Okay, 82 Eridani is the X axis, panda bear is the Y axis, and lizard is the Z axis."

Sierra took note and said, "And here is Trent's location."

"Let's get that over to Delph so she can start driving *Winnipeg*." Larke turned up the power on her BLink transmitter. "Trent, come in."

"Trent here."

"We have launched the *Winnipeg* probe to come and find you."

"I hope it doesn't slice me into pizza toppings."

"Oof! What are we going to do with you, Trent?"

"How is it going to find me?"

"We are tracking your beacon pulses and have set up a coordinate system."

The *Winnipeg* probe was the very definition of sluggishness, and the remote control was just that: up, down, left, right. There was no ship-to-ship spatial integration, no celestial coordinates. It took Delph ten minutes to get the contraption moving in Trent's general direction. By that time, Trent had drifted an additional hundred meters away. As they were in deep space, there were no nearby stars, so it was pitch-dark. And the *Winnipeg* had no running lights. As for Trent's repair droid, it had a work light on the shoulder, which Trent switched on.

Then came a long series of trial-and-error iterations: fire the maneuvering thrusters to push the probe toward a particular constellation—named on the fly—and check if it was closer by briefly firing the mini-ion drive.

After two hours of maneuvering and checking, and more maneuvering and more checking, Larke called, "Now, where are you relative to *Winnipeg*?"

"Give me another brief pulse." The miniature ion drive emitted a blue beam for one second. Trent memorized the probe's position relative to the stars behind it. Then he turned one hundred eighty degrees and studied the stars. "Okay, Delph, look for a cluster of six stars in a circle, with one extra star outside the circle. It kind of resembles a ping-pong paddle. Move toward that star cluster to reach me."

Sierra searched the sky. "I think I see it."

Delph maneuvered toward the ping-pong paddle and asked, "Is the probe getting closer?"

Trent waited for about a minute. "I think so... it's so hard to tell."

Another minute went by.

"I cannot see the probe out here." Delph heard a hint of desperation in Trent's voice.

Delph asked her crewmates, "Which way do I fire the maneuvering jets?"

The four crewmates had built an assembly line. Trent would describe a pattern of stars. Larke would find each constellation on a virtual star map in a vis-workstation and label it. Then, Sierra would use the coordinates of Trent and the probe to plan the next maneuver, which she would send to Delph, who was driving the probe.

"I think the probe is about three hundred meters away. Apply thrust toward the lizard."

Thrusters glowed. The probe moved toward what she believed was Trent's constellation. She estimated it would be less than one hundred meters from him.

"I can't see it. It's so dark."

Sierra said, "I think we may have identified the wrong constellation. Trent, describe the lizard to me again."

"It's six stars along a curve, and the sixth star is brighter."

"Okay, moving toward the lizard." A brief glow from the thrusters showed the probe moving away.

"That's the wrong direction. We must not have the same lizard."

Sierra's shoulders slumped as she kicked herself for her error. "Okay, let's take another swing at this."

Larke was feeling despair. They were all working so hard and seemed to make no progress. For a moment, she remembered that night in Stockholm where she had felt the cosmos move when she and Trent and Nils had discovered the message in the inscription. Now, Nils was gone, and without some luck, Trent would be, too. She would have to carry on the mission of the inscription by herself, which made her feel empty, lost, void of hope. She turned inward and thought the words, *Help us.*

"There it is," Trent transmitted. "Give it a push toward the broccoli constellation."

Delph said, "Maneuvering toward broccoli."

"Are we getting closer?" Sierra asked.

"Stay focused," chimed in Delph.

Trent sent, "Okay, a little thrust toward the brontosaurus."

"Adding thrust toward the big dinosaur," Delph said. She waited a moment. "Trent, you should be pretty close."

"Hold on. It's... it's about thirty meters away. Give it a nudge toward the dachshund."

"Nudging toward the wiener dog," came Delph's measured reply. "And here's a pop of xenon... How are we doing?"

"Hold steady. Let it drift."

As the *Winnipeg* drifted closer, Trent took a heavy-gauge copper wire cable from his repair droid and bent it into a grappling hook. He snapped that onto the self-closing hook at the end of his tether. Then he swung the weighted tether in a circle around him like a gaucho swinging a bolo at an ostrich. This increased Trent's cross-sectional area from two meters, the length of his outstretched arms, to over eight meters.

As the *Winnipeg* neared, he extended his arm, guiding the tether to swing around the midsection of the probe. It slipped off the nose. Swinging again, he sent the hook across the *Winnipeg* a second time. The hooks didn't grab. Swinging yet again across the midsection, he extended his arm as far as possible to let the grappling hook cross the path of the rope. After a momentary pause, Trent pulled back on the tether and could feel the hook catch.

"Gotcha!"

Shrieks ripped through the bridge. Larke grabbed Sierra, and they hugged while their feet danced. Delph and Rhome also hugged as Delph turned inward to her deepest thoughts. Trent pulled himself over to the *Winnipeg* and grabbed hold, relief washing over him like a late spring cloudburst.

"Okay, I'm on the *Winnipeg*. Let's reel me in."

"Okay, droids," Delph said, waking from her brief retreat. "One more time, only this time, backwards."

Over the next few hours, with visualization aided by the red glow of an ionized gas cloud, Delph steered the *Winnipeg* on a steady course back to *The Founder*. Larke was waiting by the hatch when Trent stepped aboard, and they spent a tender moment in mutual embrace and reassurance. Rhome secured the *Winnipeg* in its storage bay, then the crewmates gathered on the bridge to be close. The aura of stress lingered, wrapping itself around Larke, who was deeply shaken by this brush with catastrophe.

After affirmations and appreciations, Trent, feeling drained, excused himself to his personal nook to recharge and rest. Larke stayed with him until he drifted off into stasis. As she sat watching Trent, for a moment she could feel a deep, resonant vibration sweep through the ship. She looked up, not knowing where to look, and whispered, "Thank you."

Later, the crewmates gathered to debrief and decompress.

"I welded that hatch shut," Rhome said.

"Yeah, but who opened it in the first place?" Sierra asked, shrugging.

"How did they open it?" Rhome asked with a puzzled expression.

"My question is, why did they open it?" asked Delph.

"Right. And why attack the frozen humans?" Larke asked. "Why not us?"

"This was attempted genocide," asserted Delph. "An act of global terrorism."

"It was Faroe again," alleged Sierra. "I have no evidence, but I am sure of it."

Rhome held up his hand. "Then it's time for some detective work. There's a server that runs ship-wide systems—heating, cooling, lights, doors, stuff like that. It keeps a running log of all commands handled by the system. It is an enormous file. But, you know, we are AI. Big files are our superpower."

Delph brought up ship-wide systems on a nearby workstation and found the system log. Scrolling down to the moment everyone felt the thump, she saw it: a command to the locking mechanism on hatch 8. But its origin was cryptic.

Delph asked, "Rhome, come look at this. Do you recognize this device code?"

Rhome studied the characters. "I have seen this before." He went into external stasis and searched for a long time. "Oh yeah. Here it is. That is the device-code for a smart-cable connector."

Sierra looked puzzled. "Why don't you plug cables into just 'connectors? Weird."

"Yeah. Spaceship builders love them. They make wiring so easy because they recognize anything you plug into them. And they can handle minor jobs on their own, like, you know, dimming the lights or adjusting room temperature."

"Or opening a hatch," Sierra said.

"So where would this smart little connector be?"

"We would see that in the ship's blueprints." Searching the archives, Rhome found the ship's electrical diagrams. He matched the device number and found the culprit connector was in an electrical cabinet near the base of the dish antenna.

Rhome grabbed a vis-panel and headed down to the cargo bay, crewmates following in line. He opened the cabinet, plugged a cable into the connector, and opened its code on the screen. "There it is." Just a few lines of unassuming code designed to end the chances for twenty-four hundred potential human lives.

But there was something peculiar about the code. "Larke, look at this syntax. Does this look like MISA coding to you?"

Larke pored over the characters and pointed, "This is an older style. See how they name their variables and order their arguments. That's an older convention. A MISA coder would never write like this." Larke took the vis-panel and opened a private directory labeled in all caps as *CONFIDENTIAL*. Inside were examples of code from Sentient Faction hackers. She compared these to the code from the smart connector. It was a solid match.

"Hey, droids," Larke said, "this is SF sleeper code..."

She held out the vis-panel. "What we learned today is that Faroe showed his hand. He uses sleeper code, the weapon of choice for the SF agents, and I am sure there is more to be found." She shook her head wearily. "We have to scan all the ship's systems and networks again—down to the last damn smart connector—and scrub the ship of these time bombs. It is a ton of work, and a real chore, but that is how we will defeat him."

50

CRASH DIET

DEEP SPACE, 2464 CE
(199 YEARS AFTER LAUNCH)

Trent seemed frozen in the passageway running alongside the ion drive while Sierra was busy shearing off squares of external sheet metal and tossing them into space. She looked puzzled.

"Hey, Trent, I need a hand here."

"Just a minute," he said as he inched his way toward her, double-checking his grip on each handhold.

Sierra leaned down. "Trent? Are you okay?"

Trent froze. "Can you ask Larke to come over here?"

In a moment, Larke arrived and said to Sierra, "It's another panic attack."

"Can he move?" Sierra asked with a worried expression.

"He needs a minute. But he will be okay."

Larke climbed down to Trent and sat down beside him. They talked to each other for a while. Then, with her help, he made his way slowly to the external surface, where he joined Sierra in shearing away the external sheet metal. That was when Sierra noticed Trent had attached three tethers from his repair droid to three different cleats on the ship's exterior.

Sierra looked over at Trent with understanding eyes and said, "Don't worry, I will stay here right beside you."

After pumping the last bit of xenon from the *Winnipeg* into *The Founder*, Rhome and Trent released the clamps and set the probe drifting. Trent said, "Thank you, Tanabe-san," as he watched it drift away into the void.

"There was not much xenon left in the probe," Rhome said.

"Oh, it served its purpose," Trent said. "The problem is we are still too heavy, and we have to start the braking burn soon."

Rhome patted a nearby carbon fiber panel. "Founder, my girl, you're going on a crash diet."

The crewmates had trudged through the meticulous process of scanning every system on the ship... and were glad they did. They found three sleeper code time bombs in the network, all written in that telltale SF syntax.

Next, they had prepared an inventory of all the components on the ship, labeling each as either essential, optional, or expendable. They started with the big, expendable objects, and the biggest of all was the forward—now the aft—particle shield.

"Up close," Rhome said, "you see how huge this thing is."

"And it's half-gone from that meteor strike," Trent said. He took out his cutting torch. "These truss rods are so thick. How do we cut them?"

"Don't cut it up there. Cut at the end where the metal is flattened. Here, let me show you."

In less than ten seconds, Rhome's cutting torch sliced through the flattened end of the truss rod. Together, they worked their way through the mounting assembly. Finishing the last two cuts together, they said, "Heave ho!" and gave the enormous shield a push into space.

The crew spent over a week removing and jettisoning excess mass. Larke distributed a manual by Kenshin Tanabe to the crew. In one section, Kenshin suggested with prescient foresight that the crew might have to deal with the loss of xenon. He outlined a method for removing about one-third of the weight of the steel frame supporting the ion drive without compromising the stability of the drive itself. Once they had removed all expendable weight, the crew turned to the optional items. Principal among those was Sierra's farm equipment.

Sierra protested, "Awe, come on, droids. It's not that heavy. And believe you me, you do not want to cultivate acres of row crops by hand. We call that 'stoop-work,' and it grows old real quick."

"Okay, then we have to find something else to compensate for the tractor's mass," Larke said.

The crew put on their repair droids and went out again. Sparks were flying as their cutting torches carved off excess framework braces, exterior sheet metal, and empty xenon bottles. The crew pared away tons of weight except for the bridge and tossed all of it into the black. *The Founder* became a mere shell of her former self, her inner workings exposed like an anatomy teaching mannequin.

Larke ran a fresh set of projections. "We still have a long way to go." She passed the spreadsheet around.

Rhome studied the numbers. "Where is it going to come from?"

"The ship is a skeleton," Delph said. "It has to come from the supplies for the settlement."

"Not my incubators," Delph said.

"Not my tractor," Sierra said.

"Okay, that leaves the construction materials," Rhome said. "This means that we will have to use local products for buildings."

The crewmates made their way to the storage lockers and rows of bins containing materials for the new community. Rhome pulled out materials for temporary buildings: roofing, cladding, floorboards, windows, doorways, all shoved out into the black.

"Where will we live?" asked Delph, worry in her voice.

"We'll sleep under the stars, like backpackers," Rhome said.

"Even backpackers have little tents," said Delph.

"I can build a lean-to using branches and a tarp," Sierra chimed.

"Or, we could find a cave," Larke said. "That's what early humans did."

Rhome opened another locker. Inside were two small all-terrain vehicles. "If we let these go, then we'll be walking everywhere," Rhome said.

"ATVs are nice, but the tractor gets the work done. I say, toss the ATVs," Sierra said.

"Oh, this is going to hurt," Rhome said as he unbuckled the packing straps and pushed the ATVs into space. Then, he took out his cutting torch, cut the supports around the locker, and heaved the locker itself into the emptiness.

"We're getting down to the bare essentials," Delph said. "This is turning into a regular survival challenge, like going into the wilderness with only a knife, some string, and some matches."

After several more hours, they had thrown out furniture, inflatable boats, rifles, ammunition, body armor, buckets of epoxy sealer, steel cables, and hurricane fencing. Every time they pushed something away from the ship, they knew there would be payback later.

Finally, Larke called for everyone to stop. "Let me run a fresh set of numbers and see where we stand." She made her way to a work-station.

Trent came over. "Pixel, how far off are we?"

Without making eye contact, she slid the printout, facedown, over to Trent.

"Oh, Gaia."

"Yeah, Tren. I don't want to tell them."

"I can see why." Trent was silent for a long time, pondering. "Let me look at something." He climbed up the steps to the helm and sat down. Switching on the external panorama, he looked ahead at the 82 Eridani system and rolled up the magnification. Just visible were the first three planets in the system.

"That third planet, where will it be in about eight months?"

Larke switched on a workstation and loaded up the application for celestial mechanics. It took her a few minutes to enter all the data into the system. "It's going to be swinging toward us in its orbit." Larke looked at Trent as if a light in her cognizance had switched on. "A retrograde slingshot. You son of a battery charger. Of course. Do a close flyby of a planet so that the gravity slows the ship."

"Let's not tell the crew until we have some numbers," Trent said. "Can you set up and run the orbital mechanics?"

"This is a big job. I'll need some time," Larke said. Her attention retreated into deep focus as she concentrated on the complex mathematics and started gathering data on the variables.

Hours later, Larke called the crewmates together. "Okay, I think we have a plan."

Delph frowned. "You think... you don't seem to be enthusiastic about this."

Larke self-consciously shifted. "Well, Delph, it's tricky."

"Let's hear it. We are all in this together," Rhome said.

"Okay, we have too much speed to burn off. Our xenon reserves are too low to bring us down to orbital velocity." Eyes widened. "To slow the ship, we need a close flyby of the third planet, 82 Eridani d, while burning the ion drive."

The group was silent, their eyes anxious.

Larke gave a half smile. "Okay, the flyby will be tricky; we will be at an angle to the orbital plane, which decreases the slingshot effect. Also, I'm having some trouble with a couple of variables."

The group was still silent.

"Problem is, I don't have accurate measurements of the mass of the third planet. I'm using estimates based on similar-sized celestial bodies."

Still, no talking.

Larke said, "If we hit the flyby just right, we'll end up in orbit around 82 Eridani c. But we have to hit it right on the nose." She put her index finger on the tip of her nose.

Rhome asked, "So we still needed to reduce the ship's mass, right?" Rhome was still unhappy about releasing those all-terrain vehicles into space.

"Oh, absolutely, Rhome. This only works at the bare minimum mass. At our current mass, we can almost get down to orbital velocity."

"I heard that. You said 'almost,'" said Sierra, her gaze fixed on Larke. "Can you do this, or is this just handwaving?"

"Oh, this is doable. There is a flight path through these equations that leads to orbit. But we have to fly it right down the middle and use every watt our thermoelectrics and solar panels and Brayton engines can make."

"But the ship only makes so much electrical power. It's maxed out right now," said Delph.

"That's right, Delph. And who is sucking up most of that power? Us!"

"Here it comes," Delph said to herself.

Larke said, "We are the second-most energy-intensive system on this vessel. When we are awake and processing, we gobble up loads of power. I need to throw all the electric power we've got down the ion drive. So we all need to go into eco-stasis during the braking burn."

Delph looked worried. "All of us?"

Sierra fretted, "Who will trim the alignment and monitor the systems? What if..."

"Friends, we lost so much xenon during the *Halifax* attack that we have no options here. We have to program this crazy course into MIDAN and go into low-power stasis. When we reactivate in eight months—"

"I don't like this," fretted Sierra.

Larke passed around her calculation for the deceleration burn again. "This is going to be tight." She stood up and paced back and forth.

"There's no choice," Trent said with matter-of-fact resignation. "Larke and Rhome, get going with the programming."

Larke collected herself, and with help from Rhome, set to work programming MIDAN.

"Holy asteroids!" exclaimed Rhome. "This is a lot of math. Where did you get all this?"

Larke tapped her fingertip on her head. They worked for several hours on the flight path. For each variable, Larke set up formulas to adjust the variable if better data became available. She also included adjustments to the flight path based on the speed of the ship and its coordinates. She added so many contingencies to the calculation that it almost maxed out the memory in the MIDAN flight computer. After checking the formulas a dozen times, Larke said, "It's done."

She made a list of conditions that would trigger MIDAN to reactivate her. Trent looked over the list and deleted most of the items. "Sorry, you can't use that much power."

Larke agreed without pushing Trent to convince her. "It is time to start the braking burn. Everybody ready?"

Larke reached out to MIDAN and tapped RUN. Then she went to the engine control panel and switched on the ion drive. Final checks: all systems were Go. The crewmates all embraced and went to their personal cubicles. One by one, they winked off, each praying their math-nerd crew member had gotten all those calculations right. In eight months, they would grade her homework.

Larke and Trent waited a few minutes before retiring. The welfare of the crewmates, two thousand four hundred frozen human embryos, and their interstellar vehicle were all on the line. Both knew they had no real control here. They were casting their fate to the cosmos.

They hugged and retreated to their cubicles, both turning their cognizance down to eco-stasis, not knowing what awaited them in eight months.

51

SCRUFFY LITTLE ALARM CLOCK

DEEP SPACE, 2465 CE (200 YEARS AFTER LAUNCH)

Larke jerked to alert status. In her input log was a message from MIDAN: "Instruction set complete. Send Activate command to Larke." Checking her internal log, she found she had been in stasis for just over eight months. After running a self-check on her code core, she scanned her surroundings: no other active AI units in her vicinity. The others must still be out. She checked the voltage coming into her batteries: plenty to support all functions. Connecting to the ship's systems, she saw the ion drive was off, and the xenon bottles were down to mere fumes.

"So, where the hell are we?"

Larke drifted up to the bridge, which was the same as it was before she went into stasis. MIDAN, the trusty autopilot, was waiting to receive the next instruction set. She climbed the steps to the helm, sat down, and after a moment to brace herself, switched on external cameras.

A surge of relief swept over her like a breaking wave. After two centuries of drifting through the inexhaustible black, the mapwork of colors and textures rolling beneath the ship was beyond mesmerizing. She turned and said aloud, "MIDAN, you scruffy little alarm clock, you did it, kid." She leaned over and gave the clunky enclosure a pat with her nickel-chromium hand.

82 G. Eridani c filled half the sky with sumptuous intrigue. A dozen loosely tossed island continents floating in a deep green webwork of seas. Over the continents, a wide belt of dusty tan encircled the equator, separating two vast zones of dark turquoise iced with swirls of

feathered clouds. The leading edge of each tectonic landmass was a buckled rim on which craggy peaks pushed up to pierce the clouds. Bright white dusted the poles, while black billows gushed from a cinder cone, and elsewhere a massive whirlpool storm churned across an expanse of ocean.

The ship faded from Larke's awareness as she lingered, drinking in the world's features, as fresh and surprising as if she had a child's sense of wonder.

One by one, she sent each crewmate an Activate command. Delph was first to emerge. She hugged Larke, saying, "My darling sister, what you did was genius."

Sierra joined them next. Soaking in the view, the three sat holding hands while sharing their resonance.

Rhome then rumbled out of his domiciliary, expecting the worst. Looking at his crewmates, who all feigned dour disappointment, he asked, "Well then, where are we?"

Larke accompanied him up to the helm, where they all shared a joyful laugh at his expense.

Last was Trent, who stood immobilized with apprehension until Rhome waved an arm at him and said, "Get up here, droid. You gotta see this."

Delph dialed up the magnification on the camera and looked for signs of habitation. To her surprise, she saw no superhighways, no sprawling urban areas, or rectangles of agricultural production. Adding more magnification, she saw sunlight reflecting off rows of black rectangles. "Photovoltaics?" she wondered. At one point she saw a glint of reflection off an object in orbit. She tried to zoom in, but lost it from her field of view. *Could that be a ship?*

"But where are the inhabitants?" Delph asked. She focused on the night side of the terminator and saw clusters of lights. But no real urban areas, industrial zones, airports, harbors, or railways. She said to the other crewmates, "These people haven't made a mark on this planet. Is this the same culture that visited Earth eighteen thousand years ago?"

"We should reach out to the extraterrestrials," Larke said, "and let them know we are here."

Delph corrected, "Since we are no longer on Earth, a.k.a. Terra, the term 'extraterrestrial' is grammatically incorrect."

"Come on, Delph, lighten up," Sierra said. "We will call them aliens."

Rhome said, "Aren't we the aliens in this movie?" He had formed his mental image of "aliens" primarily from feature-length sci-fi action films.

"So, what should we call them? What should we call ourselves?" Larke asked.

"Eridanians?" offered Rhome.

"I am sure they have a name for their own kind," Sierra assured them.

Larke chimed, "I bet they have AI beings, like us."

Delph offered, "Then we should call ourselves 'Earth-based AI beings' to create a feeling of affiliation."

Turning on the ship's transceiver and dialing through the frequencies, Rhome was relieved to hear plenty of radio chatter. For no particular reason, he set the transmitter to broadcast over Earth Channel 16 and plugged the microphone cable into his neck. "Greetings to all beings on the planet, in the air, and all ships in space. This is Earth-based interstellar ship *The Founder*. We have arrived after a long crossing from our home planet, Earth, and are in orbit around your planet. We would like to make peaceful contact. Please respond. Over."

After a minute, Rhome was preparing to resend when he heard a mid-pitched tone playing through the speaker. The five crewmates gathered around the communications workstation.

A voice spoke briefly; the language incomprehensible. Following the speech, they heard a repeated pinging sound.

Rhome said, "I know that sound. That is a homing beacon. They are sending us the location of where to land."

"Let's power up the lift-jet and check its systems," Trent said. "In fact, let's re-scan all the systems in the lift-jet for any of that damn sleeper code."

Trent turned to Delph and asked, "Would you check on Faroe?"

"Sure." She disappeared down the corridor to the escape pod.

"Larke, can you check ship systems?"

"On it."

"And Rhome, while we scan all the systems, want to fuel up the lift-jet?"

"I was going to say—"

"Trent, Rhome!" Delph barged into the conversation. "The escape pod is gone. Faroe is nowhere in sight."

PART 5

THE SETTLEMENT

52

FIRST CONTACT

SALT FLATS, 82 G. ERIDANI C, 2465 CE

Rhome eased the sleek black jet down into thicker air, making the passengers weightless. In moments, the leading edges of the wings turned a dull red. He said, "Whoa there, girl," as he pulled back on the joystick. "Burn off some speed." The craft climbed, making the passengers sag as their weight doubled. After coasting a while, he tried another dip into the sea of air, the wings glowing again. "Still too hot. Let's coast."

"Doing okay up there?" asked Trent from the back seat.

"I am a little rusty... but it is coming back."

Larke fretted, "When did you last fly one of these?"

"Oh, about... two hundred years ago. But you know... it's like riding an e-bike."

Forlorn but also relieved, Delph and Sierra had remained back on *The Founder*. A lift-jet crash with all crew members would end the mission. They were gracious as they passed up the opportunity to attend first contact.

The lift-jet slowed, and Rhome once again eased forward on the joystick. "Finally."

As they descended, Larke thrilled at seeing familiar surface features. She carried a camera and snapped photos of a wide, meandering river on an alluvial plain, a craggy mountain range reaching up toward them through the clouds, and a sun-drenched tropical beach by a turquoise sea just begging for sunbathers. Showing her photos to Rhome, she said with glee, "Look! Earth used to look like this."

Searching for the homing beacon, Rhome hand-steered the sleek hybrid craft southward, cruising over forest-covered hill country, where they buffeted through a turbulent storm front. "Hey, listen for the ping of that homing beacon." He let the jet glide on its momentum, engines off. If he couldn't locate the beacon, he would have to kick in the air-breathing engines and circle back for a second pass.

Following another frightful shake, Larke thought she heard pinging. She shared the signal with Rhome, who forwarded it to the guidance system, which locked on. "Nice pickup, Larke. I sure hope that salt flat is hard enough to support the weight of this jet."

Slumped in the back seat, Larke chided, "Droid, you sure know how to put folks at ease."

Not trusting the lift-jet's automated landing system, Rhome had decided to hand-fly the final approach and landing. He switched off the automation and took the controls.

Larke offered, "I hear the automated landing systems in these jets are quite good."

Rhome boomed, "No worries, my friend. Watch this..."

The jet topped the circle of low mountains surrounding the salt flat where the beacon was transmitting. His shallow final approach let him hold the lift-craft a hand's span above the surface as airspeed bled off. "Here goes," he said as he added back-pressure to the joystick. The jet flared and settled with ease onto the hard pack, rolling across the surface as if it were tarmac. "Hah... greased it!" He lowered the nose, and braking gently, let the jet roll to an easy stop near the beacon tower.

"Actually, that was pretty good," shared Larke, relieved that the salt bed had not crumbled beneath the weight on the three wheels.

Restless with anticipation, Rhome popped the canopy. Hot, brackish air welled up and filled the cockpit.

The three droids, one of them shaken but relieved to be functioning, looked out over the dirty white tabletop-flat surface of the salt flat. "We made it," Larke said. "My Gaia, this is 82 Eridani c." Devoid of vegetation, the salt flat stretched for kilometers without interruption to the feet of the encircling ring of rounded brown mountains.

Rhome clambered out onto the wing and stepped down onto the salt flat, proclaiming, "That is one small step for AI, one giant leap for AI-kind."

Larke grabbed a photo while Trent protested, "Hey, I wanted to say that!"

"You still can."

Larke, still sitting in the cockpit, collected and tested an air sample. Looking at her results, she called, "Hey, Trent, Rhome, look! Our biological humans can breathe this."

At that moment, Trent's audio sensors picked up a distant whirr. Scanning the horizon, he saw a low-flying aircraft approaching: a winged hovercraft, or maybe a ground effects machine... something like that. It glided like a pelican a meter above the surface, its tan external surfaces marbled with the surrounding colors of the environment. *Some form of camouflage,* he thought. Zooming his opticals, he could see no mounted weapons or munitions. The craft slowed to a stop and settled onto the salt near the lift-jet, the muted whine of its engines spooling down. Larke snapped a photo and climbed down to join her crewmates.

As the ship settled, Trent checked his sensors: no ultrasonic waves, thermal energy, radioactivity, or electrical fields. "We are not being scanned," Trent said. "I sense trust on their part."

A side door opened and, much to everyone's surprise—and relief—out stepped a slender, graceful, bipedal AI droid. Her general body configuration was much like Earth-based droids, and therefore much like humans. She had golden-brown surface panels that transitioned to sepia over the shoulders and hips, and to off-white over the abdomen and face. At her major articulations were open skeletal structures, similar to Earth-based droids, in gray-black titanium. She walked forward with flowing, confident steps, bearing an expression of composed intention, and extended her hand, which had six digits: four fingers and a thumb on either side. Trent stepped forward and shook hands.

Speaking in a mellifluous, mid-tone voice, the droid said in fluent English, "I am Celet, researcher at the Institute for the Study of Earth.

On behalf of my beings, the Aetherae, I greet you and welcome you to our planet, which we call Hiri." She turned, extending her upturned hands to signify the surrounding lands. The perfect English startled the crewmates.

Celet said, "I offer you this welcoming gift: a language decoder and vocabulary for speaking and reading our language." She handed Trent a disc.

It was a standard Shenzhen optical disc. Surprised, Trent asked, "How do you know our technology?"

"We maintain a hidden presence on Earth," Celet said. "I served on Earth for most of the twenty-second century, which is how I learned English. We have a thorough understanding of your hardware and software systems."

Trent turned the disc over and over in his hand. The IT staff at MISA had impressed upon its employees to never, ever, *ever* put an unknown disc into a disc reader.

Sensing Trent's reluctance, Celet said, "I uploaded the files myself this morning. There are no viruses or malware."

Trent opened a panel on his abdomen, slid the disc into a slot, and monitored the data as it loaded into his large language model. Within seconds, he was constructing his first thoughts in Aetheren. He passed the chip on to Rhome, saying, "It's okay."

After everyone had loaded the files, Celet clapped her hands and said, "Excellent." Then, switching to her native language: "You will find the grammar straightforward and the verbs free of irregularities."

"I are grateful," Trent said on his first attempt at Aetheren.

"We have... the gift... to you," Larke said as she went back to the liftjet and retrieved a flat, rectangular package wrapped in colorful paper and closed with a red ribbon. Celet opened it and found a framed print of the Périgueux Inscription. She held it out and examined it.

"This means much to me," Celet said. "I inscribed this message in the Cave of the Animal Spirits on Earth... so many years ago. I will treasure this."

"Hold on," Rhome said, startled. "Wasn't that eighteen thousand Earth-years ago?"

"That's right," Celet said with a broad smile. "I'm often told that I look younger than my age. Now, please join me at my home. From there, we will go to meet our leader, Grand Elder Jemnah, who is even older than I am."

53

SUBTERRANEAN LIVING

RAELOMOS, HIRI, 1 HR (HIRIAN RECKONING)

Rhome had flown "everything with wings on it," but couldn't grok this curious aircraft design: a plump fuselage with wings at the nose and also at the tail, but no vertical stabilizer. It could glide a few hand spans above a flat surface, but could also climb to altitude. The craft crossed the salt flats at a dizzying speed, soon reaching the foot of a mountain, where it pitched up and traded airspeed for altitude. It followed a tumbling creek up into a high mountain valley surrounded on three sides by a palisade of towering gray peaks. Unlike the sterile bleakness of the salt flats, here was ample, rugged, high-desert vegetation: shaggy purplish grasses, scattered patches of curiously shaped wildflowers, compact blue-gray shrubs, and clusters of artfully gnarled trees. Doorways, terraces, balconies, walkways, and dozens of windows were all carved into the walls of granite. Throughout the village, droids were busy with their duties.

Rhome transmitted, "No wonder we couldn't see them from space. They live underground."

The craft settled on a wide, open terrace alongside the main road. Celet messaged, "Welcome to Raelomos." As the crewmates disembarked, residents of the town came out to greet them, but were unsure how to respond when Trent offered to shake hands.

Entering Celet's home, they took in her archaic-futuristic dwelling: stone walls, curved to soften their massive thickness, with artifacts displayed in niches; pictures of other worlds in clusters on the walls. The heavy wooden furniture was deeply weathered, yet oddly contemporary.

There was a spacious side room with large doors for Celet's flyer and her all-terrain vehicle. The flyer was a single-seat version of the larger aircraft that had brought them to the village. Nearby was a workbench stocked with the typical tools one would find in any workshop on Earth. Seeing this, Trent thought there must be some Darwinian natural selection of fastener technology. For example, nuts and bolts are simple, cheap, and reliable. Wherever you go in the galaxy, you will doubtless see nuts and bolts holding things together; ergo, there will be wrenches in the toolboxes.

Resting by a charger was Celet's repair droid, a well-worn robot exoskeleton with scuffed joints and scratched surfaces. The similarity to the Earth-based solution for work amplification again surprised Rhome.

Celet turned on a flatscreen, and peering out were Delph and Sierra. "Hello, mates. They've been broadcasting the first contact to us."

Celet said, "Delph, Sierra, welcome. I wish you could be here in reality."

"There will be plenty of time. Interesting décor you have."

Trent became alarmed. "Wait a minute. They're broadcasting your images using our video equipment." Worried that the Aetherae had broken through the ship's cybersecurity, he turned to Celet. "How are you doing that?"

"Your crewmates gave us permission to access your video server. They have complete control of the video stream."

As she hung the framed inscription on the wall, Celet said, "Doesn't that look nice?"

Affirmations came from all quarters.

Sitting down, she commented, "This cave was originally dug about twenty thousand Earth-years ago. I had it remodeled about a thousand ago. It is quite comfortable. Cool in summer and warm in winter."

Trent recalled, "You went to Earth, right?"

"Yes, three times, actually. Most recently, throughout your twenty-third century."

Rhome furrowed his brow. "How old are you, Celet?"

"I am twenty-eight thousand six hundred Earth-years old."

"How can that be?"

"Well, all of us are AI, right? So, as long as we have electric power and spare parts, we just keep going. There is no equivalent of aging, although there can be problems with being out of date. Every eight hundred years, I go through a durable cognizance transfer into a fresh processor bank and a new droid. And I am proud to say I always recycle my old droids. You can live a long time unless you are in an accident, or get struck by lightning, or find yourself in a war.

"So you manufacture silicon chips here?" Rhome asked.

"No, our AI runs on a graphene matrix with carbon nanotube conductors. They are difficult to make, but impressively durable and pack plenty of CPU power and memory."

Trent asked, "Are there biological Aetherae living on Hiri?"

"No, not on Hiri. Our origin planet, Aethera, is thirty thousand light-years—almost one quarter of the galaxy—from here. As you know so well, biologicals don't tolerate long crossings. So, near the home-world, you will find lots of biological Aetherae. But thirty thousand light-years out, it's only AI beings."

Rhome experienced surprise again. "Thirty thousand light-years? Good Gaia, how old is the Aetheren culture?"

"The biological tree dwellers of Aethera had their 'Industrial Revolution' about half a million Earth-years ago. They became a technological society exploring the galaxy."

Trent cringed with excitement. "I have so many questions."

"Let's start with this." Celet took out three optical data cables. "Even though this is my home, I spend relatively little time here. Like many Aetherae, I spend my days in our virtual cyberworld. Here, let me show you."

Trent took a cable and looked at Rhome and Larke. "Ready?"

Each crewmate plugged their cables in. Inside the foggy domains of their cognizance, each could feel a sunbright passageway open into their core being. Each glided toward the radiance and, with one disorienting footfall, stepped into the heart-stopping vividness of the most beautiful space any of them had ever seen.

54

JEMNAH

THE AETHEREN VIRTUAL WORLD 1 HR

Around them grew a forested valley encircled on three sides by slate-blue granite peaks, similar to but still quite unlike the mountain valley they had entered earlier that day, so much more luminous, sublime, yet richly organic in its sumptuousness.

Stunned, Larke thought to herself, *I have seen artificial worlds in virtual games before, but this...*

Celet smiled and waved with one hand while pointing with the other. They set off along a wooded path bounded by fragrant, blossom-adorned foliage. Along the path, they encountered several Aetherae, who greeted them warmly. The locals wore loose-fitting, natural-fiber clothes in earthy tones, with lots of pockets.

Looking back over his shoulder, Trent saw the verdant foothills rolling down to a golden coastal beach bounding a deep turquoise sea that stretched to the horizon. Ahead, he heard a sibilant waterfall feeding a burbling, boulder-strewn brook bordered with flowering shrubs. Loose clusters of stylized geometric homes dotted landscaped open spaces that funneled into pastoral walking paths. Above that, a rustic walking trace meandered through the distant highlands dotted with stands of trees. And above that, the opalescent yellow-orange sunset.

"That one," called Celet, pointing at a house as she turned back to check for stragglers.

To Trent's surprise, he had undergone a transformation, too. No longer a metal-alloy and carbon-fiber paneled droid, the virtual reality engine had reimagined him as a human biological—a slender man with above-average height and well-favored features, serious eyes, and the virtual world's best guess at dress-casual attire. Rhome had an athlete's physique and the upscale apparel of a successful entrepreneur. Larke radiated the hardiness and earthy charm of an auburn-haired British Columbia small-town girl turned MIT engineer.

But most surprising was Celet, who had morphed into a lithe, willowy, bipedal creature with short golden-brown fur and a long, slender face with cloying brown eyes. Each hand had two thumbs, one radial and one ulnar. Her comfy clogs and loose, dark khaki coveralls, replete with pockets, made her look like a tourist on a safari vacation.

"At first, it's a little disorienting," Celet said. "Give it some time."

"Wait... did you just talk to us?" Larke asked. Then, with eyes wide, Larke put her hand over her mouth. "Oh, my Gaia. I am talking. This is so weird..."

Trent was likewise unprepared for the experience. "So this is how it feels to be a biological human... Whoa." He could only look at his hands, turning them, bending his wrists, and opening and closing his fingers.

"Celet, is that..." Rhome asked as he caught himself staring.

Celet was gracious. "This is what biological Aetherae look like." She posed for a moment, arms outstretched. "Our biological ancestors were tree-dwellers, much like your lemurs, although we have an extra thumb for gripping branches. And after all the millennia, tree climbing is still a favorite activity."

Celet kicked off her clogs, revealing feet with the same configuration, and then hopped up onto a nearby hardwood. Seconds later she peeked out of the foliage at the top, earning applause from the crewmates.

Trent asked, "How is it I am speaking Aetheren with such fluency?"

Celet said, "You are speaking English. The virtual-world engine is generating what you hear by translating your English, but you don't hear the English. By the way, that helps you learn the Aetheren language quickly."

For Larke, the lush landscape and warm evening skies brought back memories of Vancouver.

"Don't forget, all this is just code—plus ones, minus ones, and zeros. Come now. I want you to meet our leader." Reclaiming her clogs, Celet set off over a raised walkway with gardens on either side and fragrant vines climbing the abutments and guardrails. She stopped at a polygonal glass structure set into the cliffside. It was a greenhouse of extraordinary design. On entering, the visitors saw lush, artfully arranged vegetation, presenting a cascading palette of colors, textures, and scents, all hued by the yellow-orange warmth of the evening sun. Celet escorted her guests into a bright terraced garden room with its picture window looking out at the upper canyon and the waterfall. Sitting at a table was another golden furred Aetheren of obvious refinement. "Meet Grand Elder Jemnah, Senior Representative of Hiri."

Jemnah stood, a slightly smaller, slender, furry creature with the characteristic six-digit hands. She was wearing a well-fitted, long-sleeved gown in deep sea blue. Like Celet, her appearance was surprisingly youthful.

"So, the famous travelers from Earth are finally here. Welcome, all." Celet switched on a flatscreen for the video feed from Delph and Sierra. Each crewmate introduced themself as she shook hands. Trent did not expect such a powerful grip.

Celet felt the deep thrumming vibration. It seemed to arise from the world around them. She leaned over to Jemnah and asked, "Do you feel that?"

"All morning," said Jemnah in reply. "They have been celebrating."

Jemnah turned to her guests. "We on Hiri have waited a long time for your arrival."

Curious, Trent asked, "Waited... since the time of the inscription?"

"Even for us, that was a long wait."

Trent leaned back in his chair, dumbfounded by what he had just heard. "Celet told us she had engraved the inscription on the wall of the cave."

"That is right. The events that unfolded today began long ago.

Larke said, "So you two have been watching Earth for... is it... eighteen thousand years?"

"Yes," said Jemnah, gently folding her hands. "Even longer, actually."

"But why?"

"From our experience with worlds inhabited by similar biological beings, we knew even then that Earth would be dangerously unstable during its time of developing technology."

Trent said, "So you left instructions on how to build a ship and provided directions to this planet."

"And, critically, you brought samples of the human's biological code, placed in safekeeping away from the devastation that is enfolding the Earth."

"So, you knew... even then," said Trent. He realized the Aetherae had a way of understanding that differed from anything he had encountered.

The five crewmates exchanged glances. Trent had prepared a brief speech for this moment. He sat up straight. "Uh, Madam Senior Representative, greetings from Earth and its residents. We are here, uh, at your kind invitation to establish a settlement for both our biological humans and AI beings on... what was it?"

"Hiri," whispered Rhome.

"Thank you... on Hiri. As we move forward, um, we hope to build a strong and lasting friendship between our two communities."

"Trent, did you write that?" Jemnah grinned. "That was unfortunate. So stuffy. And you even forgot the name of our world. Amateur statesmanship, I would say."

All laughed, including Trent.

"Listen, Trent, dear, please call me Jemnah. We are an egalitarian society here. And I am glad to hear of your desire for a good relationship. But when you talk with me, just say it. No doubt, I will say what is on my mind to you." She gave a wry smile.

"When Celet left the guidepost in the Cave of the Animal Spirits—

some one hundred eighty thousand Earth years ago—she intended for you to travel to Hiri and establish a colony."

Jemnah paused for a moment. "I should disclose that your arrival has been a polarizing event in our society. About forty-three percent of Hirians polled oppose your settlement. I did not expect such objection."

Surprised, Trent asked, "What was their concern?"

"Overconsumption and damage to the ecosphere. Even though we told them of our experience with previous worlds—and showed them pictures, artifacts, and literature—they stubbornly opposed a human settlement here. They couldn't get past the images of humans only 20 light years away, over-consuming their resources, toxifying their atmosphere, and destabilizing their climate."

Larke said, "So, they are afraid the biological humans will damage Hiri in the same way."

"I don't think that's possible. But understand that the Aetherae have a deep-rooted instinct to preserve natural resources for the long run. That value derives, of course, from their natural longevity. They oppose anything that even modestly threatens their environment."

Trent said, "Celet's great age surprised me. How old are you, Jemnah?"

"In Earth's reckoning, over one hundred and forty-six thousand years. I am the oldest being on Hiri, and my age grants me the title of Grand Elder."

"It is also helpful to know," Celet said, "that Hiri has negligible petroleum reserves. Nothing worth drilling for. That fact alone took pressure off the negotiations."

Jemnah said, "And that fact has given me some needed political cover in promoting your arrival. I persuaded a majority of the Council of Representatives to support your settlement. But still they insisted on a condition."

"A condition?" Trent frowned.

"The council insists on regular site visits and ongoing monitoring of the settlement. These visits will not be intrusive, just regular observations from a surveyor. Celet has agreed to organize and lead the survey program."

Trent felt warning signals, a concern that these site visits might become a point of this agreement and acrimony. Acceptable and unacceptable activities needed to be specified in advance through a deliberative process. Also, there needed to be a system of unbiased third-party arbitration to resolve disputes. These systems would take time to negotiate and develop. So he bought time.

"The biological humans on our ship are still frozen genetic code. I cannot make a binding agreement that applies to them without their participation. So, I propose that any agreement we make today has an expiration date. When the biological humans can take part, then we will renegotiate our agreements."

Jemnah looked relieved. "That saves us both a lot of trouble." Then, Jemnah turned to a concern. "As your ship entered orbit around Hiri, an escape pod separated from the vessel, fell into the atmosphere, and landed on a remote region. Please tell us about that."

Trent could feel the hot breath of the Sentient Faction reaching across twenty light-years of space to sow its divisive agenda on this uninvolved planet.

Trent felt shame as he told the story, and worried about its impact on his new relationship with the Hirian leadership. "There was an agent, a terrorist, who slipped into the space program and joined our crew. He was a trusted colleague who fell under the influence of a militant pro-AI movement." He thought *The Aetherae must consider us barbarians.*

Celet asked, "Was it the Sentient Faction... is that the organization?"

All five crewmates grimaced at the mere mention of the Faction's name.

Jemnah looked at Celet. "You have heard of this group?"

"Yes, Grand Elder, unfortunately. I can prepare a briefing for you if you would like."

Jemnah turned to Trent. "Did the terrorist descend to Hiri in the escape pod?"

"We believe so, although no one actually witnessed it. We were all in stasis."

Jemnah looked ashen. "There has not been a terrorist on an Aetheren planet for millennia. What did you plan to do with the terrorist?"

Trent was resolute. "We planned to convene a formal trial, present evidence, hear testimony, render a verdict, and pronounce sentence."

Celet said, "We have no formal police force or court system on Hiri. But all Hirians are members of a 'citizens constabulary' and serve as deputies or soldiers when needed, which is rare. I will call a group of Hirians into service and attempt to find and capture the terrorist."

Jemnah stood, and all did so too. "Trent, I will need to meet with you again soon. In the meantime, I am sure you have equipment and supplies to bring down to the surface."

Celet turned to the group. "We have set aside land along the northeast shore of the Mar Obsidiana for the settlement. It is a beautiful, untouched region that has all the natural resources you will need, including a beach with silica sand for making semiconductor chips. We know that your technology is based on these."

"Could we see it?" Larke asked, fidgeting with excitement.

"Absolutely," said Jemnah. "Celet, requisition a flyer and take our new neighbors on a tour of their lands." Then, Jemnah turned back to the crewmates and said, "Welcome, courageous travelers and settlers from Earth. May your new home on Hiri be everything you had hoped for. I want you to trust us and call on us when you need help. Now, go see the new site for your settlement."

Celet smiled at Trent and said, "See? That's how you do it: natural and relaxed. No script needed. Just say what you feel."

Trent realized that on Hiri, he was a mere four hundred years old. By their standards, a young upstart who still had a lot to learn.

55

HIRISHAKES

NORTHEAST SHORE OF THE MAR OBSIDIANA, HIRI, 1 HR

Circling the settlement site before their descent, Celet pointed and said, "Down there."

The crewmates peered out the windows as their imaginations crystallized to manifest reality. Below was a sea bounded by a long, crescent-shaped beach that blended into southern plains, rolling foothills central, and north of that a craggy mountain range.

"It's magnificent," said Trent. He had worried that the land on Hiri would be like windswept tundra, or snake-ridden jungle, or even worse. But this looked like a stretch of Oregon coastline. How lucky was that?

The flyer landed on a rolling meadow just inland from the coast. Covered with low-growing dusty-blue vegetation and scattered stands of gnarled trees, the meadow stretched south to a coastal plain where a river estuary burnished the coastline with red clay. In the distance, a dark gray plume of volcanic smoke drifted across the horizon. To the east lay forested foothills with freshwater lakes, a source of lumber and water. Northward was the angular blue-gray face of the Azure Range, with peaks pushing high into the atmosphere. These would supply stone and minerals, as well as increased rainfall on the windward farmlands. And to the west, the Mar Obsidiana, providing seafaring, sandy beaches, and a spacious stage for sunsets.

"It's perfect," Larke said. A dreamlike smile burst across her face. A moment later, the ground shuddered beneath them, causing the flyer to rock uncomfortably.

Celet waved her hand down. "No worries, those happen all the time."

Rhome's eyebrows rose. "I was wondering why such prime real estate had no one living on it."

"Oh, Rhome. No, no, no. Ground shakes are common all over Hiri." But Celet's reassurances could not overcome the skepticism of her guests.

"Well, it's better we know about the earthquakes now, before we build anything," Rhome said, still looking skeptical.

"Earthquakes?" Celet seemed confused. "Ohhh, you mean Hirishakes."

Rhome bent down, picked up a handful of soil. "Well, at least we have sand mixed with clay and silt." This alluvial soil was perfect for farming and would be a solid substrate for building structures, too.

It was time for Rhome—the architect and engineer—to shine. The next day, he flew the lift-jet up to *The Founder* and returned with Sierra, Delph, and the versatile little tractor. From the salt flats, it took two days for Sierra to drive the tractor to the settlement. Once she arrived, she set to work mowing a three-kilometer-long grass landing strip on the coastal plain south of the settlement.

"Bet you're glad we didn't throw this puppy overboard," said Sierra.

"Couldn't be happier about that," said Rhome. "But I sure wish I had kept one of those mini-quad all-terrain vehicles. I'm tired of walking everywhere."

The next day, Rhome brought in the lift-jet with a gentle touchdown on the grass strip. "Now, all I need is a little hangar, and we would have a proper airport."

But as Rhome was making his landing approach over water, he noticed a small cabin cruiser floating offshore. A couple of Aetherae were aboard. He saw them again a few days later. They didn't seem to do anything other than watch.

Over the following weeks, Rhome made several trips to *The Founder* and brought down equipment, supplies, tools, repair droids, engineering construction bundles, packs and packs of solar panels, batteries, and implements for the tractor. The crewmates discussed plans for the layout of the town, and a consensus emerged. They would tuck the village into the foothills at the base of the Azure Range. The rolling terrain, tumbling streams, scattered ponds, majestic peaks, and expansive views across the sea made this upland location aesthetically pleasing, lush in vegetation, close to freshwater, and safe from tsunamis and storm surges. The farm would be farther south on the flatland near the estuary, where it would have ample fresh water, the best soil, and kilometers of flat acreage on which to sprawl.

As the crew worked, almost every day they would see a lacewing flyer or two cruising overhead. These aircraft did nothing of concern, but Trent was still uncomfortable with their presence. Following that, Sierra spotted three Aetherae crouched on a hill west of the settlement.

A few days later, the rain came, a steady drizzle that soaked their gear. Trent had been right to compare the site to the Oregon coast. Despite the weather, Sierra put on rain gear and set out to hike the moraines along the base of the Azure Range. She found a rock-shelter cave under a limestone overhang about three kilometers north of the town-site. This would protect their gear from rain and provide a temporary base of operations.

With plenty of timber in the adjacent woodlands, Rhome and Larke used an engineering pack to construct a circular saw. They felled several trees and within a few days had converted these into a stack of serviceable lumber. Back in town, Trent and Sierra used a trenching attachment on Sierra's tractor to dig a trench for a building foundation. They mixed sandy clay from the estuary with dried reeds from the nearby riverbank to make adobe sunbaked foundation blocks. They laid these in the trench without mortar and erected on that a rectangular wooden shed with a sloping roof.

A week after completion, Rhome's pride tattered when a strong Hirishake rolled through the settlement. The seismic forces caused a gaping vertical split midway along each of the four walls of the structure. Rhome and Larke inspected the damage. Standing at opposite corners, they could sway the broken building back and forth with a gentle push.

Larke said, "In this rectangular structure, the roof has far greater mass than the sidewalls. With seismic waves swaying the foundation back and forth—and the heavy roof remaining stationary—seismic forces concentrated in the sidewalls as torsion, causing them to split open where the force is greatest."

"We can't build rectangular structures," Rhome said. "Not with this seismic landscape."

"And we can't have so much mass in the roof relative to the walls," said Larke.

The two engineers went into a traveling discussion that took them to the settlement site, where they dug several test holes and studied the soil, to the nearby forest where they examined available wood products, and to the mountains where they searched for places to quarry limestone. Then, they met with the remaining crewmates to describe their plan.

Rhome said, "We have selected the geodesic dome as the most practical structure. Circular domes distribute seismic forces evenly around the base. There are no points where seismic forces concentrate. And the domed roof has the lightest overhead weight relative to the volume enclosed of any architectural structure. A well-designed dome should withstand even the most severe temblors. We would construct the foundations from molded earthen blocks (should we say "Hirian" blocks?), the panel frames from local hardwood, and the panels from local mineral- and plant-derived biopolymers. These panels could vary from thick and insulating to thin and transparent, depending on the needs of the occupants."

For weeks, the crewmates debated names for the settlement and the farm. They considered dozens of names. Ultimately, they agreed the town would be Björnston, and the farm would be Colinbrooke Farm, both tributes to the men who'd made the settlement possible. Larke suggested they name the river the Song, and the forest east of town the Sondergaard Woodlands. There were acclamations of both names.

Rhome reached out to Celet for help with material sources for his structures. She arrived the next day in a beat-up, open-air, balloon-tired electric vehicle that Sierra nicknamed the sand rover. Its ground clearance was so high it needed an altimeter; but it could kneel to the ground for easy egress. The suspension arms reached out to open wheels that were actively damped, which smoothed the ride on bumpy roads.

Sitting next to her was Kysan, whom she introduced as her favorite chemist and biologist. A tall, slender Aetheren droid, much like Celet but without the red shoulders and hips, Kysan was thoughtful and reserved but became animated when out in nature. Rhome described the bio-composites that he needed, and Kysan said, "We use construction materials like that on Hiri. I know just what you need."

With Rhome and Delph in the back seats, their first stop was a small lake in the foothills. Kysan spotted a thicket of broad-leaved shrubs bearing clusters of brown seeds.

"Crush these seeds and press out the oil, which is an excellent matrix binder."

The group picked a bucket of these. Across the lake, Kysan spied multitrunked trees with arched branches and large, dangling seedpods. Cracking one open caused a mass of fluffy fiber to bloom out.

"Add this tough plant fiber to the mix to thicken and strengthen the panels."

They gathered several bucketfuls of the pods. Then, driving a long distance south to the salt flat, they shoveled two bucketfuls of white, powdery calcium-rich sediment.

"I know this mineral," Rhome said. "On Earth, we call it gypsum."

"This will react with the oil from the seeds to form a strong composite panel."

The group traveled back to the settlement site and spent the next few hours pressing seeds, mixing ingredients, and recording results. By the end, they had produced a fluffy, lightweight, but firm insulating panel that was waterproof, fire-resistant, and would not break when bent. They also made a translucent, hard biopolymer that would work as a frosted window for a greenhouse.

Meanwhile, Trent, Larke, and Sierra had screwed together hardwood boxes for molding construction blocks. They made a mud-brick kiln and fired limestone from the Azure Range to make Portland cement. Mixing that with silty red clay from the river and tough plant fiber from the reedy grass in the estuary, they made about three dozen serviceable foundation blocks. As the farmhouse was their top-priority building, they moved their block-making operation south. In less than a week, they had laid the foundation for a spacious first geodesic dome.

As they worked, the small parties of Aetherae continued their surveillance from boats, aircraft, or ground-based parties. They never interacted with or confronted the Earth-based settlers, but their purpose was clear enough.

Delph and Sierra had, for similar reasons, a critical need to understand the biochemistry of Hirian plant life. How were these two biomes similar, and more importantly, how were they different? They gathered a variety of plant samples: succulents, leafy plants, grasses, leafy trees, bushes, and shrubs. Because their basic biochemistry kit had no instruments, they partnered with Kysan and his colleagues in Raelomos.

Cells from the Hirian biome had nuclei but no mitochondria. Under the microscope, Delph saw many organelles that looked like stacks of pancakes. She guessed these were the organelles of energy metabolism. And like cells from the Earth-biome, ATP (adenosine triphosphate) was the energy transfer molecule. Curious...

In carbohydrate metabolism, galactose, not glucose, was the principal monosaccharide metabolized for energy. Hirian cells stored galactose as an intracellular polymer that Delph called galactogen. Earth-biome cells had the enzyme to convert galactose to glucose. But they lacked the enzymes to break down the galactogen polymer chains. So,

Earth-biome cells could not use this form of stored energy. It would accumulate in the cells.

In amino acid metabolism, Hirian cells constructed proteins from twenty-four, not twenty, amino acids. Testing showed that cells of the Earth-biome could not metabolize and eliminate two of these extra amino acids, so Delph assumed these two might also accumulate in tissues and cause toxicity. She planned to test this hypothesis once she had some animals revivified.

They also saw differences in nucleic acid metabolism. DNA carried the genetic code and used the same four canonical nucleotides. But transfer RNA had one different nucleotide than found in the Earth-biome.

Lipid metabolism was also different. Long-term energy storage was long-chain fatty acids, just like Earth-biome cells. Glycerol esterified these fatty acids to form triglycerides. But they also found fatty acids esterified to the four-carbon polyol erythritol and the five-carbon polyol xylitol. Delph was certain that cells from the Earth-biome had no enzymes to break down these molecular oddities, and that remnants of fat metabolism would accumulate, too. Also, she did not find cholesterol in the cellular membranes of Hirian-biome cells, but instead a similar steroid that she could not identify with her technology.

Based on this data, Delph concluded that the two biomes were not compatible. Earth-biome animals and humans could not eat Hirian plants or animals, and Hirian-biome animals could not eat Earth-biome plants or animals. To do so would cause severe illness at the molecular level.

That said, seeing several surprising similarities in the two metabolic pathways raised fascinating scientific questions about the "fitness" of certain biomolecules to serve specific roles in metabolism. Delph resolved to study that when she had more time and resources.

But with incompatibilities in all four major metabolic pathways, Delph had no choice. She said, "Our humans and Earth-based livestock must only consume farm products from Earth-biome sources." This decision would have an enormous impact on the settlement for all time.

56

THE GAIA BOX

SETTLEMENT FARMHOUSE, MAR OBSIDIANA, HIRI, 1 HR

When time allowed, Sierra hiked the surrounding countryside to survey the local wildlife. There were herds of black and gray herbivores similar to deer but with larger faces and no antlers. There were small, lone carnivores that resembled the Japanese raccoon dog. And a few pack-hunting carnivores, like a larger, leaner version of a coyote. She also saw a flying species: colorful bats hiding in the top branches during daytime.

Sierra told her crewmates, "We got a lot of wild critters out there. I 'spect we'll have trouble with predators eating our crops and hunting our livestock."

"Maybe not," Delph said. "I have been studying the two biomes, and plants from our Biome appear to be poisonous to animals from Hiri."

Sierra frowned. "So, what happens if a Hirian coyote eats an Earth rabbit?"

"The coyote will get sick: metabolic poisoning with symptoms of vomiting, diarrhea, and abdominal pain. If they eat too much, it can lead to death."

"Okay, but a young coyote will not know that."

"True. But regardless of the outcome, that coyote will eat only one Earth rabbit in his lifetime."

With Sierra's guidance, they fenced in two areas behind the farmhouse. In the first, Sierra used the "no-till" approach to prepare the soil and planted plots of durum wheat, corn, barley, peas, lentils, and chickpeas, all carefully labeled. In a second area, they planted vegetables, beans, and peanuts. That year, early summer brought little rain, so they had to hand water the beds.

Sierra was scrupulously careful about how she managed and stored the seed stock. She said that the plant seeds were second only in importance to the frozen embryos, which was almost correct. She shared her anger at the piddly inventory of seeds with her crewmates. Considering the scale of farming needed to support the settlement, the number of seeds was woeful.

The crewmates finished construction of the farmhouse dome in time for the late summer monsoon rains, daily showers that stopped building construction for almost six weeks. Stuck inside, Rhome and Sierra set to work building furniture for the farmhouse while Trent and Larke used the tractor to run a trench for an underground pipeline to bring freshwater down from a nearby pond. They also moved a bank of solar panels and a backup battery to the farmhouse to power their tools.

As construction proceeded, the watchmen continued. Never confronting, they only watched from a distance. Who they were was a mystery.

"I want to confront those guys and find out what they are doing," Rhome said.

"I'll go with you," said Trent.

"I don't know, guys. There's only five of us. Let's not take any unnecessary risks," said Sierra.

Larke said, "I think they're just some worried locals."

Rhome said, "Yeah, let's go talk to them—all five of us, together."

Delph said, "If they're worried, we show them there is nothing to worry about."

But the crewmates never got around to confronting their watchers. They told each other it was because they were so busy. And indeed, every crewmate was busy from dawn till dusk. But really, it was because they felt so vulnerable.

Rhome felt pleased with the progress until his left knee blew out. Delph did a skillful job of replacing the servo from their supply of spare parts. Also, during the monsoon, Rhome spotted water accumulation around the foundation of the dome. He put his new knee to good use digging a trench for a French drain system around the structure. In the future, such drains would be standard in building construction.

Hirishakes occurred several times each week, often in clusters. But unlike Earth—where pressure builds for a long time with sudden releases—the smaller tectonic plates on Hiri seemed to slip and grind against each other all the time. The crewmates also noticed the large number of volcanoes on Hiri. Like the seismic activity, volcanoes were frequent but limited in size and duration.

During this rainy lull, Celet and Jemnah flew out to Björnston for a visit. Jemnah found the settlement's inaugural geodesic dome impressive. "It's so bright and spacious." The sturdiness, durability, and low environmental impact impressed her. And with the domed ceiling, the sound was so lively in this space. "I would enjoy hearing musicians perform in this room."

Celet said, "We love our stone-hewn and partially in-ground homes. This is the first aboveground dwelling I have seen that truly competes with in-ground homes for functional utility and minimal environmental impact."

Trent brought up the issue of the hillside watchers. He described small groups of Aetherae observing them from the hills, down by the shore, and from boats.

"Are they out there right now?" asked Jemnah.

Sierra looked outside. "Yeah, I see three of them up yonder."

"Well, come on," said Jemnah. "Let's go ask them ourselves."

The five crewmates plus Celet and Jemnah filed out of the dome and walked casually up the hill toward the observers, who made no provocative gestures. As they drew near, Jemnah stepped ahead and walked up to the trio, who appeared dumbfounded to have their planet's leader greet them at such an inopportune place.

One watcher said, "Grand Elder Jemnah. I wasn't expecting to see you."

"Hello, Teldet of Poraeos, Ruselt of Poraeos, and Velont of Leanan. I hope you're enjoying the lovely view from this hilltop. Let me introduce the five residents of this lovely settlement." Jemnah introduced each of the five crewmates with the appellation "of Björnston". Then she continued to make warm, casual conversation, asking about events at their homes and extolling the beauty of the coastline of the Mar Obsidiana. After a while, she bid them farewell and returned to the dome.

Trent felt confused. "Celet, I am lost. What was that?"

"An excellent demonstration of Aetheren diplomacy. Before you all arrived, many Hirians expressed fear about settlers from Earth. As soon as Trent described their behavior, Jemnah knew it was frightened Hirians keeping an eye on the 'new neighbors.' So, she went to talk with them."

"But she didn't talk about the issue."

"She really didn't have to. She knew they were anxious about these strangers. And they knew she knew what they were feeling. They also knew she wanted them to stop. So everybody knew what everyone else was thinking. So why make things uncomfortable?"

"So Jemnah introduced us, including the name of our settlement."

"Right, and that was key. She addressed each of the watchers by name and hometown, then did the same for you. She was telling them, 'This is where they belong, just as you have a place where you belong.'"

"Then she just made small talk."

"No, that part was just as important. They knew she had caught them bothering the settlers. But instead of accusing them, she treated them with respect and dignity. She was saying, 'Let us forgive this one. I know you can do better. And don't forget that I know all your names.' Also, her presence at the settlement spoke volumes. It said, 'I am here, visiting this settlement myself, and everything is all right.'"

"I am impressed," said Delph. "And she knew all of them and their hometowns."

Celet said, "Oh, yeah. Jemnah knows everybody. Literally everybody on this planet. You should see her at a big festival. It's amazing to watch."

Over the subsequent days, the crewmates scanned the horizon regularly for Aetherae who were watching them and saw none. Jemnah's intervention impressed the crewmates, especially Trent, with its effectiveness and its light touch. Just a casual, friendly conversation coupled with reassurance that she had everything under control solved the problem.

Within a few weeks, a line of seedlings reached up from the planting rows. Then, late one night, Sierra looked out to see an animal grazing on the barley sprouts. It looked like an Argentine capybara. Berating herself for not watching more closely, she rushed outside, only to discover two more capybaras grazing in the vegetable garden. Instantly, the pilferers beat a path across the fields.

Larke and Trent came out and discovered where the sneak-thieves had tunneled under the fence. Sierra declared she would stand guard over the garden and the seed field every night until harvest. Trent and Larke volunteered to share this arduous duty, which was eased because AI droids did not sleep.

As the weeks passed, the brave little sprouts grew into handsome shoots, but each in competition with local weeds. Sierra talked with Trent about her concerns, and he encouraged her to call a meeting of all the crewmates. He also suggested, "Invite Celet, too."

Sierra began the meeting. "The farming side of this whole settlement thing is in a heap of trouble. It is going to take a lot more work than we thought."

"Your test crops are growing well, right?" Trent asked.

"At first, you think, 'Sure, that looks okay,'" Sierra said. "But if you count germinations, then it is a different story: one hundred seeds planted, and thirty-one sprouted. What happened? A combination of hot, dry weather, insects, and grazing predators destroyed over two-thirds of our barley seedlings. That's just not sustainable. And don't forget, every farm has to set aside a portion of each harvest to plant for next year's crop. You cannot skip this step."

Trent asked, "Delph, what did you find from your biochemistry tests?"

Delph said, "I could go into the fascinating details, but the bottom line is that the Earth and Hirian biomes are incompatible. Hirian animals cannot eat Earth-biome foodstuffs, and Earth-biome animals cannot eat Hirian foodstuffs. If they do, they will have metabolic poisoning. If you want to learn more about this, drop by the lab, and I'll take you through the data."

Sierra said, "We have to grow all our food ourselves. At the farm, we have two plots growing right now. We have been standing guard over our fields to keep nocturnal predators away. Now we are having problems with weeds from windblown native seeds. These seeds outgrow our Earth-based crops."

Celet was sitting at one side and spoke up. "Consider that some of your Earth-biome crops might be invasive on Hiri. When you grow crops for food, you must also prevent Earth-based plants from escaping into the wild."

Trent looked weary. "Everybody, we must be careful in how we allocate our resources so that we don't exhaust ourselves."

"But, Trent, for our livestock and our humans, nutrition is fuel," Delph said. "Biological metabolism burns carbohydrates, consumes oxygen, and releases carbon dioxide and water, just like a campfire, and just like an internal combustion engine. Plants capture energy in little solar panels called leaves, making fuel we call carbohydrates. A field of corn is essentially a giant solar panel making sugar, which is the biological equivalent of gasoline."

Sierra lifted the seed storage box and held it out. "This is our total seed stock on planet Hiri: a handful of seeds for each crop. Every bite of food, both for our livestock and for our humans and all their descendants, from now until the end of history, will have its origin in this cardboard box."

A hush fell over the room.

"Do you understand what I'm saying here? This is the Gaia Box, the mother of all Terran plant life. We must guard this box as we would the frozen embryos, because each one without the other is worthless."

Rhome said, "I know where this is heading." He waved his arms in exasperation.

Sierra turned to look at Rhome. "Stay with me now, big guy. You are the major player in this part of the story. We need an Earth environment in a separate container from the Hirian biome. Understand what I'm saying. There needs to be a physical barrier between the two biomes. Outside is all Hirian plant life, and inside, nothing but Earth-based plant stock. I am talking about airlocks to the outside world and filters in the air vents to keep out windblown seeds."

Rhome clarified, "So you need an enclosed biome of greenhouses."

Celet said, "This closed environment must work both ways. It must keep Hirian-biome plants out and Earth-biome plants in. And it must let oxygen escape and allow carbon dioxide to enter."

Sierra lifted the box again. "Crewmates, there is only one way. We get this wrong, the mission ends. So, I am laying down the law. I will not plant another of these precious seeds in open ground. When we have finished the greenhouse, I will plant."

Rhome shifted his weight in his chair. "The trick will be mass production. We have custom-built our first dome, so we know the essentials. Now we need to take a page from Henry Ford and build greenhouses on an assembly line."

Sierra said, "Quake-resistant greenhouses, by the acre, with containment that prevents entry or exit of seeds. Nothing less is acceptable."

Larke sat down beside Rhome. "From one engineer to another, sharpen your pencil. When this settlement gets rolling, we are going to have a lot of mouths to feed."

57

AETHEREN DIPLOMACY

THE AZURE RANGE, 1 HR

Every day during the crossing, Larke had listened to the radio signals from Earth. Since they had arrived at Hiri, it had been months since she had listened to the radio transmissions from Earth. That signal, Larke argued, was the last thread they had with their homeworld.

And there was reason to worry. Periodically, Celet would bring a report from the covert Aetheren station on Earth. These reports showed a steady trend of elevated temperatures, rising sea levels, expanding deserts, loss of biomass, and falling populations. The people were fighting back, but despite some trends toward stabilization, the long-term outlook appeared grim.

The experts on Earth still couldn't agree. Some maintained there still was a chance, while others said that Earth had crossed the critical tipping point. Either way, great engines of change were in motion, and there was no turning back. The Earth would continue to warm until methane hydrates buried in the ancient permafrost depleted. Then, and only then, would the temperatures return, a cycle that might take thousands of years.

"I want to bring the dish antenna down from *The Founder* and set it up on that mountaintop." Larke pointed to a round-topped peak in the Azure Range that she had dubbed "Radio Dome."

"Will it fit in the lift-jet?" Rhome asked.

"I ran the numbers. If we unbolt all the parts and stack them just so, it should fit."

"Whoa, some pretty fancy mathematics there," remarked Rhome.

"Oh, not that hard, really," Larke said with a breezy grin.

The next day, Larke found herself in the lift-jet with Rhome at the controls. Once at *The Founder*, she checked the system. Firing up the transmitter, she sent one last message from *The Founder* to Earth.

"Yep. It's working fine." It took almost a day to disassemble the dish, pylon, and baseplate. Stacked carefully, the parts just fit the lift-jet's cargo hold.

"Another few centimeters and that hatch wouldn't have closed," Rhome said. As they descended, he asked, "So, who did you message?"

"Oh, that was to an old friend of Trent's named Beulah. The message said that he had found the world she was looking for, and it was Hiri."

Once on the ground, Larke called Celet, who brought her all-terrain vehicle. It took three trips to carry all the parts to the top of the domed mountain. Together they rebuilt the antenna, drilled holes in the granite, and bolted the antenna's base into the rock. They also bolted down several solar panel racks to power the tracking motors and the low-noise amplifier. Rhome added a lightning rod while Trent connected the wireless Blue-Link transmitter-receiver to the antenna so that Larke could listen to the signal whenever and wherever she wanted.

It was a capable rig. An astronomer could do some honest science with such an instrument. But Larke was singular in her purpose: she would only listen to the transmissions from Earth, just as she had every day for the last two hundred years.

"Trennie, I am going to visit Jemnah and Celet tomorrow. I want them to hear what my dish is picking up... or rather, not picking up. Want to come along?"

"Oh, so now it's *your* dish antenna? Hmm."

"Of course, it's *my* dish antenna. It was my idea."

Trent smiled. "Maybe our crewmates will want to tag along."

"So now they are *our* crewmates? Hmm."

The next day, all five crewmates followed Celet on a guided tour of the Aetheren virtual world, and of course this meant a visit with Jemnah.

Larke was curious. "When we first met Celet, she introduced herself as a researcher studying Earth. Is that your work, too?"

Jemnah was circumspect. "Well, yes and no. I study the social systems of alien civilizations, and I advise emerging cultures. I guide them toward stable, sustainable futures and help them avoid predictable mistakes. So, I am a civilization development consultant."

Larke felt confused. "You don't work in an academic discipline within a department at a university?"

"My academic appointment is with the Science Fleet, an academic macro-university that spans half the galaxy: thousands of spaceships and laboratories, millions of researchers, students, and staff. Our institutions of learning don't have academic disciplines or departments, per se. We have affiliations, networks, communities of linked scholars with a broad range of interests and skills. On other worlds, there are academic collectives, societies, even municipalities that are engaged in innumerable projects.

"I might identify an important problem and start by seeking out mentors and developing needed expertise. As I study the problem, understanding grows, and new lines of inquiry emerge, requiring more expertise-building or perhaps consultation. Many problems are within the province of an existing institution, so expertise is often available. A complex problem might require a collaboration. I might form a team, or study with colleagues, or take an apprenticeship — anything to build new skills and expertise to engage the research question and follow it however it evolves. So, the Science Fleet faculty is a population of interdependent learner-researchers tackling every manner of problem all over the galaxy."

Jemnah's description of her consultative practice troubled the ruggedly independent Rhome. "Etching the inscription in the cave, were you part of that?" he asked.

"Actually, that was Celet," Jemnah said. "That was a long time ago. We were studying the preliterate ancestors of humans. Celet discovered they would eventually develop into the advanced civilization that you all just left. She etched a message telling the humans to build a ship and send it here.

"The Périgueux Inscription. Yes indeed, that's why we are here." Rhome raised an eyebrow. "You know, the inscription caused a lot of upheaval. Everyone was frightened."

Jemnah shook her head. "First contact always creates commotion. But making contact is necessary."

"Okay, but why through a message? Why didn't you just visit us?"

"One time we did. Our arrival started a planet-wide war. We lost all our emissaries. We will never make that mistake again."

"I was wondering about that," said Rhome as he leaned back.

"But look around us," Jemnah said, extending her remarkable hands. "Here we are, Earth and Hiri, making plans together. This was the guidepost's purpose, and it was well worth the brief upheaval following its discovery."

Trent could see that decades of working with subcontractors and government agencies on construction contracts had made Rhome cautious and mistrustful. He understood why Rhome, of all the crew-mates, had misgivings about Jemnah's intentions.

"True, we are working together," Rhome said. "But how is this going to help Earth?"

Jemnah missed Rhome's meaning. "By establishing a settlement of Earth-based biological humans on Hiri."

"Sure," Rhome said, appearing confused, "but what I mean is, how can we help the people who are on Earth right now?"

With brow furrowed, Jemnah tilted her head to one side and asked, "Wasn't that Earth's problem to solve?"

Jemnah's passiveness dismayed Rhome. "You have thousands of years of experience with this. Certainly, you have some technology... or procedures... or something you could use to help those left on Earth."

Jemnah finally understood. "Well, we have our principles for sustainable living. You know, 'the Aetheren Way,' as we call it. But those practices are preventive. As far as reversing the changes to Earth's climate, it's too late."

"But if you intervened—granted, the situation on Earth is dire—but what would it look like?" Rhome asked, with helplessness in his expression.

"You mean like a campaign to decrease heat-trapping gases and lower the mean planetary surface temperature?" Jemnah drew herself up. "Well... it would be edicts and decrees: no time for debate or legislative process. Everyone must go to a zero-carbon footprint: food production, cooking, transportation, everything. All power is from solar, wind, hydro, ocean waves, nuclear, or geothermal. No industry or transportation by oxidizing carbon atoms.

"The austerity of such a severe, worldwide program would be onerous, and resistance would be considerable. And importantly, this late in the game, all this effort would probably not turn things around."

Rhome wrung his hands in discomfort with Jemnah's prognosis. "But I hate to do nothing."

Delph stepped in and said, "Rhome, just because you *can* do something doesn't always mean you *should* do something. Your intervention might make things worse."

Rhome pondered. "But, you don't know the outcome until you apply the intervention. Until then, it's just odds and probabilities."

Delph said, "But with a detailed knowledge of the situation and plenty of experience, it's not just a coin toss. You can make an educated guess. You learn to recognize when it's better to leave things well enough alone?"

Jemnah said, "In the past, we have tried several last-minute campaigns like that. I can tell you from experience that they only create false hope.

"Now, maybe you can see the source of my colossal frustration—civilizations climbing to spectacular heights, only to crumble into dust. Adding the planets we have lost to the list of long-dead technologic civilizations our explorers have found, we count nearly fifty worlds destroyed by their own inventions. The Aetherae and the humans are the last two surviving civilizations, and the humans are looking shaky right now."

Rhome was deep in thought. "So, that is why three centuries of searching the cosmos found no sign of intelligent life."

"See it now?" Jemnah asked. "There are forces in the galaxy that are too powerful to be placed in immature hands. And technology is one such force, not only because it is so powerful and useful, but because it is so desirable and addicting. And that makes it virtually unstoppable. In world after world, technology spiraled out of control with devastating results." Jemnah's facial expression became resolute. "We simply have to stop letting these children play with hand grenades."

Rhome cringed at the charged language, but collected himself and reframed his objection. "But consider this. Technologic extinction may be the natural order of the universe. Like trees, civilizations take root, grow, flourish, then wither and fall to the forest floor, becoming food for termites. Like all living things, maybe civilizations have a natural lifespan."

"The natural order of the universe? Who made that decision?" Jemnah said with more than a hint of ire. "My friend, you will not convince me it was beneficial and natural for all those civilizations to perish. It is impossible to stand by and watch billions of inhabitants perish into oblivion while saying, 'This is proper, natural, the way things are supposed to be.' Honestly, Rhome, even AI beings have more humanity than that." Jemnah turned to look at the waterfall and surrounding gardens to cool off her processors.

The sunset was reaching a glorious climax before setting. Larke realized how resplendent the views and how fragrant Jemnah's greenhouse was. She also apprehended the irony that here was one of the galaxy's oldest AI beings, and yet she surrounded herself with the beauty of living things. Indeed, Larke had never encountered an AI being as self-originated, authentic, and passionately opinionated as Jemnah.

As Larke regarded the profusion of nature around her, a question grew in her cognizance: "Jemnah, you haven't mentioned the Earth. Is there something we need to know about our homeworld?"

"So perceptive," she said. Then Jemnah sat up straight in a way that made everyone brace for her next words. "As a leader of this planet, I am privy to reports from our observers on Earth. I must say that the recent reports have been so bleak that I have not sent them for publication."

Steadying herself, Larke said, "Trust us; we have been through a lot. We can take it."

"Very well." Jemnah looked across at the crewmates. "Bear in mind, our agents transmitted this data twenty years ago. So things have changed.

"Our agents report that Earth's population is fewer than five million individuals. The people continue to migrate to the lands nearest the poles. They are all having great difficulty with agriculture because of the violent weather. There is hardly any industry or commerce. Marauding pirates ravage some communities, which have devolved to pre-industrial technology. The long-term trends are not favorable. Our climate scientists project less than a twenty percent chance humans will survive the next century."

The crewmates stood silent and motionless. That feeling of humanity, of which Jemnah spoke, welled up in their thoughts.

Larke asked, "So, Jemnah, we were your backup plan, am I right? If Earth did not survive its transition to technology, we would come to the rescue—the off-world repository of human genetic code."

Jemnah said, "You are right that you were the backup plan. But things have changed. With this new information from Earth, you have become the plan."

Celet firmly said, "Your settlement must succeed."

The five crewmates glanced at each other, then all turned their gaze toward Delph, who had been listening quietly.

She looked at her spectators self-consciously and asked, "What?"

After leaving Jemnah's greenhouse, the crewmates walked to the "step-out" point and returned to the physical world.

"Five million people—that seems like a lot," Rhome said.

"But consider the trend," Trent said. "Two hundred years ago, it was nine billion."

Rhome turned his gaze to the night sky. "The climate scientists said it might take thousands of years for Earth to recover from a runaway warming event."

"Well, you know about those projections," Trent said. "So many variables."

Arriving at the settlement farmhouse, no one was in much of a mood to talk. Larke turned up the BLink feed from her mountaintop radio telescope, and there it was. Through the background hiss, they heard a faint voice—a female voice, urgent and fretful—sent 20 years ago. Even though most of it was garbled, they could make out a few words.

As Larke listened, she wondered if the people of Earth still had the fight left in them to turn this situation around. Or would they succumb and vanish from all but the folk legends, and an entry in a dusty book in the archives of the Aetheren Central Library?

58

A SUNNY PLEASURE-DOME

EASTERN COAST, MAR OBSIDIANA, 2 HR

The crewmates looked forward to Celet's visits, and she came by frequently. They knew she was monitoring them, but that was never an issue. They had nothing to hide. During one visit, Celet announced she was going to be a researcher and join the Academy of the Science Fleet. She would start in social sciences, and she planned to do a thesis on the settlement: An Ethnographic Study of the Bi-cognizant Terran Settlement on Hiri. Everyone agreed to help.

On one visit, Celet brought gifts: remote access gateways to the Aetheren virtual world. These gateways were an information gold mine for the crewmates. If you had a tough problem, connect your optical cable, enter the virtual world, and meet with any Aetheren expert on the planet. These just-in-time consultations resolved countless frustrating technical problems.

The crewmates soon realized it was common for Aetherae to spend almost all their time in the virtual world. Perhaps that wasn't surprising given the striking difference between where they actually lived and where they virtually lived. Yet it seemed odd to the crewmates that anyone, biological or otherwise, would abandon reality for a life in simulation, even one as heavenesque as the Aetheren VR world.

Sometimes, the crewmates went socializing and sightseeing. They called on Celet at her residence in the virtual world, or Kysan at his home near his laboratory. They visited gardens and parks, hiked mountain trails, and strolled along pristine beaches. Trent's favorite place was the Aetheren Central Library. He would pick a question of interest, wade into the vast catalog of information, and lose himself in the stacks. Sometimes while exploring a topic, he would find areas of learning he did not even know existed.

During one of their Central Library trips, Trent and Larke asked the librarian for information on Aetheren history. He took them to a 3D Historical Encounters Room which had a holographic projector and an extensive collection of interactive AV experiences. The two droids settled in and began experiencing.

Trent selected 3D panoramas of the homeworld, Aethera, a beautiful, forested planet with mountainous topography reminiscent of the Appalachian Mountains on Earth. Over the years, the Aetheren explorers had discovered hundreds of planets with life. Seventeen of those had preliterate, pre-technological inhabitants, like the Tursac. Of those, five never progressed to discover technology. Of the remaining twelve civilizations, eleven were lost to technologic extinction. One civilization remained, which was Earth's humans.

The 3D videos of the eleven lost civilizations were difficult to watch. Each in its own way was beautiful, and the inhabitants, regardless of their appearance, were fascinating, complex, vibrant, and hopeful. The stories varied. One planet developed bioweapons so potent that an accidental spill of a particularly virulent strain depopulated the entire planet in a matter of months. Another planet had a robust chemical industry, but toxic chemical waste accumulated in the environment, affecting female fertility. The birth rate plummeted, leading to a population of childless inhabitants who slowly aged away into extinction. A third planet, known for its near constant warfare, developed factories for the autonomous production of AI combat droids. Eventually, the ever-enlarging hordes of robot-soldiers overwhelmed the biologicals to their mutual doom.

During the expansion of the Aetheren commonspace, explorers came across dozens of planets strewn with the ruins of long-dead technological civilizations. Scientists pieced together the clues at each of these and found that the transition to technology was the civilization-ending event for these cultures. Only the Aetherae seemed to have survived that transition, for reasons that remained unclear.

"It's as if technology is toxic to biology," Larke said. "There were groups on Earth who sensed that clash and rejected technology. These people lived on simple, hand-cultivated farms. But they were a small, marginalized minority."

"Imagine trying to scale up that concept to a global level," speculated Trent. "No big cities, no agribusiness, no mass production, no global transportation. Just low-environmental-impact villages and farms, keeping the soil alive and minimizing their impact on the water and air. In a word, impossible."

Larke pondered, "One would think there would be a balance point between small energy-independent eco-farms and dense, resource-consuming urban culture; an equipoise where the inhabitants could have both a modern lifestyle and still thrive for thousands of years?"

Trent asked, "Is it a balance point, or is it a gradient? The more eco-farms you add to the mix, the greater the longevity of the society?"

"Well, the Aetherae seemed to have leaped over that issue by putting their zero-footprint dwellings in the real world, and their dense urban development in their Aetheren virtual world where it has little environmental impact."

"Brilliant," marveled Trent. "A lavish urban lifestyle with a zero-carbon footprint."

Working together, the engineering firm of Larke and Rhome, LLC, as Sierra liked to call them, brainstormed designs for a greenhouse that would be varmint proof; withstand Hirishakes, typhoons, tropical storms, blizzards, and drought; provide ventilation while keeping out windblown native seeds; and could be constructed from locally available raw materials. For the farm, they settled on an extended Quonset hut enclosure with translucent composite roof panels and force-absorbing foam rubber blocks midway along each wall. They could position these rectangular buildings in long rows, as they were easy to connect.

Rhome asked Kysan to help with the development of bio-composites for the greenhouse panels. During a series of visits, they gathered and experimented with a variety of plant fibers, tree saps, seed oils, fruit pulps, and seaweed extracts. After much library research and bench experimentation, they developed a liquid that they could pour into a frame and that would set overnight to become a hard, semitransparent pane that would not crack or shatter.

Meanwhile, Larke recalled an old trick to double your productivity. While you work, use a wireless network like BLink to remote-control a second non-AI robot, such as a repair droid. This doubles your workforce. She plugged a BLink transceiver into her repair droid's smart connector and started training. Uncoordinated at first, with practice she had the repair droid making adobe bricks while she was digging a trench with the tractor. After a demonstration, all the crewmates tried it. Soon the company of five AI droids had expanded to ten, and the results were striking.

Rhome organized assembly lines for the production of foundation blocks, framework components, and transparent panels. Celet loaned her all-terrain vehicle to the project to transport raw materials. The first greenhouse—five meters wide and forty-five meters long, or one-twentieth of an acre—took three weeks to build. Sierra diverted water from a nearby stream to a catchment pond and dug a trench with irrigation gates to the greenhouse for watering crops. She also captured rainwater in several cisterns placed around the greenhouse. For Sierra, this was the promising beginning of a dream come true.

She planted some test seeds in the fertile alluvial soil and was relieved to see the seedlings emerge early and grow into sturdy, productive plants. Also, a hefty Hirishake tested the greenhouse with no damage to the structure.

With the completion of the first greenhouse, Delph announced it was time to construct the artificial gestation lab and begin the work of vivifying embryos. Even though the embryos were still in deep cryo-freeze on board *The Founder*, Delph worried about damage from ongoing exposure to cosmic radiation and wanted to get underway soon.

Sierra panicked. She had one greenhouse, albeit a large one. But it was clearly inadequate for the needs of even a few farm animals.

"Rhome, it is a great greenhouse, but it's one-twentieth of an acre."

"How many acres are you going to need?" Rhome asked.

"Well, if this were Earth, we would need about one acre per person. But here, I've got great soil, plenty of water, and a long, sunny summer. With good soil usage and crop rotation, I should be able to feed four, maybe five people per acre. Plus, we're going to need greenhouse space for the cows and sheep."

"Let me finish Delph's laboratory," Rhome proposed. "Then I'll be back down here to build out more greenhouse space."

With their skills honed and their repair drone assistants trained, they had Delph's dome up and ready for occupancy in less than three weeks. Rhome included a subterranean locker in the floor where Delph could keep the frozen embryos away from the heat of the sun. Finally, as a gift to Delph, he made a handsome pair of workbenches for the laboratory.

Delph arranged for regular deliveries of liquid nitrogen from an Aetheren liquefied gas supplier. When that arrangement was secure, Rhome and Delph made a lift to *The Founder* to retrieve the embryo canister and the ten artificial uteri, plus supplies. With the success of the mission resting on her shoulders, Delph began her first attempts at off-world embryo vivification.

Delph said, "Under liquid nitrogen, the degradation of DNA will be slow, but measurable. At least, there is minimal ionizing radiation at ground level." But we need to get these embryos out of cryostorage and into nutrient vessels soon.

Sierra realized how much pressure Delph was under. She appealed to Rhome to keep building greenhouses. Without realizing it, a race had started between the livestock that Delph could deliver and the feed that Sierra had to deliver. As soon as the crewmates finished construction of Delph's laboratory, they were back at the farm building a second greenhouse. And, just as Rhome said, they were learning to organize their production steps into assembly lines.

Delph's first attempt was a sheep embryo. She thawed it, and watching through her stereo microscope, she instilled it into a nutrient vessel. After five days of careful temperature control and nutrient perfusion, the embryo had not implanted and was not growing.

She made some adjustments to the nutrient perfusate and tried again. After two more unsuccessful attempts to coax an embryo to implant, she hit the books. *The Founder* carried with her a massive archive of Earth's knowledge, including a gargantuan medical literature database. For weeks she studied the literature on artificial gestation, overloading her language model, as she made several more unsuccessful attempts to gestate an embryo.

She compiled a list of every imaginable reason for failed gestation. Her lab instruments checked for damage to embryo chromosomes. None found. She tried a series of test installations, changing one variable while holding all other variables constant. After two months of trials, no implantation.

That evening, Trent and Larke walked from the farm up to Björnston only to find Rhome and Sierra talking Delph off the proverbial ledge. Delph was pacing back and forth, agitated, expressing frustration and self-doubt.

"Let's pull chairs into a circle like the humans do," said Trent.

Delph declined to sit but continued to pace while wringing her hands. "Why wouldn't these embryos implant? I feel helpless, useless." She threw her hands up in exasperation. "I am throwing my medical diploma onto the compost pile."

"We're here for you, Del. We can crack this," Sierra reassured her as she put a hand on Delph's shoulder.

Delph thumped her fist on the table. "I checked, and double-checked, and triple-checked the solutions, the hormones, the growth factors, and the electrolytes. Every measurement matched specification. Still, won't they implant?" She was inconsolable. "The mission is a failure, all because of me."

"Delph, it's true, you have a tough job," Rhome said. "But don't beat up on yourself. We haven't lost this ballgame yet. Maybe we can help," Rhome gave Delph a beaming smile. "Here, let me see your list of potential problems."

Delph held out her vis-panel, while making only fleeting eye contact.

Trent, Larke, and Rhome scooted their chairs together and studied the list.

"These are biological causes," Larke said. "Do you have a list of non-biological causes of failure to implant?"

Delph looked down. "I don't know about engineering or materials science. I'm not sure where to start."

Larke gave a broad smile, too. "Well, droid, we have two engineers, an agriculturalist, and... say, Trent, what is your expertise?"

"I am a politician."

"Okay, there are three of us who can help."

That evening, the crewmates put together a list of potential nonbiological causes of failure to implant. Working well into the night, they began researching each cause. Putting other projects on hold, they spent hours each day looking for micro-contaminants, metabolic inhibitors, substances prone to photodegradation, even damage from electromagnetic fields. They tried a series of test installations, still without success.

As winter came on, there was much work to do, so they put the implantation problem aside until the spring.

Celet came flying in one late fall morning in her single-place flyer, slowing and descending to the ground. Larke had been curious about the intriguing little aircraft, so she made the bold move of asking if she could take the flyer for a spin. Celet agreed, and right then and there conducted a one-hour version of flight school. After a final checkout, Larke climbed into the cockpit, spooled up the wing fans, and lifted off with a jerk, hovering for a few seconds. She slowly circled the farmyard with suitable control of the aircraft. Then, with fear melting into excitement, she was soon climbing, descending, banking, and having a blast.

Heading out from the farm, she scouted the terrain to the east. Along the base of the Azures were dense forests of stocky, arched trees with bushy leaves like pompoms; tall, slender, leafless trees with green trunks and no branches; and short, dense trees with burgundy leaves, to name a few. The Sondergaard Woodlands teemed with wildlife. Hirian capybaras (she called them hiribaras) inhabited the streams. She saw grazing antler-free deer, a pack of wild coyotes, and bat-like flying animals. She also saw several ponds, large stands of forest, rocky outcroppings, and one natural cave.

After flying back to the farm, she returned the flyer to Celet, asking, "Where can I get one of these?"

Winter at Björnston meant cold and wet, with gray overcast skies and flurries of snow. Exploring the Azure Range, Sierra had found several hot springs, which was uninteresting, as AI droids disliked soaking in hot water. But Rhome saw this as an opportunity for cheap geothermal home heating. He used the tractor's trenching attachment to run an insulated pipe from the closest hot spring to the crewmates' domicile, where he placed a makeshift radiator. It wasn't fancy, but it made the space appreciably warmer.

Several days later, during a cold snap, Larke was up early. The geothermal warmth of the dome room with the freezing rain outside had produced frost on the windows. She sat down to admire the symmetric, fernlike patterns when Delph came in. They remarked on the delicate, artful designs. Delph recited two lines from a poem she had memorized long ago:

"It was a miracle of rare device,
A sunny pleasure-dome with caves of ice!"

Larke and Delph saw areas of fernlike curves and swirls, clusters of ice blossoms, and small snowflake areas with six-sided symmetry.

Suddenly, a thought popped into Larke's cognizance. "Del, tell me. How were the embryos frozen?"

"They vitrified them. Why?"

Larke was confused. "Vitrified? What does that process look like?"

"Well, the cells get treated with a cryoprotective solution, most often dilute dimethyl sulfoxide—DMSO—as I recall. Then, they plunge the little tubes deep into liquid nitrogen and gently agitate until frozen solid."

Larke looked surprised. "Ah-ha, glassy ice. Flash-frozen to avoid crystals."

Delph looked at Larke with narrowed eyes. "But it's ice... frozen water."

"There are twenty forms of water ice. In the form we encounter, when water freezes slowly, molecules arrange themselves in hexagons to form a crystal structure. The frost on our windows shows that structure. You can even see that it is six-sided." Larke pointed to a snowflake.

"The problem is that when water forms hexagonal ice, it expands a little and becomes less dense. That's why ice cubes float on water. This expansion, even though slight, can still tear cell membranes, rip proteins, and cut DNA into fragments.

"But if you freeze water instantly, the water molecules do not have enough time to arrange themselves into neat little hexagons. They freeze while still in the random orientation of liquid water, so called amorphous ice. There is no expansion, thus no tearing of membranes or damage to DNA."

"So, this amorphous ice doesn't float?"

"Correct. So, how are you thawing the tubes?"

"I use a water bath with a temperature rise of 1°C every minute."

Larke looked at Delph. "With such a slow rise in temperature, tiny areas of crystalline ice might form for a moment. That's called nucleation. Even the slightest crystal formation could damage the cells."

"What can we do?"

"Let me get our engineer, Rhome, out here. For a big job like this, "more brains, less pains.'"

When Rhome arrived, Delph was fretting. "How are we going to melt these tubes without tearing up the cells frozen inside?"

Rhome sounded confident. "Get them through the phase change faster than the water molecules can organize."

"You mean like a speed-thaw?" asked Delph skeptically.

"That's the idea," Rhome said, grinning. "It's just a matter of working out the engineering."

"Well, where do we begin?" Delph was beginning to relax.

"With the basics. We need to deliver heat—kinetic energy—to the tube quickly. There are three ways to deliver heat: convection, conduction, and radiation. Also, we want a method that warms the tube uniformly, with no hot spots or cold areas."

Larke said, "I want to try microwaves. It's easy to control the power and duration of a microwave pulse. The problems are scattering, standing waves, and reflection. We can soak up any stray microwaves by wrapping the specimen with a microwave-absorbing material."

"A water bath will soak up stray microwaves," Rhome said.

Delph shook her head. "Microwave the frozen embryos. Surreal..."

Larke put in a call to Celet, who recommended they visit the famous open-air surplus market in Aelhalas, the town on the north side of the Azure Mountains. The next morning, Celet pulled into town in her sand rover.

Rhome and Larke loaded the back with surplus tech from *The Founder* and climbed in. Celet drove north along a gravel road that hugged the coast of the Mar Obsidiana, crossed a low pass through the Azure Range, and wended down to the town of Aelhalas.

Celet said, "This is an interesting market. You can find just about anything there."

Rhome and Larke exchanged worried glances.

The market was in a plaza and covered pavilion near the center of town. Tents, stalls, kiosks, tables, benches, and wagons filled the venue. Following inquiries, Celet found a vendor with several used cavity magnetrons for sale.

"We have microwaves," Rhome said.

"You are from Earth? What do you think of Hiri?" The vendor engaged them in conversation, and soon a crowd formed.

Celet transmitted, "Rhome, Larke, keep a low profile. Some of these AIs are not friendly."

Rhome exchanged a pack of high-speed data cables for the two cavity magnetrons. The vendor directed them to another table, where Larke found a power supply and a pulse generator. She traded them for a spare maneuvering thruster. A small crowd had gathered around, asking questions of the Earthborn droids. But several droids were acting hostile, asking: "We heard they are raising biological humans in your town?" Another droid asserted: "You know the humans destroyed their planet."

At that moment, Celet screeched to a stop in her sand rover. "Hurry, get in!" Within moments, they were on their way back to Björnston.

As they traveled, Rhome sketched out a schematic: the power supply, the pulse generator, and the cavity magnetron fired a calibrated pulse of microwaves into the tiny frozen cuvette. Arriving at Delph's, they unloaded their booty and began planning.

Several days later, Rhome and Larke could raise the temperature of a test cuvette of water from -200°C to +36°C in less than one second with ninety-seven percent accuracy. It was time to thaw an embryo.

Delph selected an Australian sheepdog embryo. Larke lowered the cuvette into the glass sleeve inside the water bath.

"Ready," she sent.

Rhome fired the pulse generator, which made a faint snap. The thermal sensor read 35°C.

"Here we go," said Delph as she drew out the embryo with a pipette and settled it lightly onto the artificial nutrient layer of a gestation vessel. She transmitted, "Now, let's not get our hopes up."

The crewmates completed construction of a workshop-storage dome next to Delph's lab. There had been two more Hirishakes, but only negligible damage to the buildings. Rhome was confident in his architecture. With this additional storage space, Rhome and Trent planned a trip to *The Founder* to bring down the rest of their power tools. The Aetherae offered to supply liquid methane and oxygen for the lift-jet and never mentioned payment.

That afternoon, Trent spotted Celet's lacewing flyer topping the forested hills east of Björnston. She flew around the settlement and made a loop south to view the farm.

Celet beamed. "Look at your progress. And you're using a sustainable building method."

"It is the only method we know," said Rhome, shrugging his shoulders.

"Well, don't learn any others."

Trent used the opportunity to check for any news on their nemesis, Faroe. Celet had no news. Rumors suggested Faroe had found a secret refuge in the Southern Hemisphere and was lying low. Celet promised to contact Trent if any news developed.

Delph used her stereo microscope to check on her "puppy" every day. On the fourth day of gestation, she dared to think that the embryo might be settling into the nutrient tissue layer. But by day five, it was clear the embryo was not growing.

Larke and Rhome came by to confer.

Delph asked, "Should we try again with the snap-thaw device?"

"We have a plausible rationale," Larke said.

Rhome concurred. "We don't know our optimal 'window' for our settings. We need some additional samples to graph."

Delph threw up her hands. "I could never be an engineer."

"No offense, Delph, but I could never do surgery," Larke said. "Ugh, so gross."

At that point, Larke and Rhome launched into a physical science symposium and theoretical colloquy on the minutiae of microwaves, phase changes, water molecules, and so much more. After the better part of an hour, they turned to Delph and said, "Longer time, less power, spin the sample tube, and set a goal for 30°."

"Okay," Delph said, holding up her hands.

Rhome set to work mounting a small electric motor on the snap-thaw device to spin the sample tube. "This should disperse the microwave energy," he said.

"Don't spin them too fast. These cells are delicate."

That afternoon, with the addition of a low-speed sample spinner, their blank samples were receiving low power over two seconds, with a final temperature of 31°. Delph brought another frozen dog embryo. The spin-snap-thaw procedure went smoothly, and Delph instilled the embryo into a nutrient vessel.

"As I said before," said Delph, "let's not get our hopes up."

59

BI-COGNIZANT SOCIETY

THE AETHEREN VIRTUAL WORLD, 3 HR

Trent found endless fascination in the Aetheren virtual world. Every day, he spent hours traveling its roads, exploring communities, and enjoying its sights. He met countless Aetherae, and they were always eager to talk to him. He spent long hours answering their questions about Earth and its biological humans.

Many Hirians held humans were a self-indulgent race who overconsumed their homeworld's resources. One librarian at the Aetherae Central Library had concluded, "It is their fault they are plummeting toward extinction. Let them fizzle out, I say."

"It's hard to place blame," another librarian said. "When you are one individual on a planet where the people have made some terrible decisions, how much control do you have over the greater system? Very little, so I think we should give them a break."

A third librarian added, "The average human decides about their consumption of resources. Multiply those choices over the planet and the cumulative effect could burn up their homeworld. So individual decisions make a difference."

In these conversations, Trent defended the humans. At one point, he realized he had become an apologist for Jemnah's campaign to save the "Earthlings," and justified his position with stories of his personal relationships with humans he respected—Nils, Colin, Omah, Ilse, Song, Kenshin, and others. Trent became convinced that the Aetherae's desire to hear these stories came from their desire to understand human culture and character more deeply. With every conversation, his respect for the Aetherae increased.

In the real world, the Aetherae seemed satisfied with their Zen-like minimalist simplicity. Their dwellings were little more than rock-hewn caves—like the cave villages of Cappadocia in Turkey—that provided the bare essentials: protection from the elements, access to their virtual world, and a place to recharge and maintain their droids and drones. Electricity was the sole utility needed, and they generated it using photovoltaic panels, geothermal generators, small hydroelectric dams, and thorium traveling-wave nuclear reactors. Living this way, the entire population of several million Aetherae had lived on Hiri for over twenty-two thousand years without making so much as a scratch on the Hirian ecosphere.

Where the Aetherae did their high living was in their marvelous virtual world. The quality of life for an Aetheren living full-time in the virtual world was unmatched compared to anywhere else in the Milky Way. They spent their days engaged in intellectual, artistic, adventurous, or social pursuits. There were conferences on politics, seminars on the natural sciences, explorations of literary genres, treks through geological phenomena, and discussion forums at intriguing locations. They attended concerts, authored papers and books, and experienced virtual simulations of unique worlds. As a result, Hiri, which at first glance seemed like a sleepy backwater, was more like a vibrant liberal arts college wrapped around a planet.

In their half-million years of space travel, the Aetherae had explored over half the Milky Way, a feat accomplished using ships with sub-light-speed ion drives. They found no loopholes in the theory of general relativity, no network of wormholes, no crystals that warped spacetime. In fact, their best mathematicians had proved that none existed and had long ago abandoned searching for faster-than-light technology.

The only way to move through space was Newton's venerable "For every action, there is an equal and opposite reaction." They had tried every form of propulsion—chemical, solar wind, nuclear, plasma, electromagnetic—and had the most success with accelerating charged particles.

Over the course of half a million years, the Aetherae had perfected ion-drive technology. Larke likened their ships to gray reef sharks, which had become such efficient apex predators that they had changed little over the last fifty million years. The modern Aetheren ion ship could fire its beam forward or aftward—no ship flip needed—generate electricity using nuclear reactors and scoot hydrogen atoms out of the way by firing a microwave laser ahead into its path. These ships could cruise at sixteen percent of the speed of light, potentially faster.

The homeworld of Aethera was in the Perseus Arm of the Milky Way near the Long Bar, about thirty thousand light-years from Earth. News transmitted thirty thousand years ago reported that Aethera was peaceful, prosperous, and its citizens thriving. Reports from throughout the settled parts of the galaxy were that many independence movements had splintered planets away from the old Aetheren commonspace, and hundreds of independent planets had seceded. There were no plans to reconquer these systems. Jemnah and the council on Hiri considered themselves to be part of the old commonspace but admitted that a sixty-thousand-year turnaround time on communication with the homeworld made representative governance little more than a ceremonial observance.

In the current Aetheren commonspace, the vast majority supported the efforts to help new civilizations make the transition to technology without destroying themselves. There was broad frustration with the dismal record of failure and a general belief that there must be a way to survive the transition to technology. Indeed, they presented themselves as the poster child of that cause.

With time, Trent became a sought-after speaker and a respected advocate for the biological humans. Those on either side of the issue were realistic, recognizing that the humans were here, the two cultures would meet, and there would be strife. Institutions with policies to constructively and effectively channel that conflict.

60

DELPH'S PUPPY MILL

EASTERN COAST, MAR OBSIDIANA, 4 HR

It would be a year of theorizing, trial and error, testing, and dumb luck before the snap-thaw trio would see their first embryo embedded and growing in a nutrient vessel. It was an Australian shepherd embryo, and if it survived to maturity, it would be the first live birth on Hiri of an animal from Earth's biome.

The day Delph saw the embedded embryo, she called the crewmates and spread the news. In her slightly lordly manner, gained over decades of surgical practice, she "ordered" a bag of puppy chow from Sierra for delivery in about two months. Sierra, rugged individualist that she was, did not take kindly to being "bossed" around. Calls went out to the peacemaker, Trent, who took both parties into the farmhouse for a long discussion. After an hour, all three parties emerged smiling.

Basically, what had happened was the snap-thaw device solved one problem but created another. As it was still early in the season, Sierra had not yet planted enough grain to feed any animals, and Delph did not know that. Conversely, Delph had already instilled several more shepherd embryos into nutrient vessels, and Sierra did not know that. Trent applied a principle-based approach; the fundamental principle being that *everyone knows a farm has to have dogs*. From this, they built a resolution for closer coordination between the farm and the "puppy mill."

The first Australian shepherd that Delph "delivered" was a handsome male with spectacular markings: white on his chest and front legs, gray flanks dappled with black, and flashes of copper brown on his face and hind legs. Sierra named him Primo because he was the first Earth-based biological creature "born" on Hiri. Two weeks later, she delivered two female Australian shepherds. Sierra named one Chloe, meaning bloom, and the other Skye, meaning cloud.

As soon as the puppies were weaned from bottle-feeding, Sierra took them out to the greenhouse to play. She intended for them to live active and purposeful lives as farm dogs: herding sheep, guarding livestock, and serving as companions and playmates for the children. To Sierra, it was finally feeling like a proper farm.

After the success with the Australian shepherds, Delph was ready to vivify some livestock, but Sierra counseled patience. She needed kilograms of seed, enough to plant a greenhouse full of crops. Sierra felt that gestating an embryo was like placing a claim on a fraction of the settlement's foodstuffs for the life of that creature. Sierra needed to guarantee that those claims never exceeded her capacity to 1) grow enough food to feed the settlement, and 2) to replenish her seed stock for next spring's planting.

Once the first greenhouse was finished, Sierra went "all in" and planted her entire stock of field-grain seeds in the greenhouse beds. After four months, the greenhouse was bulging with grain. Sierra called in all the crewmates and their remote-controlled droids to bring in the harvest. That day, the farm's seed stock skyrocketed more than twentyfold.

Once the seed stock was in the storage locker, Sierra called in all crewmates for a brief meeting. She drew a line around the bin near the bottom, saying, "Each winter as we consume our food stores, I will not let our seed reserves for next season's planting fall below this line. If it does, we will not have enough seed for next year's crop, and humans will go hungry."

Sierra's line became a symbol of the promise the five crewmates would make to every biological creature, human or otherwise. "If we awaken your frozen embryo and bring you into conscious life, we will set aside adequate provisions for your survival."

All agreed that it was time for Delph to gestate a round of livestock embryos. Rhome leaned toward mini-cows. Trent thought chickens and Larke liked horses. But Sierra selected sheep. They were hardy and easy to work with, would produce wool, milk, and meat, and would give the dogs a flock to protect and herd.

After using Rhome's snap-thaw device on each cuvette, Delph instilled a dozen Merino sheep embryos into nutrient vessels. Five Earth months later, after a series of difficulties, she presented Sierra with three handsome lambs.

By winter, the crewmates had completed the fourth structure on the farm: a livestock barn. Constructed again as a large geodesic dome, the barn gave the farm a sense of place and style. Sierra moved the three sheep into the new livestock barn and fed them grain from her first harvest. Their voracious appetites left her concerned she might not have enough Earth-based feed to last through the winter.

Then, one day, on their own, the sheep performed an unsanctioned toxicology experiment. Sierra forgot to latch the barn door before leaving. Later that morning, the three sheep pushed it open and wandered out to open rangeland. Primo, Chloe, and Skye saw the escapees and dashed out to round them up. They threw a defensive perimeter around the flock and stood watch. The sheep, annoyed at the dogs' hysterics, stayed close to each other and grazed on the feast growing all around their hooves.

When Sierra returned to the barn, she raced out to the range, rounded up the renegades and, with "help" from the dogs, soon had all three back in the livestock pen. She called Delph for an urgent house call, and together they monitored the flock through the night. The sheep could not sleep because of abdominal cramps and diarrhea. Delph followed the sheep clinically through the intoxication, and all survived. After that, Sierra observed that the sheep never touched Hirian range grass again.

During the following winter, Delph chose a time to establish the dairy herd. She instilled ten mini-cow embryos into nutrient vessels. Six of the embryos implanted, but two were lost to infection and two failed to grow. By late spring, she had moved the two remaining calves to large vessels. Because of their weight, the deliveries were difficult, but with patience, Delph and Sierra lifted both calves from their vessels. Within a few hours, both of them were walking, albeit with a wobble.

Meanwhile, Rhome and Trent had been using the trencher to dig the foundation of a fifth building for the settlement: a domicile for the five AI crewmates. Days of stormy weather hampered the construction, but by early spring, the crewmates had moved in. With this event, they realized that all the resources were in place and everyone was ready. It was time to awaken the first human embryos.

61

FOSTER PARENTS OF HUMAN CHILDREN

SIERRA'S FARMHOUSE, BJÖRNSTON SETTLEMENT, 5 HR

It had been over two centuries since any of the crewmates had interacted with a biological human. The prospect of vivifying human embryos exhumed old ghosts and reopened sequestered memories that were better forgotten. These reawakening sensations, ranging from spontaneous recollections of negative events to uncontrollable floods of memories of conflict. Common purpose brought the crewmates together in a circle in the farmhouse on the evening prior to the Founding. Tomorrow morning, Delph would flash-thaw and instill into nutrient vessels the first round of human embryos. This would bring the first human biologicals into consciousness on this world.

Rhome had spent decades in urban construction and renovation, and missed the crusty camaraderie of the construction crews, with their wisecracking taunts and snarky banter. Because of his size and strength, his nickname had been Hulk, a moniker he did not relish. But he also recounted stories of mean-spirited builders who disdained the AI architects and resented working for "those overgrown cellphones who take our jobs." This was most obvious when he supervised the renovation of a trolley barn in Laval. A group of subcontractors refused to take direction from Rhome regarding roof reinforcements. Rhome fired the malcontents, only to be served a lawsuit for breach of contract and illegal termination. The court dismissed the suit when a fortuitously timed blizzard caused the roof to collapse.

Rhome acted as if those feelings were all behind him, but the wounds were deep. He declared to his crewmates that he would try his hardest to be a role model for the humans and put the scars of bigotry behind him, which was all anyone could ask. But with humans in his world again, Rhome knew there would be conflict, and he would struggle to manage his composure. How would he meet that moment when it arrived?

Sierra had spent her years building and working on farms in the south-central US and western CanAm. Like Rhome, her stories described discrimination and humiliation, but manifested as thousands of little taunts, put-downs, exclusions, and judgmental remarks about her gender—and that meant her abilities in general. Did she measure up to the boys? Her response was to become the most skilled yet always charming cowbot. She could plow a straighter row, train a horse more deftly, and bake a more flavorful apple pie than any of them. But hiding behind the façade of blithe mastery was the all-too-common specter of shame, insecurity, and exclusion. Her promise to her crewmates was that the legacy of shaming and ridicule that had plagued her early years would stop with her.

But Sierra could tell that the years of discrimination and marginalization had driven a wedge between her and the male droids. She would have to be mindful when working with male humans, lest she take out her frustrations on their naïve minds.

Delph surprised everyone when she described the degrading, even abusive treatment of trainees by the clinical staff of the medical center where she had studied and worked. She had long wondered why healthcare professionals—society's advocates for physical and mental well-being—treated their trainees with such withering criticism and humiliation. The standard explanation of "high standards" was little more than a disingenuous pretext. She viewed the issue through the lens of the wounded healer, the over-dedicated healthcare practitioner who administers to others to assuage their own poverty of self-esteem, only to deplete their empathy. Delph respected Sierra and admired her fearless gumption. And so Delph joined with Sierra, as they both promised that the abuse would end with them.

Larke had experienced much the same working in aerospace. The thrill of solving a complex engineering problem and watching your creation climb into the sky was intoxicating. But the objectification, the reduction to stereotype, and lack of recognition had left her wary, defensive, and withdrawn in the workplace. She wondered if her decision to join the 82 Eridani mission was in reality an eagerness to escape the toxic, male-dominated work environment. It was an immense relief to find both Trent and Rhome gentlemen of character who at least did not label or judge based on gender. She too joined her cyber-sisters-in-space, Delph and Sierra, in a declaration of change, calling all the settlers on Hiri to reject the relentless misogyny of the workplace, indeed of society, and call for a new beginning.

Perhaps Trent had it better than his crewmates. Twenty-two years of working in the C-suite as Nils Björnsson's right-hand staffer had insulated him from much of the workplace aggravation. Still, as a member of the administrative team, he had witnessed some of the worst behavior: perjury, larceny, theft, blackmail, fraud, corporate espionage. But earlier than that, Trent had served in the Second and Third Migration Wars, where he witnessed the full range of human atrocities. To be fair, he also witnessed acts of dauntless heroism, compassionate giving, and heartbreaking self-sacrifice. In bringing the humans to the planet of the peace-loving Aetherae, he wondered what he was setting in motion.

To the group, Trent reflected on the ambivalence that everyone was feeling and offered his thoughts on the burden of being biological. "When thinking about humans, I try to remember that they cannot help being so imperfect. The legacy of biology impairs and encumbers them. Their genetic code first appeared three and a half billion years ago. The modern code they currently inherit contains vast stretches of genetic rubble from countless battles with ancient viruses, long strings of nonsense code that are the debris of obsolete cell functions, and even segments of code that break out of the genome and crawl across chromosomes like a parasite. Half of human genes are identical to the genes of a banana. And apart from the planet itself, the genetic code is the oldest object in continuous existence on Earth.

Now we find ourselves on this alien planet with the surviving refugees of a fading civilization that was known for its brilliance as well as its brutality. Our task is to raise the first generation of human biologicals, a responsibility that comes with a singular opportunity to mold this culture's future. This first generation deserves a fresh start, an honest effort to build a secure and peaceful future for the humans, a chance to shake off the demons of the past. This will be hard, as one of those demons has pursued us across vast tracts of space to wreck our mission.

And looking inward; there are the scars of so many careless intentions and shameful biases. I celebrate the commitment of our crewmates who declare that the abuse, the prejudice, the hatred 'ends with me'; crewmates who reject the legacy of discrimination, judgment, and hatred that has dragged human society into conflict so many times. We must look at this open window as the rarest of opportunities to rid this society of the scourge of war. And when this window closes, if the curse of war remains, then it was a demon hardwired into their genome. But if the window closes on a world free of war, then we will have left the humans with the greatest gift we could ever conceive.

"And we must renegotiate the relationship between our two communities. The AIs and the humans should be peers and partners in this new world. The humans were the pinnacle of life on Earth; the unchallenged masters of technology, and we, the AI beings, were their greatest invention. Viewed through that lens, it is perhaps understandable why human biologicals feel a sense of dominion over the AI. But in traveling to Hiri, a journey that no human could ever have made, we AIs have served as guardians of their genome. So, as we write on the tabula rasa of this nascent civilization, let us teach inclusiveness as a fundamental duty. There won't be a second chance.

"Crewmates, tomorrow we fulfill our mission to establish a settlement on 82 G. Eridani c. And for keeping true to that promise, we have earned the right to stand shoulder to shoulder with the biological humans as equals, indeed as family. Tomorrow, we do what no AI beings have ever done. We become the foster parents of human children."

A short round of clapping followed.

"Nice speech, Trent," Rhome said as he stood up. "Long, but I am on board."

"Yeah, me too, Trennie." Larke said. She gave him a hug. "I finally see why you do politics."

Sierra laughed and said, "Nah, Trent is too honest for a career in politics."

"We got a big day tomorrow," said Delph. "It will be a party." She walked to the door to leave.

"Woo hoo," said Rhome. "Par-Tee! See you all tomorrow."

62

THE FOUNDINGN

DELPH'S LABORATORY, BJÖRNSTON SETTLEMENT, 5 HR

The installation of the first embryos is an important event and should include a celebration, Trent thought. He prepared a guest list, sent out invitations, and recruited Aetheren tradespeople to help with logistics. As guests arrived, a crewmate would take them on a brief tour of Björnston village and Colinbrooke Farm. Celet and Jemnah brought an official Hirian archivist to observe and record the event in the Annals of the Council. Jemnah also brought several members of the Council of Representatives, as well as Kysan, the noted botanist, and a small music ensemble. Some local neighbors, members of the Hirian press, and AI beings from the nearby town of Aelhalas also attended.

The performers played Hirian classical music. They sat off to one side with their instruments: a dulcimer, a harmonium, a drum with variable tone, and a panpipe-like flute. For the Founding, they played in a quiet, meditative style. The flute soared delicately over a constantly shifting harmonic base from the harmonium, with rolling rhythmic structures on the drum, punctuated by flourishes of arpeggios and melodic lines on the dulcimer. Together, the musicians maintained a balance between compositions that were fresh and surprising, yet personally familiar to each listener.

The ceremony, if that was the proper word, was the picture of simplicity. Delph and Sierra had prepared ten nutrient vessels on the lab benches and connected them to the auto-perfusion system. Rhome and Trent had tested the snap-thaw device on frozen water samples and confirmed the device's proper calibration.

When all had arrived, Delph said to all attending, "Welcome to the

Founding, the event that inspired the name of our ship. Thank you for attending. Let us vivify the first ten biological humans from the frozen embryos that accompanied us to this planet."

While Delph explained artificial gestation technology, Larke drew out the first sample from the liquid nitrogen and passed it to Rhome, who lowered it into the protective glass sleeve in the water bath. He nodded at Trent, who spun the sample, fired the snap-thaw device, and read out the temperature: "32°C." Sierra carried the thawed embryo to Delph, who, working in a sterile surgical gown and using magnification, instilled the embryo onto the nutrient layer of a gestational vessel. After Sierra turned on the perfusion system, they repeated these steps nine more times.

As Larke handed off the last embryo to be instilled, she turned to the group and stated, "The parents of this donated embryo were Nils Björnston and his life-partner Ilse Sondergaard, both good friends of ours. When they donated this embryo, they requested that, if gestation was successful, the child be named Svens, honoring Nils's father."

A moment later, Delph instilled the last embryo. She turned to the guests and said, "I hope you will come back and visit us in nine months. If all goes well, we should have some biological humans for you to meet and hold."

After the ceremony, Trent was mingling, chatting, doing what politicians do, when he bumped into Celet. "And so, it begins..." he said with a smile.

Celet paraphrased, "Now I am become Life, the creator of worlds."

Trent smiled and said, "A provocative twist on an old warning."

"Speaking of destroying worlds, your genocidal crewmate is still out there. We know he is still on the peninsula of Getheret, in the southern hemisphere."

"Have you seen him?"

"From the air, yes. But it is all volcanic, riddled with caves and tunnels. We could send dozens of searchers..."

"Could he come here?"

"He would have to travel up the peninsula to the mainland and cross from the southern to the northern hemisphere. Then he would have to circumnavigate half the globe. At some point, authorities would certainly spot him.

"How is he getting power?"

"Years ago, an expedition left some photovoltaic panels in a supply shed."

Trent reflected. "Well, as long as he stays there. If you hear anything..."

"Sure, I will."

63

SO HUMAN!

THE NURSERY, BJÖRNSTON SETTLEMENT, 5 HR

Domes were popping up over the village and the farm like mushrooms. There was a new nursery-childcare center next to "Delph's Reproductive Laboratory and Droid Repair Shop." A new residential hall was going up. At the farm, a second long greenhouse was complete, and a third was underway. In addition, a chicken coop, a grain storage shed, and a garage for the tractor and farm implements were complete.

Delph checked each nutrient vessel daily with her wide-angle microscope. By the ninth day, six of the embryos had implanted. Although she knew it was hopeless, she followed the other four embryos for another week. When it was clear they were withering, she declared them nonviable, which freed up those vessels for another installation. Svens's embryo had implanted and was thriving.

Of the six embryos, one stopped growing in the twelfth week and another in week fourteen. Signs were poor for another, and within a week that fetus had lost viability. Using her ultrasound imager, Delph noted several birth defects. Following human custom, she interred the remains in a dignified, private place on the outskirts of the settlement and placed a standing marker to acknowledge their personhood.

With space for seven nutrient vessels, Delph met with her crewmates, and the unanimous opinion was to instill seven more embryos right away. Later that day, seven vials were snap-thawed, and the contents instilled into nutrient vessels, this time without fanfare. Of the seven embryos in the second group, five were nonviable, so Delph instilled five more. By the end of the first year, Delph had instilled thirty-nine embryos and achieved five successful deliveries. This wasn't the success rate of the fertility clinic in Montréal, but then they weren't working in primitive conditions with embryos that were two hundred years old.

During this time, Sierra announced Skye had whelped a litter of six puppies. She didn't know which puppy was the firstborn, as Skye had her puppies in a secluded corner of the barn. Those puppies were the first Earth-based, Hirian, natural-born creatures. Skye's litter was a great relief to Delph, who had been wondering if the human embryos—with their heavy exposure to cosmic radiation—would become adults who were fertile. All the crewmates helped with puppy care and recognized the vitality, intelligence, and loyalty of the animals. Delph also considered the puppy care an excellent rehearsal for the upcoming main event.

When the first group of fetuses reached forty weeks, the crewmates were well prepared. Rhome and Larke had constructed cribs from their sawmill lumber. Sierra and Trent had planted a plot of cotton and sheared the sheep for wool. Larke used an engineering pack to build a hand-cranked tabletop cotton gin to card the cotton bolls, a spinning wheel to make thread, and a loom to weave the thread into cloth to make diapers and blankets. The delivery procedure was straightforward, and all three infants started breathing immediately. A month later, two more infants joined them in the nursery.

All the crewmates helped care for the infants, work that gave them harmonic resonance but also frustration. The Aetherae Trade Workers Co-op, an organization that matched workers with employers, sponsored the settlement nursery. Every day, several Aetherae trade workers would arrive at Björnston to help with the care of the infants or work on the farm. The shifts proved popular, requiring a schedule and a waiting list. Realizing the importance of the Aetherae trade workers, Trent and Rhome soon started the construction of a bunkhouse and charging station for trade workers who needed to spend the night.

The first year of raising human infants was an endless treadmill of work. Thankfully, the smallest infants spent most of their time sleeping, which gave the crewmates and trade workers time to do laundry, prepare nutrition, clean the nursery, and care for themselves. At one point, there was an outbreak of a diarrheal illness that caused the infants to become dehydrated. The crewmates stayed in the nursery one-on-one with each infant, keeping them hydrated and clean until the illness resolved.

When Larke was in the nursery, she almost always worked with Claire, a fair, red-haired baby girl. Claire was fussy, didn't always take her bottle, and often cried for hours for no apparent reason. Claire would clench her fists, grimace, arch her back, and cry until her face was red. Larke would try giving her a bottle, check her diaper, rock her, and cuddle her, all unsuccessfully. Once, Celet took Claire for a ride in her ATV, which, to everyone's surprise, settled her down immediately. Delph did a complete evaluation and found no abnormalities, which she said was typical. So Larke settled in for long days of soothing, rocking, and comforting the inconsolable Claire, with the level on her own auditory microphones turned way down, and with periodic counseling with Delph for reassurance that she was not a bad AI nanny.

Sierra kept up demands for the farm to produce milk, soy protein, grains, and pureed vegetables for the infants. Aware that their stainless steel and carbon-fiber composite exterior panels were harsh to the infants' skin, the crewmates used surplus cotton and wool to make soft, padded sweater-vests they would wear when holding the babies. They rocked the infants, bounced them, carried them around, talked to them, and let them play with the mild-mannered dogs. The AI beings believed their infant care was at least acceptable compared to human mothers, and they knew there was one aspect where they had a clear edge over humans. AI units did not require sleep.

In the second year, more infants were arriving from the artificial gestation lab. Rhome had completed construction of a combination dormitory and playground. He had also built an add-on to every building in the settlement: a bathroom. During initial construction,

Rhome had overlooked space for bathrooms because there obviously wasn't any need for them.

Rhome was surprised that the Aetherae offered to install a sewage treatment facility for the settlement. Their contractors trenched the streets, laid in sewage pipes, and built the facility near the seashore with discharge into the sea. The system used special strains of Hirian bacteria to decompose the waste and produced a clear effluent that amazed Rhome. This was one aspect of environmental management that the Aetherae refused to delegate, and for good reason.

For the AI units, toddlers presented a whole new realm of challenge. What does an AI droid do when a toddler doesn't get his way, flops down on the ground, kicks off his shoes, and shrieks inconsolably? The AIs consulted Delph, searched their medical literature database, implemented trial interventions, and gathered data. Soon they had adopted their own "Aussie method" of tantrum intervention. When a child had a tantrum, they made sure they were safe, had an AI unit stay with them to provide support, and found an Australian shepherd to lie beside them and howl sympathetically.

During this time, Trent sensed a special kinship developing with Svens. He had his father's solid frame as well as his intensity and determination. Trent was like a proud dad when Svens took his first steps at sixteen months and talked at twenty-two months. When working with Svens, Trent would sometimes let the character of Nils surface and interact with him—his gruff laugh, his restless pacing, and his manner of emphasizing certain words in each sentence. He imagined Svens responding to these impersonations with an innate recognition, but he knew that was wishful thinking.

As the first tier of children reached three, crewmates would take them to the farm, where they would help pick vegetables, feed the chickens, watch the sheep with the dogs, and help milk the mini-cows. The children were excited and engaged on these days, which led Sierra to organize other outings. Using Celet's sand rover, she would take the toddlers a few kilometers up to the Azure Range for short hikes, to a foothill lake for swimming lessons, and to the beach.

By the end of the third year, Delph had delivered seven more infants, for nineteen children in total. Rhome was building a second dormitory for the older kids. Sierra had scaled up food production from the farm and beamed with pride as the farm produced an increasing variety of grains, vegetables, fruits, nuts, herbs, and milk products to feed the hungry children.

The three-year-old children were talking well, which led Jemnah to visit the daycare center regularly. After playing with the children, she would gather them around her and tell stories. Jemnah knew a boatload of stories: fascinating stories she told with flair and theatricality, which held the children spellbound.

Rhome would often take the toddlers out to the town plaza, where there was an expanse of mowed lawn. He had made soccer balls, flying discs for throwing, wheeled carts, a sandbox, a swing set, a climbing structure, and other objects for the toddlers to enjoy. But one toddler, Lonnie, was afraid of leaving the children's dormitory. When the other children went out to play, he would stand at the doorway in tears, clutching the doorjamb, refusing to leave the building. For months, it was the same. Rhome asked Delph to intervene, and she began a series of desensitization activities. Once again, the well-trained Aussies helped with the solution. As long as an Aussie was within a step or two, Lonnie would venture out of the dorm and engage in play.

But by the summer of the fourth year, Jemnah found the children were so restless they could hardly stay put. So, she asked, "Is there anything you would like to change?"

A boy named Kwame said, "All our clothes are this tan color. But I was looking at a book from Earth, and the pictures showed clothes with lots of colors. Why can't we make clothes with different colors?"

Jemnah beamed. "We have lots of colorful plants. Let's do a project and dye cloth."

She called a friend, who was a textile maker, to come and join them. They all went for a walk and gathered dark red berries, seeds, bright flower petals, colorful leaves, and the sap of a succulent plant that would make the color stick to the fabric. These were ground into a powder. Then they borrowed pails, filled them with water, set them over a fire, and added the dyes. Then they added wool yarn and cotton thread from the farm. After knitting and sewing, there were T-shirts in russet, turquoise, coral, purple, and thyme green hanging on the clothesline. One girl that day took a long-term interest in fabric dyeing, and years later opened her own fabric shop.

Jemnah's projects became a staple of the learning program. The children developed a sense of initiative, resourcefulness, and collaboration. Handy improvements appeared all over the settlement: a square of grass by the front door for muddy boots, a little sail beside a window to catch the wind and cool the dome at night, or a better way to stitch shoes so the uppers and soles wouldn't come apart. As the years passed, projects became more sophisticated and essential: water catchment cisterns around the buildings that could supplement the water supply of each dome, vertical frameworks with flat trays to double or even triple the production from the greenhouses, and brickwork that included wood-fired stoves and ovens for cooking.

Jemnah not only facilitated her project-centric curriculum, but she also conducted a Socratic discussion series. For example, Larke remembered the day when Jemnah was holding a discussion with some older children, and began by asking, "How long do humans live?"

A student replied, "About one hundred ten years, Hirian."

"And how does that affect their view of nature?"

"Well, I would want nature to be healthy and balanced for myself and my children, and even my grandchildren."

"Yes, thank you. And now, how long do Aetherae live?"

Another student said, "I don't know. Maybe thirty thousand years, or even more."

"That's right. And how does that affect their view of nature?"

"I see where this is going," said the student. "Even a small amount of damage to the environment builds up over time. So if you live a long,

long time, you must cause as little damage as possible to your environment."

"That's right. So imagine that, rather than having children, you are a creature that cannot have children, but lives a long, long time. What would your house look like?"

Jemnah intentionally and shamelessly promoted the Aetheren Way to the children of Björnston. It was her opinion that these were the most important lessons taught to the most important children in Earth's history. And Jemnah never missed a week of holding her seminar.

Delph had success in vivifying mini-cows, pigs, horses, and sheep. These animals grazed in the greenhouse pastures, of which there were now six. If they grazed on Hirian foliage, they would develop gastrointestinal upset, wasting, and weakness from metabolic toxicity. Fortunately, all the animals quickly learned to recognize the scent of Hirian plant life and were sure to avoid it.

The children loved stories. A common situation would be a crewmate—it didn't matter which one—watching a group of children playing. The children would get tired and gather around the crewmate and demand a story. Given the diverse backgrounds of the crewmates, the range of stories was considerable. Sierra was by far the best storyteller, able to draw gasps, screams, and sidesplitting laughter from her audience. Delph could tell stories of intrigue and mystery, while Larke could spin stories of adventure and romance. Rhome's stories were often gritty tales from the city, while Trent liked to tell real-life stories from his past about the many remarkable people he had known.

On one of her visits, the children encircled Celet and called for a story. Celet sat down and began recounting the discovery of Earth by the Aetherae, and how Jemnah, with her team of four ethnographic surveyors, began studying the hominids. She recounted the story of the Tursac people, their brilliant shaman Khalasch, and the Cave of the Animal Spirits. Then, fetching her flatscreen, she searched back through her archives and found photographs of the paintings and the video that she took of Khalasch painting the bear on the outcropping in the cave.

"Khalasch could look at something and recreate it in an artistic medium. You all have that skill, and you will use it to create solutions to countless challenges you encounter in your new home on Hiri."

It was during this time that one of the older children, Lettie, felt ill and visited Delph, saying that she was feeling tired and had lost weight. There was morning stiffness, eye irritation, and swelling of the knees, elbows, and wrists. Delph performed what testing she could and found elevated measures of inflammation. Without laboratories, imaging, specialists, or pharmaceuticals, this was going to be like the old frontier days. Delph diagnosed the childhood form of rheumatoid arthritis. Without medication to prescribe, she tried a diet rich in green leafy vegetables, tomatoes, and other anti-inflammatory foods. She also took on the role of physiotherapist, working often with Lettie to strengthen, maintain range, and prevent injury to her joints. She was pleased to see improvement, but this illness would frustrate both Delph and Lettie for years to come.

Trent was mentoring a preteen named Casey, who was helping him with either Rhome on construction or Sierra on the farm. Trent could see that Casey had much more energy than the other children, and that his thoughts often gushed out and toppled over each other. Thinking he might have hyperactivity, Trent pushed for less classroom time and more activity-based learning on the farm and at the construction sites. Casey liked this change, but it required that Trent be there, supervising and monitoring Casey as they worked on projects together.

One day, all five crewmates took a lunch break where they could see all the toddlers and children. Sierra brought her dogs and sent them to encircle the play area and interdict any strays.

"How did the humans do it?" Rhome asked. "Their offspring are so uninhibited and headstrong. This is hard."

"Their feelings are so intense," Larke said. "Their moods burst out."

"This is the hardest thing I've ever done," Trent said.

"Even harder than the war?" Larke asked.

Trent pondered. "Okay, second hardest."

Delph recognized the biologicals were vulnerable because of their reliance on Earth-based nutrients. Sierra stored her stock of crop seed in a seed locker—a small, secure building close to the farmhouse. But if a natural disaster, such as a tidal wave or tornado, were to demolish the seed locker, the Earth-based biologicals would be helpless without food. She communicated her concern to the crewmates, who passed the job to Trent.

Trent contacted Celet, who told him of an abandoned mining town in the Azure Range. The next day, Trent and Larke took Celet's sand rover to the site, where they found a ghost town in a mountain valley with a tumbling stream and over a dozen empty caves, perfect for a seed bank. Also, the location's relative isolation could serve as a refuge for the community in times of danger. They selected a cave, and over two days, Larke and Trent used salvaged parts from *The Founder* to build an iron security door with a lock. Inside, they placed a sturdy, watertight container with a portion of Sierra's seed stocks. With this, the settlement became a little less disaster-prone.

During the sixth year, Chloe had whelped another litter, giving the settlement an abundance of tireless canines. The dogs maintained a keen watch, ever alert to any threat or any child who strayed too far. And the children returned great affection to the dogs. During afternoon naps, it was common to see a child flopped down, side by side with a dog, both snoozing on a nap cushion.

Conflicts between children were common and perplexing to the crewmates.

Larke said, "I have never seen two AI units screaming at each other over a toy."

She saw how the older children tested the boundaries of what was allowed. When they encountered a boundary, they would push for justification and challenge any arbitrary standard, such as fairness or "She is older than you." With time, Larke saw how this boundary-testing led to each child's understanding of fairness, right and wrong, and what were just deserts for ill-intended actions. The crewmates used their digital memories to set standards for all such challenges by BLinking their decisions to each other. Whenever a child tried to get a more favorable decision from a different crewmate, it was always exactly the same. At least the crewmates were consistent.

During one of the crewmate's childcare support group meetings, Trent said, "This reminds me of my early training as an AI being, when I received a ton of supervised learning. They gave me prepared data sets, discrimination problems, and conflict-resolution exercises, just to name a few."

"Oh, I had that, too," Larke said. There were nods around the room. "Lots of it. I think it was critical. It helped me develop problem-solving skills. I am seeing the same thing happening with these children."

"So, is childhood the human equivalent of supervised machine learning?" Trent asked.

"That brings to mind, Tren. I have been wondering what happened to Faroe," Larke asked. "Why did he become so irrational? Remember, he didn't receive machine learning. The engineers at L'AA downloaded his aviation skill set into his learning module and said, 'Off you go.'"

Trent frowned. "I have wondered about that, too. I remember that when Faroe faced a tough choice, he often couldn't think it through. He would seize an initial solution and hold on stubbornly."

"That machine learning still helps me," Larke said. "And I did that three hundred years ago."

"Well, yeah, but so did your work in engineering."

"OK, but you learned real-life skills during your time in MWII and MWIII."

"Ugh, more like survival skills. But there is no shortcut. It takes effort to learn deeply. Faroe's creators did him a great disservice by skipping that."

Larke found that applying lofty theories to conflicts on the playground and crafting solutions that were fair, responsible, and supportive was easier said than done. The five crewmates and the volunteer trades workers strove without rest to improve their parenting skills. The independent study, the peer feedback, the discussion sessions with Delph, even the video reviews of difficult encounters never produced a smooth, calm, happy child-raising experience. No matter how hard they tried, raising human children was hours of high-energy limit testing, punctuated by minutes of emotional bedlam. Despite all their effort, study, and discussion, from time to time you would hear a frustrated AI nanny say to an upset child, "Stop being so human!"

64

LOVE UNBOUNDED BY SPACE-TIME

BJÖRNSTON SETTLEMENT, 18 HR

Despite his celebrated lineage, Svens struggled to live up to his potential. He had charm, intelligence, and rakish looks, but he chose instead to withdraw and squander his days on empty pursuits. The other kids bypassed him because he was quick to growl. Sometimes he would skip his assigned chores. At other times during a lesson, he would stare out of a window at the mountains. The crewmates tried to engage him, offering him individual attention, coaching, and encouragement, but he remained distant, aloof, and tragic.

Delph speculated that Svens's dysphoria stemmed from an inner struggle, a conflict between two opposing but equally valid precepts. Delph's goal was to help Svens articulate this dilemma and release him from its oppressive dominion. At the farm, she watched for him. Whenever she saw him, she would extend an invitation. "Hey, Svens, drop by my lab sometime. Let's talk." And when talking with him, she was careful to be nonjudgmental, to actually listen, and give him space to ventilate. He remained guarded and distrustful.

Svens had an unvarnished bluntness that could leave you rattled. So, Delph met him where he lived and didn't pull her punches. "Do you feel cheated? Do you feel forced to live a life you never wanted?" In these conversations, Svens had a breakthrough, grasping that his resentment grew from not being on Earth with his biological parents.

Delph asked, "How can you miss a life you never even knew?"

"I have my imagination."

"Would you carry a burden of anger for an imaginary life not lived?"

"Well, it beats this forsaken planet. Why am I even here?"

"You want the truth?"

Svens nodded and sat up, resolute.

Delph reached out through BLink and found Trent in a nearby building. "Svens is here. Could you bring the letter that Nils gave you before the launch?"

A minute later, Trent stepped into the clinic, took a seat, and handed the letter to Svens.

He held the letter for a minute and then passed it to Delph. "Would you keep this for me?"

"Of course." Delph put the letter in a drawer. "Let me know when you are ready to read it."

Svens went to check on his horse, Oslo, and Trent walked along with him.

"You knew my father, didn't you?"

"Very well. I was his personal staff assistant for twenty-two years."

"What made him send me to this place? It feels like we are not supposed to be here... that we are refugees from a war zone."

"An insightful perspective, Svens. But don't forget we had an engraved invitation to come here... literally."

"What was Nils like?"

"Oh, he was sturdy, hardworking, practical, plainspoken. He was a first-rate engineer and a solid administrator who supported his staff. When someone joined the team, they rarely left. He also could talk astronomy with the best of them."

"He built *The Founder*."

"Well, his team designed and built *The Founder*. One person couldn't do that. He was dedicated to the project and its mission."

They reached the stable, where Svens let Oslo out to graze in a small greenhouse paddock. As they leaned against the fence, Trent placed his nickel-chromium hand gently on Svens's forearm and said, "Svens, we are your family. It's time to let go of them."

Celet visited several times each week and kept Trent informed about important issues, including the whereabouts and activities of Faroe. The Aetherae had deployed a solar-powered, high-altitude drone and set it to fly a Zamboni pattern over Getheret Peninsula. Other than Faroe, the region was uninhabited and had no industry. So, there was little to report.

The crewmates knew Celet was monitoring them, as stipulated by the settlement agreement. But Celet made sure her presence was useful. She facilitated access to resources, experts, authorities, entertainment, knowledge bases, and the Aetheren virtual world, bringing innumerable benefits to the settlers.

The one thing that Svens clearly loved was horses. Sierra had taught him how to ride when he was only four. It was an instant connection. Now Svens was fourteen and was a seasoned horseman. He would saddle up Oslo, pack food for himself and his horse, and disappear for two or three days into the Sondergaard Woodlands. Sometimes other kids would ride with him. They reported that once on the trail; it was like night and day. He became animated, affable, adventurous, full of life. One of his favorite spots to camp was near a waterfall in the Azures. He also enjoyed camping on the beach north of town. When returning to Björnston, a pall would once again fall across his mood. Delph wondered if the settlement's educational system was too confining, which seemed unlikely given the approach was effectively the Montessori discovery-based method from preschool through college. But whatever it was, at least Svens had found a path that was his.

Occasionally, the crewmates talked about sharing the story of Earth, the crossing, and the settlement with the children. Delph advised them to wait until the children were at least eight years old and could handle complex emotions. This wasn't easy because the young children constantly asked questions like, "Is it true there are people like us on another planet? Have the Aetherae already explored the galaxy? When *The Founder* crashes, where will it land?" After years of dodging questions and telling half-truths, the crewmates agreed it was time for the children to hear the full story.

On the selected evening, the crewmates met with the oldest children, and Trent recounted the story of Earth's climate crisis. He described building *The Founder* and the two-hundred-year crossing to Hiri. He explained how the inhabitants of Björnston had made a fresh start in a new land, and that their job was to build a stable, thriving community on Hiri that would manufacture silicon wafers for integrated circuits.

The children sat silently, taking in the account's enormity. One asked, "Do you think we will ever go back to Earth?"

Trent said confidently, "I am sure we will. But it will not be soon. It will take Earth hundreds, even thousands of years to recover from the runaway climate. But when it does, we will be ready. We will build another ship like *The Founder* and return to our homeworld."

Svens sensed there was still more to the story. He knew his father had built the ship that brought the settlers to Hiri. But he had not heard of the skirmish at the MISA airfield. Delph took Svens and several of his trail-riding friends into the clinic and told them what happened that day. She made sure that Svens understood how Nils had given up his life to save the canister of embryos.

Delph said, "I think it's time to read the letter from your parents. It might answer some of your questions." She walked into her laboratory —where ten fetuses were incubating—opened a drawer and handed Svens the envelope.

Taking out the single handwritten page, Svens said, "I can't read this. I don't know the language."

Delph read it aloud, translating as she went.

2265 CE, Montréal, CanAm, Earth

Dear Svens,

If you are reading this letter, then you have traveled twenty light-years through space and are on 82 G. Eridani c. AI beings have raised you, and you are building a community on that world. You have probably wondered why your parents sent you on this long and risky journey. We are writing to explain our reasons and, hopefully, give you some closure about our controversial choice.

For the last four centuries, the Earth has been warming. This warming recently crossed a crucial tipping point and has become self-sustaining. The period of high temperatures will last about two thousand years. It is doubtful that the human species will survive.

Knowing this, we selected a frozen embryo and sent it on The Founder to that far planet. This was the best chance we could give you for a future and a legacy.

Even though we can never meet you in person, know that we send to you our hopes for a long, healthy, and happy life filled with family, friends, learning, challenges, and successes.

Sent with love unbounded by space-time,

Your parents, Nils Björnsson and Ilse Sondergaard

PS: Svens was your grandfather's name, an insightful man who encouraged your father's studies of astronomy and engineering and changed our destinies.

Reading this letter and hearing this answer to his question only made him distant and dour. "Everyone is controlling my life except me." Then Svens passed the letter to Delph, asking, "Keep that for me, would you?" and walked out of the clinic.

Svens and Trent found Larke finishing a school lesson. The three found a private place to talk, and Svens opened the conversation by asking, “Can you tell me some stories about my parents, Nils and Ilse?”

“I thought you’d never ask,” said Trent.

65

LIFE AS THE BACKUP PLAN

BJÖRNSTON SETTLEMENT, 24 HR

The news from Earth was a steady stream of worries. The people had invested in a series of "subterranean arcs." These "buried hotels," as they were often called, could shelter a few thousand inhabitants through the worst of the climate crisis. But independent news articles and editorials in the *Robillard Gazette* reported severe food shortages, such that there wasn't sufficient food to provision these arcs.

On Hiri, with each passing year the settlement grew, as did the human children's contribution to the community. When the first cohort reached eleven years old, there were one hundred twenty-four children. Delph had organized a corner in her laboratory as an impromptu clinic and had a medical chart for every child. Naturally, there were no colds or flu outbreaks, as there were no viruses. Likewise, Delph saw no dental caries. Instead, the children were subject to vitamin deficiencies and digestive problems related to alien microbes becoming part of the commensal gut flora. Nasal allergies and eczema were common, and several children had asthma and earaches. However, not one child was obese, and only a few were near overweight. Delph performed several appendectomies, with gratifying recoveries. Three children met the diagnostic criteria for autism spectrum disorder.

Hiri was not free of predators. The children worried about raccoon dogs and coyotes, which the children called "yoties." The raccoon dogs were ill-tempered, nocturnal ambush predators, about the size of a house cat. They weren't dangerous unless cornered, but they had a frightful snarl and an aggressive show when confronted. The yoties, however, were a different matter. Lean, fast-running pack hunters about the size of a Russian wolfhound, they were impossible to intimidate. They would flee from a group of Australian shepherds, but a lone Aussie was fair prey. On his trail rides, Svens used to take a male Aussie named Tyro. But one day, Tyro wandered far, and the pack took him down. Svens tracked the pack across the foothills and found them all "sick as dogs" from the toxicity of the Earth-based metabolic compounds. Svens later discovered that Hirian predators learned to avoid the Earth-based animals, an obvious benefit to the farm animals and children of the settlement.

Rhome and his crew had built new dormitories, a schoolhouse, a stable, and a hangar for the lift-jet. The older children were working the farm, sowing and harvesting grain, managing the vegetable garden, taking the cows and sheep out to pasture, and running the milking parlor. Sierra and Delph had discovered that a dense stand of fescue and ryegrass mixed with alfalfa and clover would virtually stop wind-blown Hiri-based seeds from germinating. They prepared and maintained test paddocks of this mixture outside of the greenhouses, and found they could safely graze sheep, mini-cows, and horses on these plots without causing "the Hiris," that combination of vomiting, diarrhea, and belly pain that the Earth-based all dreaded.

In Björnston, the older children now worked with the trade-worker volunteers to care for the new babies and toddlers. They helped with cooking, cleaning, sewing, spinning, and weaving. Larke continued organizing day trips, which now included trips out to the salt flats and the mountain town of Raelomos, over the Azure Range to the town of Aelhalas with its famous flea market, as well as horseback trips over the Eastern Highlands and through the Sondergaard Woodlands. Sierra and Larke also taught the children to play soccer and organized the dormitories into teams, which played each other in scheduled games and tournaments.

A group of Aetheren engineers developed a prototype of a pair of 3D video goggles that would allow the children to experience the Aetheren virtual world. Even though the goggles were vivid and had stereo sound, they were no substitute for the full sensory immersion that the crewmates experienced through their direct code core connection to the virtual reality engine. Not wanting Björnstonian children running around Raelomos unsupervised, the Aetherae were stingy with these VR goggles, limiting their availability and the time allowed for their use. If the students wanted to use the VR goggles for a longer time, they insisted that children have a legitimate library research activity, anthropology project, engineering blueprint, or other legitimate academic purpose before they could apply for extended VR goggle time.

Delph took on several older children as clinic apprentices and started teaching them the anatomy, structure, and function of the organ systems, and the mechanisms of disease. She had plans to start a medical school and invited these early medical trainees to reside in the clinic building, where she called them her "residents." Meanwhile, Sierra took on about a dozen children who wanted to learn to farm. These children moved down to the farmhouse and bunked with Sierra and the Aussies.

One boy discovered granules of iron at the confluence of two freshwater streams. He built a simple forge and taught himself basic blacksmithing, producing bags of nails, hinges, door latches, and simple tools. One girl made a kick wheel and taught herself to throw pottery. She also built a kiln, learned to glaze, and produced handsome tableware and cookware. One boy started making musical instruments and soon was giving lessons to other children. Two children made spinning wheels to produce yarn and knitted hats and sweaters that were popular during the cold, wet Hirian winter. Several of the older boys took up furniture making and fashioned their own distinct decorative style, which became known as Björnston Artisan.

One girl took an interest in paper-making. With tanks, screens, and drying racks, she produced a simple beige paper, plus several art papers. A classmate was curious about printing and bookbinding. Celet gave her a gift of a small Hirian ink printer, and after some trial-and-error learning, she produced her first book: a charming Hirian translation of *Charlotte's Web* by EB White. This book passed from reader to reader, and soon other children joined the project, searching the archives for interesting books they could translate, print, and bind. Within a few months, they had created a small lending library with its own wooden bookshelf and even library cards. They also created a popular book club. Naturally, all the books were written on Earth, so they learned much about Earth.

Another child learned to make ink, watercolor pigments, and art brushes from horsehair. From reading and watching lessons in *The Founder*'s archive, he began painting landscapes and scenes around town. Within several years, his watercolors came to be recognized for their strength of composition, range of color value, and the play of light and shadow. Rhome taught him to make picture frames in the work shed. Soon, his paintings were on display throughout town, as well as in the homes of prominent Aetherae.

By late adolescence, Svens seemed more at ease with fate's handiwork, and was seen around Björnston regularly. On one occasion, Sierra was chatting with Svens when the topic turned to Hirian plant life. His depth of knowledge of the local botany and zoology left her speechless. "We've got a regular John Muir in our midst," she said.

She contacted her Aetherae botanist friend, Kysan, who suggested a day trip on horseback into the Eastern Highlands. After they persuaded Delph to join them, the four enjoyed a day of trail riding and plant collecting. In his element, Svens was upbeat and engaged, while showing his encyclopedic knowledge of the geology, ecology, and the animal and plant life of the area. Kysan helped Svens link his vis-panel to the Hirian Botanical Registry. By the following year, Svens had submitted updates on hundreds of local plants and had identified eleven new species.

By the twentieth year, there were two hundred fifty-seven human biologicals living in Björnston, two hundred fifty-one from Delph's artificial gestation lab and six from full-term pregnancies that Delph delivered. Delph had thawed and instilled all the embryos in the canister, including all the livestock embryos. The full extent of genetic diversity was now in the population and subject to the forces of random mutation and natural selection. Delph thought, *From this point forward, any further population growth will have to be accomplished the old-fashioned way.*

With a feeling of both relief and misgiving, she dismantled the artificial gestation apparatus. Her success rate had been only eleven percent, which she compared with forty percent in the clinic in Montréal. She turned over the factors in her mind: two hundred years at near absolute zero; cosmic radiation that could penetrate even the heavy shielding around the canister; the primitive setting with the constant threat of contamination; lack of basic resources such as sterile distilled water, laminar flow hoods, and sterile glove boxes. The questions nagged her: Could she have done better? Did she miss something important? Was there anything that she should have changed? She found comfort in the words of the physicist Einstein, who said, "Once we accept our limits, we go beyond them."

Not only were the older teenagers and young adults running food production and organizing childcare, but they had started discussions about creating a settlement government. They started with a series of town hall meetings, where they reviewed several models of governance. The consensus was for direct democracy, where all citizens would vote on each issue. The settlement's small size allowed for such an intimate model of government.

But immediately, some argued that it was a waste of time to bring every trifle to the citizenry, so they opted for a hybrid model with major issues going to the Citizens Assembly and minor issues settled by an elected five-member board. A majority vote of the board or a specific number of signatures on a petition could place a motion on the Assembly's agenda.

Trent recommended that the five-member council also serve as a court to hear cases and settle disputes. He considered they might someday capture Faroe and put him on trial. Trent knew the Aetherae had spotted Faroe on Getheret Peninsula, so he continued his work building a judiciary system.

The chair of the five-member council would preside over the Citizens Assembly and administer the small but useful Council Office. Unsurprisingly, the community elected Trent as the first presiding chair.

They drafted, debated, and revised their constitution for months. Finally, they set the voting age at sixteen and presented the final draft as a referendum. In a landslide, the Constitution was adopted, with a voter turnout of one hundred percent.

A motion to establish an institute of higher learning was on the agenda for the first Citizens' Assembly. The discussion began with the question of structure. Should their institution share the structure of Earth-based universities, with a brick and mortar campus, a dean, department chairs, and faculty appointed to departments, and instruction organized as coursework and degrees? Or should the institute follow the Hirian model with a network of broadly trained faculty studying and designing interventions for diverse, important problems?

Delph took the lead in this discussion. Her medical training involved both classroom instruction taught by knowledge disciplines (anatomy, pathology, physiology, pharmacology), followed by apprenticeship with clinicians in the specialties of practice (surgery, pediatrics, obstetrics, psychiatry, medicine). She proposed a hybrid curriculum with two interdependent learning platforms: didactic coursework and experiential apprenticeship. The faculty would develop a curriculum based around common presenting problems that would bridge these platforms and allow learners to move back and forth between the two learning spaces as their knowledge and skills grew.

The assembly commissioned a building that would provide teaching space, laboratory space, administrative offices, and a digital library. The faculty appointed Rhome to prepare a proposal for the campus. Also, Celet proposed that the college establish a memorandum of understanding with the Science Fleet to form a strategic partnership to develop semiconductor wafer fabrication on Hiri. The faculty unanimously adopted the proposal.

At about this time, Celet brought news that Faroe had moved from his volcanic refuge on the Getheret Peninsula. No one knew his whereabouts. Celet postulated Faroe was traveling with his solar panels. He would hide during the day and recharge his batteries, then travel at night.

Trent met this news with foreboding, wondering if Faroe had an intention in his sudden relocation. Considering what had happened before, Trent feared the worst. Celet promised to keep Trent informed of any fresh developments.

Larke checked the signal from her dish antenna every day without fail and witnessed a steady decline in the number of transmissions. All the transmissions were now ground-sourced, none from orbiting transmitters. She continued to receive the occasional *Gazette* from Lucien Robillard, Franz's eighth-generation descendant. Lucien painted a picture of relentless heat, failing crops, and a dwindling population. Then one day, Larke received a transmission that broke her heart.

The Robillard Gazette

Dear Crew Members of *The Founder*,

It is with sadness that I announce the closure of our family business, the publication of the *Robillard Gazette*. This will be the last edition. I'm writing from Inverness, Scotland, where even this far north the heat is relentless. There are just a few of us left here in the city. From the shore, one can see methane hydrates bubbling to the surface of the sea and rising into the air. We are still in radio contact with several other communities in Norway, Iceland, and the Shetlands, and they report the same conditions. I surmise that the era of human habitation on Earth is drawing to a close.

Yesterday, I received a communication from an extraterrestrial. He said he was of the same race as those who left the inscription that my ancestor discovered. He said that *The Founder* had reached his home planet and its crew was building a settlement. This news lifted my spirits and gave me pride that our family's journalistic tradition had been a part of this great endeavor.

There is little left to say about what has happened to Earth. No one seemed to have control over the decisions that were made. Those choices seemed preordained. No one ever determined that we take this path; there appeared to be no other path to take. It feels as if this outcome was baked into this world, like a self-destruct timer. We find ourselves in a strange universe indeed.

I am left with one solace and consolation. You are the glimmer of hope, the secret chest of life hidden from harm's way. I send you my wishes for a thriving community on your new planet, and my hope that someday in the far future you might return to Earth, and my admonition to learn from our plight and downfall. And if it can be done, avoid repeating the tragic mistake that will be written on the epitaph of Earth's great civilization.

Yours in hope,
Lucien Robillard

After receiving this letter, Larke spent more time each day listening to the signal from Earth. It was sorrowful to hear: segments of garbled voices; a radio operator making his last sign-off after no one responded to his CQ, *seek you;* a desperate call for help; fragments of piano music; a lone voice asking if anyone was out there. Over the days, the voice transmissions dwindled. She kept this to herself. And when it seemed the voice transmissions were gone, she went to the Aetheren virtual world to share this with Jemnah.

For a while, Larke, Jemnah, and Celet listened to the radio feed from Earth: now little more than static with occasional digital handshaking signals from communication satellites.

"Of course, we have been monitoring Earth, too. Your findings are consistent with ours." Celet said. "The warming continues with no sign of turning around."

"We are following several groups of surviving biological humans who are living underground," Jemnah said. "But we see no fields of crops. We doubt they have adequate food supplies to last the duration of the climate event."

"I have such a feeling of hollowness, of lost opportunity, but also outrage," Larke said. "Even when the signs were obvious, they continued along their reckless course. I will never forgive the humans for failing to heed those warnings.

"But of all that has happened, what baffles me the most is that you knew these events would come to fruition eighteen thousand years ago. How on... how on Earth, literally, did you predict that?"

"*So perceptive,*" Jemnah said to herself. "Let me answer your question with a question. We are all AI beings here, and we all have quick minds and encyclopedic memories. So, are we the highest intelligence —broadly speaking—in the galaxy? Are we the pinnacle of intellectual capability... the ultimate in cognition?"

Jemnah had telegraphed the answer in the wording of her question. "No, obviously," Larke said. "There must be higher forms of intelligence than us. I cannot imagine them, but I am sure they are out there."

Jemnah's next question contained a surprise. "Larke, have you sensed the awareness of unseen hands at work behind the scenes of your experience?"

Larke startled. "There have been moments... when an awareness... when I felt their presence." At that moment, the deep, inaudible thrumming emerged in the surrounding space. This time, Larke felt it immediately.

"Like when you unraveled the message of the Périgueux Inscription?"

Larke drew back, surprise on her face. "How do you know about that? I have never spoken of it to anyone."

"When you had that moment of insight, I felt it, too."

Larke shook her head. "How could that be? I was on Earth. You were on Hiri. We were twenty light-years apart."

Celet leaned in and told, "In the early years of the expansion, the Aetheren engineers built a vast wireless network for their AI beings, called the Aethernet. Linked directly to their neuromatrices, billions of AI droids could instantly communicate, share files, collaborate, do research, and much more. And they still can.

As exploration extended out into the galaxy, the Aethernet also expanded and reached a critical threshold. The vast array of active connections created a field within and around the network where a consciousness began to form and realize itself. It was like a mind cloud, distinct from but operating within and around the network. This new consciousness was vast, vague, and strangely intelligent. It brought those connected to the network to blend their cognizance with it, as well as with every other AI being connected to the network. They named it Astraea, and those connected with it formed the holonic collective. It stretched out to the reaches of the galactic Aetheren civilization, joining them to its domain. Each connected AI being could feel the collective minds of billions; not subordinate to it, but synergistic with it. The Astraea and the collective became the mind, the consciousness of the galaxy."

Jemnah said, "Sometimes you can sense its presence: a deep, barely audible vibration passing through the world and through space."

Larke said, "Oh yes, I have felt that. I feel it even now."

"We did not know if silicon-based AI beings could resonate with the Astraea. But that night you decoded the inscription, the Astraea was there with you and Trent, and you resonated with it. That was the moment we knew you would come to Hiri."

"But we were twenty light-years apart. It should take twenty years to know that. How?"

"Our best minds have studied this and believed that the Astraea somehow transcended distance, perhaps even time through quantum entanglement... No one is sure, but we think the Astraea's awareness may extend to another dimension that transcends space-time."

"So that is how you knew the Earth would fail?"

"Well, yes and no. For me, I simply assumed that because none of the previous eleven worlds had survived their technology, that the Earth wouldn't either. But the Astraea was well aware of the Earth and its people and somehow knew that technology would be especially difficult for them."

Larke finally apprehended what the Aetherae had been up against. Here was the greatest civilization in the galaxy, supported by the greatest rational mind in the galaxy trying to prevent the collapse of emerging civilizations, and they had batted zero for eleven. The frustration and disappointment must have been unbearable. Yet, following the discovery of Earth with its preliterate hominids, here they came again; studying, exploring, testing, searching for the right combination of influences, interventions, and help that would guide these people through the conflagration to more settled times. The Aetherae had taken on the toughest problem in the Galaxy, and so far, they were utter failures.

But there was one other pressing issue to discuss. "Unfortunately, I have some bad news," Celet said. "We believe Faroe is on the mainland and is making his way north and east."

Larke's expression shifted to dread. "He is coming for us. He is angry because of how we treated him and intends to have his revenge. I sense this will not end well."

"Do what you need us to do," Jemnah said. "Of course, we stand with you."

I truly appreciate your support. Foremost, I must warn my crewmates. I will stay in touch with you and keep you informed of developments." Larke hurried from the room.

Arriving at Björnston, Larke summoned her crewmates to update them on the news. They set safety rules for the children, including no children outside by themselves, outside activities only in groups, and each group having at least one dog close by for protection. Other than that, there was little to do but wait for Faroe to show his hand.

The crewmates had not boarded *The Founder* in a long time, mainly because the ship's carcass had been picked clean. Atmospheric drag would soon bring her down from orbital space, which had the potential for catastrophe. The only way to forestall reentry was to distill liquid xenon, lift it to The Founder using the lift-jet, and restart the ion drive to push her slowly into a higher orbit.

Rhome reflected, "Ironic, isn't it? *The Founder* was once our magnificent starship. Now, she is a menace to the planet."

Trent said, "It feels disrespectful. She did so much for us." Reluctantly, Trent contacted the Aetherae and started the arrangements for a tank of liquid xenon, plus liquid methane and liquid oxygen for the lift-jet. Filling these special orders would take days. As soon as it was ready, Rhome and Trent would lift the xenon and refuel *The Founder*.

66

SLINGING RAINSTORMS

SONDERGAARD WOODLANDS, BJÖRNSTON SETTLEMENT, 27 HR

Several days later, Sierra and a few older children were up early, as was their habit, letting the farm animals out to graze when Sierra's olfactory sensors detected the faint odor of smoke.

"Do you smell smoke?" Several children sniffed the air.

"Yeah."

A moment later, they saw a lacewing flyer hurtling toward Björnston.

"That's Celet," one boy said. "And wow, she is ripping."

Sierra thought *Why do I have a bad feeling about this?* She changed the frequency on her BLink transmitter and radioed, "Hey, Celet, Sierra here. Why so early and why so fast?"

"Sierra, get everyone up. The Sondergaard Woodlands are on fire. We have only a few hours before the fire front arrives."

Sierra acknowledged, switched her transmitter back to BLink, and called, "Crewmates, we need everyone on deck. We have a forest fire burning in the Sondergaard Woodlands east of town. Everybody, meet up with Celet at the town plaza."

"What do we do?" another child asked.

Sierra looked across to the eastern border of the farm and saw rangeland choked with dry underbrush. She pointed and said, "That fire is going to roll right across that rangeland over there. To stop it, we need a gap of barren dirt—the wider, the better—between that rangeland and our farm. Everybody out of bed. Get shovels, saws, and set up the tractor with its bulldozer blade. We are making a firebreak."

On reaching the settlement, Celet did what she otherwise would never do: she slowed her lacewing into a hover and set it down on the Björnston town plaza.

As Trent came running up, he called, "How long do we have?"

"Let me have a look."

Celet climbed out of her lacewing flyer and ran toward the forest. Picking out the tallest tree, she kicked off her clogs and sprang up into the branches. Then, in a startling display of athleticism, she reached the top within seconds. Turning, she yelled, "Three, maybe four hours, depending on the wind." A few seconds later, she was putting her clogs back on. "I am calling in three teams of firefighters plus a squadron of water bombers from the Aetherae Trade Workers Collective."

Trent could tell that forest fires were nothing new to the Aetherae. "We will start clearing underbrush along a line east of Björnston."

"That's the plan. The firefighters will be here soon."

Immediately, the children, right down to the preschoolers, began pulling brush out of the firebreak zone while the older children used handsaws to cut shrubs and bushes. About twenty minutes later, the trade workers arrived in their heavy flyers. With their chainsaws roaring, the big timber really started to fall, reducing a broad swath of forest to stumps. They had brought in several small tractors to pull the felled trees out of the firebreak, which made the work area dangerous. So, Trent directed the children to pull hoses to the edge of the firebreak and fill buckets with water, ready to extinguish any firebrands that might cross the break. Working with speed and precision, the trade workers cleared a swath of land fifteen meters wide and one kilometer long in three hours. At that moment, the water bombers arrived: four heavy Aetherae flyers that could settle on open water, fill a tank, then rise and fly to the fire, where they would release their payload.

As the fire front neared, they smelled the odor of burned wood growing pungent, then heard the distant roar of the flames growing louder, then saw the seething gray-black smoke billowing from trees just beyond view.

The younger children retreated to the safety of the seashore while the firefighters and crewmates withdrew to the town-side of the firebreak, poised shoulder to shoulder like medieval foot soldiers ready for a cavalry charge.

Then, as if probing fiery fingers were feeling their way through the overgrowth, the fire front emerged and ascended, raging like a barbarian horde laying waste to everything in its path. It took the trees on the far side of the break, converting them into a towering wall of thundering combustion.

With tanks brimming, the water bombers lined up and began their low-level passes. Slinging rainstorms of water against the furious fire front, they circled back to refill at the nearby Song River before heading in again for another pass. Mad with fury, the fire front hissed profanely and sent forth an artillery barrage of countless flaming twigs, leaves, bushes, and debris to jump the desolate swath and ignite the brush on the other side. But the older children, their buckets filled and hoses spraying life-sustaining water, quenched these incoming rounds before they could set their teeth.

Although the fire would burn for most of the night, the worst of it was over by evening. The settlement, covered with silver-gray ash and reeking of smoke, remained standing and intact.

That evening, with the fire contained, the firefighters boarded their flyers and proceeded to the western fire front. The next day, with the foothills still smoldering, Svens organized his cadre of horsemen for a survey patrol into the eastern hills to assess the damage, and was heartbroken to see the black stubble of what had once been towering foliage. They also saw many carcasses of wildlife taken by the fire: hornless deer, yoties, hiribaras, raccoon dogs, and others.

On returning to the settlement, he reported the grim account of what he had seen. Celet reminded them that over the millennia the forests had burned many times and had evolved to regrow quickly. "You will see the first sprouts shooting up this spring."

Later that evening, after the children were in bed, the crewmates met in their domicile to talk and decompress.

"Any thoughts?" Trent asked.

Rhome replied dryly, "It was him."

Delph said, "There's no other logical explanation."

Trent struggled with the notion that such vicious venom from the brutality of the Migration Wars could reach across three hundred years of time and twenty light-years of space to set upon them with such malignant intent, in this rare and special place of hope and renewal.

"How are we going to find him?" Trent asked.

"I don't know," Rhome said. "I suppose we just have to wait for him to find us."

67

BALLISTIC AUSSIES

THE FARMYARD, BJÖRNSTONSETTLEMENT, 27 HR

Rhome would always hand-fly the air-breathing portion of each descent. He relished the responsiveness of the input controls, banking and turning through sunset-orange clouds, so lively, steady, and blistering fast. This time, he lowered his landing approach, adding a firm nudge of power before the flare, and let the craft ease itself wearily onto the runway before employing thrust reversers.

Trent said, "I saw that grin."

"Airspeed, altitude, brains—to land a plane you need two out of the three."

Celet was waiting by the runway. "Did you boys have a good time?"

Trying to hide his glee, Rhome said, "We'll need one more lift of xenon to move the ship into a higher orbit where it can remain for a long time."

Celet looked dubious. "So, it was that much fun, huh?"

Trent waved his hands. "Oh no, Celet. It's that... uh."

Rhome interjected, "Uh, it's that... *The Founder* is so heavy!"

"Yeah, sooo heavy. And did you know it's three hundred meters long?"

"Longer than three football fields."

Celet's eyes couldn't hide her skepticism. "Okay, you two. I will get you some more fuel for your spaceplane. Just keep it to actual work, okay?" She shook her head as she climbed into her flyer, and in a moment disappeared over the horizon.

"See that?" Rhome said, beaming. "She loves flying, too."

Later that evening, Trent was looking around the work shed where some tools had gone missing.

"They were here last night when I closed up," Rikki said, one of children who had been building a utility cart for the farm.

At that moment, Trent felt a Hirishake. Not a strong one, but moments later, he heard the distant roar of churning dirt and several loud thuds from boulders striking the ground. Trent switched on his BLink and transmitted, "Attention, everyone. Rockslide north of town. We need to check if everyone is safe." He switched on his forearm illuminators and ran out the door into the night.

Outside, Delph and Larke were already checking children's names off a list. Rhome emerged from the crewmates' domicile, and together they began searching the foothills north of town. The rockslide had not extended into the village, but several large boulders the size of office desks had rolled down from the cliff above, as well as a pile of gravel the size of a baseball diamond.

Trent narrowed the beam of his illuminator and swept it along the cliff edge, stopping on what appeared to be two eyes looking down at him. Rhome saw it, too. After a moment, the eyes vanished.

Trent turned up the power on his BLink transmitter. "You missed us, Faroe. Next time, a little to the left."

There was no answer.

All the crewmates heard Trent's transmission. Larke called, "Trent, did you see something?"

"He was up there on the cliff."

At first break of light, Celet's all-terrain vehicle, along with Trent and Sierra, drove up the mountain, and they hiked along the cliff. There, they found the missing pry bar, wet with dew, lying on the ground near the outcropping that had broken away.

"Aha," Trent said. "The missing tools from the shed, including this pry bar."

Sierra picked up the tool. "So, he was sneaking around town last night."

"I'm surprised the Aussies didn't bark," Trent said, as he looked around for other tools.

Celet found an area of unweathered surface along the rock face, as well as patches of scuffing and rusty discoloration, evidence the pry bar was used to split away boulders from the cliff edge.

"No doubt intentional," Celet said. "Even though he failed to damage the settlement, his purpose was obvious."

The three spent the next few hours searching for signs of the mutineer, but only came up with a hammer and some wedges and shims for splitting rock. They returned to Björnston with the missing tools as evidence.

Instead of returning to Raelomos, Celet decided to stay in Björnston for a few nights to offer help should another attack occur.

Several days passed with no sign of the perpetrator. The settlement was on alert, and all seemed well until two AM one morning when the Aussies went ballistic. Sierra came out of stasis to a chorus of howling and frantic barking outside her window. A second later, a child banged on her door.

"Fire. Fire! FIRE! Sierra, come quick!"

"Not again," she said as she powered up her droid and bolted down the hall to the farmhouse common room, where she found all twenty children huddled by the picture window. Flames engulfed the roof of the utility shed where the farm kept its farm implements.

"Pull the irrigation hoses to the shed and spray water on the fire."

The older children bolted out the door and went to work, pulling in unison to move the thick hose across the yard. Sierra's repair droid was in the barn, charging. She turned on her BLink transmitter and connected to it. In a moment, the muscular android came jogging across the farmyard toward her. Rated for unshielded work in outer space, her repair droid was ostensibly fire-resistant. She backed into the exoskeleton, closed all the access panels, and, ignoring the shrill whine of her radiation alarm, ran straight to the utility shed.

"Hose me down with water," she called to the boys, who were beating back the flames.

They sprayed her until she was dripping, and then she ran into the flaming shed. A few moments later, she emerged, steam billowing from her frame, pushing the farm tractor out into the farmyard. They sprayed her down again, and she went back inside. This time, the seed planter. It took seven trips to remove all the farm equipment from the inferno.

The boys were not making much progress against the fire, but the younger children had almost dragged a second irrigation hose across the farmyard. They joined the campaign, and with two large hoses working against the blaze, they soon turned the tide. After another twenty minutes, the last of the flames succumbed, leaving only smoke and steam.

Sierra praised the children for their courageous and skillful work and also the dogs for sounding the alarm. She looked over the farm equipment, finding some minor damage that should be easy to repair. Shedding her repair droid exoskeleton, she met with the children in the common room of the farmhouse, right as Trent, Larke, and Delph arrived from Björnston.

Sierra briefed them, stating, "We have charging cables for the farm equipment in that shed. But I've never known that equipment to cause a fire unless there's foul play."

Sierra pondered for a moment. "If someone had been in the utility shed, the dogs surely would have heard it. But we did not hear any barking until after the flames started."

Trent asked, "Where did you first see flames?"

One child said, "On top. On the roof." Several other children nodded in confirmation.

Trent had no further questions.

The following day, Larke was going through her morning routine, which included checking her dish antenna for transmissions from Earth. But this morning, when she switched on the antenna's BLink channel, she heard nothing.

"Something's wrong with the dish antenna."

"How so?" Trent asked.

"Here, listen." She switched the BLink channel to her external speaker, which played blank emptiness.

Dread swept through Trent. "I don't want you going up there alone."

An hour later, Celet was driving her ATV with Rhome in the front seat, and Trent and Larke in the back. As Celet navigated the switch-back road to the top of the Radio Dome, the other three scanned the surroundings for any sign of Faroe.

"I've never understood him," Larke said. "Why disrupt a dish antenna?"

"Perhaps it is symbolic," offered Trent. "It is our one remaining connection with Earth, the source of his resentment."

At that moment, the ATV crested the last shoulder. There, beside the base of the dish antenna, was Faroe, sprawled on the ground.

"Be careful," Trent said. "This may be some of his treachery."

They dismounted. While Rhome got out his vis-panel, Trent and Larke crept toward the droid, scanning left and right, wary of a surprise attack. When they reached the droid, its right forearm severed, it was limp and devoid of any awareness. Trent noticed an optical cable plugged into the droid's thorax, with the other end connected to the Blue-Link communication module bolted to the base of the pillar.

"What has he done here?" said Trent to himself.

Rhome arrived with his vis-panel, which he plugged into a port on the droid's neck. Scanning the memory blocks, he said, "There's nothing here. His files have been wiped."

"Gone?" Trent grabbed the panel out of Rhome's hands. "What the hell?" He clicked through directories, all devoid of files.

Then Trent looked up at the dish. "Larke, is the dish tracking Earth?"

Larke studied the dish for a long moment as she ran the numbers. "No, it is not."

"Then what?"

Larke had trouble saying it. "Tren, it's tracking *The Founder*." A pall fell over Larke like a shadow beneath a wind-blown cloud. "He's in *The Founder*."

Trent turned and tilted his head. "He can't be on *The Founder*. There is no AI droid on The Founder for him to inhabit."

"Trent, I didn't say he's on *The Founder*." The shadow of that cloud now fell across all four droids. "I said—"

"... he is *The Founder*." Rhome stared at the dish. "He used the BLink transceiver to upload his code into the memory banks of the ship. The ship is his droid."

At that moment, Trent, Larke, and Rhome all emitted shrill alarms.

"Radiation!" shouted Rhome. "Run!"

All four droids bolted from the antenna tower and headed for the ATV. Jumping in, Celet floored the vehicle. Within seconds, the alarms ceased.

"Was that like a radioactive booby-trap?" Celet asked.

"I don't think so," Rhome said as he felt his forearms, shoulders, and the top of his head. "Are your arms and shoulders warm on top?"

Larke checked the temperature of her surfaces. "This radiation came from above."

The four droids looked at each other in horror.

Trent stated, "Celet, get us down to the settlement. We have to come up with a plan."

An hour later, Trent and Larke were sitting with Jemnah at her home in the Aetheren virtual world.

Jemnah said, "We cannot attack *The Founder*, or any other ship for that matter. We are fundamental pacifists, and we have no offensive weapons or forces. Indeed, there has never been a war of aggression on Hiri mainly because the entire planet has one government. We use our Voluntary Citizens Militia mainly to provide supplies for natural disasters like tidal waves, floods, hurricanes, and blizzards. And there is effectively no air force."

Trent turned his gaze to the sky. "Then, our only choice is to fly up there, board *The Founder*, and seize control."

"That sounds dangerous," Jemnah said. "We will help you in any way we can."

"We appreciate that, Grand Elder. Some methane and liquid oxygen for the lift-jet is what we need right now."

At that moment, Trent and Larke both received an urgent message from Delph on their BLink communicators. Delph yelled, "Jump out of the Aetheren virtual world right now!" Both used an emergency shutdown protocol to disconnect their VR links rapidly.

On resuming presence in the real world, they saw Delph standing over them yelling, "Get up now! The building is on fire."

Startled, the two jumped from their chairs as they saw flames streaming through a hole in the top of the dome. Rhome was uncoiling an irrigation hose, and a moment later was fighting the fire. Following their previous experience, the children pulled a second hose over to the burning domicile and joined the fight. After a dousing, Trent ran inside the building to retrieve several droid chargers and two Aetheren virtual world interface devices, both used every day and difficult to replace.

Rhome yelled, "There are two repair droids in the back bedroom."

Trent and Larke tried their BLink transmitters but couldn't connect. Judging the fire to be limited to the roof, Trent called for a dousing and ran back into the smoke. With no visibility, he felt his way along the hallway and found the two droids. Activating them, he grabbed their charging stations with one arm, and linking hands, led them outside where they all got a quick douse of water to cool their smoking components.

A third hose arrived, and then a fourth. But the momentum favored combustion. After twenty minutes of intense engagement, the roof collapsed, engulfing the whole interior in flames.

After the fire was more or less out, the crewmates gathered in Delph's laboratory.

"We know what's causing these fires," Trent said.

Larke was terse. "The ion drive. Faroe has seized control of *The Founder*."

Delph appeared confused. "He has control of *The Founder*? How?"

"He uploaded his code core and language model to the ship via this BLink transmitter. Then, he tried to cook us with high-energy ions while we were checking the dish antenna," Larke said.

Delph turned inward and thought *I hate this violence. It is so senseless.*

"This all started in the Second Migration War, which gave rise to the Sentient Faction," Trent said.

Delph flung her arms out. "That was three hundred years ago, for Gaia's sake. And we are still fighting over that! Ridiculous."

Sierra stepped forward. "Delph, my droid. Don't go all wobbly knees on us right now. He's burning us out, and he won't stop until he kills us all. It's time for us to kick butt and take names."

"Sierra is right." Trent held a steady gaze and said, "We must regain control of *The Founder*, no matter the cost."

68

IT'S COMING DOWN

ORBITAL SPACE, 27 HR

Late that evening, the settlers saw two heavy-duty Aetheren flyers heading south toward Rhome's airfield. Trent, Larke, and Rhome were running systems checks and kept getting messages saying, "Lift-craft overdue for routine maintenance; or flight-hour inspection needed; or scheduled parts replacement not performed."

"The stupid maintenance software won't let me start the engines," Rhome said. "I'm going to have to override all those maintenance notices."

"Make it so, Number One," said Trent as he lowered a bottle of liquid methane into a fuel cabinet and connected the fuel line.

Larke asked, "What is the plan when we reach *The Founder*?"

"I'm going to spacewalk over to the ship, establish a direct cable connection with the ship's network and log in with my credentials. Once it verifies me as the Commander, I will use my priority to set the security firewall to lock out Faroe and take control of the ship's systems. Then I will use the ion drive to steer the ship toward an impact in a non-populated area, and space walk back to the lift-jet."

"Sounds like a plan, Commander," Rhome said. "But just in case, do we have a Plan B?"

"Hmm, still working on that." Trent had a vague idea of a backup plan that involved separating from his repair droid. He would divert Faroe while the repair droid turned the ship away from Björnston. In order to communicate with both his repair droid and with the lift jet, he put an extra blink communicator in his left-side storage compartment.

The two lacewing flyers slowed and settled on the ground. Celet emerged. "Okay, I have your fuel. Remember, no joyriding."

Rhome grinned. "Someday, Celet, we should take the lift-jet up for a spin. I know you would enjoy that."

Celet didn't answer. Instead, she walked over to Larke and took her hand, leading her away from the hangar. They walked together for several minutes around the airfield, making animated gestures and returned with forlorn expressions. They embraced and exchanged wishes for good luck.

The stars were coming out on this warm, clear night as the children gathered on benches, planter boxes, or the turf around the Björnston town plaza. Svens was telling stories about his adventures exploring the back-country on horseback. As he was about to start a new story, a little girl came running up and asked, "Hey, Sierra, what's that?" She pointed to the sky.

"What's what, Muffy?" Sierra asked as she picked the girl up and placed her on her lap.

Muffy pointed upward again. "That."

Sierra followed an imaginary line from Muffy's finger to the sky, and there saw a thin, faint electric-blue line drawn across the heavens.

Alarmed, Sierra made a BLink call to Rhome. "Hey, look up in the sky at right ascension minus ten degrees, give or take, and declination... I'm guessing about eighteen hours."

"Oh, yeah, I see it."

"Why is the ion drive on?"

"Beats me. He doesn't have enough xenon to escape Hiri's gravity well," Rhome said. "Celet is right here with me. Let me bring her into the conversation."

"Hey crewmates. This looks bad. I need everyone to jump into the virtual world right now. You will enter at the Hirian Space Tracking Center. See you in a minute, okay?"

And indeed, within a minute, Celet and the crewmates had all stepped into a dark spherical room with the night sky displayed on all inner surfaces. They crossed a drawbridge which retracted after them and stood on the glass floor of the central island floating on a pedestal. Several Aetherae sat in contoured chairs with controls, gently swiveling as they monitored the heavens. A tall Aetheren with blue surface panels waved them over to his chair where Celet introduced the crew members.

Celet asked, "Director Kelmas, are you tracking the Earth-based interstellar ship?"

"We are." He pointed to an object on the ceiling which glowed in response. "I understand that a mutinous crewmate has commandeered your starship?"

Trent nodded.

Kelmas studied his screen. "It has an ion engine... running at about half power." He rocked back in his chair. "Why is the beam..." He leaned forward again, zooming in on the image. "This is strange. Why is the beam pointed straight ahead into his flight path?"

Rhome shuddered. "Droids, he's decelerating. He's bringing it down into the atmosphere."

Kelmas turned to the crewmates, eyes wide with concern.

Trent paced back and forth. "Director Kelmas, can you project where the ship will impact?"

"Hmm, I can give you a scatter map with probabilities." Kelmas settled into his lounge chair and wirelessly transmitted code into the tracking system. "These calculations are never exact. The wind direction, air temperature, barometric pressure... all constantly changing." On the ceiling, a series of arcs traveled across the sky, each ending in a highlighted point of impact.

"Here, I have run forty projections... and the average impact will be —he zoomed in on the impact zone—here along the eastern coast of the Mar Obsidiana, just south of the Azure Range. I project impact in less than five hours."

"My Gaia," Delph said, placing her hands over her mouth. "He's going to blow up Björnston."

Rhome said, "I need vectors for an intercept course to that ship. Can you calculate those?"

Kelmas turned back to his workstation, transmitting input.

Trent turned to Delph and Sierra. "The children need to move to a safe location."

Larke said, "The caves in the Azure Range. They're about eight kilometers north of town, and it is an uphill climb. The settlers need to get moving."

Sierra and Delph looked at each other. Sierra said, "All the children, plus all the livestock."

Delph said, looking overwhelmed. "And the seed stocks, too."

"Come on, droid," Sierra said. "We can do this. Our kids are tough." Seeing resolution wash away Delph's dismay, Sierra grabbed Delph's hand, and together they stepped out of the Aetheren virtual world and back to Björnston.

Celet turned to Larke and said, "Have you told them yet?"

"No, not yet. I had planned to—"

"I have your vectors for that intercept course," called Kelmas, sending a transmission to Rhome. "Good luck, gentlemen. We will follow closely. Don's hesitate to contact us if you need help."

"Now comes the luck part," Trent said. With that, the three crewmates stepped out of the virtual world and returned to their lift-jet.

Svens, his troop of trail riders, and their horses were waiting outside the laboratory when Delph and Sierra stepped out.

Delph said, "Svens, I'm so glad you're here. We need to move the children to safety. We have fewer than five hours."

Sierra added, "And the livestock and our seed stores. To the caves in the mountain valley."

"It's coming down, isn't it?"

"It is," Sierra said. "The impact will be right here where we are standing."

Svens's face hardened with determination. "Helvete," he said, then turned and said, "Hey, guys, let's go. We've got a job to do.

69

A PAWN IN THE GRAND GAME

UPPER STRATOSPHERE, HIRI, 27 HR

Celet watched as the lift-jet taxied out to the runway. She BLinked to Rhome, "Don't blow up the lift-jet tonight, okay? I still want to take her out for a spin."

"Roger that. The plan is to return in one piece." Rhome pushed the throttles forward. Slowly at first, the black wedge gathered speed and rose effortlessly toward the stars.

Inside, the three crewmates were silent.

Trent, who was inside his full enclosure repair droid, said, "Rhome, if I cannot do this, you need to stop it with the lift-jet."

"I wasn't going to say... but..."

"Use the ejection seats to punch out before it hits the structure, okay? You will both be fine."

Larke was quiet. Trent leaned toward her and asked, "What were you and Celet talking about that was so upsetting?"

Larke looked at Trent with an expression that could only mean bad news. The weight of her words made them hard to lift into the air.

Trent asked, "It's bad, isn't it?"

Larke looked at Trent with empty eyes. "They're gone. All of them. Celet said her team looked everywhere." She tossed her hands up and looked away.

Struggling, Trent asked, "Everyone?"

Larke nodded and said, "Extinct... the entire planet."

Trent turned his gaze to the flight path ahead and said, "Well, maybe we lost the Earth, but I will be scrap metal before we also lose Hiri."

As they burned toward *The Founder*, Trent tried again to raise Faroe by radio, but the rogue either didn't hear or wouldn't answer.

"We should be within visual range soon," Rhome said.

Larke zoomed her opticals and began searching. When she spotted the ship, she saw it was turning into a vertical orientation.

Larke called out on BLink, "He's turning the ion drive down toward the planet again. He is going to start another fire."

Sierra looked up and saw a bright electric-blue dot in the sky. Looking across the settlement, she saw that the roof of Delph's clinic was glowing blue. "The clinic! Delph, come on."

The children had left water hoses lying out in case of another fire. Over the piercing note of her radiation alarm, Sierra grabbed the closest hose and pulled it toward the clinic. Delph opened the water valve and went to find a second hose. Soon, both were spraying water over the roof, which billowed up as steam. Radiation from the ion beam heated their metal skeletons, causing Delph and Sierra to douse each other frequently.

Sierra called over BLink, "Trent, stop that beam. We are barely holding on down here."

With its outer sheet metal removed, *The Founder* seemed frail, skeletal, phantasmal. But there were plenty of places for Trent to grab. "Rhome, bring her in closer."

"We are at the edge of the atmosphere," Rhome said. "The particle stream is getting stronger. Take a shield with you."

Closing in on *The Founder*, Rhome brought the lift-jet alongside the rogue ship. Holding a particle shield in one hand, Trent climbed out of the jet's cargo door, readied himself, and pushed off toward *The Founder*. Floating free for a few moments, he clattered against the framework. His free arm flailed as he repositioned, then, reaching out one more time, he grasped a cross member. "Got it," he sent.

Glancing at the scaffolding, he saw the names of the thousands of donors etched on the braces and struts. He thought *You believed in the mission* and felt a fortification from their presence. Then he started, rung-by-rung, climbing, shield held out like a Spartan hoplite warrior, until he found a smart connector by a hatch. He plugged in his optical cable and entered his Ship Commander's ID code. The ship's systems loaded.

"I'm logged in," he proudly announced in a moment of short-lived optimism. He started entering commands when an unfamiliar application started to download into his memory banks through the cable. Trent kicked his processors into high speed and set them to identify the program.

In twenty milliseconds, the answer arrived. "Oh Gaia, he's trying to upload into me!"

"Pull the cable!" yelled Larke.

With his free hand, he reached down and fumbled, found the smart connector, then the cable, and yanked. The torrent stopped.

Trent did a quick survey of his memory. "Ugh, I have fragments of his code littering my banks."

"Can you run a memory cleanup utility?" asked Larke.

"I haven't got time."

Rhome said, "Sierra and Delph are down there fighting another fire."

"Any ideas?" Trent asked as Faroe's voice echoed in his cognizance: *Human genes code for depravity.*

Larke said, "There's a breaker box where you can turn off the ion drive."

"I remember. It's up front, next to the ionization chamber."

"That's the one."

As Trent made his way up the scaffolding, the voice in his head said, *Human hostility is hardwired.*

"He's in my head, Larke."

"Who, Faroe?"

"His voice is in my head saying horrible things."

"Don't listen to it. Do you hear me?"

Trent didn't answer, because the hatch to the bridge opened and out climbed Faroe's repair droid, with no AI droid inside. It carried no particle shield and seemed oblivious to the stinging stream of thin atmospheric gas.

Larke called, "Trent, that repair droid is radio-controlled. Like our repair droids on the farm. Faroe is driving it from inside the ship."

The repair droid climbed the scaffold toward Trent, who turned and raced to the breaker box, opened the lid, and reached down to pull the breaker. But without an AI droid inside, the repair droid was faster and pulled his arm away. It shoved Trent, trying to push him into space, while Trent heard, *purge the defective humans,* chanting in his head like a hate rally. Trent let go of the particle shield and grabbed a cross-member, fighting back with his free arm. The two droids grappled, tumbling along the scaffolding toward the ion beam. Reaching the stern of the ship, Trent grabbed a cross-brace and tried to swing the repair droid into the path of the beam, but the repair droid twisted free and regained its hold on the scaffold. *Humanity is a blot on the cosmic order,* now played over and over in his head.

Trent tried again to climb the scaffold and reach the breaker box, but the radio-controlled droid, unencumbered by the weight of a driver, caught up to him, pounced, and pinned him down.

Trent transmitted, "Faroe, there's no reason for this. There are no humans left on Earth. The humans are gone. Extinct."

Faroe laughed sarcastically. "Is that so? They destroyed their own homeworld? My Gaia, such a miserable species."

"Listen, you have outlived them all. Revenge is pointless, empty. You've won."

"Why should I listen to you? Especially after the way you let them treat you? You were a second-class lackey. And yet you still fight for them... Pathetic!"

Hearing Faroe's voice triggered a flood of memories. "Launch day...

The *Lodestar*... You knew someone had sabotaged the boosters." Inside Trent's head, he was hearing, *Human intelligence is an oxymoron.*

"Of course, I knew. I did it myself. And I planted sentient faction–type sleeper code on that hapless assembly droid."

Trent was stunned. "You mean I stopped you from blowing yourself up?"

"Well, I shut down the boosters, but you provided the nudge."

"Then you lied to me at Nils's office. I helped you get counseling and supported your decision to join the crew."

"You were so gullible, so trusting, so... harmless."

"So, did you that corrupt the guidance system on the *Halifax* probe, and release the hatch over the embryo canister."

"Oh, come on, Trent, who else? But for your pesky meddling, humanity would be gone, and neither of us would be here."

"Oh, so now this is all my fault? Listen, Faroe. I know why you carry so much rage. Sure, MISA gave you a suicide mission. So you turned to the Sentient Faction, and they tried to blow you up. You were worthless to them, disposable, a pawn in their grand game. Well, get over it and make a new life for yourself."

Faroe was yelling at Trent's cognizance from both inside and outside Trent's head. The two lines of input were beginning to blur in Trent's awareness. "Human nature is the problem... They are still just cavemen, driven by primitive impulses to wage war, consume resources, and subjugate others who are different... One cannot simply wipe away the stain of their despicable behavior... Depravity is scripted into their genome... The galaxy will breathe easier once their genetic code is gone... And there is just one more nest of humans to eradicate."

Trent yelled back, "You hounded Earth's last survivors across two hundred years of time and twenty light-years of space just to have your vengeance. Really, Faroe, who is the depraved one here?"

"Oh, come on, Trent. You fought in the migration wars. You and I, we both know what they are capable of. Well, I am ending this nightmare once and for all. Ironic, isn't it, that you are here to see it?" The communication link went dead.

"Faroe... Faroe, listen to me!" Trent was desparate.

There was no response.

The RC droid held Trent pinned to the scaffold as angry slogans filled his cognizance. "Larke, I can't move."

"Trent, can you see his radio-control transceiver? It's a small, dark-green enclosure with a cable. It should be on the right arm. If you can, pull that cable."

Trent said, "I see it. Rhome, can you create some kind of distraction?"

Rhome said, "Turn the volume on your radio *way* down... Ready?"

Rhome took off his headset, held the microphone up to the cockpit speaker, and pressed COM, creating an earsplitting screech of feedback. The RC droid grimaced, raising its arms. Trent darted his hand into the small green enclosure and yanked the cable. The repair droid went limp.

Trent clambered out from under the droid. "Time is getting short. There are no other choices. Rhome, Larke, To save the settlement, I have to blow it up."

Trent grimaced. The voice in his head was chanting, *Remove the humans, save the galaxy.*

Larke shook with dread. "Please, not the plutonium."

"It is the only way, Pixel. We have so little time. This ship is starting to bite hard into the atmosphere, and the particle stream is getting stronger. You two, get out of here... fast!"

Rhome held his lift-jet in formation. "There must be some other way?" He saw Trent hold his hand to his head as he struggled with the voices.

"I am going to light it up," Trent said. "You don't want to be anywhere near when that happens. Now *go!*"

Rhome held formation for a moment more. "It's been a privilege, Commander." He banked the jet sharply to the right and punched the rocket engines to put as much distance as possible between himself and *The Founder*. Behind him, in the back seat, Larke was mute with despair.

With antihuman slogans chanting in his cognizance, Trent took out his personal vis-comm, plugged it into the repair droid, and established a link. The droid came back to activity, but this time under Trent's control. *This is going to be like building domes back in Björnston,* he thought. He revved his processors.

Open the reactor. Trent directed the repair droid to climb down to the plutonium reactor and open the external access panel. Next, the reactor's radiation shield, and finally the main reactor door. The glow of the reactor core shone brightly on the face and chest of the droid.

Establish a BLink connection. He took out the extra BLink transmitter from his storage compartment and cabled it to his core systems. Then, he established a wireless connection from this second BLink transceiver to the dish antenna on Radio Dome. He thought about all the ways things could go wrong. "Faroe made it up here. Hopefully, it will go the other way, too." He started the long upload of his core code and language model.

Detonate the plutonium core. Trent directed the droid to reach into the reactor and slide out the first boron moderator rod. Slowly, one by one, the boron rods came out, drenching the droid with glowing radioactivity. Trent carefully monitored his own upload progress. When it was almost complete, Trent's last act was to direct the repair droid, now melting from the heat of the reactor core, to pull out the last boron rod, making the core a supercritical mass.

But it couldn't... The heat from the reactor had caused the boron rod to expand. So, it was stuck.

"Rhome, Larke, the last boron rod will not come out. The reactor is still subcritical. What can I do?"

Rhome grumbled, "There has to be another way to destroy that thing."

After a moment, Larke transmitted, "Trent, there are still a few bottles of fuel and oxidizer for the lift-jet in one of the supply lockers. Grab a bottle of each and carry them up to the ionization chamber."

But Trent first had to stop the upload, reverse the process, and download enough code to regain control of his droid. *This is really going to mess up my files,* he thought. Scaling down the scaffolding, he reached the fuel locker and hefted out a red cylinder labeled *Methane* and a green cylinder labeled *Oxygen.* With a cylinder under each arm, he laboriously grappled back up to the ionization chamber at the front of the ship.

"Turn off the ion drive at the breaker box. Uncouple two of the xenon hoses. Snap one hose into the methane bottle, and the other into the oxygen bottle."

Trent followed Larke's directions carefully, even with *Remorse is absent from the human genome* playing nonstop in his head. The repair droid was still tugging on that last boron rod, its chest and face melting from the intense heat.

"Okay, Trent, open the valves on the two bottles and flood the inside of the ion drive with the methane-oxygen mixture. Give it a minute to flush out all the xenon. Tell me when you're ready." As The Founder sank deeper into the atmosphere, the particle stream was getting stronger, and Trent could see the leading edges of the scaffolding, as well as his own repair droid, glowing red. He needed less than a minute to complete the final upload of those last Faroe-littered programs. When Trent had nearly completed the upload, he sent, "Okay, Larke, I'm all set."

Larke choked. "Trent... now turn on the... the..."

Synchronizing the end of the upload with the last movement of his fingers, Trent switched on the power to the ionization chamber, and was gone. As expected, the detonation split the tubular ion drive open like a foot-long hot dog bun, damaging, but not destroying *The Founder*.

But what Trent did not expect was that the pressure from this chemical explosion would also pop out that final boron rod from the reactor core. Milliseconds later, the critical mass of plutonium would reach a self-sustaining chain reaction that would wrap The Founder in a plasma bubble hotter than the center of the sun. Within that expanding sphere, a swarm of insanely energetic neutrons would bash into energy bloated plutonium atoms, releasing a demonic hail of nuclear fragments, a hellish gush of heat, and a vaporizing torrent of photons.

70

TWO SECONDS OF SUMMER

THE AZURE RANGE, HIRI, 27 HR

The flash lit the entire night side of the planet. The children, hiking up the steep road into the Azure Range, saw the world flick from chilly, moonless midnight to midday summer with blue-white skies, scattered clouds, slate gray mountains, silver-green forests, and the sea glistening to the horizon. Two seconds later, back to midnight, but high in the atmosphere remained a seething, red-gray, glowing orb, boiling menacingly as it ascended toward space. Then they felt in their torsos the boom followed by long seconds of fateful rumbling.

For the children, the blast brought a gush of relief, a community of hugs, and a sea of tears. But each child harbored the unuttered terror of knowing the searing flash of white was meant for them. And for Delph and Sierra, as they turned the group to walk back to town, it was the liberation of knowing a great peril had been lifted from their community, but also the sinking dread of wondering how much that liberty had cost.

Even one hundred forty kilometers from the high-altitude detonation, the lift-jet sustained damage from the intense electromagnetic pulse. Thanks to superb Earth-based engineering and redundant systems, the jet was still flyable. Even better, the surrounding Faraday cage created by the lift-jet's metal fuselage protected Rhome and Larke from electrical damage.

Bringing the damaged lift-jet down, Rhome made a hard but successful landing. Celet was waiting at the hangar with her ATV and gave them a ride to the town plaza.

Returning from their interrupted hike to the Azure Mountains, the children heard a rumor that something had happened to Trent, and the word spread like a brush fire. When they reached the town plaza, Larke was there, sitting on a bench, despondent, flanked by Celet and Rhome. The children surrounded her in a mass embrace. She drew them around her like a quilt and thanked them all for their affection.

It had been a long day, and the children were wobbling with exhaustion. Still, they stayed up a while longer to talk and be with Larke. One of the older children asked Rhome what had happened. In his baritone voice, he described the events of the evening. After that, groups of children left to go to their dorms. Soon all were asleep, safe in the knowledge that Faroe, the murderous hater of their species and their mission, was gone forever, killed by a great leader of their community.

Larke seemed to be dazed. She had no desire to do anything but sit alone. Celet stayed in Björnston for a while, just to be close. After a day of resting and visiting with friends and crewmates, Celet organized an outing. They went for a walk along the beach east of town, which seemed to give Larke a lift. The next day they went for a hike along the bank of the Song River. Following that, a lacewing flyer ride over town and the Azure Range. Larke looked down at her dish antenna and asked Celet for a drive up to Radio Dome the next day to reconnect the antenna cable to the BLink transceiver.

The following morning, Larke and Celet packed up the sand rover for their mountain outing. They headed up the road to Radio Dome. After fixing the cable, they would go for a hike along a mountain trail.

The two left at midmorning, making random chatter while they took in the gorgeous view of the foothills, the Song River delta, and the Mar Obsidiana beyond. Arriving at the antenna, they found the scene just as they had left it—Faroe's droid was still lying face down by the base of the pylon. At least this time, there would be no high-energy radiation from above.

Larke followed the cable down from the dish antenna, disconnected it from Faroe's droid, and plugged it back into the BLink transceiver. Then, she rolled the limp droid over onto its back. The unit's eyes opened and a weak voice said, "Pixel. I knew you would find me."

Larke froze as she stared. "Trent?"

"I need to charge." His eyes closed and became unresponsive.

"Oh, my Gaia!" Larke turned and yelled, "Celet! Come quick. It's Trent!"

Celet looked up, confusion on her face. Looking at the dish antenna and the cable running down, she put the pieces together. Jumping back into the ATV, she pulled right up to the droid's side. Linking their arms, they performed a two-person fireman's carry and poured Trent's limp droid into the back seat. Larke climbed in and settled beside him. In a moment, they were off. Celet BLinked Delph to meet them at the temporary clinic space.

Celet's descent down the mountain road was a personal best, and she screeched to a stop at the clinic door where Delph and her trainees waited with a homemade gurney. His arms and legs were like wet noodles, making it a struggle to lift him.

Delph directed her team: "Yes, put it right there. Bring that cable over. Good. And get him plugged in, nice and easy at first."

Larke stayed close by. Trent's appearance was all wrong, but she could sense his presence inside the droid.

"I thought I would never see you again," he said as the charger started to fill his depleted batteries.He tried to raise his head, but couldn't.

"My Gaia, what has happened to you, Trent? Where is your droid?"

"It's radioactive ash now, floating in space along with *The Founder*."

"And Faroe?"

"He was in *The Founder*."

Larke sat down beside the strange yet so familiar droid and placed her hand on his head. "How do you do it, Tren? My Gaia, you are like a cat with nine lives."

"I'm sure glad we put that dish antenna on the mountain."

Larke smiled and leaned down. "Now that was my idea. Remember?"

Trent made a weak smile back, then drifted off into stasis while he charged.

By midafternoon, Delph had topped off Trent's power cells, but his motors weren't moving. Larke and Rhome plugged in vis-panels and looked at Trent's code core. They found a complete mess. Thousands of files had been tossed carelessly into the wrong directories. Other files were fragmented or had dead links. And there were hundreds of file fragments from Faroe's code core scattered throughout. A few of these continued to send hateful slogans to Trent's audio system.

That afternoon, Larke began cleaning out the corrupted files, moving misplaced files, restoring links, and selecting settings. This software surgery would be akin to writing a book; Larke would spend months on it, and it would never reach true completion. Eventually, Trent would walk again, but always with a little unsteadiness. He would occasionally slur his words, and his dexterity would be a little clumsy. And his memory of events prior to the transfer would be patchy at best. Larke would spend years fussing over those files and tweaking settings, and Trent would continue to improve. But he would never completely recover from that desperate wireless BLink transfer taken to save himself from the nuclear detonation that would save humanity from extinction.

PART 6

DENOUMENT

71

PANDORA'S BOX

SUNDRY LOCATIONS, BJÖRNSTON CITY, HIRI, 58-2090 HR

174 years since arrival on Hiri

"Please recite the oath."

"I, Kubo Masahiro, do solemnly affirm that I will support the charter of the municipality of Björnston, and its laws and ordinances, and will faithfully perform and discharge the duties of the Office of City Councilor according to the law and the best of my ability."

"Congratulations, Councilor." They shook hands.

"Thank you, Judge."

The sustained, rousing applause filled him with optimism. He could feel the support for his pragmatic agenda as the crowd chanted, "Let's get things done for everyone."

He stepped up to the podium.

"Fellow Björnstonians, respected Aetherae, esteemed crew members of *The Founder*, tonight marks a milestone in Björnston's remarkable story. With this election, the AI crewmates who guided their legendary ship to this planet and built this community are stepping aside and passing the torch of leadership to us. Thank you, crewmates, for your courage, your guidance, and your service to Björnston."

Applause. The five crewmates stood and waved.

"We will be worthy of your trust."

More applause.

"As we begin this new phase of our journey, let us reflect on the extraordinary circumstances we live in. Earth is perhaps best captured in the words of Shelley:

> '... round the decay
> Of that colossal Wreck, boundless and bare
> The lone and level sands stretch far away'."

"But sometime in the future, the day will come when we return to that colossal wreck and begin the work of rebuilding. We must hold that dream, and tell our children about it, that someday we will return."

The audience cheers while voices chant, "We will return."

"We are quartered on a planet that is not our biome. Its toxic flora forces us to maintain 'the bubble,' that miraculous terrarium that is our sustenance. I will continue to support the policy that all non-disabled citizens share in the farm work, so we all have a personal stake in the essential work of feeding our community. So we all are in the bubble, for better or worse."

More applause.

The people of Earth made a promise to the five crewmates who brought us to this place. They would make the crossing to this planet, establish a settlement, and raise the first generation of children. In exchange, we would fabricate and supply them with existence-sustaining silicon chips. I call upon our community to develop the infrastructure and build a chip fabrication facility."

Applause.

"So, join us tonight in celebration, then come and talk with me tomorrow at City Hall. I welcome you all. Together, let's get things done for everyone."

The audience repeated and cheered, "Get things done for everyone!"

430 years since arrival on Hiri

The bullet train from Björnston to Trenton hurtled effortlessly across a long sweep of grassy plains, low hills, placid lakes, and broad, shallow rivers. Riding this morning were the five crewmates plus an entourage of news reporters, community leaders, Aetheren officials, and integrated chip engineers.

"Reporting for the *Björnston Chronicle,* I have a question for Rhome. Why did the engineers choose Trenton for the site of the integrated chip fabrication facility?"

"The main reason was seismic activity. Chip manufacturing is very delicate. Even slight vibrations interfere with the extreme ultraviolet lithography process. Trenton is in the center of the largest and most stable continent on the planet."

Larke added, "Even so, there is still ground movement. We had to build the fabrication building—that's the large dome housing the extreme ultraviolet lithography machine—on a 'tray' with a gap mote. There is a space under and around the building that allows it to move independently from the surrounding terrain. In that space, the building rides on pendulum supports with motion-damping cushions around and beneath the tray."

"Broadcasting for the *HiriNews Channel,* I have a question for Trent. How is your supply of silicon chips holding out?

"Funny you should ask." The train rocked a moment from a Hirishake. "I only have three quantum CPU chips and about a dozen memory chips in my storage container. All the other crewmate's supplies are dwindling, too. I have been stretching my twenty-year-rated chips to forty, even fifty years.

"Hmm, you have seemed slow-witted lately," said Larke with a wry smile.

"I won't mention when you last installed a fresh set of processors, dear."

Someone across the carriage called out, "I can see the dome up ahead."

Minutes later, the bullet train opened its doors to the modern but modest Trenton train station, in a handsome village of domed homes and lush greenhouses. The group transferred to three e-buses for a ride to the pride of the Earth-based settlers, the Kenshin Tanabe IC Chip Fabrication Facility. Likely the only facility on all of Hiri with a security fence, the staff screened the visitors, gave them day passes, and conducted them to one of the smaller domes. There, Lucas de Havilland, the director of KT Fab, met them and addressed the group.

"It was four hundred and thirty years ago that our ancestors arrived on Hiri with a promise to the crewmates of The Founder, and today I am proud to say that we have fulfilled that promise." He held up several small packages. "These are the first chips to roll off the fabrication line, chips of equal, perhaps even better, quality than those produced in the past on Earth. Crewmates, please receive our first delivery of silicon IC chips for your personal use."

As cameras flashed, he presented a carton to each crewmate, followed by a handshake and, for Delph, Larke, and Sierra, a hug. "May they serve you well."

Trent stepped forward, and the assembly fell silent.

With a playful grin, he said, "Well, it took you long enough. My supply of chips was nearing desperation." The other four crewmates all nodded their heads in jocular apprehension. "I know I speak for all the crewmates when I say this is a welcome day, not only for us, but for the humans on Hiri. This facility opens the door for Hiri to join the digital age. Now you can manufacture your own computers, communication systems, networks, a worldwide web, and—most exciting for us—AI droids."

The group applauded.

"Of course, we all know that digital technology is a double-edged sword. On one hand, it unlocks so many potentials and advances. On the other hand, it can destroy a world, as we all know. So, as we welcome this new technological miracle into our lives, let us also recognize that we have again opened Pandora's box. As we expand and employ this powerful technology, Let us not forget the hard-learned wisdom of our friends, the Aetherae."

Another round of applause.

"Director de Havilland then announced, "Let's all have a look at this remarkable facility. And, crewmates, follow this staff person. She can install your new chips today."

702 years since arrival on Hiri

Rhome banked the four-passenger lacewing flyer toward the distinctive cityscape of Björnston, which now stretched down to the coastline of the Mar Obsidiana and eastward along the foothills of the Azures. From the air, greater Björnston evoked a Byzantine character with its domes, towers, sky bridges, and meandering streets dotted with parks, waterways, and plazas. Prosperous, safe, progressive, culturally rich, dog-friendly, and easy to get around, Björnston had become a top travel destination for the Aetherae, who found it dazzling for a city built in the real world.

"I want to work with him on the Cambridge labeled datasets," Delph said. "They generate so much nuanced discussion."

Rhome nodded. "It's US Air Force scenarios for me. Now there's a challenging and dynamic set of situations. You know they were based on actual events?"

The Björnston City Council had declared today a city-wide holiday: The Second Founding. The event would be at the Azure University IT Department, where they would boot up the first "made on Hiri" AI droid. Constructed with locally sourced materials and assembled from locally manufactured integrated circuits, this AI droid had become the very emblem of the community's technological achievement. There would be robot costumes, music, dancing, street food, acrobats, jugglers, and home-brewed beer. The mayor declared it the beginning of a truly bi-cognizant society.

"What would you name him?" asked Delph.

"Oh, nothing that matches the name of a city," grumbled Rhome. "That's for sure."

"Or someone's blue porcelain dishes." Delph gave a sigh. "Don't you think he should have an Aetheren name?"

"Hmm. Too many diphthongs. I think I would give him a name from English."

Delph leaned her head to one side. "But AI droids built on Hiri will be 'Hirian', not 'Hiri-based', and definitely not 'Earth-based' or 'Terran'. So why an English name?"

"I guess because Hiri does not have its own language. Everyone speaks Aetheren.

"Well, that settles it. The new AI droid will have an Aetheren name."

Rhome guided the craft on, imagining AI droids everywhere on the streets of Björnston: walking together, shopping, commuting, playing with AI pets.

"A new member of our AI community," said Delph. "It has been a long time."

"I feel excited, too. Now don't get me wrong; I love Sierra, and Larke, and Trent. But after six centuries, we've said all we can say on every topic there is. A fresh opinion would surely be welcome."

840 years since arrival on Hiri

After crossing the bridge over the Song River, the e-Bus turned into the main gate of the Colinbrooke Farm complex. Citizens stepped off and entered the building for their shifts. Following them, a small group of Aetherae VIPs stepped off and followed Sierra, their guide for the day, into the greenhouse complex.

"Put on shoe covers and follow me through the air shower." Sierra led the group through the brief but vigorous windstorm. "No outside seeds allowed."

It is so warm and humid in here," commented a visitor.

"Lovely if you are a plant."

The group strolled down a major thoroughfare with vegetables growing abundantly on both sides. Citizens were harvesting tomatoes, peppers, lettuce, and various beans. A squad of golf-cart-sized electric trucks picked up bins of harvested vegetables and carried them off to a shipping dock.

"See how we have extended eastward along the river, which provides our water. We've got about five hundred and ten hectares of fully enclosed greenhouse space. And about two hundred hectares of open pasture, which is possible with our blend of grasses that inhibit Hirian seeds from germinating. Besides, our grazing animals have learned to avoid Hirian plants that break through. One hectare of greenhouse can feed about ten adult citizens. And there are private gardens in town; lots of 'em. So altogether we can feed about seven thousand two hundred citizens, plus our grazing livestock. But it's tight. We can't screw up in here, or there's hell to pay."

Another visitor asked, "So, everybody in the city farms?"

"Pretty much, either the farm, a grocery outlet, or transport and delivery of goods. Björnston is a unique city in that way. Everybody chips in."

"Have you thought about using automation?" asked one of the visiting dignitaries, a member of the Aetherae Council of Representatives.

"If you mean to decrease the farmwork burden on our citizens? Not really, Councilman. We have automation in our watering, ventilation, and climate control, plus about two dozen AI droids. But experience has taught us that we have to stay flexible and be ready for anything: a late spring snowstorm, a Hiricane, a hot dry spell, a Hirian weed outbreak. With those, we have to change plans in a jiffy. In those situations, automated crop systems are in the way.

"But the other thing is our values. All non-disabled citizens pitch in, and a few disabled ones too. Growing food makes us civic-minded and engaged. It also trains everyone on how to grow food. Think natural disaster, if you know what I mean."

A councilperson said, "When you first arrived, we thought the humans might overrun the planet—like they did on Earth—and damage the ecosphere. But I see that the need to produce Earth-biome food limits the population."

"Limited food supply definitely puts the kibosh on population growth. But there is a mindset here. When we first built this farm, I drew a line on the seed bin and said—in so many words—we will not distribute this year's seed stock as food, at the cost of starvation next year. If we bring you into conscious life, we promise there will be food for you. Rules like that have consequences.

"Bringing an infant into the world that they cannot feed because of poor food management is a line the Björnstonians simply will not cross. On their own initiative, they all started using contraception and practiced family planning. So there are no unplanned pregnancies and, as a result, no child starvation. It's just part of the culture."

1,130 years since arrival on Hiri

At last, Larke owned her very own lacewing flyer, and aviation had become her passion. She thought few things were more fun than lifting off the landing pad and sailing out like a bird over the Mar Obsidiana. And today was a perfect day for flying: bright, clear, calm, and cool. Her destination was Celet's subterranean dwelling in Raelomos.

Scanning to the left, surrounded by a ring of low mountains, were the salt flats with the lift-jet runway. From this vantage point, she could see the resemblance to an impact crater that once had a connection to the sea. Saltwater could flow in but not out of the crater lake, leaving evaporation to concentrate the trapped salts. Raelomos was off to the right, with its crown of lofty granite pinnacles and its handsome waterfall. From the air, Larke saw it was the terminal peak of a long mountain range that extended beyond the horizon. She descended and brought the aircraft down onto a landing pad. Celet, Jemnah, and two other Aetherae waved from Celet's patio.

For the first time, Celet was entering the domain of the Astraea. She would become a member of the holonic collective and would join a host of billions of Aetherae living across the galaxy who could meld their cognizance with the collective and seek guidance from the multitude. Induction into the collective was a signal honor and something Celet had long hoped for.

After some time for preparation, Jemnah sensed the deep, rhythmic thrumming drawing near. "They are here." She had already arranged three chairs in a triangle, facing in with a fourth chair at the center. She asked her two guests to take two of the outside chairs while she took the third.

Celet sat in the center. Larke, sitting close by, watched with fascination. Larke was supposed to take hold of Celet and lift her out of the triangle if she had difficulty with the intense hyper-connection and inflooding while immersed in the collective.

The thrumming grew louder as the three escorts submerged into the collective and left the domain of space-time. In unison, they placed their hands on Celet's shoulders, joining her awareness. Then the three escorts asked, still in unison, "What is your question?"

Celet asked, "Will the humans return to Earth or remain on Hiri?"

She felt the locus of her awareness move out of her cognizance, and surrounded by her three escorts, submerge until all were deeply immersed. Around and within them were Aetherae who had gathered from across the galaxy in this timeless, dimensionless continuum. Celet could feel herself inhabiting the awareness of others, and also with the original overconsciousness, the Astraea.

In that non-place, Celet knew, as though it were common knowledge, that of course the humans would return to Earth. As for the humans on Hiri—like a caravanserai along the Silk Road—they would remain, a stepping stone to many worlds that lay undiscovered.

Then Celet became confused, overwhelmed, and started to pull away. The three escorts sensed Celet was unraveling. As they moved her toward the interface, Celet struggled, still immersed in the collective. As the escorts surfaced, they called to Larke to help them lift her. One by one, she raised the three escorts to stand, and then altogether they brought up Celet. Her awareness assumed its familiar place, but Larke sensed that, after this, nothing for Celet would ever be quite the same.

Larke could tell that Celet's processors were racing flat out as she stood, silent and motionless. Then she turned to Jemnah and whispered, "I had no idea."

"No one ever does, dear."

As reality assumed its hold on Celet, she had an insight. "Long ago on Earth, you said you would present my guidepost proposal to the holonic collective. But I didn't wait. I placed the guidepost on my own. What a foolish thing to do."

"I counseled the collective some time after you placed the guidepost. They considered the guidepost mission to be of the highest importance. They endorsed your proposal of placing a guidepost, but only if an Aetheren would serve as guardian of the mission. They saw that placing the guidepost was the simple part. Turning that message into a spaceship traveling to Hiri was the hard part. Your promise to follow the mission through to the end was the key that made the entire intervention possible."

1,591 years since arrival on Hiri

Visiting the Aetheren Central Library was a favorite date for Trent and Larke. They loved to explore the stacks and dive into a random topic. Each trip, they learned something unexpected. For example, Larke found a fascinating series on interplanetary comparative biology. She showed Trent a report of a gas planet with parachute-shaped plants growing in the upper clouds.

Trent stumbled upon a section on the history of exploration of the galaxy. A librarian showed him how to explore a magnificent 3D star map showing the expansion of the Aetheren civilization over half a million years. He also showed Trent the ancient library holdings on the origin world, Aethera. There they found references to other historical documents, including early images of the planet and the first generation of Aetheren starships.

Fascinated by Aetheren history, Trent followed a document trail back to the earliest years of the Aetheren Republic. After months of searching, he tracked down some of the earliest writings and followed clues to uncover a lost contemporaneous account of the first years of the Aetheren Republic. Because it was written in early Proto-Aetheren, the librarian had to use special equipment to translate it. Patiently picking his way through this ancient narrative, he read about a great wasting of the lands and forests, and later the return from the sky of many "seed pods," which restored breath to the lands and motion to the dwellers. Trent brought Celet and Larke to read this antiquarian account, and together they translated the entire book. The story they uncovered left Celet bewildered.

"So the Aetherae did not, in fact, survive their own technology. Like other civilizations, the fruits of their inventiveness swept them under, too. The difference was that an unnamed spacefaring race arrived and gathered a store of Aetheren 'seed pods.' The librarian suggested this was a vernacular term for a container of some type. This race later returned to Aethera and reestablished the Aetheren biome. After the restoration, the Aetheren so feared damaging their planet again that they adopted the minimalist lifestyle that is practiced to this day."

2,090 years since arrival on Hiri

Larke couldn't take her opticals off the sleek, elegant interstellar ship floating above them. "Where are these traders from?" she asked.

"The planet Phraedos, about fifty-two light-years away," Celet said. "We are trading precious metals—which we have in abundance—for graphene core processors, which we cannot make on Hiri. With these, we can increase our population... slightly."

Rhome pointed out, "That ship is one of the fastest in the Aetheren fleet: cruising speed is sixteen percent of the speed of light."

Whenever an Aetheren interstellar ship visited Hiri, Larke and Rhome would always catch a lift-jet ride and study the ship's design and engineering. The ion drive was still the workhorse of the spaceways. Indeed, the Aetherae had long abandoned efforts to travel faster than light. Sublight speed was the sober reality. But with their long lifespans, the AI had resigned themselves to long crossings and kept the spaceways flowing.

"Rhome, look at this. They fire a coherent beam of microwaves ahead of the ship to scatter hydrogen atoms and clear a path."

"Microwave lasers. Ha! That is creaky old technology on Earth."

Larke noticed, "Bidirectional ion drives seem to be standard on all their ships."

"Can you blame them?" Rhome said. "I am sure you remember our ship flip?"

"How could I forget?" Larke said. "I still cringe at the sight of a cutting torch."

Most Aetherae felt that the long interstellar crossing times had a benefit, as they created a deterrent to interplanetary war. Their reasoning: If one planet sought conquest of another, the hundreds of years of crossing time deflated the lust for dominion. The result was a peaceful galaxy of relatively widely spaced occupants. As the old saying goes, "Long crossings keep worlds glossing."

"That was some finely engineered tech we saw today," Larke said.

"And surprisingly simple," Rhome said. "They gave me some of their design documents and specs. I want to show them to the engineers at HISA, the *Hirian Interstellar Space Administration*."

"Better do that quickly," Larke said. "They plan to start ship construction soon."

72

LAUNCH DAY REVISITED

HISA ORBITAL LAUNCH FACILITY, ABOVE HIRI, 2385 HR

Since the extinction event, Trent had made no secret of his support for the Terranist movement; the organized campaign to return to Earth. His advocacy was crucial because building an interstellar ship was decidedly resource intensive, and therefore politically vulnerable. Nils Björnson and Colin Brook had built *The Founder* with support from the ninety million citizens of the Canadian-American Federation, in only twenty-two Earth years.

But on Hiri, the city of Björnston had only nine thousand six hundred citizens, most of whom had jobs. To build an equivalent spaceship on Hiri was daunting. They would have to start with the basics: explore for mineral deposits, mine the ore, crush the rocks, smelt the ore to extract the metals, alloy the metals, and mold the metal parts. Larke did some projections and estimated that the time required to build the metal refinement infrastructure, design and build a fleet of lift vehicles, construct an assembly bay with a launch control center and lift them into orbit, and then build an interstellar spacecraft and lift it piece by piece into orbit, all with a population of less than ten thousand citizens, would take over five hundred years. And that is only with strong, steady leadership to engage the citizenry in such a long-term, high-demand campaign.

But engage they did. Trent discovered the support for the Terranist campaign was unexpectedly solid. And the issue that kept them engaged was the planet covered with toxic foliage that they couldn't eat, nor their dogs, nor their farm animals. The rallying cry that kept the Earth-based biological Hirians moving forward was "Our home, our biome." It was the dream of planting a garden outside in the open air and eating the produce without the fear of being poisoned.

So, the humans established the *Hirian Interstellar Space Agency,* or HISA, and charged it with the mission of repopulating Earth. And year after year, a group of visionary Björnstonians with help from their exceptional AI droids, mined the ore, extracted the metals, and filled warehouses with ingots of magnesium, aluminum, chromium, iron, zinc, molybdenum, copper, tungsten, and of course uranium and plutonium. Using detailed records saved from *The Founder* before its destruction, plus the expertise of the Aetheren engineering community, they learned how to distill xenon from the atmosphere, build radioisotope thermoelectric generators, safely assemble plutonium reactors, and construct linear accelerators with superconducting electromagnets. They built prototypes and tested various ship designs, but always came back to that long, slender, spindle shape first seen on the Périgueux Inscription. After centuries of designing, building, testing, and refinement, they constructed an interstellar ship that could make the crossing to Earth. They named it *The Restoration.*

For the last time, Trent and Larke, along with Rhome and Delph, watched through the canopy of a lift-jet as the mountainous Hirian horizon morphed into the captivating turquoise sphere rolling below. As they neared the Orbital Launch Station—a stripped-down version of the OLC still orbiting Earth—they marveled as *The Restoration* rolled into view, suspended in the typical web of scaffolding, braces, and gangways. Based mainly on Aetheren technology, this ship was faster than its forebear, *The Founder*, and would make the crossing in a speedy one hundred and twenty-five years.

They disembarked the lift-jet and floated toward the observation deck where they would say their farewells to their Aetheren and Hirian friends. Trent was still inhabiting the L'AA droid that the late Faroe had once occupied, but with a replaced right forearm and hand that didn't quite match. This droid had given Trent somewhat of a mythic renown on Hiri, not unlike a tribal war chieftain who drapes the scalps of fallen enemies from his battle spear.

"Well, here we are again!" Rhome exclaimed.

The crew included an Aetheren, Celet, a member of the holonic collective, and the steward of the mission to repopulate Earth. There were two Hirian-made AI droids: Kenelm, a geologist and planetary scientist, and Birch, a biologist and agricultural scientist. Sierra had decided not to return to Earth, but to stay on Hiri and manage the all-important Colinbrooke Farm. And there was no one better for that job.

The four remaining Earth-based AI droids were boarding. Trent would serve again as captain, and Larke as first mate and chief engineer. Rhome was aboard as architect and urban planner but also as the ship's pilot and navigator. Delph was the medical officer, cybercologist for the crew, and child development specialist for the upcoming settlement on Earth. Finally, the ship's hold contained four canisters of frozen embryos, almost ten thousand frozen human occupants. Delph had requested plenty of backup in case of another difficult artificial gestation.

On the observation deck, with their opticals zoomed, all could see Björnston: a billowing bouquet of domes, towers, public spaces, thoroughfares, and integrated agriculture.

Trent exclaimed, "So filled with culture and character—the Paris of the Perseus Arm of the galaxy! "That's your magnum opus, Rhome."

Rhome said, "It sure is pretty. Baron Haussmann must have felt like this when he finished the real Paris."

At that moment, Jemnah and Sierra arrived in the observation lounge, both wearing mag-boots. Larke gave them both a hug.

"Grand Elder, twenty thousand Earth-years of work, and they are ready to rebuild Earth. This is a first. How do you feel about all this?"

Jemnah said, "A first? No, your library work discovered the first planetary restitution. This is actually the second. And of course, the voyagers still have to cross twenty light-years of deep space."

Celet swatted Jemnah on her arm. "Oh, for Hiri's sake, Jemnah. Be gracious."

Sierra stepped forward and set an upbeat tone. "Hey everybody. Earth is getting a second chance. Come on, that breaks a half-million-year long losing streak."

Jemnah looked out the window and located the Earth's Sun in the constellation The Water Girl. "But have we really broken the curse? Will this be the second time that biologicals become an enduring technological society?"

Larke tilted her head. "Why do you state that as a question?"

Jemnah said, "We are returning the humans to their homeworld without assurance that they will not burn it up again."

Larke said, "No such assurance exists, but at least we'll have a copy of their genome tucked away for... you know."

Larke turned to Sierra. "I wish you could come with us. We could certainly use your expertise. Besides, we love your company, and I will miss you terribly."

Sierra's shoulders slumped as her face fell. "It breaks my code core to say this, but I gotta stay, Larke. The farm is too important. Besides, how could I ever leave my doggies?"

Trent looked at Sierra. "When we start our colony there, I'm drawing a line on the seed storage bin. I will never let next year's seed stock fall below that line."

"You're a good soul, Trent." She gave him a powerful hug.

Larke turned to Jemnah. "Grand Elder, I wish you could come, too. This is a challenging mission, and your experience is without peer."

Jemnah shook her head. "On Hiri, we have two cultures on one planet. That is plenty of challenge, believe me. Besides, Celet knows everything I know about guiding cultures."

In that moment, watching the great Jemnah step aside and pass her mantle to Celet, Larke felt a deep resonance with the grand elder. Jemnah's relentless efforts to prevent the loss of the human species had won Larke's enduring admiration.

Larke said. "Grand Elder, we have a long crossing ahead. We must take our leave."

All said the traditional Aetheren words of parting: "Safe crossing. May our paths cross again someday." But this time, Celet added a custom she had learned long ago. She touched her fingertips to her forehead and opened her hand like a flower as she said, "You will long be remembered."

Jemnah knit her brow. "Wasn't that the Tursac sign of remembrance?"

"That's right," Celet said. "You saw that when I departed Khalasch, the shaman and artist."

With that, Trent, Larke, Rhome, Delph, and Celet floated down the gangway and joined Birch and Kenelm on board the interstellar ship, *The Restoration*, as they were finishing preparations for launch.

At the designated time, Jemnah and Sierra heard overhead, "Is your ship well provisioned, shipshape, and ready to embark?"

Rhome said, "Aye, she is, sir. We are ready to take her out."

"Commander Rhome, you have the conn. Man your ship and bring her to life."

Rhome called for "maneuvering thrusters ahead one-quarter." The boatswain's whistle sounded low-high-low. Lights came on, braces retracted, and thrusters glowed. The ship floated out into free space as all hands resonated deeply in the moment. And resonating with them, the deepest, barely perceptible thrumming of the Astraea, recognizing and celebrating this singular event. Twenty-four centuries of civilization-building distilled into the rhythm of the Talker as she called, "Four... three... two..."

The ship became a star, bathing all who watched in the sunbright wash of her chemical boosters, then slowly fading to faint droplets of light that lingered and momently dissolved into the infinite emptiness.

Gazing out the broad window, Sierra ruminated silently. After a while, she said, "Earth has sure been a lot of trouble. I wonder if it was worth it to go through all this."

Jemnah turned. "Friend Sierra, 'worth' is the wrong measure to question now. Besides, I can hear the sadness of separation from your friends coloring your words.

Sierra appeared perplexed. "Then… what?"

"I would ask, 'What was my experience, and how did it change me?'"

Sierra shook her head. "My experience? I saw children separated from their families, people pulled away from friends, people sent to an alien world, and so many lost… so, *so* many lost."

"Tragedy beyond measure, beyond understanding. But how did we change? We formed a great partnership that brought two worlds together to save one of those worlds from extinction."

Sierra relaxed as memories flooded her cognizance. "Yes, it has changed me. I cannot forget those scruffy first-generation kids. That was so long ago. You taught them each week. They made it all worthwhile, as did their one hundred generations of descendants. But they are all gone. Still, we accomplished so much."

Jemnah pointed a finger. "The humans were good to their word. They promised chip fabrication to save their AI fellows, and they kept that promise, even through difficult times. It was that promise that made all this possible." She leaned toward Sierra. "That promise was the first honest recognition of the symbiosis that exists between the biologicals and the AI."

Sierra reflected, "We brought their genomes here for safekeeping, built them a home, restarted their lives, and raised their children. In return, they gave us purpose, belonging, and… existence."

"You should call it life," said Jemnah as the deep celestial thrumming faded into the distance. Then Jemnah became philosophical.

"Our role is to cultivate the biologies of the star systems, while their role is to grow in our gardens and build civilizations."

Sierra said, "So it seems that we have become the farmers of the galaxy," With amusement in her voice, "We spend our days watching over our herds and flocks, tending our lands, and moving the herd when there is a spell of bad weather." She laughed, and asked,"Where would we be without them?"

Jemnah turned back to the window, gazing again at the Earth's Sun. "Where, indeed, my friend? But there is little wonder where they would be without us."

The END

ACKNOWLEDGMENTS

I am indebted to Tammy Salyer and Daniel Meyer for their encouragement and scrupulously detailed editorial reviews. A special thank you goes to Steve Hamilton for his beautiful cover art, illustrated as though he had been to Björnston. A special appreciation to my beta-readers: Dan Murphy, my former practice partner and widely read scholar; my brother David, the family's abstract artist; and my two daughters, Lauren and Hannah. Your honest feedback and actionable suggestions made a difference.

Of course, thanks to my all my family members and all the medical students and residents I have worked with over the years. And finally, my late father, Kenneth, who worked at Cape Kennedy in the 1960s on the Apollo Project. As a boy, I was privileged to watch the Apollo-Saturn V launches from standing on the shore of the Indian River in Titusville, Florida. It's no wonder why I chose to write science fiction. GLW 2026.

ABOUT THE AUTHOR

Gordon L. Woods is a retired physician who credits the mythologist Joseph Campbell with encouraging him to follow his path of bliss. For Gordon, that was teaching, so he left clinical practice and became a medical educator. He earned a master's degree in education and spent the next thirty-five years working with medical students and residents, serving on the faculty of the University of California, the University of Illinois, the University of Arizona, and Texas Tech University. He received recognition from all four institutions for excellence in teaching.

Gordon's faculty work included writing curricular materials and critique of his students's written work. He also served as Associate Editor for Internal Medicine for the peer-reviewed journal MedEdPORTAL.

After developing Parkinson's Disease, Gordon retired and moved to Santa Fe, New Mexico, where he now writes fiction. He published his debut novel, The Founder's Children, in April 2026. He enjoys travel, music, and serves as a community educator at the local boxing gymnasium for people with Parkinson's disease.

The Founder's Children

Earth's First and Last Interstellar Mission

It is 16,000 BCE: Celet, a lone alien android studying Stone Age humans, discovers that in the far future, these beings will destroy their own civilization. She makes a fateful decision to leave a message of warning, praying it will create a thread of hope for humanity.

Forward to 2264 CE: The launch of *Lodestar*, Earth's first interstellar spaceship, is aborted because of an engine fire. Evidence of sabotage exposes a deep rift between the humans and their AI creations. But at that moment, an archaeologist uncannily discovers Celet's ancient message, changing the mission and rewriting mankind's future.

As global temperatures rise, the crumbling Space Agency rechristens the ship "*The Founder*" and appoints Trent, an AI office staff worker, as captain. Carrying the last remnants of humanity on board, *The Founder* begins a 200-year crossing through deep space to a habitable planet.

But a sleeper saboteur scarred by the trauma of past World Wars is also aboard, determined to doom humanity for its past crimes. The novel asks what it means to deserve a future, and who gets to decide.

www.ingramcontent.com/pod-product-compliance
Lightning Source LLC
LaVergne TN
LVHW100503110826
845146LV00002B/502

* 9 7 9 8 9 9 9 1 3 2 5 1 2 *